# I Am That I Am

## With Sci-Fi Implications

## Lee A. Drayer

Trafford
PUBLISHING

Author photograph used by permission of:
Hansen Fine Portraits, Orange City, Florida

This is a fiction story. Names, characters, places and story situations
have been created by the author's imagination and are purely fictional.
Any resemblances to actual events, locations or persons, living or dead
are entirely coincidental.

Order this book online at www.trafford.com
or email orders@trafford.com

Most Trafford titles are also available at major online book retailers.

Note for Librarians: A cataloguing record for this book is available from Library
and Archives Canada at www.collectionscanada.ca/amicus/index-e.html

Printed in Victoria, BC, Canada.

ISBN: 978-1-4251-8629-6

Our mission is to efficiently provide the world's finest, most comprehensive book publishing
service, enabling every author to experience success. To find out how to publish your book, your
way, and have it available worldwide, visit us online at www.trafford.com

Trafford rev. 8/12/2009

 www.trafford.com

North America & international
toll-free: 1 888 232 4444 (USA & Canada)
phone: 250 383 6864 ♦ fax: 812 355 4082

Appreciation to

Steph Waller

A friend who convinced me to write this story

# Contents

# CHAPTER 1
## RETIREMENT, HUMBUG

**M**atthew and Julie live a quiet and peaceful retirement life near Knoxville Tennessee. They purchased a small home just a few miles west of the city. The large front porch was what attracted both to this particular house. Growing old together, rocking away on the porch on cool summer evenings was what they envisioned retirement life would be. That was the goal they genuinely believed most old folks would have, to sit quietly on the front porch, rocking away the time with the love of their life.

Julie and Matthew have grown very old together, but for now, sitting on their porch is not a pretty sight. For months life has become sour for humans all over the world.

The actual problems began about a year ago when for some unknown reason the world began feeling the gradual effects of nuclear radiation poisoning. Geiger counters were clearly showing alarming amounts of radiation present in the atmosphere.

At first the scientific community thought there had been a meltdown of a nuclear reactor somewhere in the world, but they had no idea the origination of it. World leaders and many scientists speculated the United States must be testing some type of nuclear device. That was proven not to be the situation because comprehensive accounts of the nuclear radiation were coming from troubled regions around the world. The United States was accused of testing a nuclear war device in international waters. The U.S. government reassured the world the United States was not the source of the radiation because even the United States was feeling the same effects as their neighboring countries of Canada and Mexico. What was the source was the big question?

Matthew and Julie were in what *had been* the security of their home, yet to look at them; it was obvious their bodies were deteriorating rapidly. Their peaceful and serene days are now filled with unbearable pain and misery.

Before her retirement Julie was a nurse many years ago and through her hospital friends, she was able to get pain medication. However, the medication is no longer available because the hospitals are rapidly filling with far more needy patients than she and her husband. Even the doctors and nurses are having the same health problems as the rest of humanity. Day by day people are dying by the hundreds, no, not hundreds, but by the thousands. The world, as we once knew it, is beginning to shut down.

Television is displaying horrible situations from around the world. There appears to be no solution as to the source of the radiation. "Is it possible," The television reporters from around the world are saying, "could it be we are being bombarded from outer space? Is it possible earth's protective shield from radiation has vanished?" These are but a few of the unanswered questions. There have been no answers, only guesses.

# CHAPTER 2
## CHILDHOOD HAD ITS MOMENTS

**M**atthew's mom and dad lived in a small town in Pennsylvania, Frackville to be exact. To be precise, it is located in the coal mining region, midway between Pottsville and Hazelton.

Their house is a very modest, half a double, located just outside the downtown area. Like most other houses in town, it is a grayish weather beaten place that needs considerable repairs. The small front porch roof leaks and many of the floor boards are split, revealing the dirt below the porch. Several of the steps leading up to the porch from the sidewalk below are split and broken as well. John Wilson, his father was heard saying more than once to his wife Thelma, "One of these days I got to fix `dis place `fore somebody falls through da floor."

To which Thelma would always reply, "Sure John, one of these days."

It was in this town that Matt, or as he prefers, Matthew Franklin Wilson was born to Thelma and John Wilson. President Franklin D. Roosevelt was John Wilson's hero. President Roosevelt was beginning to get the country out of the depression, hence the middle name, Franklin for John's new son. Some years later Matthew learned that his birth took place in an upstairs bedroom of his mom and dad's house. A neighbor lady assisted with the birth.

Times were tough. John Wilson worked in the local coal mines. He said he hated every minute of it, but it was the only work available for the men of this small town. There is no other industry. If you had a car you could drive north to Hazelton where industry was beginning to locate, but Matthew's dad didn't have a car.

The time period was when the United States was thinking about becoming active in the war between England and Germany. The talk around town by the men focused on joining the military to serve their country and help the English people survive the brutal onslaught of Germany.

However, then the unthinkable happened. Matthew was now about four or five years of age, the time when a child begins to have memory of life events. Matthew's mother was getting little Matthew out of bed on a Sunday morning when she heard a commotion below the bedroom window down on the normally quiet street. A newspaper kid was yelling at the top of his lungs, "EXTRA EXTRA READ ALL ABOUT IT! THE JAPS BOMBED PEARL HARBOR, THOUSANDS KILLED! EXTRA EXTRA!" The paper boy went on and on yelling the horrific message.

Dad and mom hurriedly went downstairs and turned on the radio, their only connection to the outside world. It was true; the Japanese had, in fact bombed Pearl Harbor and sank several U.S. war ships sending thousands of sailors to their death.

Later that day, President Roosevelt came on the radio and echoed the terrible act that placed the United States at war with Japan. During his radio address to the nation that terrifying day, the President exclaimed, "This is a day that shall forever live in infamy!"

It didn't take long for thousands and thousands of men from cities large and small to volunteer to join the United States in the war efforts.

"It is our patriotic duty to volunteer," John Wilson said.

Furthermore, John did volunteer and joined the army along with hundreds of men from the little town of Frackville, Pennsylvania.

Suddenly, the small town of Frackville became a woman's town. About the only men left were the elderly and a few frail men that couldn't pass the military physical examination. There were of course, a lot of frightened children that couldn't grasp what was happening. The only thing the children knew was their dad's were gone and mom's were now the bosses in the families.

In this small town, military industry, that had to do with the war effort sprang up almost overnight. The reason was not good, but it did bring work to the women left behind by their service men husbands. Prior to the introduction of the military jobs, the left behind families had no money for anything. Finding food to survive became a very real challenge.

Matthew's mom began working at a parachute manufacturing plant along with many other adult females from town. She was amazed how quickly she learned to attach the strings and ropes to parachutes in the new Quonset hut factory buildings located within walking distance of her house.

"I was glad to do it for our soldiers and for the good pay I received. Without that money, we would have starved."

There was very little mail from John. When a letter came, Thelma would sit in the kitchen reading the letters over and over. Then she would cry for a time, trying to hide the tears from her young son Matthew. Sometimes she would pull Matthew into her lap and hold him as she began to pray that his daddy would be home safe soon. Before John went away, Thelma and John constantly argued about silly stuff, like money and how poor they were. This was a new side of mom Matthew had not seen and it made Matthew cry also. He surely did miss his dad.

The little reddish-orange flag, with one white star in the middle flew proudly in their front window for all to see. It was a signal to all that the houses flying the little flag had one in the military, proudly serving their country.

As near as Thelma could tell, John had been shipped overseas and was on a battlefield someplace in Germany. Matthew thought the war was with Japan, but his mother explained that Germany was also in the war with the United States.

Thelma was getting extremely upset that she had heard nothing from John for nearly nine months. Her husband had been good about sending news weekly, even though censored by the government. She reasoned that he was in battle someplace and simply couldn't find the time to write.

One day there was a knock at the front door. Two very tall, neatly dressed army men appeared on the front porch. Women at work had told Thelma about the visits from these special military men. When she saw the men at the door, her knees began to buckle because Thelma Wilson knew why they had come. As she tried to regain her composure, she pushed the squeaky screen door open and invited the two inside. They were very quiet and somber as they announced that John Wilson had been killed in battle. The two went over the details of how he would be returned to the states as soon as possible for burial. The little flag in the window would now have a gold star in the middle to indicate that their house had lost one in the war.

Now it was just Thelma and her son. They both cried for days. It took months for Matthew to realize that his dad would never return home. In the meantime, Thelma kept working at the parachute factory. She needed to continue working, as she said to a fellow worker sometime later, "I have to keep busy, if I don't, I'll go crazy. Then what would Matthew do if they took me to the crazy house."

Months later Matthew told his mother. "When I get old enough mom I'll go to work and help you all I can; we'll get along mom, just you wait and see."

As an only child, being raised through his grade-school years and without a father, you would think Matthew would become a rather unruly boy. For Matthew, this was not to be. In every possible way, he obeyed his mom's strict rules. Matthew realized, as a young boy, helping mom around the house seemed necessary. One might think this strange, but his mother even took time to teach him how to cook. "Much later in your life Matt, knowing how to prepare a meal will come in mighty handy." Little did he know that his mother expected him to have dinner ready when she came home from work each evening?

After the war, Thelma was promoted to a supervisor at the factory where she worked. This was the same factory where she had worked during the war attaching ropes to parachutes. The building was now being used to make the newly invented, injection plastic molding containers for food storage. Thelma loved her job and was making considerably more money which allowed her a decent life of modest luxury.

Very seldom did Matthew ever rebel. The paddle that hung on the wall by the kitchen doorway was still in its original place. After Thelma had the house remodeled she placed the paddle back in the kitchen doorway as a reminder to Matthew to behave. For sure, Thelma wasn't afraid to use it.

By this time Matthew was in the sixth grade, and he was at the critical age of thinking for himself. Most children at this age, begin the grown-up attitude, thus he decided it was time for him to correct his mom about his name. He felt, if your parents give you a first name, everyone should respect and use it. Nevertheless, because his first name is Matthew, everyone wanted to call him Matt. He hated that! His mom would scream at him if he did something bad. "Matt Wilson," she would yell, "you get in here *right now*."

One day, he made the mistake and screamed back, "Mom, *my name is Matthew!*"

"Well Matt," Thelma said using her calm, but determined voice, "I strongly believe it's time for you to get my paddle.

If you're going to scream at me like that, I'll just hafta teach you some respect. Now go to the kitchen and get my paddle." Knowing what was to follow, most kids would quickly run out of the house to get away from the punishment.

"Like an idiot I would go to the kitchen where the paddle hung, get it, and give it to mom." It was one of those foot long, thin jobs with extra holes in it which gives it that extra sting. Then, as promised, mom became a professional paddling champ, after which my bottom hurt and burned for a long, long time. After three or four of those paddling's I decided that Matt would be an okay nickname. I still didn't like it, but I never sassed mom again.

Grade school and into high school was great. Most kids hated school, but not Matthew. He studied hard and received mostly A's and an occasional B. His favorite subjects were math and science. While in high school his mother would bring problems home from work and ask for his help to solve complicated situations that involved math. A few times his mother invited him to visit her work-place to see first hand how the complex machinery that made the plastic containers worked. He was fascinated with the mechanics of it.

The years flew by and when he became a high school senior, Matthew tried to locate a college that would give him scholarship help. He applied to several, but the one he wanted most was Penn State. On graduation day Matthew Wilson was given a grant that paid all of his tuition, room and board at his chosen college. Matthew was ecstatic to say the least. The only thing he had to pay for was books. His mom said she would help with that.

He entered college as a business major and, in addition, a nuclear science engineering program. Prior to entering the school he had meetings with those responsible for helping him pick the proper courses based on one's scholastic abilities. Because of his extreme math achievements in high school, they suggested nuclear science engineering. This was a new course for the college and they were having trouble finding students qualified. Lucky Matthew!

Even for Matthew, the studies were difficult. It seems most of the students wanted to party every night. He was asked several times to participate, but after a bit, the invitations ceased. He was not opposed to the drinking and partying, but learning this science stuff required him to spend considerable time in the library and in his room, buried in his books. After all he said, "I am a guest of the college and I appreciate that very much." Most of all he wanted to make his mother proud.

Matthew's last day at Penn State, graduation day, Thelma came to see him accept his diploma. "It was good to see Mom come and bring along her man friend. I didn't know Mom was seeing anyone. He seemed like a nice enough man and if mom is happy with him, I am happy for her. She has only had me for a long, long."

During the last year of his post graduate studies at Penn State, a professor mentioned to Matthew that Oak Valley Nuclear Research Facility was looking for a degreed person to head their engineering department. The professor said to Matthew, "Because of your business and nuclear engineering degrees, you would be the perfect person for the job." With the professor's help, Matthew Franklin Wilson applied and was accepted as the Senior Chief Engineer of Oak Valley Nuclear Research Facility located in Knoxville, Tennessee. Not bad for a kid from the small town of Frackville Pennsylvania.

# CHAPTER 3
## A NEW BEGINNING

**M**atthew Franklin Wilson began his working career as the Senior Nuclear Engineer Manager of the Oak Valley Research Center. He is the new man working with several hundred research engineers. The facility has been looking for years at new methods to make nuclear power safe, but have never come up with an actual fail-safe nuclear power plan. For sure, they improved some existing methods, a tweak here and a nip there. However, after the March 1979 Three Mile Island reactor meltdown problem, nothing they came up with seemed to satisfy the Washington Nuclear Energy Committee. The NEC is the group that oversees the activities and the finances for Oak Valley.

The Oak Valley Research buildings are located about a mile and a half north of the main highway that runs from Knoxville Tennessee, west to Nashville, and about ten miles west of downtown Knoxville. Unless you actually know the location, you would probably pass by it because it is nestled in a grove of fifty year old oak trees which completely hides the buildings from the narrow two lane road that passes by.

The U.S. Government property is completely surrounded by a high chain link fence with barbed wire running along the top to keep intruders from jumping over it. Matthew says in a questioning manner, "I don't understand why all the fence protection. We no longer have anything secret to hide from the outside world. If you want to come inside, you need only enter the large parking lot and park in the visitor parking area, come through the front door and try to get past the receptionist."

Christy is the reception screener that filters curiosity seekers and salesmen from venturing beyond the front door. She is just over five feet and somewhat heavy in stature. She has been the receptionist for Oak Valley, as she says, forever. She takes her job very seriously, and she is mighty good at it.

The main single story building is massive, about the size of a football field. The office portion of the building is where the senior engineers and Matthew's office is located. Matthew would smugly say, "My office is smack dab in the middle of the building, on the fifty yard line if you will. I mention this only because at the end of the day my legs and feet feel the result of walking, what feels like, miles as I survey the work of my engineering team."

Matthew's office is small when in comparison to offices of executives in the outside business world. "That's okay," he would say as though apologizing, "since I spend very little time in it. At least I have two windows that face the parking lot."

Matthew continues, "Two of my assistants occupy the other two offices located on the north side of the main entrance, but they have no windows. They complain often about not being able to see daylight, so I suggested they knock out some of the walls building blocks and make a window. Of course that has never happened. I remind them that they are there as the engineers support team and shouldn't be looking out of the windows anyhow."

The interior of the offices are very plain. Matthew believes the government must have had a lot of battleship gray paint left from some other projects because every wall in the huge complex, including the offices, is gray. The offices have a few chairs and an old severely scratched desk, large enough to place an in and out box and lots of clutter paperwork. In the end of each office is a large table used for displaying the large, work in progress, equipment blueprint drawings. On the other end of the room is a fire proof safe file cabinet where the blueprints for work in progress are kept. Matthew comments from behind his desk and from his somewhat aged swivel chair, "At least they have a goodly amount of fluorescent lighting. You must have lots of light to read the confound drawings."

The only room that wasn't painted gray was Mary's office. Somehow she managed to get the painters to paint her office a soft bright yellow. Mary is the office assistant to Matthew and his two assistant engineers, Marty and Jim. Everything that happens in the front offices goes through Mary. She knows all the two hundred engineers by their first names and most names of the members of their families.

Before Matthew arrived at Oak Valley, it was interesting to hear Mary and Christy talk about the new college kid that was coming to become the Senior Engineer of the entire facility. One day Mary said to Christy in a rather huffy tone, "Imagine, a snot nose kid just out of college coming here to run this place. What was Washington thinking?"

When Matthew first arrived at Oak Valley, he immediately sensed Mary's hostility toward him which made him realize he must find a way to change her attitude. From his arrival beginning Matthew included Mary in every meeting with his staff. He wanted her to see first hand that he was more than capable of the job given him.

As Senior Nuclear Engineer, Matthew's job could last for years as long as Oak Valley is included in the federal budget's annual fiscal spending program. Presently, Matthew is working on their funding budget for the next year. Annoyed by the massive amount of paperwork involved, he complains saying, "This is the annual part of my job I detest most." He knows the projects they currently have in house and the newly proposed projects, but wording them in terms, and dollar amounts the budget committee wants to hear is quite another thing. One misplaced word can doom a very necessary project and worse, require downsizing of his working manpower. "I know the Finance Committee is supposed to understand what we do, but do they? Humph!"

## Late 1960

Life in college had been great for Matthew, but boring. Often he would say that it would be nice to get together with his fellow college friends to go out and party, but he just didn't have time to do the fun scene.

Now, with his new job at Oak Valley, he was free to do what he wanted. He had found new friends at work that loved to party on the weekend. The only problem was Mary, his ever vigilant office assistant. Mary would say as Matthew, Jim and Marty left the office on Friday night's, "I hope you boys aren't going to party all weekend."

To which they would reply, "No Mary, we promise to be good at least on Sunday. On Sunday's in Knoxville, bars and liquor stores are closed because of the state's Blue Laws.

Night life in Knoxville was very good for the young studs. Friday and Saturday night in town was a blast for the threesome. Matthew and his friends would go to town and raise all kinds of, well you know. Of course that was before Matthew and Jim were married. Marty was already married, but he just wanted to party regardless of what his wife thought. Some Sunday mornings after the wine, women and song on Friday and Saturday night, they had no clue as to how any of them ever got back to their homes.

On one of those bleary party nights Jim and Marty decided they wanted to go to a University of Tennessee football game. Matthew wasn't much for football, or any other sport, for that matter. His friend and colleague, Marty mentioned that there was cheap booze and lots of pretty women. So, guess what, Matthew went along.

Marty Glessner and Jim Adams are two of the top nuclear engineers at Oak Valley. Matthew immediately made friends with these two. He said that he needed people that were dependable and knew their engineering job. These two needed to respond to engineering problems within the massive production laboratory quickly and efficiently.

Matthew, in a somewhat bragging manner said, "Having good assistants you can trust in this business is so important. Yes, we have our irreverent moments, but those moments are never discussed within hearing distance of any of the hundreds of other engineers."

Marty has been married for about three years, but still likes to look at the girls. They have no kids, so he says that until there are children in the mix of things, it shouldn't bother his wife if he goes out from time to time and blows off some steam. For sure his wife doesn't agree with that, but he does his own thing regardless of what she says. His defense is that the tremendous demands of the job are the fundamental reason for going a little crazy on the weekend.

As Matthew tells it, "Marty is a good man to work with because when I am stymied while working on a grand scale type of job, Marty has the good sense to stand back and look at it from a distance, and then he comes up with possible realistic solutions." Matthew feels he couldn't do without him.

Jim, on the other hand, is single, quiet and a cool person in everything he does. Jim is a good dresser, always looking like a man without a care in the world. He lives at home with his mother in a rather well to do neighborhood, about a mile from the office. That's a good thing because on some of the wild nights, Matthew and Marty rely on him to get them back to their homes in one piece. Jim rarely drinks hard liquor, which is very good. He has good common sense and can tell when the other two are about to get into trouble, the kind of trouble that would have them placed in the slammer. He is also good at negotiating with the bad guys that want to punch out Matthew and Marty's lights. Jim is very good at preventing clashes.

I mention all this because that is the reason the three of them go to town together. Not that they need a reason, but as was said before, women and drinking. Marty cautioned, "And don't forget the food. You need to eat something, otherwise when you get sick from drinking; you have nothing to throw up."

Long before the games start the three of them have their own version of a tailgating party. Marty and Matthew begin by chug-a-lugging beer to see who could get a buzz on first. As usual, they both became extremely obnoxious after half-dozen beers. Jim is different. He can nurse a bottle of beer for nearly an entire game. Jim felt it was dumb to get so sick and also because it's so expensive. He watches his money closely.

On the nights when they attend one of the Tennessee football games, one of them would decide when the game was over. Not necessarily at the obvious end of the game, but simply when it's time to leave the stadium. Afterwards they would go down to the Main street bar rooms where they would finish the night trying to get lucky.

That never happens because as Jim says, "No decent girl wants to go out in the company of a guy that is smashed out of his mind, extremely drunk." Matthew agrees with that, but it was always fun trying.

On one particular night, the trio had to take a cab to the stadium. Jim said his car was in the garage and he wouldn't get it back until sometime Monday. Jim seemed to have a lot of work done on his car because he rarely had it available to take them to town. That was especially true since Matthew got sick in it some weeks ago.

As a result, how will the boys get home on this particular night? It is obvious, after the night of carousing they will go home the same way they got there, by a taxi. Cab drivers that recognize them won't pick them up because of their past cab ride incidents. Marty and Matthew stand out in the street yelling all kinds of nasty things at the cabbies as they drive by, but they won't stop. Jim, however, is determined and never gives up. Eventually, he finds an unsuspecting cabbie who is excited to take them all the way to their homes in West Knoxville. Jim assures the driver that the three will be okay.

The driver soon finds out that all is not okay. The cabbie keeps insisting that Matthew try to stay in the cab while it's moving. Actually, all Matthew wants is some fresh air. Drunk as he is, he still knows it isn't polite to throw up inside the cab. He knows cabbies get very angry about that so Matthew keeps opening the door, trying to get out. The driver continues pulling him back inside. The cab is now on the main road out of town, so Matthew's only other choice is to hang his head out of the window. The fresh air seemed to work, but it sure does make a mess on the side of the man's cab.

"Oh well," Matthew says as he falls to the ground once the cab stops at his house. "Imagine that, and he still expects a big tip."

On Monday morning Matthew could be heard saying to Jim and Marty, "I have to tell you boys, it always amazes me that we get to the lab dressed in our white shirts, ties and our nice, cleanly pressed suits and shiny shoes. It truly is impressive!" Probably the reason is that the three of them have all day Sunday to get sober.

Then there was another time Matthew went to the game alone. Marty's wife absolutely forbids him from going. Matthew had difficulty understanding why she got so upset about a night out with the mischievous partying boys. Nonetheless, she was really upset and had no problem saying as much.

When Matthew got to Marty's house to pick him up, his wife screamed and cursed at Matthew, even before he arrived at his front door, "All you guys do is get drunk and flirt with the girls and Marty is not going tonight." The air was blue with curse words leaving Matthew to wonder what happened after he left. Even so, leave he did. Jim, on the other hand had made a commitment to take his loving mother to visit a close friend at the nearby Knoxville hospital. Jim felt he owed his mother some quality time, so he refused to go along to the game.

Yes, Matthew did go to the football game, but alone. Later he said, "I guess Tennessee played a good game. I certainly must have enjoyed it." For Matthew going to the football game, as has been said before, meant tons of food, beer and best of all, beautiful or not so beautiful women. Of course he didn't remember the women part. As far as he was concerned, finding any woman willing to spend time with him was good. Then there is the other side of the extensive drinking. Having consumed a huge amount of alcohol that night there were the severe consequences of not feeling well. Matthew did the not feeling well thing often that night.

# CHAPTER 4
# THOUGHT I DIED AND WENT TO HEAVEN

On this particular night, Matthew did in fact meet a woman. In reality, he doesn't remember the meeting part. The lady found him passed out near the restroom door. She genuinely assumed he was dead because he wasn't moving. As Matthew found out later, she was an emergency room staff nurse from Knoxville Baptist Hospital. With some laborious help of several spectators, she managed to get him into her car and eventually took him to the hospital.

At the hospital the doctors and nurses were extremely busy tending to several automobile accident victims. They had little time to notice a severely intoxicated man the ER nurse had placed in the waiting area. After most of the accident victims had been attended, the nurses noticed Julie sitting alone in the waiting area with Matthew. Often the ER received over indulged men and women after the football games. The unusual thing in this picture was she was one of their own nurses that had brought this person to them. For what reason remained a mystery until the ER returned to near normal.

It was then the ER nurses laughed and proclaimed loudly, "You do know Julie; you brought a seriously drunk man in, and for what? Is he a relative of yours?"

To which Julie replied in her nonchalant voice "No, I never saw this man before in my life."

After a brief pause of disbelief at hearing Julie's answer, the attending nurse said to her. "Surely you have heard of alcohol poisoning? Just by looking at this man, I can see that is his problem. Take him into room three and we'll do the usual stomach pump. You know Julie, that's about all we can do."

After considerable time, Matthew's green facial color began to turn almost pink. Confused as to where he was Matthew saw for the first time his savior, Julie Karns. He had no idea that the lady standing before him was the one that rescued him from, he knew not where.

His thoughts however were not affected by his lingering drunken state as he said out loud, much to the embarrassment of Julie, "Wow, you are such a beautiful lady! On a scale of one to ten, I'd say, you have to be a twelve."

For safety reasons, no woman in her right mind would take a person, much less a drunken man she had picked up at a football stadium to her house. But for reasons known only to Julie and much to the chagrin of her fellow workers at the hospital, Julie did just that.

She drove Matthew to her house, cleaned him up and put him in her bed and patiently remained in an armchair by his side until he had become completely sober. Hours later when he awoke, to his surprise, he realized that under the covers he was wearing only his birthday suit. Needless to say he was very confused. Not only that he had no clothing, but had no idea where he was. Being as drunk as he was on this night would make a person want to go to the next alcohol anonymous meeting.

Julie had placed him in her own four poster bed. As Matthew much later tells the story, "I truly thought I had in fact died and gone to heaven although I knew that wasn't possible considering my past life." Matthew had always pictured himself going another direction and he is not talking about going west.

To hear Matthew tell the story, Julie truly was a Florence Nightingale. Julie, being the cool, calm and collected person she is never once mentioned the drunken state he was in when she found him. Nor did she mention that he was passed out and near death beside the bathroom door at the stadium. Instead, the two of them casually talked for hours on end about what he did for a living and what she did. For Matthew it was a most enjoyable evening.

At some point during the talk that night Julie introduced herself as Julie Karns. Earlier, while Matthew was sleeping off his drunkenness, Julie felt she should find out the name of the stranger lying in her bed. Although she felt it an invasion of his privacy, she decided to check his wallet for a driver's license. Matthew Franklin Wilson. She said to herself, realizing the hospital nurse could have told her his name, but didn't.

Finally, after hours of talking to his newly found friend, Matthew got up enough nerve to inquire, "So Julie, the thought of what happened to my clothes has been going through my head."

As politely as she could she explained, "You're clothes had become extremely soiled and I took them off you and put them in my washer and dryer. They're hanging right over there in the corner. If you would like, I'll leave the room while you get dressed."

"Why? You obviously took them off me so why should I be embarrassed for you to see me like this ... naked. After all, you are a nurse and I'm sure you've seen it all, all parts of men and women."

Not a bit shocked by his reply Julie said, "That is true Matthew Franklin Wilson, but I'll leave you alone while you dress." The last time Matthew heard anyone use his full name was way back in time when he lived at home as a child.

After Julie dropped him off at his house, Matthew made an unannounced commitment to himself that he would never again go out with the boys and get so insanely drunk. His days of making a complete fool of himself were over.

Julie Karns had, as a teen, found a husband. She seldom talked about how the marriage was going because her mother was so anti-divorce minded. Her mother felt the boy she married came from such a nice Christian family and Charles would never do anything to hurt her young Julie.

A year or so into the marriage, Julie found, as many young people find, marriage is something that requires give and take by both the husband and wife. Julie found the marriage quickly became an, all Charles way, or no way. She felt she had rights also, but after she rebelled several times her husband became extremely hateful. He became a mean person who, after many arguments, which were usually about money, he began to physically and severally beat her. Charles felt he should control all of the spending and she shouldn't be entitled to any of their incomes. For days after the beatings Julie had facial bruises along with black and blue marks all over her body.

Julie's father became extremely angry and called the police several times, but the investigators explained that they could do nothing unless Julie filed a complaint. It was her father that suggested Charles get help from a counselor. Charles wouldn't have any part of that and instead became even more brutal because, as he said, she had told her dad about how badly he beat her. It was her father that suggested divorce and paid the lawyers fee that ended the marriage.

Time was ticking for Julie. Many women, at that time, feel if you can't get hooked up with a man before forty, you will never get a man. Of course that is not true, but Julie actually believed it. She would often say to her friends, "I just want to find someone that will love me for who I am, not for my body or for the money I don't have." Then she would laugh along with whomever she was talking with.

It was true, Julie did not have large amounts of money stashed away, but she felt she was a woman with fair looks and she dressed conservatively. Actually, she was a knockout in her white starched hospital uniform. She was average height and weight with a figure that attracted many of the men she worked with at the hospital.

From time to time she would accept a lunch or dinner date with a doctor, but as she soon found out most of them were married. Besides, she felt romance should be with someone outside the work area. That had been drilled into her head when she attended nurse training. At some of the luncheons with doctors their main complaint was they never get to see their wives because of their brutal work schedules and the long hours. Hooking up with a doctor, what kind of a life could that be?

A short time after Matthew met Julie in such an awkward fashion, they decided to take a chance and try having dinner together. She suggested they lunch at the nearby, small Italian restaurant near the hospital that, she said, has great food. That dinner led to several luncheon meetings. At first they dined in the open area of the restaurant. Eventually they would ask to be seated in a quiet, dark romantic corner. After each meal they talked about their lives prior to meeting. Matthew felt he had found the love of his life. In reality, Julie had found him. Nonetheless, Julie was also feeling the pangs of love evidenced by the light kiss Matthew would give her when she left to go back to work.

For months Matthew was off the alcohol and all the misery that goes with it. Julie truly had cleaned him up, inside and out. He never realized that people like her existed. Julie was such a loving lady in every way. She loved her job, as well as all the doctors and nurses where she worked. Very few people love their jobs as she does. It bothered Matthew that she worked and associated with the wealthy and very well to do doctors daily. She was so beautiful one assumed she would have hooked one of those rich doctors. But she didn't, Julie was waiting for a kind, sweet and charming man and she felt Matthew was that man. At least that is what she kept telling herself. Hearing her thoughts about that made Matthew almost laugh out loud at times. So the obvious question in his mind was, would she willingly take him as her reliable friendship partner?

Her response to that, "God has a reason and I'm glad he has chosen you to be my friend at this time. God has a clear view and a clear picture of everything that takes place in our lives. We need to stop and listen to His direction always."

With most men there comes a period when he realizes, it is time. It is time to really settle down and definitely allow life to begin. That realization ended his horrible nights of getting so drunk he had no recollection of who he was, much less where he was.

There were times when Matthew was weaving his way home in his car and the cops would stop him and say, "Matthew, you know you're too drunk to drive don't you?"

Without delay he would say, "Well I certainly am not too drunk to drive, maybe too drunk to walk, but certainly not too drunk to drive, so just get out of my way and let me go." Of course they didn't. They all knew him and would take him home. He knew that wasn't right, but they did it anyhow. Nice people those Knoxville police officers.

The time had come to think about marriage. For these two unmarried people marriage seemed to be eluding them. One day Matthew began to realize their relationship was getting serious and in a rather awkward manner he said to Julie, "I just want you to understand that I believe we are coming along with our relationship just fine. My feeling is that it is time for us consider settling down and maybe ... *live together*. What do you think?"

Taken back by the statement Julie said "You know Matthew, we've been going together for quite some time, but I've never heard you mention anything about marriage."

"You're talking about the big *M* thing. What about it?" Matthew said trying to recant his previous statement. "I assume things are going along just fine without having a piece of paper to express that we've been declared a couple. Why would you want to mess up this whole beautiful relationship? Julie, don't you enjoy the free love we have?"

"Sure Matthew, but you do know I have very powerful religious convictions about my church and my church family. Religion plays a seriously large part in my life. At this time of my life I feel as though I need to become a family person and yes, I do love you very much. But without marriage, I'm afraid we can't continue as we have been. I know God sees what we are doing and it is not right. I'd like to fix that now. *Marry me Matthew!*"

By this time both of them were so connected, he was putty in her hands. Whatever she requested of him, he did his best to please her. It was obvious he'd have to do something about this marriage thing so he asked, "Julie, what do you want me to do? You know I love you so very much and I certainly owe you everything, including my life, so what's next?"

"If you are saying you will marry me," Julie said with renewed confidence, "I'll make an appointment with my minister and he will discuss what steps we should take and answer any questions the two of have about marriage."

"I do, so very much want to marry you Julie. But couldn't we just go to the courthouse for the ceremony?"

"Sure, but I would prefer our marriage be performed by my pastor. He knows about the heartaches of my first marriage and I would like him to meet you."

Clearly, Matthew had given in to their first serious discussion they had ever had about marriage. "Julie I love you so much and if this is what it will take to continue this bond, point me in the direction." He agreed to meet her pastor at the small Baptist church just off route forty. For Matthew, that was handy for him because route forty came within two miles of his house.

Pastor Bill, as she called him, was a big person, not a tall person, about five-seven, but big in all other areas. When Pastor Bill talked, you listened because he seemed to be in touch with the realities of life.

He pulled no punches as he spoke to both of them. "Matthew, I fully understand Julie's conviction of wanting you and me to have this discussion. I've known her for a lot of years, actually since she was about ten years old. I tried to help her through her unsuccessful early marriage. That is a long time to know a child, and I've known her mother and daddy for just as long. They are a God fearing family. But Matthew, I just met you today for the first time and I definitely don't know where you stand with our Creator."

As always, Matthew tried to joke around as he tried to explain his past and some of the stupid stuff he had done. "I know I've been a bad guy, but a person can change and Julie has been the reason for me to clean up my act. Pastor Bill, I'm ready for a long and lasting relationship."

Pastor Bill then explained the link between God and man and how to be certain we would be with Him when life here on earth is over. "As a married couple, where you spend eternity is very important Matthew. Permit me to carefully ask you a question. Matthew, if you died today, do you for sure know where you would spend eternity? The choice is either in heaven or hell."

"Well, I don't think I have ever heard such a direct question," said Matthew. "I don't know, I've never been asked that before. In the company of people I recently ran with, heaven and hell were not concerns we had to deal with. Quite frankly Pastor, is there a significant charge for going to either place? That has never been part of my travel plans and honestly, if there is a charge for going to either place I'll have to take the less expensive trip.... But wait just a minute, it sounds like you're speaking about dying. You mean *that* heaven or hell?"

With a serious look of determination on his face Pastor Bill firmly says, "That's the place I'm talking about Matthew."

Scratching his head Matthew said, "I've always believed that if you die, that's it, *right*?"

"No Matthew, *that's not it.*" Speaking with a very serious voice Pastor Bill said. "I just want to be sure if you die, you and

Julie will be reunited in Heaven." Pastor Bill described to him the pathway to meet God when life is over. Listening to the Pastor's message, Matthew willingly accepted his new life with Him.

With an excitement in his loud voice Pastor Bill said, "I'm really glad the two of you are here right now because in this day and at this time, life is so uncertain. Julie, I thank you for bringing Matthew today and thank you Matthew for coming."

"You're a nuclear scientist aren't you Matthew?" Pastor Bill said.

"I guess I qualify as one. I have a large piece of paper on my office wall that plainly says I am. I spent four years plus a few others at Penn State to get that piece of paper, but don't hold that against me Pastor."

Julie was amazed that Pastor Bill had been able to keep Matthew's attention so long. Sometimes Matthew had difficulty talking about anything that was not related to his work.

"Matthew," Julie said, "if I want to do something bad or something good I get this inner feeling that makes me realize something is either right or wrong. Eventually you will begin to have those same feelings. Those feelings are the Holy Spirit of God working on your inner self. You see Matthew, when I saw you lying on the floor at the stadium, those feelings told me to stop for a second and see if I could help you. That is how I found you Matthew, and that is how God has put us together. It is not an accident that we are here now. My first task has been to show you the road to an everlasting new life." The discussion ended with Pastor Bill, Julie and Matthew in a firm friendship hug.

They both readily conceded it would be a simple marriage ceremony. In attendance was Julie, Julie's mom and dad, Matthew, the Pastor and Pastor's Bill's wife who acted as a witness. In the state of Tennessee, and in the entire universe, Julie and Matthew could begin their life as man and wife. The exact date was Friday, April 15, 1964.

# CHAPTER 5
## THE LADY LOOKS SO GOOD

**J**ulie had a small house and Matthew, a somewhat larger one. Matthew felt his house was the better choice to live in since it had three bedrooms and a small spare room that could be used for just about anything. Perhaps the extra room could be used as a sewing room or a craft room, not that Matthew ever did anything crafty. Julie, however, did a lot of sewing. Many of her dresses were hand made and she also liked to do quilting. Julie liked the idea of a spare room she could call her own.

It was Julie who made the decision as to where to live. Although her house was closer to the hospital, she decided that Matthew's would be the nicer place to live. The attraction she said was that his house was in the country with the beautiful Western Knoxville hills behind it. She also liked Matthew's house because of the small stream that ran close behind his large lot. The front porch ran across the entire front of the house and on it, a creaky old swing for two as well as the two large white rockers. She loved sitting on the swing, listening to the swing screech. She could feel the romance of the two of them swinging or rocking away in their retirement years. Now, as never before, she could enjoy a view. She could see the trees, the clouds and hear the nearby stream and hear the birds as living objects that He created. She just loved his house.

Her house in the city sold quickly and she used some of the money from the sale to furnish the inside of Matthew's place. It seemed that Matthew had it fashioned, as would be expected, as a bachelor pad.

Matthew didn't care what kind of a fix up she did so long as there was a comfortable recliner for him in the living room. After a month or so, the house had new carpet, drapes and some new furniture including a queen size bed and two large dresser drawers for their large bedroom. The old bedroom furniture was placed in the second bedroom. The two bathrooms were updated with entirely new fixtures. The kitchen was also made new to reflect the appliances of the times.

When all was finished Matthew showed his approval by saying, "Julie, I would have done all this myself, but I just don't have time. Thank you so much for giving the house your expert women's touch. It's beautiful." Matthew used a masterful choice of words instead of expressing his real thoughts. His very real thoughts were *the cost*.

It was clear Matthew was proud of Julie. Often he talked about Julie saying, "My goodness, He really created a beautiful woman, but I suppose I've said that before." They were close to the same age, she a few years younger than Matthew. For Matthew, the few years of carousing had not yet begun to show on his face.

He still had most of his long brown hair, and there always seemed to be a small wisp of hair that was constantly hanging on his forehead. He sports a soft, slightly olive-tan complexion that makes his six foot body stand out in a crowded room. The stress of his job had begun showing ever so slightly, small crow's feet around the side of his dark brown eyes. Still, when he went out with Julie to dinner or to church, dressed in a suit and tie, Matthew looked like the good looking young man he is.

Julie's slightly wavy hair laid softly on her broad, but feminine shoulders, light ash brown and so silky, it had what most

I AM THAT I AM

women want, a smooth bright sheen always. There were times when it fell across part of her face covering one of her bright dark brown eyes. Actually Julie's eyes were beautiful, large and nearly black. It was interesting to watch her talk because she always looked directly at you, never looking past you as some people do. It's very difficult to tell a lie when a person looks directly into your eyes. Her face was nearly square and the skin so soft and smooth, not a wrinkle on it. Julie was perfectly proportioned, top to bottom. To look at her, one would say she has a near perfect body.

When she was dressing, there were times that he just sat on the edge of the bed and stared at her the whole time. That made her nervous so she would say, "What are you looking at Matthew?"

"Oh nothing," he said. "Your legs, they're so well proportioned and your leg muscles are so firm and tight."

At times she interrupted him and said, "Yes, and they go all the way to my hips don't they." Then they would both laugh.

But she was correct. They do go all the way up to her slender hips. When Julie put on high heels and stood up, her leg muscles would stand out as though she was intentionally flexing them. Matthew would say, "As you can tell Julie, I am a legman."

Matthew has been known to say that his Julie is put together at the top just as well. In the summer when she slips on one of those flimsy peek-a-boo dresses, he finds it almost impossible to keep his hands off her body. Julie always wore a dress. She said she wanted nothing to do with all the modern stuff like slacks and short skirts.

"You have to leave a little to the imagination. Slacks do nothing for the imagination and short sirts, well; you might as well go out in a bikini or just go naked." Oh yes, the loose thin dresses would turn Matthew on a whole bunch.

Her dresses, he would say, "Are just short enough to expose those beautiful legs and loose enough at the top to show her perky cleavage, but just a little."

Matthew would brag saying, "In her perfectly pressed nurse white work uniform, Julie is a knock out. Kind of makes me want to be one of her patients." At times he fantasized as his thoughts began to wander, pretending he was one of her patients.

During a fantasy moment in their bedroom he would say, "Oh nurse Julie, would you come here a moment. Please nurse come closer, bend down and check my neck. There is something wrong with my neck."

In his imagination she would bend down and always say, "There is nothing wrong with your neck, you just want to look down my blouse." That would be the end of his imaginary moment.

Yes, you must be thinking that at her age her body must be sinking, just as most women do, but they haven't had children yet so things have kind of stayed in their original place. Early on in their relationship they talked about children and decided not to have any. Their decision was based on the fact that in this disturbing time, they felt it best not to have children.

# CHAPTER 6
# THE FUTURE INVESTIGATED

How would Matthew explain to his fellow engineer scientists, the new Matthew? "Guess I'll just have to trust Him to show me a way." He said talking to himself, so he decided to just say nothing and allow his actions to do all the talking about the new Matthew.

At Oak Valley, work is beginning to get hectic. Washington is again beginning to put pressure on him to come up with a failsafe plan for the nation's nuclear power plants. His answer to that has been in the past, and still is, that as long as man makes the nuclear stuff they put in those systems, things, really bad things can happen. It doesn't matter how much the technology has progressed. What Congress really wants is for his office to give them a plan that has the appearance of perfection as it pertains to nuclear power. In other words, if something goes wrong he and all his engineer scientists get the blame. Matthew would say, "We are the ones that get hung for the results of whatever happens."

The fact is however, the world, not just the United States, is quickly running out of oil, coal and gas reserves. An action of some kind to address the problem must be acted upon quickly. Even if the nations of the world begin building hundreds of nuclear power plants today, it would be at least twenty years before they could be placed on-line. In ten or twenty years our natural resources, for the most part, will be gone or at the very least, severely reduced. Then what? Transportation as we know it today comes to a halt. Included with that is the love affair man has with his adorable automobile.

As Matthew and his fellow engineers tell it, that is just a tiny portion of the problem. Nearly everything this country needs to survive in life is manufactured using some kind of an oil based product. Building more and more nuclear power plants only temporally solves a small portion of the big problem. This country, as well as the rest of the world needs solutions that go beyond the huge nuclear power plants. Nuclear power gives us electricity for our homes and industry, but the world needs to think beyond that. Matthew's reasoning is that it is time for all nations to get together with each other and share their future energy knowledge. Share any and all ideas with each other concerning the long term energy solutions.

Matthew knows other nations around the world are exploring all kind of possible solutions to the energy crisis. He also knows the United States has been working on an, until now, classified project in Idaho called The Idaho Project, or simply called 'The Site.' It has been going on for about seven years and would appear to have real potential. The problem is that it is also nuclear.

The people of this country continue to think that nuclear cannot be made reliable and fail-proof. Unfortunately our government has the same mindset. It appears to Matthew, trying to get money to advance the Idaho Project is nearly impossible. The Senate Appropriation Committee says the people of the United States won't tolerate money spent on any kind of nuclear projects. With that said, he decides to ask Marty and Jim their feelings of inviting a few high level U.S. individuals to meet with them for a mini energy idea conference.

The next day Matthew called Marty and Jim and asked them to meet him in his office. He also asked Mary, his executive office manager to join them. It seemed proper to ask Mary to join because she seems to know where any important Washington people, in their business world, are at all times.

Most of the time, Mary is a very likeable person, but certainly not a push over. She knows her job and does it very well, just don't get in her way when she is doing it. She would often say to Matthew, "Matthew you ask me to do something, now allow me to do it in my way. If you want things done your way, do it yourself." Then she would go to her desk, sit down and glare at him until he left her office. "That's Mary," he would say. "I love her like a mother."

In nearly every office there is someone that looks out for all the little things and Mary is that person at Oak Valley. She always remembers all the workers birthdays. She knows more about the people that work in the building then they know about themselves. If there is an office party, and they have them often, she is the one that keeps the party orderly. At times the parties would get sort of out of hand. Mary has a way to get it all back in line or if need be shut down the occasion. Always in a gracious way, but you definitely know the party is over.

Mary has the appearance of a frumpy, older person. She dresses very conservatively. Always in a long dress, never slacks. She wears large wide heeled shoes. Matthew used to tease her and sing, 'Those boots are made for walking.' Of course she would react by swinging her foot at him as though trying to kick him in the butt. Matthew stopped teasing her about her shoes, "I don't do that anymore ever since she hit me once where it really hurt."

After hitting his mid-body the last time, she apologized over and over, then gave him a big motherly hug and added, "Matthew, you deserved that but I'm so sorry."

"You gotta love that woman."

Meanwhile back to their meeting. "Marty, Jim and Mary," Matthew said, "I think it is time for us to venture outside our tiny little cocoon here at Oak Valley. Let's invite some world energy leaders from outside our nuclear energy field to come here for a *think tank* session. It would appear to me that nothing will ever begin to be done about long term energy solutions unless someone of importance makes some serious noise. It is time for our side of the equation to be heard. You both know and I know that nuclear is not the only solution to solving the world's fossil fuel dependence and the global warming issues."

As Matthew raves and rants on and on Marty is tapping his fingers rapidly on his desk, anxiously waiting for Matthew to finish. When Matthew ends his message Marty claps his hands as he says, "Jim, I do believe Matthew is on his soap box today. Frankly Matthew, you are talking to the choir. What you are saying Matthew sounds good to me, but how are you going to get the energy people you suggest to come to a meeting here in little ole Knoxville? Quite honestly Matthew, I've wondered why you haven't suggested such a bold move like this long ago. There are so many others in the energy business; it would be good to hear some of their long term solutions, if they have any. God knows this country has none."

"Here, here!" Jim echoed Marty's last statement.

"Before you answer even who or how would you get them to meet with us Matthew," Marty continues. "I've been reading some of the research articles about our own Idaho Project and future fuel solutions from other parts of the world as well as their alternative energy possibilities. You and I know if we are not careful, in just a short time the United States could find itself looking in from the outside. It appears other countries around the world are considerably far more advanced in these matters than the U.S."

"I read the same research articles as you Marty and that's what I'm talking about," Matthew exclaims. "Sometimes our country remains sheltered in our comfortable little nest, afraid to venture into the new areas we see going on in other parts of the world. My guess is that our politicians don't want to make waves that would take away their precious, secure jobs. When new methods happen, there can be life changing consequences and that could mean losing our jobs."

After a time there was a pause in the conversations giving Mary an opportunity to inject. "I don't know if you men are aware that Catherine Hamilton, our U.S. Department of Energy

34

Secretary and the daughter of former President Hamilton, is coming to Knoxville tomorrow morning. She is coming along with Congressman John Gandy and a few other noteworthy people. As you know Matthew, John is the Congressional Chairman of the commission investigating why our energy prices are going through the roof."

"I know who they are Mary, I have to deal with Hamilton almost monthly and who cares about the price of gas. They had better care about even having gasoline." says Matthew using a rather haughty tone as he speaks.

Mary added, but feeling a bit stepped on, "Well I just thought I would mention it."

"I'm sorry Mary for being so short with you." Matthew said as though apologizing. "Would you call them and request they meet with us before they leave town tomorrow?"

"I would be happy to," Mary replied. Mary left the room to make appropriate preparations for this very small, but first step meeting. As she left the room she thought to herself, *this is what I enjoy most about my job. I get to do something significant once in awhile, not just the every day boring paper stuff for these guys.* "Oh my," she said, looking at her watch, "it's much too late to be calling them in Washington tonight, but I'll at least find out where they are staying while in Knoxville and call them first thing in the morning."

Back in the conference room Matthew was still talking. "Gentlemen, Congress and their political committees are so short sighted. I guess if I was a Congressman I would feel the same way. If you expect to be re-elected you have to say interesting things your constituents want to hear. The simple truth is they are constantly looking for a quick, short term political fix. It will be interesting to find out the other people that will be here with Hamilton. Actually, I am more interested in where and what our national and foreign energy suppliers are up to. I don't know why I'm thinking this, but the fact that we weren't invited to their meeting makes me believe their meeting is with some of our U.S. energy suppliers. If that is who Hamilton and

Gandy are meeting, perhaps we can find out just how far into the future these people are thinking. These two and their committee's are some of the ones that control the billions and billions of tax dollars that could fix our future energy shortages."

"Marty and Jim, I especially need you two to brush up on what we discussed earlier, you know, some of the other promising energy solutions. Marty, you know where we are going with our nuclear energy programs. I'm sure Hamilton knows also, but put together a presentation that shows where the United States is going as it pertains to our existing nuclear energy needs. Be certain to include the Idaho Project. Until tomorrow gentlemen, this meeting is over."

On the way home Matthew had to reflect back on his last encounter with Christine Hamilton. He had sharply criticized her for not going along with the new research lab he was trying to get for Oak Valley a few years back. He had lobbied for months about the essential need for new, more modern equipment and space. In the end she firmly declared, they had not shown any research results that warranted such expenditures. As far as she was concerned, Oak Valley didn't deserve the annual money they were already getting. That really riled Matthew. As he reflected back on her comment however, he had to almost agree with her. What really upset him was that Congressman Gandy, the local Congressman, readily agreed with her and voted against any additional money for Oak Valley. So now Matthew was wondering if Mary would be able to get them to visit their local office tomorrow. Mary was good at convincing stubborn people to do what she asked. He was guessing she would succeed.

Who is John Gandy? Back in the old days, before Matthew stopped drinking, John Gandy was an upstart politician from the Knoxville region. Matthew describes him saying, "We would party for days together. But then one day, just like that, he sobered up. And just like that, he decided it was a critical time to get serious about his political life. John carried out a good election campaign and to my surprise, he won the senate race." Matthew believes what helped him win the race was the women, they love him.

He is a tall, over six foot man and has exceedingly good looks that distinguish him from the ordinary man. When he enters the room, everyone seems to gravitate toward him. For a man his age, he has a full head of wavy dark hair and wears it slightly like Kennedy. Gandy always has on a well tailored and very expensive suit. His before D.C. life as a prominent lawyer positively gave him the proceeds to support stuff like that. Matthew felt that's why the women liked him; he dresses well and has the looks of considerable success. He has a smooth bronze complexion with hardly a wrinkle on his face. The booze has not yet spoiled his boyish appearance. Every place he goes there always seems to be a lady hanging on his coat tail. They are always real lookers, as Matthew recalls.

It was the women that occasionally caused John and Matthew to have a falling out. About nine years ago John and Matthew parted ways, except for occasional business meetings. Somehow Matthew managed to pick the one woman that was John's favorite. I believe her name was Nancy.

She and Matthew would end up at the bar where they would drink and dance for hours and always ended up in her hotel room, which was *always* at John's expense. That's probably what irritated John the most, he was stuck paying the bill for Matthew's nights of carousing with his favorite girlfriend. John Gandy was married, but, "So what" he would say.

"One day he informed Matthew that if he didn't lay off his Nancy, he would see that his projects would never receive another cent from Washington. That didn't bother Matthew though because at the time John was not yet a senator. After he did become a senator however, he did keep his promise of cutting funding. Regrets, regrets, Matthew had none even though John did, at times, make it rough on Oak Valley, but they usually were able to get around most of the proposed budget cuts."

Matthew enjoyed talking about the Washington people that he must deal with occasionally. Catherine Hamilton is one of them. The only comparison you can make to John Gandy is that Ms Hamilton consistently has a professional look about her appearance. In public John is the same, always wearing an expensive suit. Catherine wears, what would seem to be the best attire money can buy. But then why not, she has scads of money. At least that is what the public records indicate. Business attire always, unlike some women of position who wear leisure clothes but not Catherine Hamilton. Only once has Matthew seen her in anything but an executive business suit. She always wears a well tailored skirt, cut just below the knees and always, a separate suit jacket to match and usually wears a well fitted blouse. At times she wears a matching hat. The hat look seems to be the trend with the women of this time. Women want to wear a hat just like the ones worn by Catherine Hamilton. Hamilton could make a bundle if only she would allow a hat manufacture to put her name brand on their merchandise. Being the lady she is however, she would not allow that.

As mentioned earlier Matthew saw her once in something other than executive business attire. Matthew and his wife, Julie were invited to a rather fancy after election party in Washington. Matthew tended to shy away from such affairs, but since most wives have their way, Julie convinced him that being noticed in such places can do nothing but help with job security, so they both went.

In strolled Catherine Hamilton on the arm of the Vice President of the United States. What an entrance, all eyes turned toward the arriving couple. Actually, all the men's eyes focused on Catherine and even Julie exclaimed, "Wow!" Because of Julie's exclamation, Matthew believed that meant he could stare also, and he did. Apparently Catherine had purchased her dress directly from Paris. It was an extremely flimsy low cut and nearly a see through dress, not quite see through, but almost. When Matthew mentioned earlier that her clothes were well tailored, he meant this one was extremely well tailored.  Not much left to the imagination.  She wore what appeared to be a scarf around her neck, although Matthew didn't know why.  It was certainly not for warmth.  It was compelling to note that it gently flowed across the front of her body, close to hiding her somewhat youthful looking cleavage.  The gown was extremely loose fitting on the upper region of her figure.  Matthew seriously wanted to take a closer look, but Julie kept tugging at his coat to hold him back.  Instead Julie wanted him to notice that she had on very stylish shoes and the rich color of the shoes matched the lavender colored gown she wore.  The heels were only about three inches high.  Matthew felt that was to keep her below the height of the Vice President."

What a good looking woman.  At one point Matthew moved close enough to count the rings on her neck?  That is his way of telling the age of a woman, or anyone for that matter.  With Matthew's system you count the neck creases or rings, one ring for ten years and a partial ring for the years in between.  Julie used to tell him people are not trees.  What she meant was the rings of a cut down tree shows its age.  But the reality is, you can almost always tell a person's age if you count the rings on the neck.  Catherine Hamilton was about forty five according to his system.  Now however, each time he sees her, he gets images of her in that outstanding evening gown."

It is seven in the morning as Mary leaves her house to begin another day at the office.  As she is driving the short distance from her house she is considering what Hamilton and Gandy would say about meeting with Matthew's group.  The night before Mary had no luck finding out where the team was staying in Knoxville.  Once at the office, she went about her job of trying to track them down.  Finally Mary located them by going through their operational office assistants in Washington.  Mary found out they are staying at the Knoxville Hotel. *That wasn't too difficult*, she thought; *perhaps they will be in a good mood and readily agree to come to our office.*  There is only one way to find out so Mary made a call to Hamilton's room.

It is early in the morning so Mary's thoughts are to catch both of them before they begin their meeting. The telephone rang and rang in Hamilton's room. Finally an answer on the other end, "Ms Hamilton, this is Mary Grainger, the executive assistant to Matthew Wilson at the Oak Valley Laboratory."

"I was just on my way to breakfast Mary, don't tell me Wilson needs more money for Oak Valley. That is all he ever wants when I hear from him."

Mary came back quickly before the discussion came to a quick end. "No, he and several others at our laboratory hope to meet with you and Congressman Gandy before you leave Knoxville to talk about where the United States is going concerning future renewable energy needs. Matthew is calling it an energy crisis *think tank* session."

"Now that is interesting Mary," Hamilton said. "Actually that is exactly why we are here. We are meeting with several major players in this nation's oil and gas supply chain and a few major foreign suppliers to discuss just that topic. I'm wondering how Wilson picked up that we were coming to Knoxville in the first place. We assumed we could just sneak in and out without being noticed."

"To be honest Ms Hamilton," Mary said. "In this era of crucial information and communication, not much happens around here that I don't know."

"Mary, I wish I had a person like you in my office, one that always has their ear to the ground listening to what is going on around me." Hamilton, admiring Mary's dedication said, "Mary, since Matthew believes he knows why we are here, why doesn't Matthew and his assistants meet with us at the hotel. Our conference will begin today just after lunch. If he wants he may meet us about twelve and join all of us for lunch."

"That would be great. I'm sure that will be okay. I know he is looking forward to meeting you and Congressman Gandy again. Thank you so much Ms Hamilton."

Mary could hardly wait for Matthew to get to the office so she could tell him all the good news about why Gandy and Hamilton are in town.

Matthew, Jim and Marty usually arrive at the office about the same time, just before eight every morning. This morning Mary is beaming, pacing anxiously as the three of them arrive. Before Matthew, Marty or Jim have an opportunity to take off their coats, Mary blurts out, "Matthew, I have good news. I'll bet you can't guess why Hamilton and Gandy are in town."

"Let me guess Mary, they are coming here to talk with a team of U.S. energy moguls about the coming world energy shortage."

"Know it all. That is exactly why they are here." exclaimed Mary. "They wanted to meet some place away from their political, all ears environment back in Washington. Oh, and you should also know there are several foreign oil suppliers with them. She didn't say who they are."

"What did I tell you Marty? The most significant question Mary is whether it would be possible to meet with them today or must we schedule another time?"

"It is better than that Matthew. The three of you are invited to meet with them for lunch. Their meeting won't take place until after lunch. Be at the Knoxville Hotel dining room about twelve o'clock."

"That is better than I had hoped Mary. Thank you for doing an excellent job."

"Jim and Marty, bring the presentations you planned for our meeting along to the hotel. I just hope we have an opportunity to use them."

The three arrived at the hotel about eleven-thirty not sure what to expect. Meetings like this have a way of going no place so they weren't assuming anything. Marty and Jim had a briefcase full of related information in case they were given the chance to speak. Matthew felt the information his two assistants had collected would be useful. His expectation was that

Ms Hamilton would generously give his team some time on the floor to demonstrate their points of view.

To the surprise of the three, they were warmly greeted at the door by Hamilton and Gandy who took them immediately to the hotel's private dining room. Both appeared unusually happy to see Matthew, considering all the bickering he had with the two them in the past.

The dining room had a few people Matthew had never met. Mary told him the NRC Chairman was going to be attending. It has been several years since Matthew had spoken to him in person. Matthew was anxiously looking forward to seeing Chairman Johnson of the Nuclear Regulatory Commission face to face. As they entered the room, Matthew was surprised Johnson was not present.

Trying not to be too surprised by Johnson's lack of attendance Matthew asked Ms Hamilton, "So where is the most high and mighty Chairman Johnson?"

She replied, overlooking Matthew's rather malicious question, "He said he would be late, but hopefully he'll arrive in time for the meeting."

"Very good," Matthew said and left it at that. He has found from his past experiences not to express his opinions of negativity concerning trivial circumstances. In this case, as to why the most important person is not present.

Those already seated were the real surprise to Matthew. Senator Gandy went around the table introducing each person as though they were all his personal friends. That is Gandy's method of operation; he wants to be the star of the show.

"Our first honored guest," said Gandy, "Vice Chairman of Quantum Fuel System Technology Worldwide, Inc., Franklin Jonquel. His company is working on new methods of creating bio fuel from waste. His primary business office is in Germany." This was a person Matthew had never heard of and up until now, had no idea what his firm did.

"Next I would you like to meet, Karl Mercedah from Iceland.

Mr. Mercedah is CEO of a company working with the newest and latest technology, hydrogen fuel cells." That name struck a familiar ring with Jim Adams. Recently Jim had read an extensive article written by Mercedah published in Modern Technology magazine.

The real surprise to Matthew was the introduction of the French Director of Energy and Raw Materials, Claude Rafferty. He has known Claude for years and his overwhelming zeal for nuclear power in France. What a surprise to see him in Knoxville.

The fourth person introduced was a lawyer representing a major, unnamed Middle Eastern oil supplier, Mr. Jon Lunsborg, also from Germany. How bizarre Matthew thought, *a bit of international suspense.*

"Last, but not least is Ms Catherine Hamilton," Gandy said. "Most of you know our very own, United States Secretary of the Department of Energy.

I've been told," Gandy continues, "William Johnson, Chairman of the U.S. Nuclear Regulatory Commission is running late, but will arrive shortly."

The luncheon went on with a lot of small talk, mostly light personal things and about their wives and children. When the informal talk came in Matthew's direction he told them about his wife Julie. About his children, he said, they had tried, but thus far were unsuccessful having one. That was a lie of course, but the ones in attendance had no way of knowing that. Actually Julie and he decided early in the marriage that they definitely didn't want children.

To Matthew's surprise it was interesting that the foreign attorney, whose home is in Germany, had seven children. *Whew,* he thought, *glad that's not me.* With all his world wide travel, Matthew did wonder how Jon managed to have that many kids. Jon eventually answered the question Matthew was thinking by saying he was not traveling every day. I guess not, since he had a child for each day of the week.

After about an hour and a half the luncheon began wind-

ing down, Ms. Hamilton informed the waiters to begin clear-
ing the tables. Then she announced, "Gentlemen let us stand
and tip our glasses to a meaningful conversation about possible future energy solutions." With that said, there was a clink
of glasses and a resounding voice of enthusiastic agreement:
"*Here, Here!*"

Christine Hamilton, a nearly six foot lady, and as always,
was dressed in complete business attire continued standing
and suggested all be seated. She moved to the front of the table
to announce that she would be the moderator for the meeting.
"Gentlemen, I would especially wish to open the dialogue with
what some of you already know. The United States, as is the
entire world, is facing a disastrous, very near catastrophic future unless we can do something to solve the world's failing
supply of fossil fuel. Today, The United States is prepared to
share our secret and not so secret future energy solutions. In reality we have, for the most part, nothing new to share that you
do not already know. Therefore the floor is open to any energy
discussions at this time."

Quietly trying to sneak in the back door of the meeting room
was William Johnson, Chairman of the NRC. He tiptoed quietly and took his seat beside Catherine Hamilton.

"Welcome Mr. Johnson." Ms Hamilton said. "The meeting
has just begun and I believe you know most of those present."
For the record, Ms Hamilton reintroduced each one present.

"Thank you Ms Hamilton." Johnson said. "Unfortunately a
news reporter recognized me at the airport and questioned me
as to why I am in Knoxville. I didn't want him to know the real
reason so I simply said I was visiting a sick relative. That didn't
set well with him and he attempted to follow my cab. For not a
whole lot of money, you can get a cab driver to do some insane
things to lose the person following in his car, closely behind."
With that said, the entire room broke out in laughter as though
they had, at times, had to do the same thing.

To the surprise of all present, Franklin Jonquel announced a new project that most knew nothing about. "For the last two years we have been working on methods to set up an infrastructure for adding hydrogen to our automotive service stations throughout Europe and Asia. At present we produce roughly twenty five percent of the oil and gasoline for the international network of petrol stations in Europe and Asia."

He continued, "As you already know we have been exploring new methods of producing bio fuel made from just about any source we can find. We've used corn, sugar, waste cooking vegetable oil. You name it, we've tried it. Unfortunately, after several years of research we have finally decided that, no matter the source, the financial bottom line is that, it is not possible to make a bio fuel without causing extreme hardship to the human population."

Jonquel went on to say, "It is my personal view and that of our research engineers, the optimistic future outlook of the transportation industry will be hydrogen powered vehicles. There are some serious obstacles however. Cost of the domestic vehicle for one, but the extremely serious obstacle is the local supply line to the locations and the storage methods at the service depots. Getting the needed supplies to the stations by truck is the easy part, but storage, once there, is another matter. Actually we would like to have the hydrogen generated at the local dispensing stations. That would be the ideal method. That would resolve nearly all our problems, but to date we haven't seen that as a practical solution. That, my friends is why I am here. My expectation is that one of you can willingly help solve the hydrogen storage problem."

"The floor recognizes Karl Mercedah, CEO of his fuel cell company in Iceland." Ms Hamilton said.

"Thank you Ms Hamilton. Our country has placed a time frame of ten years from now to have an infrastructure of transportation service stations in place that can supply hydrogen for our fuel cell vehicles. At this time we are building several extraction facilities in our country. As I'm sure you know, there are several ways of splitting water into its component parts of hydrogen (H2) and oxygen (O). We have chosen the process called steam reforming of methane from our, extremely abundant, natural offshore gas resources. We chose this process because we have vast amounts of natural gas in and around the deep waters of Iceland. We are however faced with the same problem as Mr. Jonquel just mentioned. How do you store the hydrogen at the local service facility?"

Mr. Jonquel was quick to interrupt saying, "We know what you are doing in Iceland, but I have one big, big question Karl. Your plans are to use a fossil fuel to manufacture hydrogen. How do you see that as solving the fossil fuel shortage?"

"Well Mr. Jonquel," Karl said. "It is clear that some international action on the subject is necessary to approve our actions. In our country we feel our solution is a step that has to be taken immediately. Our country is within ten years of running out of oil that can be converted to gasoline. Quite frankly, Iceland refuses to be held hostage to the world's oil producing nations. To our knowledge, we are not seeing any long term practical answers from anyone in the world. The world cannot afford to wait for a perfect solution. Again Mr. Jonquel, if you have a solution to the service station storage issue, please share it with us"

"Mr. Rafferty," Hamilton said, "We understand that your country, France is heavy into nuclear power. Do you have any update on where you are going as it pertains to future oil needs?"

"As you know," Rafferty began, "France is at the present time nearly one hundred percent nuclear power. We have the natural resources to maintain nuclear power for at least the upcoming one hundred years. Our plan is to make it essential within the next two decades to have all motorized vehicles running on total rechargeable electric batteries or hybrid electric. Our very real immediate problem is the necessary replacement of our old nuclear facilities. We eventually wish to team up with the United States at their Idaho nuclear test *Site*. If the U.S. would share their information, they could save us a vast amount of time in our nuclear update process."

"Mr. Johnson, can you shed some light on the U.S. Idaho nuclear test program?" Hamilton inquired.

Mr. Johnson began, "As Chairman of the NRC for the United States, I believe I can speak openly about *The Site'* known to most now as The Idaho Project. Most countries around the modern world know that we have been testing a new generation of nuclear energy. Our present nuclear power is being produced by Generation II units. As Mr. Rafferty has stated, France desires to soon begin replacing all of their aging nuclear power plants. Here in our country we have one hundred and three nuclear reactors aging also. Within the next two decades most of these will have to be replaced, but with what?"

Johnson continued, "Until a few years ago most of what we were doing at the Idaho Project was classified as *secret*. Over the last two years however, the United States started putting pressure on a couple of Mid-Eastern countries to stop their on-going development of what they call, nuclear power plants."

"We have found they are secretly trying to produce weapons grade nuclear uranium. One of our test reactors uses nuclear uranium, enriched to ninety-two percent. Anything more than twenty percent is considered weapons grade. In view of this, we had to come forward and explain to the world exactly what we are doing. The purpose of our enriched uranium that high is to test the long term effects on our sophisticated equipment that will be used in the construction of our new, updated nuclear power plants. It is a short cut to see how long a new plant can last before replacement is necessary. Mr. Wilson can confirm that, unfortunately none of the Mid-East countries genuinely understand this as, the truth. If it is okay with our moderator I would like to turn the session over to Matthew Wilson who has knowledge of our next generation nuclear power plants."

"Mr. Wilson, please proceed," Hamilton said.

Matthew took the floor and began, "I have asked several of my associates to prepare information about the United States future strategy as it pertains to where we are and where we are headed. It appears that all here know where we are as it relates to nuclear power. What you might not know is that at the Idaho Project, we are developing a cost effective test power plant. When the Idaho Project is completed it will have supplied the necessary information to build the future Generation IV nuclear power plants. Presently at this site, we are testing a Generation III plant that is much like the Generation II plants. We are presently operating with the notable expectation that Gen III is a much cleaner and safer unit. Congressman Gandy can verify that our government has allowed $1.25 billion dollars to initially construct this experimental reactor. This will be the equivalent to the Secret Project of a half-century ago. The key difference is scientists from around the world will be working together to restructure nuclear power production, not in secrecy, but providing open information to all interested parties in all parts of the world."

"Gen III is a nuclear facility whose fundamental purpose is to test parts that will go into the next Generation IV units," Matthew continued. "A normal Gen II 1000 megawatt unit costs about $2 billion dollars and usually takes about ten years to twenty years complete. We do not have that kind of time to waste. When we eventually get the critical data needed to begin assembling the new generation units, a Generation IV can be put in place in about five years, possibly less time. The fundamental reason being, most of the operating parts will be manufactured off site and trucked or railed to the construction sites. It is like building a system with huge Lego blocks."

"The real advantage of this unit is that the steam produced has an extremely high output temperature in the range of *1650 to 1830 degrees Fahrenheit*; thus allowing the commercial by-product production of *hydrogen* by using a process called *steam electrolysis* which will result in the future dream of exhaust free cars running on hydrogen, totally independent of foreign oil. Admittedly however, this does not solve the on-site service station problem mentioned before by Karl or Franklin."

Matthew continued. "The Generation IV unit we have chosen to construct is a meltdown-proof, pebble bed reactor which uses grains of uranium encased in balls of graphite as fuel rather than nuclear fuel rods. Most of you are familiar with the method since it has been published in journals world wide. I'll only add that the benefit of this type structure eliminates the extended down time for refueling. This happens because the reactor core is filled with close to 360,000 of these *nuclear fuel pebbles*. Because the way the pebbles, known as kernels, are constructed, each day, or when necessary, about 3,000 of them are removed from the bottom of the pebble pile as the fuel is spent and fresh pebbles are added to the top. These pebbles are fireproof and practically impossible to use for dangerous weapon grade production. The spent fuel is easily transported to permanent storage facilities. The real question is, store them where?"

"Would it be possible," inquired Mr. Jonquel, "to build the Gen IV units small enough to locate, let's say, in or near every large city. If that is possible, it would certainly solve most of our hydrogen production and transportation problems."

"At present," replied Wilson, "we really aren't sure. When our testing is complete you will have a suitable explanation and so will we. If you are thinking that the price of fueling your car will return us back to the old fashioned days of cheap fuel, forget it. Recently Jim Adams, who some of you know, has put together some financial numbers that I strongly believe are going to be pretty close to reality. He is here with us and I'll ask him to disclose his findings."

"Ms Hamilton if I may." Jim Adams asked, requesting the floor.

"By all means, please do."

"Producing hydrogen as a direct by-product of nuclear electric generation, as with any new product, has tremendous hurdles to overcome. First and central is the average price of the power plant itself. A full size unit of say 250 megawatts will cost probably in excess of several billion dollars. To answer your question Mr. Jonquel, developing a smaller city size unit would be in the neighborhood of, let's say, 500 to 800 million dollars. You have to ask yourself, how many cities could afford that? The same technology has to go into the smaller unit as the larger one."

"From a positive standpoint," Jim continued. "If countries around the world would rapidly adapt this technology we would have solved, for the moment, global warming caused by the automotive and transportation industry. We would have eliminated gasoline and diesel vehicles. No more smoke from coal or fuel burning power generation plants. Smog, as we know it, would be nearly eliminated. Global warming would, for the most part, be eliminated. That would be a really big, big leap forward."

"The cost to generate electricity will come as a shock to most of us, the end consumers. The by-product of hydrogen from these local smaller Gen IV power plants might solve transportation's dependence on fossil fuel, but the financial results could bankrupt most countries and definitely their cities. Fossil oil will still be needed in one form or another to make the millions of products used daily by the human race."

"Recently I did research and have come up with a very educated guess as to the financial impact concerning the idea of smaller, city owned power plants such as you just suggested Mr. Jonquel. My estimate includes the added taxes the cities would need to pay for such a facility, the necessary trucking transportation, the tank farm storage and multiple other factors. I've included profits for the owners of the dispensing stations. I'm guessing we would see the average hydrogen vehicle fuel cost for the same miles per gallon of gasoline and diesel covered, in excess of $7.00 to $10.00 or more per equivalent gallon of hydrogen fuel. In reality a fill-up would be in the area of $140 to $200 for the equivalent 20 gallon of fuel. If we could create hydrogen as has been suggested, would it be worth the price. Personally, I think so. However, if placed to a vote of the average person in the United States, I suspect it would be voted down."

"Our petrol in France is at nearly $7.00 a liter now." Claude Rafferty grumbled.

Quietly absorbing the materials discussed, lawyer Jon Lunsborg came to life and asked several questions. "The companies and individuals I represent would never allow the world's cities and towns to operate their own private power companies. Should this program advance beyond its present state, you must understand, today's oil and electrical industries will be the businesses to foot the cost of setting up such an infrastructure, and I might add, also reap the profits."

Lunsborg went on, "Of my bigger concern is the question. Will your governments be willing to propose such drastic actions? If a politician is honest with his constituents about the end costs of such a proposal as has been discussed here, he or she would be committing political suicide."

"Do you actually believe the American congress will pass legislation allowing such energy development? To tell the American people that they are going to help save the world from global warming by creating a type of petrol that costs in excess of ten dollars a gallon. I think not."

"Thank you Mr. Adams and Mr. Lunsborg for your enlightening input." Ms Hamilton said, quickly sensing a possible argument that was about to arise. "It is interesting that the discussion has moved in the direction of small reactors. Recently I visited a senior high school near Washington D.C. to examine a science project created by a very bright senior high school student. To my surprise this boy, with the assistance of his science teacher, actually created a miniature scale model nuclear reactor. The amazing part, according to him, is that he has designed a system small enough and safe enough to be placed within the personal area of each home and business on the planet. Of course he has no clue what is being done today at the Idaho Project, but it does make one wonder if such a unit would be possible. You said yourself Matthew, Generation IV plants can be assembled much like building a Lego building except with larger building blocks. Also, that would allow each home or business owner to not only generate their own electric power, but also create their own hydrogen. Of course, as Mr. Lunsborg suggests, these units would be owned and operated by the existing power companies."

"Now just a minute Ms Hamilton," said an irritated Mr. Jonquel. "We eventually intend to build a hydrogen infrastructure of service stations worldwide. As has already been stated, the fuel industry is not going to sit by and allow anyone to take that away from them. Should such a far fetched personal home or business idea surface, Mr. Lunsborg is right, you will see a political revolution like the world has never before witnessed."

"It was only a thought." Hamilton replied. "I was of the impression that this is a session to openly examine any and all possibilities."

"You do have to wonder however Mr. Jonquel," Matthew added. "If that were possible, can you imagine the eventual elimination of all those overhead power lines? We know the havoc that we experience when severe storms of all kinds crop up. The United States has, in recent years, gone through its worst hurricane season ever. Power has still being restored in parts of this country. Ice and snow storms would not cripple towns and cities as it does now. The expense of overhead electrical transmission lines from central power stations to cities would not be necessary. In parts of the earth where there is no electric power, small independent power generation would be possible. It would eventually take years and years for the advantages to be fully realized. In reality, individual homes, having the amazing capacity to generate their own power would not be practical, but placing small systems at or near small towns and large cities could be. Honestly, there still must be a service station to supply fuel to the billions of fuel cell vehicles. The oil startup corporations would become very lucrative investments."

Matthew went on to say, "Honestly Ms Hamilton, I for one would certainly want to meet the kid who is capable of such futuristic thinking. I plan to come to D.C. in the upcoming week or so to address our recent budget proposal for next year, perhaps we could visit with the boy and his teacher."

"I'll alert the finance committee. Thanks for the warning Matthew. I'll also attempt to set up a meeting with the boy." Hamilton said.

Suddenly the door to the conference room burst open and the hotel manger raced to Ms Hamilton exclaiming that there are about a dozen demonstrators in front of the hotel. "They have signs saying *no more nuclear power* and they are loudly and almost violently chanting the same." He said he phoned the police, but strongly recommends the meeting be ended before the demonstrators get out of hand. Additionally he requested us to leave by a rear entrance.

Mr. Johnson, not surprised that the demonstrators had found him, said "Apparently, that news guy found out from the taxi dispatcher the hotel where the taxi driver dropped me off. Those news jerks will do anything for a story."

Wilson rose to his feet and said, "Gentlemen and Ms Hamilton, I believe we are for the most part, in an acceptable accord that Generation IV nuclear power is a direction the world must go sometime in the not to distant future. Now Mr. Johnson, it's up to you to sell Congress and the President the idea."

"You are all invited to visit and carefully examine the *Idaho Project*," Chairman Johnson said. "The Project is about forty-five minutes southeast of Idaho Falls, Idaho. At this time we have nothing to hide and eagerly look forward to sharing our newest state of the art technology with the world. In spite of the protests, like the one going on at this time in front of our hotel, safe nuclear generation is coming back in the very near future regardless of how the world feels about it."

Matthew then advised the group, "The hotel manager has said transportation back to the airport has arrived at the back door so please quietly exit. Thank you for inviting us Oak

Valley folks to attend this very informative meeting."

Ms Hamilton proclaimed. "Gentlemen, this meeting is adjourned. Have a safe trip home. Thank you for spending this brief time with us. For those wanting to visit the Idaho Project, please send me a note or call my office in Washington requesting a time for your visit."

Mr. Johnson paused for a moment before leaving. "Mr. Wilson and Ms Hamilton," Johnson said. "I would like to have a word with the two of you in private before you leave." It appeared to Matthew that Johnson was somewhat agitated about, Lord only knows what.

"Sure Mr. Johnson," Matthew said. "You look as though something is extremely wrong. What is the problem?"

Johnson walked to a corner of the room and waved for us to meet with him. "Wilson," he said, "I have heard about your methods of operation and some of your past boondoggles. You tend to do things without formal approval, then after you have already opened the can of worms; you come begging us at NRC to okay your projects. That is not going to happen with this hair brain idea you and Hamilton are contemplating. You must keep me informed of each and every step. Crazy as the idea mentioned in this meeting is, and assuming it is possible, I must insist you provide my committee with step by step progress. Failure to do so will inevitably lead to Congressional rejection of any plans you two may have conceived. Now, have a nice rest of the day. I must return to Washington."

As Matthew left the hotel by the rear door he said, "Ms Hamilton, that sounded like a threat."

In a rather sarcastic tone Hamilton answered. "Actually Matthew Wilson, it sounded more like a promise to me. I have to hurry or I'll miss my ride back to D.C. I'll call you after I contact the boy genius and his teacher."

# CHAPTER 7
# FORBIDDEN ROMANCE FILLS THE AIR

**I**t was late afternoon so Marty and Jim decided that they would stay in town and have an early dinner. With a little prodding from them, Matthew decided to stay and have an early dinner also. *After all*, he thought, *Julie wouldn't be home from her hospital job so why not have dinner with the boys?*

Matthew was trying not to notice some of the old off limits hangouts they passed on their way to the Franklin Room. The Franklin Room is a very respectable small restaurant located within a few blocks of the Baptist Hospital. It is a great place known for their, *all-you-can-eat* prime rib. His mouth began to water as he recalled that he hadn't had an acceptable prime rib in months. When Jim and Marty suggested eating there he quickly agreed.

Matthew isn't a particularly up to date sports fan, but it was good to just sit back and pretend to be interested talking with the boys about the sports scene. When men get together it seems that's about the only thing guys can discuss. Of course we can talk about our jobs, but why? Sports, now that's the important stuff. Who will make it to the Super Bowl and why? They argued back and forth, but never came to any real conclusions.

Out of the corner of his eye Matthew believed he saw Julie being seated in a dark corner of the restaurant and with her was a rather good looking man. No, he assumed, she is still at work, but the woman looks just like her. His curiosity got the best of him so he decided to approach the two of them. As he did the woman looked like she wanted to slide under the table. Why, because sure enough, it was Julie.

"Hi Julie, thought you would still be working so Jim and Marty talked me into coming with them for an early dinner after our meeting here in town."

Julie managed to say something after an embarrassing long pause. "Matthew, this is Doctor Frank Jordon, one of the interns at the hospital. I didn't think you would be home until late so I agreed to have dinner with Doctor Jordan. I hope that is okay."

"Sure Julie, that's fine with me. Why don't you and Doctor Jordon join us at our table?"

Matthew was sure Jordan knew Julie was married so it didn't seem to bother the doctor that he had caught the two together. Jordan seemed relieved Matthew had invited them to join his table. Jordan was a sports fanatic and carried most of the table conversation. That seemed to relieve the pressure among all present, especially Julie. Julie in a nurse uniform is a sensation so Matthew can't say he blames anyone wanting to take her out. The surprise to him was that she accepted. When he got home, to be sure, there would be a frank and lively discussion about this Doctor Frank guy.

The dinner was great. His appetite was fulfilled completely. Don't know why, but he had a healthy, or not so healthy, large piece of pecan pie. When he finished Matthew exclaimed, "Wow! What an end to a truly great meal?"

Julie had her car at the hospital so she had to leave the restaurant with Jordan. This left Matthew to wonder if she would come home or do something else dumb.

Matthew was driving so Jim and Marty left with him. Not much was said on the trip back to the office parking lot. Jim and Marty could feel the tension and fortunately said nothing about the restaurant encounter with Julie. They both knew

Matthew from the past and knew he was quite capable of losing his temper. When he did, it was not a pretty scene. By the time they arrived at the office it was almost dark so Jim and Marty went immediately to their cars without saying a word.

Matthew was home for about half-an-hour when Julie arrived. When she came in, all she said was, "That was a nice dinner wasn't it Matthew?"

"Sure." Not sure where she was going with that remark and wondering how she was going to explain Doctor Frank. "Julie, how long has this been going on, I mean, have you and Doctor Jordan done this before?"

"From time to time," Julie tried to explain, "Doctor Jordan and some of the other interns take me out. Most of them are from other parts of the country and they get lonely and just want someone to listen to their hospital work complaints. I don't see anything wrong with that Matthew."

*Hmm ... strange logic he thought. Could she be that naive?* His answer to her made him question himself as he said, "It's okay as long as you recognize you are married to me. I am your husband. Are you sure that is all there is to it Julie?"

"I love you Matthew and would never cheat on you." Countered Julie

"What you did this afternoon has all the appearances of cheating." Matthew said "The fact that I happened to find you with another man establishes the possibility that you might cheat. I should be furious, but for some unknown reason I'm not. It's getting late so I believe we should go to bed. Perhaps after a good night sleep I will forget this dastardly deed."

Time has a way of cooling off bad situations. Relationships, like those of many couples who have had unpleasant situations develop in marriages, require time before returning to normal. Still there were the lingering bad thoughts in Matthew's mind, but after several weeks passed, those lingering thoughts began to diminish and he was glad. After all, she was the one that should be questioning his faithfulness considering how she found him, not that long ago. But that was his past ruckus life style and this is now.

It had been several weeks since he heard from Christine Hamilton about whether he should plan a trip to Washington. It was nearing the time for the budget committee's review of the Oak Valley budget for the coming fiscal year. One day, as he sat in his office pondering why he hasn't heard from her, Mary came to his door and announced that Hamilton was on the phone.

"Thank you Mary," he said as he was answering the phone, "I was just wondering what happened to her." Hamilton knew the Oak Valley budget had to get to Washington within the next week.

As he answered the phone he said, "Good morning Ms Hamilton, I was just wondering if I should make the dreaded budget trip to D.C. in person or would mailing the budget proposal be sufficient?" Matthew was not fond of flying, especially when it meant facing the dreaded *finance committee*. Of course he knew he was required to appear in person, but he felt it was worth a try this one time to simply mail the yearly budget proposal.

She was quick to respond with a rather stern, "Not if you genuinely expect to keep your secure job and those two hundred plus engineers and scientists working for you."

"Saying it that way sounded as though you were listening to the nasty rumors about shutting down the Oak Valley facility."

In a rather sincere tone she continued, "Those rumors are no longer rumors Matthew. You know all about the Idaho Project. The senior directors of that project feel it would be much more beneficial to have your laboratories closer to them."

"Frankly," Matthew said, "it would be a huge monetary benefit I'm certain, but transferring all of this operation there would not be cheap and besides these engineers, including me, do not want to move to, of all places, Idaho."

"Matthew, you do know you need to hop on a jet and come

here yourself? Perhaps you can best defend your operation in person. The Finance Project Committee is in tight control of the money for the Idaho Project *and* for Oak Valley. The executive committee meeting is on Monday, so be here."

"Okay Ms Hamilton," he said realizing she was dead serious and definitely not joking. "I'll have Mary make room reservations in D.C. today and I should be on an early flight to D.C. tomorrow morning."

"Tomorrow will be great and I will pick you up at Dulles airport myself. Ask Mary to call me about your arrival time and you can tell her you won't need a hotel room. We need to talk about your proposals in detail before the meeting on Monday. Besides I have several empty rooms in my large Georgetown townhouse that should be sufficient for a day of relaxation before we go head to head with Johnson and the finance committee."

Matthew was caught off guard by her offer. "That sounds great if you're sure the room arrangement won't cause a complication for you Ms Hamilton. I have always wondered how you Washington folks live."

Later that day Mary provided Matthew and Ms Hamilton with the departure and arrival flight information. It was all set for Matthew to visit the big city of Washington, D.C. As he drove home from the office, he did wonder if he should tell Julie about staying with Hamilton at her townhouse.

Honesty is the best policy so he decided it would be best to mention it in the morning. It was late when Matthew arrived home. Why because trouble, he reasoned in his mind before heading off to bed? Finally however, he felt he must discuss the trip now.

Julie was first to ask questions. "Just in case of an emergency Matthew, in what hotel will you be staying?"

As innocently as he could he told her why he would be staying with Ms Hamilton instead of at a hotel. He explained that they needed to discuss the budget proposal before they meet with the Finance Committee.

"Sure," Julie said. "I guess this is pay back for me having dinner with the doctor."

It seemed best if he didn't answer that and that was the end of the conversation. The balance of the evening was totally void of any conversation. Gee, I can't imagine why. The bed springs were quiet in the Wilson house that night.

Jim was to take Matthew to the airport Saturday morning. Matthew thought he would tell Jim on the way to the airport about the possibility of shutting down Oak Valley, but decided not. Matthew was going to Washington to give it his best effort, not to have that take place.

The time was near for Jim to pick him up, but a phone call from Jim changed the plan. Matthew was used to change in plans. Jim had problems with his car again making it necessary for Matthew to drive himself to the airport. *Just as well,* he thought, *I really shouldn't tell Jim something negative like closing Oak Valley until it happens.* Could be my imagination is getting ahead of me.'

The flight was uneventful and left on time for a change and arrived at the scheduled arrival time. Sure enough, Ms Hamilton was there at the designated arrival pick up area as promised. It did seem a little awkward to have her as his taxi driver, but he fought off any attempts of his usual wise cracks and greatly appreciated the ride to her townhouse.

It was still very early in the morning when they arrived at her house. She asked if he wanted to have breakfast with her in her small bricked veranda area, just through the dining room double French doors. Outside, the temperature was a warmer than usual, early autumn, beautiful sunshine morning and a great place for breakfast.

The house was extremely well furnished. First class in every respect, and to Matthew's surprise, it included a butler that attended to his and her every need. Apparently he had been advised that they would be having breakfast on the veranda immediately upon arrival. The moment they came through the door he had already placed coffee on the glass top table. Shortly afterwards, bacon and eggs just the way Matthew preferred. He did wonder how he knew how he preferred his eggs, over light and an English muffin instead of toast. Matthew didn't question it, he simply went to work eating the delicious food. Later he found out that Christine had talked to Mary about his breakfast desires. In Mary's position, minute details are what her life is all about. *How nice*, he thought.

While they were chatting, Charles her butler, took his suitcase and briefcase to what was to be his room. *Just like at a hotel*, Matthew thought, *but you don't have to tip the bellman.*

Charles was a rather tall, dark skinned gentleman. He was dressed in formal butler attire, a neatly pressed black butler uniform with a freshly pressed white shirt and black tie. The shirt cuffs extended a few inches beyond the coat sleeves revealing beautiful diamond cuff links. Matthew marveled that the man should look so good, so early in the morning.

Their casual conversation was very friendly, not the type of heated exchanges he usually had with Ms Hamilton. In the past she would talk very matter-of-fact, but this time she was a very different Catherine Hamilton. Matthew enjoyed what he was seeing, Catherine Hamilton, as a real human being.

After they finished breakfast she said she would especially like to show him parts of Washington as she knew it, not just the customary tourist spots. He had a day to kill, so he thought, *why not*. When Ms Hamilton said on the phone earlier, this would be a day of relaxation, she meant it.

She was clearly known every place they went. Matthew never knew you could go behind the scenes like they did. Tourists see the Capital building and the powerful chambers of the Senate and the House of Representatives area. They, on the other hand, moved from office to office visiting Congressmen and Congresswomen without ever being stopped by security. They went to the museums, but not in the front doors, rather in the protected back rooms where displays were being made ready for public display. It gives you a whole new perspective on the demanding work it takes to get artifacts ready for viewing. The history museum and the science and technology museum were his favorite and in Matthew's opinion, extremely interesting.

She took him, of all places, into the kitchen of one of the top rated restaurants in D.C. for lunch. The workers were going, in what seemed like a hundred different directions, and all at the same time. How in the world, Matthew wondered, do the cooks and waiters ever get the delicious food orders to the correct tables?

The main chef apparently knew Ms Hamilton quite well because he said that he had created a dinner especially to honor the World Famous, Ms Hamilton. That was probably a lie, but it sounded good. Nevertheless it was outstanding and was presented at a candlelit table in a quiet corner of the restaurant. *It appears*, Matthew thought, *Catherine Hamilton was trying to come on to me.*

Usually, Matthew had a difficult time talking about anything except his work, but Catherine Hamilton made conversation flow easily. They talked for hours about everything from sports to his marriage to Julie. She inquired as to why he and Julie never had children and he told her. Early in their marriage they both decided the world is too messed up to bring children into their life. Besides he said, "We both have an enjoyable career and don't need the responsibility of kids."

Catherine was becoming a real friend. He even told her how Julie had rescued him from becoming a terrible alcoholic. "That easily could have destroyed my future as a scientist."

By now the sun was beginning to go down so they headed back to her home. He used the term home because the word house implied just a place for anyone to live. It had become clear to Matthew that Ms Hamilton's house was her home sweet home. Clearly, Matthew felt very comfortable with Ms

Catherine Hamilton.

She had what appeared to be hundreds of old movies and she suggested they watch one of Matthew's choosing. He told her that in her home they would watch one of her favorites and so they did. It was a romantic tear jerker, the name Matthew doesn't recall, but it was a good way to pass a few hours before bedtime.

Catherine was enjoying a glass of wine as a nightcap and of course, she offered Matthew one. It had been several years since he drank anything alcoholic. Shortly after the wine, the little fuzzy feeling came on him rather quickly. His past experience with alcohol reminded him it should help him go to sleep rather quickly. Catherine had another and she poured one for him also that turned out to be one too many.

Matthew was beginning to feel his oats and leaned close to her, lightly touching her shoulder, slurring his words as he spoke, "Ms Hamilton, when we are alone like this, would it be impolite of me to call you Catherine?"

"That's my name Matthew, please do."

The movie ended and he politely said good night as they both emptied their wine glasses. "Whew," he said under his breath as he carefully felt his way up the steps to his bedroom. "I definitely need to get to bed before the room begins spinning." They had way too much wine and he knew what that could do to the equilibrium.

It had been a long day and he felt the needed a quick shower before climbing into bed. A warm shower with a quick blast of cold water should help him shake off the queasy wine feeling. Unfortunately that didn't work at all so he held on to the furniture carefully as he felt his way toward the bed. Ah, he said to himself as he pulled the sheet up to his chin. It was a nice touch that Charles the butler had placed a small night light in the room because when one awakens during the night to do whatever, one must be able to find the john. He closed his eyes and fell off into a light sleep.

In what seemed like just a few minutes he imagined he heard the door to the room slowly open. It is almost impossible to open a closed door without making a slight click or the door rubbing noise on the thick carpet. *Is it just my imagination?* He thought. But as he opened one eye just a little he could see a figure standing in the dim light of the doorway. The hallway light revealed a woman standing still as though not sure if she should enter. Could it be, surely not, but there she was, Catherine. Slowly she tiptoed to his bedside. The dim nightlight revealed a woman, not dressed in her usual formal business attire, but rather, wearing nearly nothing but a very sheer nightgown.

This can't be happening; Catherine knows that Matthew is a married man. As she stood beside the bed he pretended to be asleep, but with his eyes partially closed he caught a glimpse of an extremely beautiful body. She was a middle aged woman who still has everything perfectly in place. The dim nightlight exposed every inch of her body. He wondered if she might have had surgical implants because for a woman her age, he could see she had very perky breasts. Not too big and definitely not floppy, just right. By day she proudly presents a very well proportioned body, but by night, and without the suit, she appeared to be a very trim lady from top to bottom.

Without speaking a word she slid into the bed and as she did, placed her arm over his chest. Ever so slowly she placed her hands around his head slowly pulling his lips to hers. Her warm soft lips touched Matthew's. He felt the softness of a woman's lips that wanted more than just a quiet kiss goodnight.

Before he met Julie he had dreamed of something like this happening. Rarely did it work out this way because he was usually too drunk to enjoy the pleasure that was running through his body at this time. Perhaps this is just one of those dreams guys have. If he could close his eyes, he most certainly would go back to sleep. Surely this was just a dream, but it wasn't. The pleasure went on for what seemed like hours

Matthew had no idea when she left. There was no goodnight

or goodbye. Catherine Hamilton left as quietly as when she came to his bed. Did what just happen really happen or was he dreaming? If it was a dream, he was left with a completely exhausted and very sweaty body.

In the morning there was a slight knock on the bedroom door and he heard Charles say, "Mr. Wilson it is eight o'clock. Ms Hamilton suggested that you have breakfast with her in a few minutes."

"Thank you Charles, I'll be down in about ten minutes."

Matthew again needed a quick shower, if only to clear his head of the remaining Catherine thoughts. Quickly he showered, combed his hair and brushed his teeth. The night's affair was still just a blur, even after the cold shower. What should he say to the lady that controls his entire business future life? As he brushed his teeth, Matthew mumbled almost aloud, "I'm not going to say a thing; I'll simply wait for her to say something." He reasoned that if nothing is said about the night of romance that would be the obvious end of it. Truth of the matter is she certainly knows how to satisfy a man.

Again he reassured himself that after a night such as they had, he had earned the right to call Ms Hamilton, Catherine. For sure, from this time forward, when they are alone, he felt he had earned the right to call her Catherine.

Catherine was already at the breakfast table enjoying a glass of freshly squeezed orange juice. "Good morning Matthew," she cheerfully said. "Did you sleep well; sometimes it is difficult to sleep in a strange bed, at least for me it is. You know I must travel from hotel to hotel around the world. Some beds are too hard and some too soft."

"To tell you the down right truth Catherine I rested very well, but I did have a problem dream. It was a good dream however, but it seemed so real." Matthew had the feeling Catherine was quizzing him and wanted him to say something, but he said nothing about his unusual night visitor.

"Oh I suppose the dream was just one of those delightful

matters that men dream about. It must have been the late night-cap we had before going to bed that brought it on."

"Matthew, it's Sunday and I know you always go to church on Sunday so I have taken the liberty of picking a church for both of us to attend, if that is okay with you."

"Sure, any church is fine with me."

"I'm guessing you have never had an opportunity to visit the Washington National Cathedral, I mean during an actual church service." she offered. "Most people receive the visitor tour, but that isn't the same as a regular Sunday service. You will be totally amazed at the splendor and sound of the beautiful choir and the magnificent pipe organ and of course, a splendid spiritual message. It is something everyone should definitely hear and see sometime during their lifetime"

Somehow you just don't think of a responsible person like Catherine Hamilton, in her high level government capacity, as one who goes to church. Of course that isn't fair to judge a person's private life like that. Why should anyone make assumptions of one's religious faith? Matthew wondered all of this, but he felt it was nice of her to consider his feelings concerning the matter. *Frankly*, he thought to himself, *I should be going to a Catholic Church and spend time with a priest in the confessional considering what happened with us during the night.* But that thought left his mind almost the instant he thought it.

"Catherine, I believe that would be a nice change from the small chapel Julie and I attend back in Knoxville."

"Fine," she said, "I'll meet you by my car in half an hour."

By now it was mid- morning. She remarked that the Sunday traffic in and around Georgetown and Washington is so much quieter than through the work week. She explained that this section of the city is quiet today, but come tomorrow morning the peace and quiet is no more. "Enjoy the beauty and the sunshine." She said, "I imagine, for you Matthew, it's almost like being back in Knoxville, so peaceful and quiet."

"It is that Catherine."

As they neared the magnificent huge stone structure Catherine said, "There it is Matthew, the Washington National Cathedral. For years one man has worked on the stonework that you see. It appeared he would never complete his part of the masonry. It has only recently been nearly completed. I'm not sure about this, but I think his son has picked up where his father stopped. Some of the outer stone work is still not finished, but because the father taught his son the stone craft, the stonework will eventually be completed."

The crowds were already entering the building as Catherine and Matthew approached the main entrance. As with any church, when you arrive everyone pretends to know you and greets you with, "Good morning, how are you, and this is certainly a beautiful day isn't it?" Then, before you have a chance to answer the question, the well meaning nice people move on to the next person. Catherine handles those situations by shaking their hand and holding on to it until she is satisfied she has a chance to answer what they had asked. There actually were a few people that knew Catherine and spoke briefly to her, but respected her privacy and immediately moved on.

The service was very formal. There was a lot of stand up and sit down stuff before the minister began the sermon part. Matthew had no idea what the sermon was about because he was so awe struck by the music portion of the service and the beauty of the wall statuettes, the gorgeous windows and the ceiling that seemed to go upwards at least a hundred feet. The choir and the huge pipe organ were, for the lack of any other explanation, spectacular.

# CHAPTER 8
## KIDS SCIENCE LESSON FOR ADULTS

After the church service Catherine said they were going to Virginia to visit with the student and his teacher that had built the miniature nuclear project. Until this time, nothing had been mentioned the day before about the student's project.

To which Matthew exclaimed. "How in the world are we going to contact them today, it's not a school day, you do know it's Sunday, right?"

"Yes Matthew, but I spoke to his teacher and explained that the only time we had to meet would be today, Sunday. Both the boy and his teacher were so blown away by the fact that we were interested in seeing the boy's project that they forced an arrangement with the school principal to have the building opened especially for us."

Catherine continued, "Matthew, try to keep an open mind about what you are going to see. I have seen the presentation of Mark Erickson and it truly amazed me that this student and his science teacher, Miss Sheldon Blakely would even consider something as timely as this to create."

"I have no difficulty with that Catherine, but it never has occurred to me that we could see a school nuclear science project of this magnitude on Sunday. I must admit there are times, as a research scientist, it takes viewing the simple things in life close-up. As scientific engineers, we generally look too far into the distance for obvious results that are right in front of us all the time. Who knows, perhaps we can both learn from this kid's project."

By now it was one o'clock as they drove up to the front door of the school. As scheduled, the principal, the teacher and the student are awaiting their arrival. After a brief introduction to each other they entered the building. It was clear to see that this was a top notch high school where no expense had been spared building it. The foyer was huge with Italian marble flooring and a beautiful stained glass dome that went up at least two stories. The sunlight streaming into the foyer through the reflective ceiling stained glass windows made the entire room appear like a fairyland. The beauty was nearly overwhelming.

All of the classrooms were fully carpeted. Matthew thought that this must be a janitor's nightmare, keeping the carpets clean. How does a high school achieve funding for something like this?

Nothing like this when Matthew went to school, not even in college. His grade school and high school classroom floors were old oiled wooden floors. The lighting in his old classrooms had those large white globes suspended from the ceilings. Here, on the other hand, the classroom lighting was controlled with light dimmers connected to rows and rows of fluorescent lights that came on automatically when anyone entered the room and went out when the last person left the room. Believe it or not, they actually had real live tree plants scattered throughout each room. This school was very impressive to say the least. These kids apparently live in a have it all, upscale neighborhood and want for nothing as it pertains to their school building.

The theatre like auditorium was even more amazing for a high school. The massive auditorium floor was very expensive brick and sloped downward toward the stage allowing everyone a clear view. The seating appeared to be the slide back type that was capable of slight reclining. Matthew's high school used the gymnasium as an auditorium. They used folding chairs you had to take with you from the cafeteria. After an event was over, each kid had to return the chairs back to the cafeteria. Matthew was impressed and said, "I think I might have enjoyed my school years if our school could have been like this. I wonder if these kids realize just how well off they have it."

Mark was getting a bit impatient with the principal because of our tour of the building. It was clear to see that he especially wanted us to see his extracurricular science activity. Mark was patiently pacing and smiling as we approached the two long tables that held his display. Miss Blakely was extremely proud of Mark and it showed as we all stood before his project. She wrapped her arms around Mark's shoulders as she announced, "This is Mark Erickson's Nuclear Power Creation of the future electrical needs for personal homes and business'."

*(It is important to note that as a nuclear scientist, what we are about to discuss is an overly simplified version of a nuclear power station in miniature. Many fundamental factors regarding the actual design have intentionally been omitted)*

Mark had built a model of a closed system nuclear power plant, meaning no nuclear or water vapors would ever be released into the local atmosphere. He explained that the scale model, oval shaped ten foot high and four foot round tank contained the reactor in which enriched uranium rods would be automatically raised and lowered into the chilled heavy water. This process, Mark said, "Allows the nuclear fission to take place and super heat the water turning it into steam. The steam then goes to the turbine that produces DC electricity. The DC power travels to a converter that changes the DC electric to AC electricity that is usable for homes and businesses."

"From the turbine the steam travels to an enclosed cooling tower that reduces the steam to just hot water. As the hot water leaves the tower, electric pumps send the hot water to an electrically powered chiller, a refrigeration type unit much like a super sized home air-conditioner. This system eliminates the remaining heat from the water and allows the cooled water to flow to a large, cold water reservoir holding tank. From there the chilled water returns via pumps to the reactor."

Mark had all the tanks and pumps cut open for easy viewing and had very in-depth diagrams describing each step of the electric generation process. He was quick to emphasize the fact that no steam or water escapes into the atmosphere. A real life-size of the miniature power plant, he explained, would fit on a re-enforced concrete base about five feet wide by fifteen feet in length.

Miss Blakely dutifully explained to all present, Mark's primary reason for creating the project is that in the not too distant future, our natural fossil fuels of oil and gas will be depleted. By eliminating coal, oil and gas power plants around the world, global warming would be lessened considerably.

"Of course," Miss Blakely continued, "we all know that, but Mark wants to be part of the scientific community that finds solutions to solving present fossil fuel problems. If you think about it, there would be no need for overhead power lines that get knocked down during our severe storms."

Mark picked up on her last comment, "Thousands of people that service the electric industry would be retrained to maintain the miniature power units. Servicing the units would be accomplished by retraining the thousands of highly professional, but existing personnel worldwide who are already part of the world's electric power companies. One would think power companies should welcome this because they would have nothing to lose and everything to gain."

"This would not be a cheap alternative, but it would solve the fossil fuel depletion of our precious natural resources within the not too distant future. This type of system could be available within twenty to thirty years."

It was clear that Mark had certainly thought his proposal through in its entirety, but one of the relevant issues remains, who would build these millions of units globally?

"You are probably wondering about the construction of each power plant." Mark said. He then went on to explain that once the first unit was actually produced and deemed safe, each component would be produced by independent contractors selected from all over the competitive world. The units would be built like any other production line business. When each was completed it would be moved by tractor trailer to the business or home site and placed on a concrete reinforced foundation by large cranes.

"Imagine if you will," Mark declared, "the millions of people in areas worldwide that have no electricity, they would now have the benefit of electricity. This would bring the entire world into the modern age of electronic technology. Everyone on the entire planet we call Earth would have access to television, computers and microwaves etc. The thousands of household items we in this country take for granted would now be available to all. Imagine, if you will, that distant villages in the remote areas of the world would see for the first time that there are millions of people around them."

The teacher and her student stood there beaming and very proud, as they should be. Matthew was sure if these two could attract the attention of the Department of Energy Secretary and a little known scientist that understands the inside happenings about nuclear energy, they should rightfully be proud of their academic accomplishments.

What really amazed Matthew was the fact that they were in a classroom on a Sunday afternoon as opposed to a regular work and school day. The school principal had to be very proud of this student's effort to allow them access to his building at this time.

Matthew pulled Catherine to the side and quietly said, "This kid just might be onto something. Not his idea of putting a nuclear plant in every home and business backyard, that's absurd, but some customized version of it just might be possible. Could it be possible to place a somewhat larger version of the miniature plant in or near the towns and cities? Hmm, when I get to Idaho and see everything we are doing, I might just bring up the possibilities with a few of my colleagues."

Mark apparently has very supportive parents. He announced to all of us that his mom and dad wanted all of them to go to his home for a Sunday brunch. Catherine and Matthew agreed to move on to his home because they both wished to see the parents of this boy that was this dedicated to future world science. The principal declined saying that he had a former luncheon engagement with his family.

The drive was only a few miles from the school. Catherine followed in her car behind Miss Blakely and Mark which gave Catherine and Matthew a few minutes to openly chat.

"You know Catherine," Matthew said, "with the strength and the brilliant foresight that Mark has, I would like to see if we could get him a full college scholarship into the University of Idaho at Pocatillo. That way he would be fairly close to what is happening moment by moment at *The Site*. The University of Idaho has a nuclear engineering program that attracts young people into the nuclear energy field. I'm sure you already know that's one of the main reasons Idaho was selected as our nuclear power test site."

"Obviously I know that Matthew." Catherine said rather sarcastically. "That thought has occurred to me also, but what I would like to do is invite Mark to go with us to the Idaho Project itself when we both visit it in the next week or so after we are finished with your budget meeting with the finance committee. Incidentally Matthew, please do not refer to what we call the Idaho Project as, *The Site*. The Site name sounds like some kind of secret place."

"Sounds like a plan Catherine. I wonder what his parents will say about such a sudden decision on our part. I suppose we'll have to just take it one step at a time."

Arriving at the Erickson's home only took a few minutes. "What a beautiful place." Matthew exclaimed as they entered the long driveway which ended at the front porch portico. "I wonder what his dad does for a living because this house is not the average neighborhood house."

The house was located on several acres of land and resembled a colonial three story mansion complete with a columned front entrance. Mark's mother and dad welcomed them at the door and it was obvious that they knew Ms Blakely because Mr. Erickson gave her a big hug. We were ushered into the dining room where the table was already set. Mrs. Erickson seated us immediately in the dining room then went to the kitchen and began to place a full course dinner before us. Catherine spoke saying, "I was under the impression that this was to be a light brunch, but I can clearly see it is much more. You are very kind Ms Erickson, thank you."

The luncheon went on with all exchanging compliments about their son's abilities. The Erickson's proudly mentioned that Mark was at the top of his class and was a near 4.0 student. Catherine realized that would make Mark a shoe-in for a scholarship.

During their casual conversation Catherine said there were hundreds of college grants that are never used. With parents that were in an apparent higher income level Matthew wondered why they should even suggest a scholarship. His thoughts went back to his hard earned college degrees. He recalled, even though he received a scholarship, he still had to do work at the school. He worked so hard for every day of life at Penn State. For Matthew a full, no strings attached, college grant was nearly non-existent. That was then and this is now.

Lunch was nearly over when Catherine asked Mr. Erickson what he did for a living. He was quick to say that what you see here is the successful results of his wife's business. "My loving wife is the senior director of the nation's largest division of Mary Kay Cosmetics."

"Mrs. Erickson, my hat is off to you," Catherine said. "At this time women have a difficult time rising to the top of any company, but you have certainly achieved that and more, I salute you." With that said all raised their glasses as recognition of mutual agreement.

It appeared that the time was right to talk about the scholarship and of the trip to Idaho. "Mr. and Mrs. Erickson," Matthew said. "Ms Hamilton and I would like to suggest that Mark apply for a full scholarship to the University of Idaho at Pocatillo, Idaho. It is just a short distance south of Idaho Falls. The fundamental reason being, perhaps unknown to any of you, there is a nuclear power station test facility we call The Idaho Project, about thirty minutes southeast of the university. The university supplies the personnel essential for the United States and a large portion of the modern world with nuclear technology and nuclear scientists. As we already know, Mark is an extremely sharp young man who has, what appears to be, the desire to able to help the world overcome dependence upon fossil fuel. Both Ms Hamilton and I are going to visit the facility in Idaho in a week or so and it would be an honor to take your son along. He would see first hand what is currently happening in the nuclear energy field and while there he could also visit the university."

"We have never been parents to stand in the way of his desires," Mrs. Erickson said, "but the decision to go on such quick notice is absolutely up to him. Mark, what do you think of their offer?"

"I'm impressed," Mark declared. "I have been looking around the country for a college and a visit to what they call, The Idaho Project would be extremely interesting, I'm all for it. Mother, I believe I will celebrate the good news by going to the kitchen and serve our guests your delicious German chocolate cake as dessert."

"I'll help you Mark." added Ms Blakely.

"And I need to find the rest room if you don't mind excusing me for a minute." Matthew said.

"Matthew, there is one down the hallway just past the kitchen." responded Mrs. Erickson.

As Matthew was doing his duty in the bathroom he couldn't help overhearing Mark and Ms Blakely talking in the kitchen. Ms Blakely and Mark seemed to be having a somewhat heated conversation.

Ms Blakely clearly was upset with Mark's dining room answers. "Mark, we have so much going on between us that I'm surprised that you would even consider Idaho as a college. You know that we secretly discussed you going to a school close to me. I love you and I know that if you go that far away from me I'll never see you again. Please don't consider that as your choice for a college. You could go to the University of Virginia that is only a few miles from me. We could be together always if you stay close to me. I'll take care of you in every way, please don't go to Idaho."

"I do love you Sheldon, but this means so much. I promise that we will be together when I finish college. Being a nuclear scientist is what I want, you know that. Maybe you could come with me; you could teach school there also Sheldon."

From the dining room Mrs. Erickson called, "Mark how are you coming with the dessert?"

"It's coming right up mother." Mark said.

*What an interesting conversation between a teacher and her student,* Matthew thought as he walked back to the dinner table. Honestly, who couldn't fall in love with a teacher that had the beautiful looks of Sheldon? In my school days you could never call your teachers by their first name much less say to her the things he just did. My, how times have changed.

Sheldon Blakely is a beauty for sure. Even Matthew would have wanted to get close to her if he had been in her class. Every boy that has an attractive lady teacher, at some time has had a secret fascination to explore the unknown. Sheldon was a very well dressed young lady in a tight fitting, above the knee skirt and a loosely fit lacy collared blouse. She had beautiful silky dark blond hair flowing over her shoulders. She certainly could have been a supermodel, but instead chose teaching school. Her high heels made her a few inches taller than the five foot seven she was. Mark was almost six feet tall, which is what most women want in a man. Although Mark is not yet a man, he's close to a man, but not yet, or is he?

Her body was very trim; apparently she exercised a lot be-

I AM THAT I AM

cause the muscles on her legs looked tight. Perhaps that is because of the high heels shifting the body weight slightly forward. As Matthew had said many times, show me well shaped legs and I'll show you a women that has never been someone to stand for hours on end. That's not nice to say but Matthew knows it's true. Oh, the cleavage. Not too much, but what she has appears to be just right. For a woman that appears to be about twenty-five, she is put together rather well. The one time Ms Blakely was talking to Matthew and standing near him, Matthew did notice she had two and a half rings on her neck. As he said before, that's how he guesses a persons age.

Back at the table they finished the delicious chocolate cake dessert and Mark announced that he wanted to travel to Idaho with Matthew. Catherine assured his parents that all travel arrangements would be on the government and we would take good care of their son. Catherine said that she would contact his parents about the departure time from Dulles Airport. Catherine further said that she would have a chauffeur pick Mark up for the ride to the airport and also return him to his home the following Saturday. This would most likely be a quick four day trip.

It soon became clear to Matthew that Ms Blakely wasn't fond of Mark's choice of going away without her. The scornful look she gave Catherine and Matthew as they went to their car was one that would kill. That is, of course, if she had a gun. Clearly she was not happy with Mark's decision.

# CHAPTER 9
## JOB SECURITY SLIPS AWAY

**A**s Catherine began the drive back to her Georgetown home Matthew brought her up to date with what he had heard in the Erickson's kitchen. Surprisingly, there was little disapproval for either Mark or Ms Blakely's behavior from Catherine. All Catherine said is, "What do you expect, the two of them have been working on this educational project for months either at her house or at his. His parents, I'm guessing, are seldom around and the two of them are alone at his or her home, I say again, what do you expect?" What a surprising reaction. Matthew imagined Catherine would go on and on about how awful something like that is, but no, it was almost as if she approved.

The balance of the trip was about their scheduled meeting with the fiscal appropriations committee tomorrow morning. Matthew assured Catherine he had what he felt was a reasonable financial accounting of the funds needed for the next year at Oak Valley. He had not added anything extravagant like sometimes happens with government budgets. Having to reduce the budget more would have him eliminating jobs. You are then talking about people's jobs and he surely didn't want to eliminate any of the dedicated men or women that work at Oak Valley.

Catherine decided that she would stop for a pizza. Apparently she got information that Matthew was a pizza nut from Mary. As they waited for the pizza Catherine ordered a glass of wine for the two of them. Matthew was hoping this was not to be another night like last evening, sex and all. Drinking again, he knew he has to stop it before he gets hooked on alcohol again. Julie would not be happy about that and she would quiz him as to why he started drinking again. How could he explain it, he would have to make up a lie? Julie could always tell when he was lying, he doesn't know how she knows, but she knows.

Eventually, after several glasses of wine, they arrived at Catherine's townhouse. It's getting late so Matthew was hoping they would eat the pizza and go to bed. He was not looking forward to tomorrow's meeting, so a good night of refreshing sleep would help make tomorrow seem brighter.

Everything in the pizza kitchen was on the pizza including anchovies. He now knew for sure that Catherine had gotten information from Mary because nobody but Mary would know how much he loved anchovies. He was never quite sure what they were, but from what Matthew had been told, they were salty little fish like creatures, yum, but so good. At least that's Matthew's line and he's sticking to it.

Another small glass of wine, some small talk about basically nothing and he excused himself and went to the bedroom for a restful night of sleep.

Sleep came rapidly and he began dreaming about his meeting with the congressmen who were grilling him about his past life as though he were dead. "That's odd," he told them, "but I'm not dead yet." In the dream they kept insisting he was dead and they began showing him candid photographs of how drunk he got back in the old days. "No," he said, "I have changed. I'm not like that any longer." This dream certainly couldn't be because he ate all the pizza and wine before coming to bed. Surely not, he had eaten much more many times before bed and slept quite well.

Believing he was still dreaming he imagined he felt a warm body against his. His mind was shouting, "Can't you committee people see, this proves I'm not dead. Can't you see I'm dreaming?" Still dreaming he declared to the finance committee, "look, look carefully, do you see this woman lying next to me, I can't be dead." But suddenly he realizes he was not dreaming. There really was a warm soft body lying in bed with him. "Whew, what a welcome relief, I am alive."

It was Catherine again, and again he said nothing as she moved ever so gently rubbing and touching every part of his body. It felt so good that he didn't want her to stop although he knew she should. The touching went on for a few minutes longer and then she rolled him over face to face with her

Matthew felt, it's not fair that she has gone through the first steps to get him ready for what she definitely wanted, but he rationalized that he was innocent since he hadn't touched her yet. It felt so good to have her warm body next to his. Yes, he knows it is wrong, but still it felt so good. Then as quietly as she came into the room, Catherine left and Matthew fell asleep fully satisfied, but again totally exhausted.

Monday morning Washington traffic is the pits. The city becomes extremely alive during the weekdays. What should have been a half hour trip was taking most of an hour. There was nothing you can do but just ride with the traffic.

Just as before, no recognition of the wild night in his bedroom. Needless to say he certainly was not going to bring it up. That was then and this is now.

Catherine today, all business! He came to D.C. to do his job and she obviously knows her place and her job. He did wonder if the nightly escapades would have any influence on how she would defend his budget requirements.

As they arrived at the NRC building she greeted the security guard warmly. He allowed her to enter the underground parking garage and that was it, they had arrived. They stopped on the main floor at the blind vendor's snack and newspaper stand

and purchased a cup of coffee to go. It is nearly ten a.m., time to be in Johnson's office. She walked briskly as Matthew tried to keep up, almost running, trying not to spill his coffee. He muttered a cuss, "damn ... hot," which indicated he wished he had placed a lid on his coffee cup.

As they entered Johnson's conference room, ten committee members were already seated. Most of them Matthew knew, but a few were strangers. Matthew's local Tennessee Senator John Gandy, a friend many years ago but no longer, was among those he knew. Gandy had been on the powerful finance committee for years. They gave the obligatory greeting to each other for a moment and the scheduled meeting began immediately.

Seated at the large oval shaped table were the committee members along with the executive director, William Johnson, who was seated at the head of the table. Beside him was Gandy, the Vice Chairman of the committee. Christine Hamilton took her place to the left of Johnson. The other members were along the sides of the table. Matthew's place was at the far opposite end of the table. Today this would be on the *hot seat* for sure.

Executive director Johnson began by firmly saying that each of those present had received an advance copy of Wilson's budget proposal for Oak Valley. "Mr. Wilson, your office manager was kind enough to overnight a copy of it to us. We received it Friday afternoon," Johnson continued. "Each of us has had the weekend to look it over. First, I especially want to apologize for not getting a copy of it to Ms Hamilton, but she was not home when the deliveryman attempted to deliver it to her."

"That's not a problem sir," Ms Hamilton said. "Mr. Wilson had the forecast proposal with him when I picked him up at the airport. I have already reviewed his financial proposal for the next fiscal year."

For a brief moment Matthew's thoughts wandered. *You can believe that, Catherine has reviewed every inch of me, but I know that isn't what Johnson was speaking about.*

Chairman Johnson went on declaring, "It is our decisive view that the Oak Valley facility in the past has been an extremely valuable and an extraordinary asset to this country. The Oak Valley and The New Mexico facilities took us out of forty's hydro-electric era and placed us in today's nuclear power age. And for that we salute the results made by you Mr. Wilson and the two hundred plus engineers that are there with you now."

As Matthew listened to him speak all the good things about his operation, his creative mind began to run in circles because this is not what you expect to hear in meetings like this. Matthew began to squirm a little in his chair. Everyone enjoys hearing compliments, but he began to wonder where all this is heading. Matthew knew however, there is a time to remain quiet and this seemed like one of those times.

Chairman Johnson continued, "Mr. Wilson as you know, *The Site*, or as it is commonly known by most now, The Idaho Project is in full swing. They are in need of several billion dollars more to complete the Generation IV nuclear test reactor. We have had discussions with the technical engineers and scientists at that location and have found what you are doing at the aged Oak Valley laboratory could also be done in Idaho." Matthew's heart sank because he now knew where this is going. Unfortunately, to be honest, he had to readily agree with Johnson and the committee's findings. How can you defend your property when you know they are right?

"We could have sent you our official recommendations," Johnson continued, "but we decided to bring you to Washington to tell you in person. Our decision has already been made to close Oak Valley and transfer all the projects and your personnel to the Idaho Project. Mr. Wilson that includes you if you so desire. Ms Hamilton will assist you in any way possible to make the difficult transition as seamless as possible. I'm sure you have questions, but they will all be answered in time. For now, we certainly want you to visit the facility in Idaho and formally meet the local people with whom you would be working. I expect you could do that in the upcoming weeks or sooner if you prefer. This type of message is difficult for all of us. There is never an easy way to have your roots pulled from under you,

I AM THAT I AM

but I for one would like you to make the move as soon as possible. Any of the staff at Oak Valley that chooses not to make the transfer will, of course, be allowed to take a rather lucrative exit package that we have put together. Those that accept the exit package may combine it with their retirement benefits. In a few days the complete details will be forwarded to you at Oak Valley. Included will be the information explaining the government's moving expense reimbursement plan. There will also be a section discussing our program to help each person with financing new housing in Idaho. Ladies and gentlemen thank you for attending." As Johnson said that, he immediately got up and left the room.

Not really surprised, but nevertheless stunned, Matthew arose and approached Catherine, but before reaching Catherine John Gandy gave him a glancing look as though to say, this is pay back Matthew. Ignoring the nasty look, Matthew went on to Catherine and spoke virtually in a whisper, "You knew about this all along didn't you? Is that why you treated me so well at your house these past few days?"

"Yes Matthew I did," she said modestly, "but I enjoyed your company so much and I appreciate everything, and I mean everything you did for me and to me. Now let's have some lunch before I take you to the airport."

Catherine decided to take Matthew to the Senate cafeteria located across the street from the Capital building. "Matthew, you must have some of the Senator's famous bean soup. It's the talk of the town."

"Sure, why not, this trip has been a gas; perhaps I can spread some gas on the plane as I head home. I'm sure the pilot could use some extra fuel."

There was little conversation as they ate lunch. Matthew tried to explain that Julie is not about to move to Idaho no matter how much more money the government pays him. Catherine tried to console him by saying Julie might enjoy the beauty of the mountains and the peace and quiet of the area. "You do know that Julie can take the trip to Idaho with you. It will be exciting for both of you to visit your new Idaho home, should you decide to make the move. Just think Matthew, fishing in the mountain lakes and streams. You'd enjoy that, right?"

"Sure, but I know Julie isn't going to move."

Catherine dropped him at the Dulles airport departure entrance and simply said, "Matthew, I wish you the best in whatever decision you make. Personally I would like to see you make the move to Idaho. I know it will be a hard sell convincing Julie to leave Knoxville, but there are hospitals there where I'm certain she could immediately get employment if she desires. I will be in touch in a few days about our visit to the Idaho Project. I will also take care of preparing appropriate arrangements for Mark Erickson to accompany us. You need not worry about him; I'll take good care of Mark." We shook hands and she drove off.

As Matthew walked to the departure area, his mind pictured a nearly nineteen year old boy with Catherine, a woman approaching fifty, doing as she said, take good care of Mark. *That's silly; Catherine would never take advantage of a young boy like that.* But enough thoughts about Catherine, Matthew had his own personal problems to cope with when he gets home.

# CHAPTER 10
## RETIRE OR NOT, THE BIG QUESTION

T he flight was routine, which is the way anyone that uses regular air transportation wants it. Matthew arrived safely in Knoxville late in the afternoon. The sun was just beginning to set behind the mountain range that over shadows Oak Valley. Matthew looked around at the hills and mountains and thought, only in Tennessee could you see such beauty. *Should I or should I not move to Idaho and leave the serenity of this beautiful Knoxville city.* He muttered aloud as he found the way to his car in the airport parking lot. "After all,I have enough years in government service, so why not have a go at retirement. Get out of this rat race job and take the government's exit package and retire. It's time for someone other than me to try solving the world's energy problems."

A young couple walking a few steps behind Matthew couldn't help overhearing Matthew's frustrated conversation with himself. As Matthew neared his car the young man said out loud, "Yeah! Yeah! Let someone else take the heat for the right and wrong decisions."

"You got that's right mister, I've had it with this government job," he responded as he placed his key in the car door. As the couple passed by, Matthew gave them a thumb up wave.

As Matthew approached the parking lot attendant he rationalized in his mind, announcing retirement would make the news of explaining his job to Julie much easier besides, and Matthew already knew she was definitely not going to move.

As he slowly came around the curve in the road and passed by the neighbor's farm fresh vegetable roadside stand Matthew could see the house, what a beautiful site. As he pulled into the driveway his thoughts were said out loud. "This looks like a really nice place to begin retirement ... home at last."

Earlier Matthew had called Julie from D.C. so she knew roughly when to expect him. As always, if she was at the house when he returned from a trip, she would be sitting on the front porch anxiously waiting and swinging on the old squeaky swing. This time was no exception. Julie was waiting on the porch, looking like a fresh breath of spring. She greeted him as though he had been away for months. Matthew would often say, "That's the good part of being away for even just a few days. Julie never fails to be happy to see me when I come home no matter how tired she is herself."

Although he was not hungry, Julie had prepared a great meal. She asked how the trip went and he gave her the usual answer that the visit went well, but had a few problems that had to be resolved.

She did ask how the room arrangements went with Ms Hamilton. Trying to not be overly happy about the arrangement at Hamilton's house he said, "Ms Hamilton has a very pretty and extremely well furnished townhouse in Georgetown and if you can imagine, she even has a butler. Julie, Ms Hamilton even took me to church at the Washington National Cathedral, what a beautiful, magnificent stone building. I was wishing the whole time you could have been with me."

Knowing Julie's thought processes he realized he had better get her off the questions about Catherine's house so he added, "The meeting with the finance committee was not what I expected at all. Julie there is no easy way to say this, but in just a few months Oak Valley is going to be shut down completely.

All of our work is going to be transferred to The Idaho Project. You've heard me mention it often as the place where our nuclear power testing has been going on for years. Everyone at Oak Valley will have the option of being relocated there. Or if you choose not to move, the government is offering a very good exit package."

Not expecting that kind of news Julie just sat as stunned as Matthew had been when he first heard the news. Julie's reaction was calm and quick. "So, Matthew, what are you going to do?"

"I don't know Julie, I just don't know. I suppose I could retire. I have enough time with my government service to do that."

At this point in the conversation he felt it best to just put the tough choices on the table as the best way to cope with the situation.

"Before we make any firm decisions about this you and I may visit the Idaho Falls area for a look at the housing available. You can check out the hospitals in the area for a nursing job while I visit the project. The project is less than an hour southeast of the city. The other choice is that we remain here. With the number of year's service I have I could retire with a very good income, plus they are offering a sizable exit package to any of us that do not want to make the move."

"I said it before and I'll say it again Matthew, what do you want to do?"

Truth of the matter is, Matthew was looking forward to seeing up close, the progress at The Idaho Project. There was little doubt that Julie would want to make the trip to Idaho with him, but he should at least give her the opportunity to turn it down. "At this time my thoughts are to leave Oak Valley, however I do want to visit the facility before I make any concrete commitment. Hamilton is making arrangements for both of us to visit the area in a few days."

"Just give me a day or so to get a replacement at the hospital." Julie said. "Now forget about the bad news and let's finish eating and watch the really bad news on the nightly TV news.

You wonder how news leaks to the TV news media so quickly. When Matthew arrived at the office the next morning Jim, Marty and Mary were gathered around the TV set listening to the local newscaster who was talking about the Oak Valley facility. He announced that it would be shut down in the next few months and the operation moved to a larger location in Idaho.

"Did you know about this Matthew?" Mary said as he entered the office.

"No Mary, not until yesterday. The budget commission meeting in Washington was all about how terrific we have been in the past then the bad news of the shut down. My stomach has been in knots ever since I found out." Matthew admitted. "Mary, that is the bad news, but there is good news also."

Jim was quick to pick up, "How could there be good news about having our jobs eliminated?"

"Well," Matthew quickly added, "the good news is that nobody will lose their job if you agree to go to Idaho and work at the Idaho Project. Our complete operation will be shifted to Idaho. The government will help all of us with the moving expenses and will assist us in finding and financing new housing. These days, very few companies will go that far. Usually you have to find your own housing, but from what I understand, the good news is that housing is much cheaper in that area. This move offer is to every one of the two hundred and ten of us located here. The financial committee feels that finding nuclear engineer scientists with the expertise and accumulated experience we have would be difficult. In the long run it would be far less expensive to move us, rather than look for new replacements. However for those that, for reasons known only to themselves, opt not to make the move, the commission has approved a rather lucrative exit package. The decisions for accepting that package must be made within the next two weeks. Mary will be receiving the incentive exit packages for each and every individual within the next few days. After each of you read and understand the various offers, discuss the choices with your immediate family before making a final decision."

"So what are you going to do Matthew?" asked Mary.

Seems Matthew has heard that question before. "Mary, I don't know yet. I have only known about this for just a few more hours than all of you. Julie and I are going to visit the area in the next few days. Catherine Hamilton is scheduled to meet with Julie and me at the Project. Catherine will call you Mary about the time and place we are to meet her."

"Things in Washington must have gone well with Hamilton," Mary sarcastically said, "I notice that we are now on a first name basis, hmm, very interesting."

Ignoring that comment Matthew explained, "Mary, you are included in the same benefit package as the rest of us. I'm betting that you'll be taking the retirement package rather than move."

With a little smirk on her face Mary said, "We'll see."

To end wherever Mary was going with her comment about Catherine and using his voice of authority Matthew firmly said, "Mary, I would like you to call a meeting of all those working today and request them to meet with me in the cafeteria following the lunch period. At that time I will make a formal announcement of our location closing." Pausing for a moment Matthew continued, "On second thought Mary, hold off on calling a meeting today, let's wait until the official incentive exit packages arrive tomorrow before we meet with everyone. With the exit package in hand we will have the exact information each person needs and the packets should describe in detail what each can expect."

The next day the financial separation packets arrived as promised. Mary distributed them to each and surprisingly the group had few questions. The surprise to Matthew was each person affected in the move was invited to take a second person, a spouse along to visit the surrounding Idaho region with all expenses being paid by the U.S. government. Needless to say, any projects Oak Valley were working on at this time came to a screeching halt. It seemed that almost all would make reservations to visit Idaho. Why not, get to visit where all the action seemed to be in our field and at the same time have an all expense paid mini vacation.

The following Monday Matthew was told to meet Hamilton and the boy wonder with his science teacher at the Marriott Inn in Idaho Falls. According to Mary, Hamilton said the boy's teacher would also be coming along. How interesting, how did Ms Blakely make that happen? What kind of room arrangements would be made for Catherine, Blakely and Mark? This should be an interesting few days for all of us. Matthew knew that Julie and he would be in a separate room because Mary made the appropriate arrangement, but they would all be at the same hotel. *Enough already,* he thought, as he tried to clear his mind of his recent encounters with Catherine.

While Matthew and Julie were in Idaho, Mary would be acting as a very busy travel agent for the employees wanting to visit the Idaho Project. Perhaps when they got back from Idaho, Mary will have decided her future plans as well.

Matthew knew she and her husband always talked about someday retiring and just traveling the country, visiting their friends and parts of the country they have only been able to read about in travel magazines. His guess was that Mary would retire, why not, Mary was still in good health and her husband only had a health issue or two, but nothing that would keep them from fulfilling their travel dreams. It's interesting that so many retirees wait much too late before retiring and when the time finally comes, health problems make it impossible for them to enjoy any part of their retirement.

The flight to Idaho was set for early Sunday morning. On Saturday evening as Matthew was packing, Julie told him the news that she would not be able to go along. What was the real reason? He didn't know, but she said the hospital was extremely short handed for the next week. The nurse supervisor said if she had given more notice the time off could have been approved.

They talked back and forth about the opportunity for both of them. "After all," he said, "this is a life changing opportunity. For you Julie, to relocate to a totally new hospital and who knows, with your background, you could possibly get into a nursing management position which is what you have always wanted."

"So true Matthew, but I just don't feel like starting over. I mean by that, I love our home here. I feel comfortable here, but Idaho, who lives in Idaho, name just one person. Except for the people that work at the Project, you don't know anyone way out there. For me, I have my friend's right here. I know this must sound like a teenager whose parents want to move them away from their friends, but I just do not want to move. Furthermore Matthew, we are not young any longer. For either of us to consider this move is insane. I do realize this is only my opinion, but I'm sticking to it."

What could he say; she was right. They were not young or even middle age adults any longer. "To be honest Matthew, I don't want to go to a land that, among other things, is so extremely cold in the winter."

"Julie, I'm on your side, but I must at least visit the Project and once there I will make a decision about my job future. I love you Julie and I certainly do not want to move to Idaho and leave you here alone."

Sunday morning the sun was just beginning to come up when he awakened. Still in his pajamas, he went to the front porch and sat in the large white rocking chair just to listen to the birds singing their early morning breakfast songs. *What a pleasant sound*, he thought, *the birds haven't a concern in the world. Their life consists of simply chirping and looking for food.* Of course he knew that's not all they do, but ordinary life for them appears to be very simple. They appear to have none of the worries of losing their jobs or where to find work.

Julie began to stir about in the kitchen making breakfast. Through the open front door Matthew could smell the bacon and eggs cooking. It smelled so inviting and good. In just a few minutes Julie called for him to come in. As they ate not a word was said about the discussion of the night before. She had made her point last evening and her decision not to move was settled.

"It's time to go," Matthew said. He gave Julie a big hug and a kiss and off he went to the airport.

As with all flights to anyplace, there seems to be no direct flights, especially from Knoxville, Tennessee to Idaho Falls, Idaho. If you go south, it's via Atlanta. To go west, it's through Chicago or Dallas.

The trip to Idaho via Chicago was quiet. Sunday flights seem to have fewer passengers so you can stretch out in the empty seats. The steward came by with coffee which made Matthew sit up in the seat. The steward also offered a breakfast, but Matthew declined. Instead he said, "If you have just a small Danish roll, that would be nice." After the Danish and another cup of coffee he slouched down in his seat for a short nap.

The plane touched down in Chicago on schedule. If you have ever gone through Chicago O'Hare airport and had to change airlines you know you are usually faced with the challenge of finding the gate location for your next leg of the trip. He soon learned that the airline going to Idaho Falls was a long distance walk from where he had just disembarked. "Oh well, the walk will do me good."

It seemed he had walked for at least half an hour when he heard a voice behind him calling. "Matthew, wait up." He immediately turned and looked back to see a party of three approaching. It was Catherine Hamilton, Mark Erickson and Sheldon Blakely. He knew they were also coming today, but he never thought they would be arriving at the same time as he.

"Good morning Matthew," Catherine said. "I never thought we would meet in Chicago. You know Matthew, we have to stop meeting like this people might start to talk."

In a somewhat irritated voice Matthew said, "You know Catherine, I really don't care what people say. Good morning to you too and Mark and Ms Blakely."

As they continued walking to the gate Catherine asked, "Did Julie not come along?"

"No, she is not very thrilled with this move in the first place and besides, she could not get time off from her work at the hospital."

"That's too bad Matthew she would have enjoyed the change of scenery. Have you made a decision yet?"

"I have not. I won't do that until I see what kind of job is available for me."

After a short walk they arrived at their departure gate and just in time. They had already begun boarding first class passengers. When you travel with Catherine Hamilton it is first class all the way. Again, very few passengers came on board so Catherine decided to sit with Matthew while Mark and Ms Blakely sat several seats in front of them.

Not long after they were airborne Matthew had to ask, "Catherine what happened that caused you to bring Ms Blakely along?"

"Matthew, I explained to the Erickson's that when Mark gets to Idaho Falls he will need a rental car at his disposal. His parents told me that Mark had not yet obtained a drivers license. I had not expected that, so my only choice was to allow Blakely to come along as his driver. After all, you and I will be going in completely different directions than they. I called the college and informed them of the need for Mark to briefly visit the Project. I gave the college the telephone number of our hotel and asked them call me when he is finished with his visit at the college. The college has arranged for the rental car at the expense of the college."

"It appears to me, you are encouraging the two of them to continue their spicy relationship."

"I wouldn't exactly say that, but who am I to stand in the way of their future? If I don't try to help them in some way Mark might never get an opportunity like this again. I have already contacted the scholarship committee at Idaho University and they sounded excited about meeting Mark with the possibility of enrolling him in their new, special nuclear engineering program. It is an extremely ambitious program and very few young people want to enroll in it. The University is looking forward to having him as a student. Frankly Matthew, if it takes bringing Sheldon along to insure that Mark enrolls at the University, I consider that a small price to pay."

"I do believe you have covered all the bases Catherine. I just hope it doesn't backfire. It appears that Sheldon has considerable influence over Mark. I'm sure you realize Catherine, if he is going to agree to the I.U. scholarship, Blakely must find a job teaching near the college."

"I know you will find this hard to believe," Catherine said, "but I have taken care of that also. When I talked to the college admission folks, I explained as carefully as I could about Ms Blakely. You see Mathew, I checked on Sheldon's teaching credentials. She has a BS degree and has her Masters degree in nuclear science. When I saw that I wondered why she is teaching science at a local high school. That of course is her business and I will never ask her for a reason and you shouldn't either Matthew."

"My guess is that you expect the college to offer her a job as a professor."

"You must be a mind reader Matthew. In fact, I have suggested to the University they must certainly be in need of someone with outstanding credentials like Ms Blakely."

To which the college folks replied, "We are constantly searching for bright new talent. I'm sure we could use Miss Blakely in our science center on the main campus. When she arrives, we will place her in touch with our human resource faculty employment team."

"You don't miss a thing do you Catherine?"

"It is my job to be thorough."

The rest of the trip was quiet. Matthew felt a short nap would do him well, so he reclined the seat and fell into a deep sleep. It seemed only minutes until he was awakened by the slight bump of the wheels as they touched down on the airport runway at Idaho Falls, Idaho.

The Marriott Hotel shuttle van was waiting for the three of them and a few others who also needed the shuttle to the hotel. After a quick front desk check-in they went to their pre assigned rooms. Imagine that, Catherine's room was next to Matthew's. Mark and Sheldon's rooms were next to each other also. How convenient, but at this point Matthew really didn't care. The flight had been long so he decided to lie down for a few minutes before going to the hotel restaurant.

Matthew was awakened by a slight knock on the door. He opened it but, there was no one there. Then another knock and he realized it was coming from an adjoining room door. *Oh my,* he thought, *not another performance such as the one at Catherine's townhouse.* To his happy surprise, as he opened the door, there she was, fully clothed. For an unmarried man, adjoining rooms would be a desired bonus. For Matthew however, he just wanted to get through these few days without any more lingering regrets.

"Are you ready for dinner Matthew?" Catherine said. "Mark and Sheldon are here and we are all going down to the hotel restaurant."

"Sure, I'll be right with you."

The dining room was not exceptionally large as you might think for a large hotel like this. Cozy, might best describe it, with a floor to ceiling fireplace in the far corner of the room. Matthew remarked that it gives you the impression it will be very cold in the winter. What appeared to be hand hewn timbers running across the ceiling were gorgeous. There were many slightly dimmed, multi lamp chandeliers hanging from the ceiling timbers. A huge picture window gave everyone a perfect view of the remote, but distant snow covered mountains. In the near distance you could see the cable lift that takes the skiers to the top of the ski slopes. Julie would have enjoyed the beauty of this, but that was not to be.

Matthew's thoughts were interrupted by the realization that in the winter this would be a very, *very* cold place. Perhaps Julie is right by not wanting to move here. Neither of them enjoys an extremely cold winter climate. A move to Florida might have made Julie think longer about transferring to a new location.

The four talked during dinner about all the possibilities of college at The University of Idaho. Catherine just happened to mention that Sheldon might consider working at the college. Sheldon seemed pleased about such an extraordinary possibility. It was clear that Catherine had not told Sheldon of the arrangements she had made with the university. Getting Mark enrolled in the university was Catherine's main purpose in bringing her along.

Catherine explained to Mark and Sheldon that they would be on their own to investigate the university campus on Monday. Catherine gave Sheldon maps of the area because she was the one that would be doing the driving. Sheldon thanked Catherine over and over for allowing her to come along. Little did she know that Catherine had thoughtfully opened many doors for the two of them?

Catherine was picking up the bill for the dinner so Matthew decided to take advantage of it by ordering a thick juicy Western steak, smothered in mushroom sauce. The steak alone filled his plate and was cooked to perfection, medium well done. A side order of onion rings and cheese covered Brussel sprouts, it doesn't get any better than this. "Hey," Matthew said, "some of us actually like Brussel sprouts, so stop gagging." The dessert for all was the chef's special dessert, German chocolate fudge cake.

Going to bed after a meal like that would be really dumb

so Matthew decided to take a walk outside in the fresh evening cool mountain air. He especially wanted to be alone, but that wasn't to be. Catherine, Mark and Sheldon decided to tag along. This is such a beautiful location; picture post card best describes it. Just a few hundred steps down a walkway they came to the hotel's boat dock where you could see the lake that appeared to go on for miles. Thoughts about great fishing went through his mind. The others simply marveled at the beauty of the moon as it lit up the entire landscape surrounding the endless lake. Matthew had to admit that the splendor of it created a very romantic setting. After about an hour of Matthew throwing little flat rocks in the water trying to get them to skip like he did back home as a kid, they all decided to call it a night and head back inside. Too bad Julie couldn't be along to enjoy this beautiful setting.

Mark was so impressed with his room he especially wanted us to see it. Catherine and Matthew agreed to briefly visit for a few minutes. It was evident that the maid had turned down the bedspread and placed one of those small green chocolate mints on his pillow. Apparently Mark had not traveled much because this caused him to feel like a very important guest, which is what the hotel management wants. His adjoining room door made Sheldon smile, while trying not to be obvious. How convenient, as Matthew mentally wondered what would happen in their room tonight. Oh well, as Catherine says, that's their business.

Catherine and Matthew went to their separate rooms. It wasn't long before Catherine came into Matthew's room and sat on the edge of his bed. He had neglected to lock his side of the adjoining room door.

"Matthew, you probably wonder why I acted so boldly with you at my home in Washington."

"That thought has run through my mind many, many times over the last few days Catherine."

"Matthew," she went on. "For years I have traveled all over

the world. I have met very important men, most of who tried to get me into bed. Truthfully a few of them did although I got very little pleasure from it."

"I wonder why that doesn't surprise me Catherine," Matthew said using a rather indifferent tone in his voice. "You are a very beautiful woman, from top to bottom. You have the composure of a very sophisticated lady. You have the ability to blend in with any group of assembled people; from the lowest scrum balls to the high and mighty important men in any and every situation. And I must say as I sit here looking at you, you have a rather stunning body. To be sure, very few men would kick you out of bed."

"Thank you Matthew … I think." Catherine said. "When I'm in bed with a man Matthew, I definitely need to be the aggressor. I don't like the wham, bang, thank you maam stuff. I get immense satisfaction from seeing a man turned on so much he can't help himself from going all the way with me. Matthew, if I'm going to have sex with a man, it must be on my terms. By the way Matthew, it seems to be getting very warm in here, would you mind if I remove my jacket and blouse, all this talk about sex is getting me rather hot?"

Matthew tried to reply half heartily. "Sure why not, I must admit I am getting pretty warm myself."

The bedroom the lights were on revealing what a great body Catherine has. For her age, Catherine was one beautiful lady. In his mind Matthew realized Catherine had never been married or at least never had children because she had none of the tell tale signs of child bearing. It was obvious to him, at this particular point in their relationship, that Catherine was playing the part of a woman on a sacrificial sex hunt and he was her prey.

I have to ask you Catherine though, why me? There are untold thousands of men that want their woman to be the aggressor."

"That is true," Catherine said. "But I want you because quite simply, you are here with me now. Also, because I know that you aren't going to brag to anyone about our hours together like some men do. I trust you Matthew, besides; you know how to do the interesting things that most women only get from reading women's magazines."

Having said that she reached over to the night stand and turned the light down to a low, dim light. Matthew had been caught in her web and she knew it. Escaping from her never entered his mind although he knew he should at least try.

# CHAPTER 11
## INVESTIGATE THE POSSIBILITY

**M**ondays, for Matthew have always been exciting. He loved new challenges and new solutions. For reasons known only to him he eagerly looked forward to the new week. That might sound difficult for some to believe, but Matthew did enjoy his time at Oak Valley. This particular Monday for him was different. The thought of beginning a new job in Idaho had him a bit uneasy. He wondered how he would fit into the big picture of the enormous Idaho Project. Would he be accepted as an equal to those that had been there for years or would they accept him because they had to? He would soon find out.

Catherine and Matthew were already in the dining room having breakfast when Mark and Sheldon arrived.

"Good morning," Catherine said. "Did you both sleep well?"

"Sure did," exclaimed Mark. "Slept like a baby."

"And you Sheldon," Catherine asked.

After a brief pause Sheldon said, "It took me awhile to get to sleep, I kept wondering if perhaps I could find a job in this god forsaken place. If Mark decides to take the scholarship it would be nice if I could get a teaching job at the university. As we were flying here I have been thinking I might choose to move on to a more satisfying teaching position. You know, like one that eventually would pay more money than my high school teacher job, maybe even a college professorship. Ms Hamilton, I doubt that either of you know this, but I have teaching credentials that qualify me for such a job."

"This would be a good place to start looking," Catherine said, pretending that she knew nothing about Sheldon's background. "But why would you wish to teach here, it is so far from your home?"

"Yes Sheldon," Mark asked, "your home is in Virginia and this is so far away from your mother."

"Mark, you know the answer to that, just think about it."

Catherine and Matthew left that pass without uttering a word. They both knew what she meant, so why bring it up.

Catherine quickly changed the subject as she said, "Sheldon you have the necessary maps of the area. You have a rental car so from now on you and Mark will be on your own. Your home base will be this hotel. Matthew and I will not be back here until Wednesday evening. Incidentally Sheldon, be sure you follow the schedule I have given you. You and Mark must be at *The Project* Wednesday morning at nine a.m. Mark is to take a tour of the facility before returning to the hotel Wednesday evening. If you check the itinerary it shows the location of *The Project* and also the inn where Matthew and I will be Tuesday night. We have room accommodations near The Project at a place called The Valley Inn Bed and Breakfast. If you need us for any reason Tuesday evening, the telephone number is on your itinerary."

"Matthew and I will meet you and Mark at The Project Security entrance Wednesday at nine a.m. Please be prompt because Mark's tour will take most of the day. And for sure, please be careful and drive safely. Remember Sheldon, the car belongs to a rental agency and they expect to get it back in one piece. Now stay and enjoy your breakfast, Matthew and I must leave."

The drive to the Project was only about forty-five minutes. Catherine and Matthew were both amazed at the amount of traffic on the two lane windy road. It would seem nearly everyone that lived in the small surrounding towns of The Project worked at The Project because they were all going in that direction.

They arrived about nine-thirty at the security check point where they picked up their temporary security passes. It was at the security office where they were to meet Jack Jackson, the Senior Engineer over the entire Idaho Project.

After a few minutes they were greeted by Jack. Matthew's first impression of him was that he was so young. Matthew loved guessing a persons age so he guessed Jack to be about thirty, maybe forty at most. Turns out he was actually thirty-five. *Hmm ... Matthew thought. He only has three neck rings that he could see.* I'll not explain that again. Jack is well over six feet tall and has an extremely large and very thick neck. Could be he is a weight lifter or an ex football player. Apparently the thick neck is what threw Matthew's neck ring theory off.

Jack was neatly dressed in a white lab coat and a tie and had on a large white hard hat that had his name stenciled on the front, J. Jackson. Guess that is so you can tell who is the boss around here. Everyone else was wearing a yellow hard hat.

"My name is Jack," Jackson said. "Around here we all go by first names. I thought I would try to get us off to a friendly start. If it is okay with the two of you, the lady will be Catherine and I know you to be Matthew. I hope that isn't too presumptuous of me"

"Fine with me," Matthew said, "and I'm sure it is okay with Ms Hamilton also."

"Good." said Jack, "First things first, let's go to the cafeteria for a good cup of coffee, because we need to talk for a bit."

Catherine and Matthew talked with Jack for more than an hour. Matthew had the impression by his questions, Jack was starting the interview process and he expected that Matthew was going to be, for sure, accepting the job and working with him. He had done his homework as it pertained to Matthew. Jack knew all about what he did at Oak Valley. Jack talked in depth about the jobs most of the Oak Valley engineers do. Nearly all work done at Oak Valley concerns projects related to the Idaho Project. What honestly surprised Matthew was that Jack new by first name, most of the Oak Valley engineers? If first impressions mean anything, Jack Jackson appeared to be a brilliant person and Matthew felt comfortable with him.

"It's nearly eleven o'clock." Jack said. "The people using this cafeteria have lunch breaks at multiple times and we are about to see the first group arrive so we should leave now. This self service cafeteria is for those working on reactor four. This is the newest of the three reactors, but then Matthew, you are very much aware of that."

"At this time I would like to take you and Ms Hamilton to the central production area where you, Matthew and your engineers would be working."

The three of them went outside to Jacks awaiting van. Before leaving Jack presented the two of them with their required hard hats. Matthew's had M. Wilson and Catherine's had C. Hamilton lettered on them.

As they began driving the short distance to the central production building Matthew was just now beginning to realize the hugeness of the property. As far as the eye could see there were parts of nuclear generation units in beginning or finished stages. In fact Matthew mentioned to Jack that he perceived the Project as big, but never realized it would go on for miles. Jack offered a bit of explanation that they are inside a fenced security area of about sixty square miles. In fact he added, "This entire sixty square mile area is secured and surrounded by a double fenced area, monitored by armed mobile security personnel, each having K-9 buddies riding in their vehicles. Should you try to enter the property via a climb over or under the fence, security will use any necessary force to stop the intruders. It has been tried a few times, and I might add, with deadly results."

There is nothing small at The Project and the building they

were about to enter, from the outside, appeared to be about the size of two football fields in length and about as wide.

Inside were hundreds of engineers working, a few of which Matthew recognized. Some of the mechanical projects they were working on looked familiar to him. It soon became obvious to Matthew; some of the visible projects appeared to be a duplication of what they were doing at Oak Valley. To Matthew, the transition move to Idaho had begun months ago.

"So Jack," Hamilton said, "this is where much of the tax payer's money goes that is in your budget."

"That's right Ms Hamilton." Jack said defending his enormous budget request. "Most of what you see being built outside this building initially starts in here. Without proper research and testing, the interior parts of a nuclear power plant would be extremely unsafe. In this industry trial and error cannot be tolerated."

"Where would I fit into this operation? Matthew inquired.

"Matthew," Jack said, "your office would be in the center of this structure on the third floor overlooking the entire area. Anyone having a project problem has a signal light that, when on, allows you to telephone the person or if need be, visit that distant area by using one of the small electric cargo vehicles."

"That's a help," Matthew quickly added. "Back at Oak Valley I put on many miles a day walking through our research building."

For the next hour or so they walked through the entire complex. It was an eye opener to see the new tools being used that Matthew had tried to get for years at Oak Valley. It was clear to see that most of the government funding for his projects came here.

As they entered the cafeteria for this area, most of the engineers had already had their lunch breaks. When Jack mentioned that they would have lunch in this cafeteria Matthew cringed, just a little. Eating in cafeterias is usually not his idea of fine dining. He mentioned this because usually food in these places is awful and expensive. Not so here, the servers offered them a choice of several selections of beef, rare or well done, however they wanted it cooked. Matthew was happy to see a good selection of vegetables that had not been stewing for hours. He hated mushy, over cooked warm vegetables. The desserts, wow, about anything your heart desired were still available even after most of the workers had eaten. But most impressive was that the servers brought it to our table. This place was great, but then Matthew supposed one received VIP treatment when you come here with the boss.

After lunch they toured most of the reactor's still under construction stopping for considerable time at the new Generation IV reactor.

One does have to wonder how the pieces of the big puzzle fit into the big picture. At home they work from blueprints and never see the finished product. This had been an eye opener to both Catherine and Matthew.

It is late in the afternoon and the sun was already behind the distant mountain making it seem later than it actually is. It was just a little after six p.m., but beginning to show darkness when Jack returned them to their rental car in the security parking lot. Jack gave them a map of the local area that showed the location of their overnight lodging located nearby. "Anything you want or need, just call." He gave them his home telephone number and they left.

As they approached, what was to be their overnight lodging, a light rain had begun. As they stepped out of the car you could smell the freshness of the rain lingering in the spring country air. In front of them was a very large, three story home. The house, perhaps at some time, belonged to a very wealthy or famous person. Catherine best described it as quaint. And quaint it was, freshly painted white with yellow trim. The added touch of bright yellow shutters on each window and light green and white striped cloth awnings above each window made the house jump to life.

Who could have imagined such a beautiful property located,

as this place was, in the middle of nowhere, yet here it was, The Valley Inn Bed-and-Breakfast. From the massive front porch you could see in the distance the high water cooling towers of The Project Nuclear Power Plant. One had to wonder how the Inn would get enough guests to remain in business. To their shock however, as they entered the lobby there were approximately fifteen or twenty guests having a late dinner. *So much for The Valley Inn Bed-and-Breakfast*, Matthew thought. *Apparently they serve dinner also, not just breakfast.*

"This place is drop dead beautiful," Catherine exclaimed. The tied back wine colored curtains, the warm soft lighting, not too bright and the soft two tone beige wall colors ... gave the appearance of an exquisite country cabin. The hallway of the bedrooms overlooked the dining room below. Each room coming out to a landing that wrapped around the entire second floor. The new owners of the Inn must have spent thousands upon thousands to refurbish the place.

They were greeted by the innkeeper himself. "Good evening Ms Hamilton and Mr. Wilson. I'm Fred Conners, the innkeeper, and my wife, Dorthea is the Master cook. Welcome to our humble abode. As you can see, dinner is still being presented so why not find a seat and your waitress, Catrina, will be with you in just a few minutes. If you would allow me, Mr. Wilson, to have your car keys. We will park your car and place your overnight cases in your rooms. When the parking attendant is finished he will place the car keys in your room on the night table"

"Thank you." Matthew said.

"A person could get used to this kind of service in a hurry. Shall we have dinner Matthew?" Catherine suggested. "After dinner I am going straight to bed, this has been a very tiring day Matthew."

Catrina, our waitress, suggested Mrs. Conner's home cooked beef pot roast as their main entrée. In a short time Catrina brought a shrimp cocktail appetizer followed by a small mixed salad. As the dinner was near completion the dining room had become nearly empty. Mr. Conner and his wife came into the room and inquired about their satisfaction of the meal, to which both had nothing but praise.

Matthew invited Fred and Dorthea to join them at their table. Matthew was curious as to how they arrived, as the keepers of the inn.

Fred explained, "About three years ago I responded to an ad in a magazine that listed this property for sale. Five acres of wooded land with a three story house for sale. There was a picture included in the ad and my wife and I decided to come see it. Clearly the place needed a lot of work if it was to become my dream property. We both have dreamed of having a bed and breakfast inn for years, but back home in Pennsylvania such properties are completely out of our price range."

"This place is so desolate Fred and so far removed from the population? Where do you get enough tourists ... I mean it takes guests to pay the bills.

"Mr. Wilson, as you stood on the front porch you can see the cooling towers in the distance? The Nuclear Project has thirty or forty out-of-town visitors every day. My wife and I have visited with Jack Jackson, the big man of that place. We invited Jack and his wife here several times for overnight visits and gave them meals many times. Jack suggests the visitors to the Project come here. ... Need I say more?

In his mind Matthew could see how the system works. "I suppose that answers the, who question. The other question I have is who would build such a large house in a wilderness such as this?

"Long before the project began; a man by the name of Woodrow Long, a retired early railroad tycoon owned about seventy square miles of land here. He owned the land where The Project is currently located. They say Mr. Long and his wife wanted to get away from the hustle and bustle of St Louis city life. A few years after building this place, his wife died. Mr. Long wanted a place that his children and grandchildren could visit often. A few years after his wife died he became ill himself. When the government offered Mr. Long a tremendous amount of money for much of his land, he sold it. He then moved back to St Louis to live with his daughter. This building was empty for about two years when the daughter placed it on the market for sale. That's the story Mr. Wilson and here we are."

Having satisfied his curiosity, Catherine and Matthew went to their rooms. *Finally*, Matthew thought, *an uninterrupted night's sleep and I sure am glad.*

Tuesday morning came as a dreary, misty wet day. After breakfast Catherine wanted to stay behind saying that she had a lot of paperwork to forward to Washington. Apparently her visit with the finance people she had met the day before indicated there were some serious discrepancies in their accounting procedures at The Project. The only reason Matthew knew that is Catherine discussed a few of the problems last evening during dinner. He knew someone in her capacity should not discuss such things, but for whatever reason, she enlightened him, nevertheless. It could be it was a signal that all was not as perfect as Jack had explained. Her information did make him wonder if he accepted the job, would he continue as a lead scientist in the department. Or after he moved here would he be reduced a few levels to save the department money. Surely not because Jack did say yesterday that he would be raised a few levels to a considerably higher income.

When Matthew arrived at the security building, Jack appeared to be anxiously waiting. Surprised to not see Catherine with him, a somewhat relieved Jack said, "It makes me a bit uneasy to have Washington people looking over my shoulder at the enormous amounts of money we spend here. Every activity we have is essential and anytime someone comes to examine the project we usually have our funding slashed by huge amounts. Every dime spent here is necessary and to my knowledge there is no waste."

"Jack, I'm sure Ms Hamilton didn't come here to scrutinize your operation." Matthew said, trying to reassure Jack all was well.

Jack and Matthew toured the many different departments. As they did it became obvious that Matthew would be the old man in this operation. Nearly everyone they met was in their early twenty's, thirties and a few in their forties. Again he questioned himself as to how he would fit in with these youngsters. Jack assured him that he needed someone older that these young engineers could look up to. The reality was these people had been working on the Reactor IV project for several years. Matthew had been helping also, but from afar.

Today was the day Matthew hoped to talk to Jack, and with whomever else he chose, to discuss the viability of a miniature version of the Reactor IV project.

After a bit Matthew and Jack went into a small conference room located within the huge research building. Apparently Jack had prearranged this because there was coffee and Krispy Cream's already in place. It seemed to Matthew this was where Jack was going to have him decisively commit to a move here.

Before Jack could say anything Matthew opened the conversation with, "Jack, recently Catherine and I met with a high school student and his science teacher. For this boy's senior science project he designed a miniature nuclear reactor. In your wildest imagination, do you suppose it would be possible to build a miniature Reactor IV?"

"Matthew," Jack said, "it sounds like this kid has been reading too many comic books."

"Don't be too fast to throw the idea away Jack." Matthew said. "The idea is that this could possibly be an initial start to directly solving the fossil fuel shortages that you and I both know are coming in the very near future."

"Okay Matthew," Jack said. "Let's, for the moments assume it could be possible, but humor me a bit and explain to me just how miniature this reactor would be."

Matthew followed with, "I will be glad to do that, but I would like you to invite some of the engineers that could realistically listen to the boy's proposal."

Jack immediately got on the phone and called several engineers to come to the conference room. Within minutes several men arrived.

"Gentlemen," Jack said, "yesterday some of you met Matthew, who I hope will come on board with us. Today we are talking over a new idea that has been shown to Matthew recently. I'll not say where this idea came from, but it is being brought up at this time as a serious consideration. Matthew the floor is yours."

"Gentlemen, what I am about to suggest might seem like a belly laughing idea but trust me, it is not. I have had a week or so to digest what I recently saw and realize that we are not always the best people to make quick judgments. So often we look at what we do so closely that we loose all perspective of the possibilities. Stand back and look from afar and you might be surprised at what you see."

"Here it is," Matthew continued. "Everything we do in the nuclear business is enormous. As I moved about this entire complex yesterday, that fact became extremely apparent to me. Suppose you could build, for example, a Generation IV unit in miniature. Would it be possible to reduce the two hundred foot reactor buildings and cooling towers to about eight to ten feet in height?"

Everyone including Jack had a really good laugh. After the laughter subsided one of the engineers spoke, "We all laugh at that, but I have wondered for years if something like that would be possible. My fantasy thoughts were that in time, every house would have its own individual power generation plant. But then I realized that would not be cost effective. Instead, why could we not have a somewhat larger unit placed near the towns and cities all over the earth? For example the larger units, a miniature version of Generation IV, could be placed in the location of current electric sub-stations and the by-product of the Gen IV, hydrogen produced would be stored nearby at each sub-station. That would make each reactor totally independent of the other. Hydrogen transport to service stations would be much faster and far more convenient."

"The present power employees would service the units of course, but not before extreme training in the handling of nuclear equipment. Power outages would be reduced to only the local areas instead of outages within the entire power grid. Overhead power lines would be reduced to nearly none thus reducing outages from devastating storms, etc."

"You must have seen," Matthew said, "what I saw just recently. You are describing precisely what an extremely intelligent senior high school student and his science teacher built as his senior high school science project. This boy impressed Ms Hamilton and myself so much that he is, at this time, following up on a possible full scholarship offered him by the Idaho University. He too felt that each unit would be for individual homes. In reality, that would not be, as you said, realistic or cost effective."

The assembled team talked for several hours about the possibilities. The humor had totally ceased as they began to talk about the likelihood of such a project. Engineer Mike Creamer had mentioned earlier the possibility that a Generation IV miniature electric power unit could also generate hydrogen. That fact alone seemed to excite all present, even more. By doing that, they all said, we would partially solve earth's motor vehicle dependence on fossil fuel and thus minimize the onset of global warming.

Jack seemed very excited as he said, "If such a unit is possible, Washington will surely provide the funding, especially if we can guarantee hydrogen as a byproduct."

The fascination of how to cool the steam and turn it back to usable heavy water triggered the biggest concern. Changing the reactors old fashioned uranium rods appeared to be the easiest item to deal with. Generation IV's use pebble base, enriched uranium that allows the consumed pellets to be removed from the bottom of the unit and fresh pellets inserted on top. This process eliminates the necessity of shutting the system down for refueling. The miniature units would simply use smaller pebbles, possibly a small grain type of enriched uranium.

Lunch was brought to the conference room at mid day and Matthew had to admit he was hungry. Hot roast beef sandwiches, great vegetables and pecan pie. Good coffee or whatever drink you wanted was also served. Matthew had to admit that these people eat well at the government's expense. But after being served lunch, it was back to work.

Cooling the super hot steam coming from the reactor was another matter. It seemed like they grappled with that problem for hours. Is it possible to have, what would amount to a large air conditioner type of system reduce the extremely hot steam back to cooled water thus eliminating the huge cooling towers on today's nuclear units? How would you keep the water from escaping into the atmosphere? When they reached the end of the day they had come up with possible answers for nearly every problem.

It was agreed by all that it would be worth additional investigation by structural engineers. Tons of others would further have to sensibly examine the feasibilities as well.

Jack concluded with, "This sounds like an absurd idea, but as I said before, if we can get funding to reasonably examine this, I'm all for it. For once the United States can be on the forefront of the future by seeking to solve the fossil fuel crunch."

"Don't be too fast to claim the United States is going to be first." Matthew said. "Several weeks ago Ms Hamilton and I met with several high level responsible individuals from around the world and this very idea was considered at that meeting."

"No matter," Jack said. "Given enough money to investigate this, we will be at the top of the class."

There was an excitement that Matthew hadn't seen with men of this caliber for years. *Refreshing,* he thought, to be part of a group that unanimously agreed on something for a change. Usually there are the negative opinions that make it hard to present new ideas.

"Matthew," Jack said, "tomorrow you and I will discuss your transition to our complex. I would certainly want to see you head up this new project, if it is approved. I'm actually looking forward to meeting your boy wonder who intends to save the earth's future concerning the fossil fuel shortages. I believe you said he will be here tomorrow morning at nine, right."

"Catherine and I will see you at nine in the morning, with as you say, the boy wonder, Mark Erickson."

# CHAPTER 12
## THE PRICE OF BAD BEHAVIOR

T he rain was coming down hard by the time Matthew left and headed back to the inn. Becoming head of a huge power project such as this would be an enormous challenge. But suppose he moved here and the new program failed to get funding, what then? Matthew wanted Julie to at least voice an opinion. He already knew what her opinion would be. "You must be crazy Matthew, to move into an unknown situation, and at your age." Julie told him.

It was nearly six o'clock by the time he reached the lodge. When he arrived, Catherine said she was beginning to wonder if he was going to return. Because of the rainy weather she wondered if he might have had an accident. He assured her he had not and suggested that they have a light dinner.

During the meal Matthew bubbled with excitement about the proposed mini power plant. He talked like a little boy that had received his first new bicycle. Catherine was happy to see someone that excited about a new project that, at the moment, was without funding. She was kind enough to not burst his bubble by bringing up the fact that most new projects of this magnitude have little chance of receiving even a second glance. Her thoughts were, *a lot of Congressmen would have to step up to the plate if this has any chance of fruition.*

It was nearly ten o'clock before they both decided to call it a night. Catherine went to her room and Matthew to his. No interruptions from a connecting room, so he just lay back on the bed, propped himself up on a pillow to watch a few minutes of the ten o'clock news and reflect on the days events.

After about fifteen minutes Matthew felt himself begin to doze off. *Oh no,* he thought, *not again.* Catherine was tapping on his door calling to him. "Matthew may I come in?"

"Sure the door is not locked, come on in."

There stood Catherine before him in a beautiful full length lavender velour robe. By now he was up and sitting on the edge of his bed wearing his old ratty looking pair of pajamas. He had held on to them since the beginning of time. Julie had bought him new pj's, but like a lot of men, he refused to wear the new ones, it's a guy thing, I suppose. Men like to keep old clothes. They actually don't want new stuff until it absolutely cannot be mended any longer.

"Have a seat Catherine." Matthew said.

"Thank you Matthew, I didn't want to bother you tonight, but I guess I must have slept too much today and I am just not sleepy."

"You poor neglected child," He said. "You must have had a difficult day working on all those facts and figures you gathered at the Project yesterday."

"To tell you the absolute truth Matthew," Catherine confessed, "I just used that as an excuse to not go along today, I knew what you were going to discuss and felt you could do a fine job on your own. Perhaps, if you could just massage my back a bit it might relax me enough to get me in the mood for sleep."

"I'll do my best Catherine," Matthew said. As he said that Catherine slipped off her robe, allowing it fall to the floor. *There she goes again, oh my goodness,* he thought, *control yourself, but why?*

Sheldon and Mark had a long day. Mark had been in the admission's office for most of the afternoon and Sheldon in the faculty human resource office.

As they both hurried through the rain to their rental car Sheldon said, "I suppose we shouldn't have stayed this late, but the women professors wanted me to stay for a baby shower they were having for Elizabeth. In a university where there are only five women professors on the entire campus I felt it important to attend the shower with them."

At first her last statement went over Mark's head, but then he realized what she had said. ".... Sheldon, does that mean you will be teaching here?"

"It sure does Mark. Isn't that great?" As they reached their car Mark pulled Sheldon close and gave her a loving kiss of congratulations.

Once inside the car Sheldon turned on the light and pulled out the direction map and started to study it.

"This has been a day I could only have dreamed of weeks ago." Mark said, "You getting a job teaching here and I being accepted as a student. I really assumed we would go for weeks before either of us would know the outcome of today's visit."

"Normally," Sheldon said, "it takes weeks and sometimes even months before you get responses like we received today. Apparently this was all prearranged by Ms Hamilton before we even got here."

"Do you actually believe Ms Hamilton has that much power?" Mark said.

"In her position," said Sheldon," when she says jump, people say how high."

"Well I am certainly happy she did what she did. Now you and I will be together forever. I love you so much Sheldon, I just couldn't stand it if we had to be separated for all of my college years. If you had not been placed on the staff I believe I wouldn't have been able to go through with college here in Idaho. I would be just too far from you, with me here and you way back in Virginia."

"That's nice of you to say Mark and I love you too," Sheldon said as they embraced in another kiss. "You know Mark, I'm looking at this map and we are not very far from the Valley Inn Bed and Breakfast where Ms Hamilton and Mr. Wilson are staying. The inn is close to The Project where you have to be in the morning so why don't we just go there for the night. It's much closer than driving all the way back to the hotel in Idaho Falls. Besides we can tell both of them the good news in the morning."

"Do you think there would be a room for us at the inn?" Mark questioned.

"I'm sure. And besides who would come all the way out here in the middle of nowhere, and especially on a rainy night like this?"

"You convinced me Sheldon, let's go for it." Mark replied.

"According to the map we just have a little bit of two lane road before we come to the main road. Then we go south on a four lane divided road for about ten miles. The Inn is just off the exit, no sweat."

The rain clearly was showing no sign of letting up. Sheldon located the narrow windy road leading toward the four lane highway. As she began to wind her way out of town, already Mark had laid cross ways in the car seat putting his head on her lap as she drove. His fingers were reaching for the buttons on her blouse. One by one he began to unbutton them.

"Mark," Sheldon said, "wait until we get to the inn. We will have all night to fool around."

"I can't wait that long, I've wanted you all day." As Mark was saying that, he had completely opened her blouse revealing her soft velvety, slightly tan skin. The instrument panel lights provided just enough light for Mark to plainly see her delicate body. "You are so beautiful Sheldon." Mark said as he placed his face tightly against her skin." Sheldon squirmed in the seat a bit giving him the position he wanted.

The excitement from Mark's fingers touching her and kissing her body aroused Sheldon. With her left hand on the steering wheel and the other free to roam, she began touching him, ever so gently.

"Please Mark, you must wait, it's so rainy I can barely see. Please Mark, stop, you're distracting me. This darn truck in front of us is going so slow, if I get a chance I'm going to pass it. At this speed we'll never get to the Inn so hold on Mark here we go."

"I'm holding on Sheldon. When you can, pass the thing, I can't wait much longer."

Sheldon pushed the pedal to the metal. The engine roared as she began to pass the big tractor trailer truck. The rainy spray from the trailer truck wheels were blinding her as she started her attempt to pass. It was dark, and the road ahead appeared straight allowing her to safely pass. But the road was not straight and the truck was much longer than she thought. Suddenly from over the crown of the hill, coming the other way, were headlights and they were in her lane. She pushed harder on the gas pedal, but as she did the back end of the car began to skid, first one way then the other. She couldn't get past the truck fast enough.

Believing she was past the truck, but not realizing the back right corner of her car had already hit the truck, she made a hard jerk to the right which put her car sideways, directly in front of the truck she was trying to pass.

The experienced driver of the truck was already attempting to stop, but on the rainy, slippery road his truck was not stopping. Instead the little automobile was in front of the truck sliding sideways and was being crushed as the tractor of the truck suddenly jumped on top the car. The momentum of the truck continued to push the car down the road several hundred feet. There was no way the truck driver could prevent smashing the small car.

When the sound of the crushing metal and the broken glass had stopped, the truck driver, considerably shaken, got out of his truck with his flashlight in hand and began to survey the damage. He quickly saw that the two people in the car were beyond help.

By this time the driver of the car coming in the opposite direction came running with his big flashlight in hand. He had taken his car off the road to prevent hitting Sheldon's car head on.

"I was positive I was a goner." The man said who had run off the road. "I'm an off duty state trooper, on my way to work. Good god that was a close call! Are you all right Mr.?" He said to the trucker.

"Yeah I am, but look at them, they're both dead. My truck rolled on top of them. They never had a chance."

"I can see that. Why they elected to pass here is beyond me." The trooper said. "I'll call this in right now. This is going to require a coroner, so we'll be here for a long time. You can wait in my car Mr. if you want; your truck isn't going any place for now."

"You can say that again officer. I believe I will wait in your car if you don't mind. I just want to get out of the rain and try to settle my nerves for a bit. My body is shaking so much I have to sit down before I fall down."

The trooper called in the accident report and was told to stay put. He walked back to the top of the hill and set out emergency flares to warn oncoming traffic. He also called for some heavy duty tow trucks that would be capable of lifting the truck off of the car. There was no way that the two bodies could be removed from the wreckage unless the truck was picked up and another tow truck pulled the automobile from beneath the heavy truck.

The coroner arrived before the tow trucks. There was no need for an ambulance so the corner came in the county van. Once the bodies were removed, he would transport them back to town.

By now an on-duty highway trooper arrived and began taking the usual measurements after a fatal accident scene. He began taking the statements from both the truck driver and the off duty officer.

The truck driver told the investigating trooper that he could see the car coming in his mirrors. "I never thought they would try to pass, especially with the rain pouring like this and with the top of the hill just ahead. As the car pulled up beside me, they must have seen the oncoming car so they floored it trying to get around. Then just as they were almost past me, their car started to swerve this way then that. I tried to brake to let them come back in the lane, but the rain slick road just caused me to skid and by that time their car was in front of me sideways, my truck just rolled on top of them. I'm sorry sir, but there was no way I could stop."

"I understand sir," the investigating officer said. "The preliminary look indicates that you were in no way responsible for this."

The tow trucks arrived and went about the grim task of lifting the truck off the car. The other tow truck placed a chain around the remains of the rental car and slid it forward enough that the big truck could be cautiously lowered back down to the pavement.

And now the grim task of taking away the bodies. The coroner took pictures to show the position of the bodies. "Normally," the coroner said, "the pictures are usually taken by a highway patrol photographer, but the person scheduled tonight was working another accident and wouldn't be available for a few hours." He said the photographs are used sometimes in court, to hopefully show fault.

"In this particular situation however, I don't think there is any question as to who is at fault. What a shame," coroner John said. "She looks to be about twenty five and he's just a kid. I wonder where they were going in such a hurry."

"I don't know where they were going but look at her; she is nearly naked from the waist up." The investigating officer said. "After you remove the bodies John, I'll go through the front seat of the car and see if there are any indications as to where they were headed."

The investigating officer began looking through the tangled mess for identification. "Look John ... down there on the floor, I believe I see a purse. Hopefully that will identify who they are and possibly where they were going."

"By the position of the two of them he must have been planning more than a Tuesday night ride." John, the coroner said.

Matthew began a memory rewind taking him back to his younger days at Oak Valley in Knoxville. Never, would a situation like being in bed with a lady like Catherine happen to him. The women he had fun with were either hookers or married women looking for a good time. In his wildest dreams he never thought this could happen.

"Matthew, I think the phone is ringing in my room." Catherine said.

They both stopped and listened, but heard nothing. "Oh well," Matthew said, "I don't hear it do you Catherine?"

"No I guess it must have been a phone in another room." Catherine said.

In a few minutes there was a knock at the door. "Just a minute." responded Matthew.

Hurriedly Matthew put on his pajamas and a house coat and went to the door. When he opened it, it was Fred, the innkeeper. "Mr. Wilson someone is in the lobby and would like to talk to you and Ms Hamilton."

"Thank you," replied Matthew, "I'll get Ms Hamilton and please tell them we will be down in just a few minutes as soon as I get dressed."

."I wonder what that's about." Catherine said.

As Matthew rushed to get dressed, Catherine hurried to her room and said she would be down in a minute also.

Matthew was the first to get to the lobby. Standing by the front desk was a grim faced, six foot, Idaho Highway Patrol officer. Matthew's heart sank as he tried to recall what laws he might have broken that would bring this man out so late in the evening, and especially wanting to see the two of them. By this time Catherine had arrived in the lobby with a puzzled look on her face.

"Folks," the officer said, "I'm afraid I have some shocking bad news to tell you. First, I must ask you if either of you know a Sheldon Blakeley and Mark Erickson."

"Yes sir," Catherine said, "the two of them are here as prospects for the University of Idaho. Ms Sheldon is to hopefully receive a job at the university and Mark will become a student at the university, why do you ask?"

"Well that is not going to happen. About nine thirty tonight they had an accident on the road that leads from the university to the new four lane highway. They tried to pass a truck on the rain slick two lane road and didn't make it. They have both been killed. I'm so sorry to have to bring you this news."

Both Catherine and Matthew slid backwards into the nearby sofa upon hearing the news. A look of disbelief came on their faces. Neither could say a thing.

The officer continued, "Their bodies are being transported back to the Pocatello morgue at University General Hospital, located near the university as we speak. Fortunately in Ms Blakeley's purse was an itinerary of where they were to spend the night, but we called the hotel in Idaho Falls and were told they had not yet arrived. Neither of them had picked up their room keys so I looked a bit further and found that you two were spending tonight here at the Bed and Breakfast Inn. I don't know what your relationship is to the two of them, but if you can help us in this matter, I would appreciate it. We also have no idea who their next of kin are. If you can tell us that information, our department will advise their kin of the situation."

"No need for that," Catherine calmly said. "They were both here as our guests to check out the university. I thank you sir for going to the trouble to find us. We will handle all the necessary details. Mr. Wilson and I will make the arrangements to have the bodies flown back to the Washington D.C. area. If you could provide me with the location of the University General Hospital in Pocatello, I would appreciate it."

"Just follow the signs to the hospital when you come into the town." Replied the officer

For his report the officer needed address details so Catherine went to her room and returned shortly with all the information he required. Again they both thanked him and the officer left. They both continued to sit in the lobby. To say they were stunned would be an understatement.

By now it was nearly midnight, but neither of them felt they could go back to bed. Instead they stayed in the lobby discussing how to tell Marks's parents and Sheldon's mother. Sheldon's father had passed away several years ago.

Catherine had the telephone numbers of both the parents. Then there was the unpleasant task of notifying the university that the future of Mark and Sheldon has suddenly been ended. In the morning Matthew realized he would have to call Jack and advise him that, as he called Mark, the boy genius, would not be visiting his facility after all.

Matthew has never been placed in a predicament such as this before. It became clear to him that Catherine seemed to have a clear understanding of exactly how to handle the situation. She began writing down in precise order all things that needed be done in the morning. Matthew was glad that Catherine was a take charge person. He wondered how she could think clearly at a time like this. As she was began writing down the order of things to be done, she would say aloud each one as though including Matthew in the process.

*The immediate to do list:*

1.  Call Jack to cancel the meeting with Mark.
2.  Call Mark's parents.
3.  Call Sheldon's mother.
4.  Find out where the tow truck took the rental car.
5.  Call the car rental company and advise them of the situation and tell them where their wrecked car is located.
6.  Call the airline; cancel the reservations for their return flight to Dulles.
7.  Cancel the chauffer limo at Dulles airport that was to take the two of them to their homes.
8.  Go to the morgue to identify the bodies. The officer said

that would be necessary before any preparations for travel arrangements could be made.

9. Go by the Idaho Highway Patrol and pick up an accident report. If the report is not ready, give them an address where it should be mailed.

10. Call my office in Washington to advise what has happened and tell them there will be a much higher cost returning the bodies as freight. Also advise our legal staff to get the necessary police report of the accident (I should have a copy of it when I return, possibly not) but be prepared for a possible lawsuit.

11. Arrange to take the bodies to their respective funeral homes. Get the addresses and phone numbers of the funeral homes.

12. Arrange for the undertakers in Washington to pick up the bodies and take them to their home town funeral location.

13. After getting delivery locations, make airline reservations for their flight to Dulles.

14. Arrange with the local undertaker, the flight time and the airline where the bodies should be delivered to at the Idaho Falls airport.

15. Call the school where Sheldon teaches and advise them what happened.

16. Call Mark's High School and advise them what has happened.

17. Remind both schools that the government will handle all of the costs and details concerning them.

"Have I left out anything Matthew?" Catherine said.

"The only thing I can think of is you might try to get us an earlier flight home." Matthew replied.

"Thank you Matthew," she said. "Now let's go to your room and try to get some sleep. Yes Matthew, I did say to your room. I would feel much better if I could be with you for the rest of the night and while we are at it, why not take a bottle of wine to the room. It might help settle our nerves."

Normally in a bed and breakfast operation like this the night manager would have been in bed, but given the circumstances, Fred felt it necessary to stay up with them until they went to bed. Matthew requested the bottle of wine and paid Fred for it and the two went to the room.

On the way to his room, Catherine stopped by her room to get a night gown. After a short time she returned to Matthew's room. They sat for a time in the chairs by the small table and drank and drank. The only glasses in the room were water glasses, but considering the circumstances, water glasses were fine.

They talked very little, what can you say? They did talk a bit about why the two were traveling on that stretch of road. They should have been going north on highway fifteen toward Idaho Falls. Only they knew the reason and for Matthew and Catherine to be wondering about it was useless. The accident occurred and that was that. They both decided that revealing Mark and Sheldon's feelings for each other would continue to be their secret.

This time in bed it felt good to have a warm body lying next to his although he did feel somewhat uncomfortable about it. In a few minutes Catherine turned toward Matthew, wrapped her arms about his body, kissed him and said goodnight. This had been an awful night, but as bad as this night has been, having Catherine close, felt good.

After a few minutes Catherine said. "You know Matthew I still haven't had my back massage that you started earlier"

"I know, but I thought you wanted to go to sleep. Now go to sleep Catherine, we both have a busy day tomorrow."

Matthew awoke Wednesday morning with the light of the day barely visible in the east. His alarm was set for seven and promptly at seven it broke the silence. *Good grief that was a short night*, he thought. It was then he realized that Catherine had apparently quietly slipped out of bed and went to her room.

After a quick shower and shave, Matthew was finally awake. He dressed and went to the railing outside his room overlooking the dining room to see if Catherine was there yet. To his amazement Catherine was already there sipping hot coffee. Being the mind reader she is Catherine had ordered coffee for him also. "Good morning Matthew." She said. Matthew knew for her it was not going to be a good morning, but how else do you greet someone this early.

On the table was her to do list. "Matthew, because of the time difference I won't begin calling back east until about ten."

They both had a full breakfast although neither felt much like eating. Catherine reminded Matthew that today they would need all the strength they could muster as they dealt with the list.

As Catherine talked she began pointing to the list saying, "Matthew I think the number one item for you to do is to call Jack Jackson and tell him the situation. After you do that I will call the tow truck company and the car rental company. We can do all of these things before we leave for town." She definitely had to call the airline to cancel their reservations and try to book them on an earlier flight. Then the next worst task of all, go to the morgue. While they were in town they must go to the Highway Patrol office and take care of matters there. By that time they would come back to the inn and finish the absolute worst task of all, number two and three. "Now that I think about it we had better return back here by early afternoon. Questions with the local undertaker about transporting the bodies might come up, so we will make this our base of operations for the day Matthew."

"I'm wondering with all that you must do, perhaps you might want to keep our late evening flight." Matthew said. "It will be late afternoon before the list is complete. Then we still must travel back to the hotel in Idaho Falls."

"That might not be a bad idea Matthew. We'll leave the plane reservations as they are." Catherine said.

Matthew's phone call to Jack at the Project disturbed him. Calling to tell anyone that the person they were to meet had been killed in an accident is difficult. But then why should this be a problem to Jack, after all Jack never met the boy. To him, Mark was just a name, so why should it bother Matthew to tell Jack the bad news, but it did.

Matthew placed a call to Jack's office and found that Jack had not yet arrived. His receptionist offered to transfer the call to Jack's home. "He usually comes to the office about eight thirty." The transfer to Jack's house went through.

After a few rings he answered. "Jack," Matthew said, "there has been a dramatic change of plans for today. Mark, the boy that was to meet you this morning was killed in a traffic accident last night."

"Was that the accident on the two lane highway out of town that leads to the route 15? On the news this morning they said two people were killed."

"That's the one." Matthew agreed. "The science teacher traveling with him was the other one killed; in fact she was the one driving."

"That is a nasty piece of highway especially in the rain." Jack said, but without missing a beat he continued, "But Matthew, that still won't affect what we want you to do, in fact after you left yesterday the boys and I agreed that you should be the one to head the miniature nuclear project. It will be a few months before the boys can get the numbers together, but we all agree it would, at least, be worth a look."

"I'm flattered," Matthew said, "but I still am not sure what I will do. I have to talk to my wife and I already know she is not for the move out here."

"I realize that could be a problem Matthew," Jack said, "but keep in mind, if we decide to go ahead with the project; my first thought at this moment would be to memorialize it with the boy's name, The Erickson Nuclear Power System. How's that sound? After all he is the one that brought this idea to our attention."

Matthew responded with. "I am sure his parents and his high school would appreciate that. Jack, keep me up to speed on the project, somehow I would really like to be involved. We'll talk later, but I must go now, we have lots to do."

Back at the Inn Catherine had just finished talking with the car rental company and her office back in Washington.

"How are you doing with the phone calls Catherine," Matthew said.

"Just told the rental car company where they can find what is left of their car. They said they need a copy of the police report. They need it for their insurance company."

"We must wait here Matthew until my office faxes the necessary paperwork and travel vouchers to return the bodies to D.C. That is as far as I can go 'till the fax arrives. What do you say we have another cup of coffee while we wait?"

"Good grief Catherine, that sounds so cold when you say it like that."

It wasn't long before Fred came to their table and handed Catherine the paperwork that had come over the Inn's fax machine. She thanked Fred and said to Matthew, "I suppose it's time for us to go to Pocatello, and the hospital morgue."

"I'm not looking forward to this. Matthew said"

"Me neither, but let's go."

The rain had stopped; the sun was bright and had burned off the early morning fog. Finding the hospital wasn't too difficult; just follow the big hospital direction signs like the officer said.

The town was not a huge metropolis city like back in the East. There is however a lot of traffic for a small college town. It would appear most of the traffic was going to the university. The morning classes would begin in a short time, at least for those students actually going to class. Matthew thought back to his college days at Penn State. He slept-in late, rather than attend most of his early morning classes. The afternoon classes were another thing however, those subjects required his full attention *and* attendance.

The University General Hospital was small compared to

sprawling big city hospitals. One large three floor building and that was it. Upon entering, most everyone greeted the two of them with a big smile and an enthusiastic good morning, but when Catherine asked the reception lady for directions to the morgue the smiles quickly turned to a sorrowful frown. Nevertheless the receptionist did point them in the correct direction which was to the basement.

When they arrived at the morgue desk they identified themselves and said they were told by The Highway Patrol officer to come by and identify the two persons killed in the highway accident Tuesday night. After signing several official papers the gentleman in charge took them inside the chilly room. On the walls were several stainless steel, what looked like small refrigerator doors. At this point Matthew was beginning to feel a bit queasy. He has never had to do something like this. People he knew that died belonged to someone else. It was their relations that had this task. Identifying the mangled dead was never part of his job. Julie, being a nurse, was used to seeing things like this, but not Matthew.

The attendant opened the drawer and slowly pulled the sheet back that covered the first body. Fortunately the attendant only showed the face. The attendant said the balance of the body was pretty much crushed. There was enough of the face visible that Catherine said, "Yes, that's Mark Erickson."

Then he opened the next drawer and again slowly removed the sheet that covered the mangled body. It was difficult to identify any part of the body except to see it was a woman. The only part recognizable of her was the long brownish blonde, blood soaked hair. Catherine grimly said. "For the record, I believe that this is Sheldon Elizabeth Blakely. This body did come here last night at the same time as the Erickson boy, right and did the Highway Patrol officer identify her as coming from the same accident?"

"Yes maam." The attendant said.

"Then that's it, I'm satisfied that this is Blakely." Catherine confidently said. "Both bodies are to be shipped to Dulles

Airport in Washington D.C. tonight. I have the flight information for you and if you would have a local funeral home take care of the transportation to the Idaho Falls airport it would be greatly appreciated. I'll provide you with the information you need and a government emergency transportation voucher. The voucher will cover the hospital's expense and also there is a voucher for the funeral home transportation services. The autopsy will be done in her home town which should verify for sure, the body is Sheldon Blakely."

It amazed Matthew that Catherine was so matter of fact. She handled the whole process as though she was shipping a couple of boxes by UPS. She stopped at the attendant's desk and gave him the paperwork and vouchers. The next stop would be the finance office of the hospital. Catherine explained to them that the attendant in the morgue had the payment vouchers for the hospital. She thanked the hospital staff for their assistance and they left in search of the Highway Patrol office. The pink lady at the hospital reception desk said the Highway Patrol office was only a block from the hospital.

As they walked toward the police station Matthew said, "What a waste, two beautiful kids to be taken out of this world in such a horrible way."

"When you play with fire Matthew, you can get burnt, sometimes really badly."

That statement struck Matthew in the heart. He had been playing with extremely hot fire for the last few weeks. He was beginning to wonder when and how he would get burnt.

Although the trek to the police department office was just a few blocks away they walked right by it without realizing where it was. There was no sign that identified the building, but when they back tracked a few doors, they found the address. The official name was barely visible on the door making it difficult to see from the street. Upon entering the building they questioned the uniformed officer behind the desk if this was the place to pick up an accident report. "Sure enough," the officer said. "If the accident happened in this county, this is the place. This is the Idaho Highway Patrol Office, now, what can I do for you?"

Catherine identified herself and Matthew as those responsible to the parents for the two killed in the highway accident last night. She explained that the investigating officer said they could pick up the police report about the accident this morning.

"Sure," the officer said, "if you can wait just a minute I'll make copies for you."

They left with copies of the report in hand and returned to the Valley Bed and Breakfast Inn to finish the worst part of the ordeal, notifying both Mark's and Sheldon's parents.

"Matthew," Catherine said, "I don't know what I was thinking when I said we would have to delay until ten a.m. today to call their parents. We are in the Mountain Time Zone and that makes us two hours later than D.C. time. I can't believe you didn't correct me. It is after ten o'clock here so that makes it near noon back home. Oh well, I guess I'm entitled to a mistake once in awhile."

"With all that's going on Catherine," Matthew said, "I'm surprised that you can remember anything."

"If you don't mind," she said, "I'm going to my room to make the rest of the calls in private. It's not that I don't want you around, but there is no need for anyone to hear me and you can't do anything but listen, and besides, I would like to save you the agony of listening. Why don't you remain here in the lobby and have some coffee. If anything comes up that I need you, I'll call the front desk."

"Sounds like a plan."

With all the things on Catherine's list, it would be hours of waiting, so Matthew settled back in an easy chair and took in the view of the beautiful mountains. His mind began to wander and he asked himself again, is this where he wanted to live for the rest of his life? As pretty as it is, his thoughts were not to move here. Julie, he reasoned, would never come here and for him to be here alone, well, he didn't want to think about that. Matthew loved Julie in spite of all the foolish things he had done over the last few days. Catherine, to him, had just been a roll in the hay. A good one he admitted, but that's it.

Then the really big question entered his troubled brain, should he tell Julie about his romantic affairs with Catherine? Matthew knew Julie all to well and at some point she was certain to discover his indiscretions. His thought processes were working overtime and he decided it was better to fess up, but when? Should he tell her as soon as he returned from this trip? Perhaps if he told her about the tragedy that happened, then casually bring up the affair, which might diminish the impact. *How stupid,* he thought, *to assume she would ever forgive me of my wrongdoing.* Frankly, he couldn't blame her if she wanted to leave him. On the other hand, Julie was such a forgiving person, she might get over it, but it would take a long, long time. Everyone knows you can be forgiven, but misbehavior of this magnitude is never forgotten. Matthew didn't know Julie as well as he thought.

Telling Julie that he wanted to come to Idaho to lead the Erickson Nuclear Power project might be cause enough for her to throw him out of the house. Telling Julie about his affair with Catherine would be a really dumb move.

Matthew was mesmerized as he watches through the picture window, a ski lift operating continually on a mountainside, far in the distance. It is summer-time he reasoned, the lift must take summer tourists to the top of the mountain. Once at the top of the mountain, overlooking the valley below must be a beautiful site during the warm summer months. Reality interrupted his vision of beauty as he visualized the winter scene, the same forested mountains blanketed by mounds and mounds of cold, freezing snow and ice. Matthew knew more than ever, he did not want to move here. Yes, he knew, it would mean a lot more money, but did he want to risk losing Julie over it? After all, money is not everything, Julie told him that so often. Personal happiness is what life is all about she said. "Do what you yourself enjoy, not what the world around you wants you to do. Be kind to yourself." Julie would say.

The soft sofa was so comfortable; Matthew looked at his

watch and realized Catherine would be in her room for at least another hour. There were no others in the lounge area of the Inn so he took the liberty of removing his shoes and stretched out, full length on the large sofa. Matthew did a loud yawn as he settled back for a short nap. Just as his eyes were beginning to go into never, never land he suddenly remembered something. Suddenly awakened he realized that she did miss something on her to do list. He knew Catherine must call the University and tell them about the accident, but she needed to find out if her influence was enough to get Ms Blakely permanent work as a professor and if Mark had been accepted into the University. *Oh well,* Matthew thought, *this is not something that must be done this very minute.*

In a half sleep state Matthew began to think about Mark. What a shame that the boy, with his obvious talent, would not get to apply it. But then, he had already talked to Jack Jackson at the Project and told him what happened. Jack said the boys name was to go on the project so it really shouldn't matter if the boy was accepted or not at the university. The idea came from the boy so why shouldn't he be memorialized. For now Matthew would leave the details to Jack Jackson and his team of engineers.

Those thoughts began to fade slowly and Matthew started into a deep sleep. Matthew seldom dreamed, but pleasant dream visions of his past week or so with Catherine began to appear. In the dream it felt so good to have Catherine next to him. In his dream he began to talk to himself. "Why am I enjoying this so much? I know it's wrong, but it feels so good. No, no, don't stop now. I enjoy everything you do to me Catherine, please don't stop now." Matthew is now talking in his sleep as he begins to roll and toss about on the sofa.

Suddenly in the dream Julie appears. "How did you get in here Julie? This is Catherine's room. You're not supposed to be here."

"You are a dead man Matthew Franklin Wilson." Julie said. "I realized something was wrong when you said you were staying at Catherine's townhouse instead of a hotel in Washington.

I have this gun and you will never do something like that again, you two timing jerk."

"Julie, please don't shoot me. I'll never do it again," begged Matthew. Then, in the dream, Julie pointed the gun at him and began to shoot. "No, no, no!" Matthew screamed.

"Matthew, Matthew," said Catherine shaking him, "Wake up; you was talking and screaming in your sleep. What in the world were you dreaming about? You kept saying, no, no, no!"

"I don't know Catherine, just a really bad dream, a really, really bad dream."

"These have to have been the worst hours of my life," Catherine said. "I feel so bad for Mark's mother. And Sheldon's mother too, she just kept saying over and over that Sheldon was all she had left in the whole world. There was nothing I could say to comfort her. Catherine wrote herself a note saying that when she returned to Washington she must pay Sheldon's mother a personal visit.

"I'm glad you made those calls, I don't think I could have done that. By the way Catherine, did you call the university and find out if Mark and Sheldon were accepted? If they were, that should be some consolation to both parents."

"That's right Matthew," agreed Catherine, "but I already know the answer." With a smile on her face she said. "The good news is Mark was going to be accepted based on the assumption that all of the application information checks out okay. Miss Blakely was accepted as a professor and would have begun in the science department this fall. Of course they would have checked out her credentials, but the preliminary information appeared good. They thanked me for bringing the two of them to their attention and expressed their sorrow concerning their death."

"It's getting late so we had better get back to the hotel in Idaho Falls," Matthew said.

The day had been exhausting which made the drive back to

the hotel especially long and quiet. Catherine was driving and broke the silence by saying, "The local funeral home arranged to place the bodies, as freight, on our flight. There are times you request important arrangements like this to be carried out without error. When we get to the airport Matthew, I'm hoping to see the shipment of their bodies on our flight as part of the cargo returning to Washington."

"Catherine, you have done the difficult task of making the proper shipping arrangements, why would you have negative thoughts about it?"

"I don't know Matthew. I just get nervous about something this important."

"It will be fine Catherine, relax, but not too relaxed until we get back to the hotel. We surely don't want to ruin another rental car by having an accident."

"The problem is the Erickson's and Blakely's mother had given me the funeral home names. I called both of the undertakers and told them the arrival time at Dulles. The funeral homes each assured me that all would be handled and they would make the final funeral arrangements directly with each family. It would not be good to have the flight arrive late or without the shipment."

By the time they reached the hotel they had about two hours before their flight. Just enough time to settle up with the front desk. Having successfully completed the checkout, they hurriedly left the beautiful hotel and Idaho Falls behind, as well as the horrendous past two days. After a short drive they arrived at the airport and drove immediately to the car rental return area. Catherine reminded Matthew not to say a thing about the other car she had rented. The friendly rental people could turn very nasty if they suspected Catherine was the one that vouched for the two young folks who demolished their beautiful new rental car.

The flight was beginning to board as Catherine and Matthew

approached the departure gate. First class had already boarded so Catherine decided to be among the last to board. Matthew wondered why she waited until last, but soon found out the reason. Catherine wanted to ask the stewardess about the two body boxes.

"Good evening ladies," Catherine said to the smiling stewardess'. Is there any way you could ask the pilot if two bodies have been loaded as cargo yet? It's very important they are aboard this flight back to Washington."

The stewardess' smile suddenly turned to a questionable frown as she said, "I'll ask Captain Mitchell." In a moment the stewardess returned and announced to Catherine in a very quiet voice. "Maam, if you look out of your window, the ground crew is removing the two boxes from the hearse now."

"Thank you so much Miss, now if you have anything that has alcohol in it I could use it now please. Oh and make it one for my friend also."

# CHAPTER 13
## THE DOORS ARE FOREVER CLOSED

The stress of the past two days had caught up to Catherine. She gulped down two travel size bottles of whisky before the plane had even been pushed away from the terminal. Matthew on the other hand sipped away on his bourbon and tonic water. As the aircraft raced down the runway lifting gently into the air, Matthew glanced at Catherine and saw a lady, totally asleep. Finally she had earned the opportunity for a much needed restful sleep. On the other hand, Matthew definitely desired to avoid sleep and dreaming again. He never realized that he talked in his sleep. That's not a good thing; he always thought dreams were only in the mind of the person dreaming. Spoken words aren't supposed to leave your body as sounds, but apparently they do.

How does one say goodbye to a woman that has been as close as they had been over the last few days. Because Chicago's O'Hara's airport is so massive, at some point they would have to separate as she went to her Dulles airport flight and Matthew to his Knoxville flight. As they say, the fork in the road soon came and they paused for a final goodbye hug.

"Matthew," Catherine said, "you have meant so much more to me than I ever imagined. If you ever feel like visiting me in Georgetown, for whatever reason, please feel free to call me and come by. I have never felt like I wanted a full time partner until these last few days. Matthew I will miss you so much, please keep in touch."

As those words were leaving her lips Catherine put her arms around Matthew and hugged him ever so tight. It was one of those long hugs that one receives as though it will be the last one ever. She began to release him slightly while still holding his face with her hands and kissing him on the lips over and over. The kiss felt so good to Matthew so he offered no resistance. The moment of tenderness had both of them in tears as they said their goodbyes.

The flight from Chicago to Knoxville was very quiet. No screaming babies crying, no tour information from the captain, a nice peaceful trip.

Matthew's disturbed mind ramblings were non stop however. Should he or shouldn't he move to Idaho, should he tell Julie about his escapades recently or should he not? His mind simply would not shut down. Finally the airplane touched down in Knoxville. Now he started to feel really nervous, it had come time to make some life changing decisions.

It is nearly midnight as he pulled into his driveway. The house was dark which is good because that meant Julie was probably asleep. Maybe he could sneak in without waking her, slim chance of that however; she is a very light sleeper.

No sooner had he placed the key in the door than the house lights came on. Julie was up and waiting to give him his welcome home hug and kiss.

"Welcome home Honey," Julie said. "I have really missed you these last few days. Come, sit in the kitchen and I'll make you some coffee and you can tell me all about the trip. I know you had some real excitement, tell me all about it."

"What do you mean, some excitement?" He said questioning. How could she know anything that happened yesterday? Matthew had not called to tell her about the trouble.

"Tell me about the accident," Julie inquired.

"How do you know about that Julie?"

"It was on the early morning network news this morning. They said the Department of Energy Secretary, Catherine Hamilton and Chief Engineer, Matthew Wilson from Oak Valley had taken a teacher and her student to visit the University of Idaho." The news report continued, "Apparently last night both the student and the teacher were killed in a car, truck accident. There were no details given, just that it had happened."

"Well," Matthew said, "it did happen. Ms Hamilton and I were all day today making arrangements dealing with it. This day has been a nightmare. It's too bad because, according to Ms Hamilton, it appeared that Mark had been accepted into the university and Ms Blakely, his teacher, was going to become a professor at the college."

"The news didn't say if they were the only ones in the automobile Matthew, I've been a nervous wreck all day wondering if you were okay. When something like that happens you should call me Honey."

"You're right, but it never occurred to me that news like that would ever make our local Knoxville news. I appreciate the coffee Julie, but we really should go to bed."

*Good*, he thought, *so far so good*. Now if he could just get to sleep without talking in his sleep.

Before going to sleep Matthew has thoughts about tomorrow. He was anxious to get to the office to find out just how many of his engineers were going to take the pay buy-out offer the government has made. Unfortunately he was also wondering how much grilling Mary would do about the trip with Catherine. Mary was always up to speed on everything that goes on here and also in Washington. He was hoping she didn't ask too many questions about Catherine. Finally, much needed sleep conquered his weary body.

Nothing much was said in the morning. Julie kissed him as she always did before she went to work at the hospital.

Apparently he said nothing in his sleep, so far, so good. After a shower and shave he left for work as usual. He did feel a bit of apprehension as he went out the door and headed toward the office, not knowing what to expect when he arrived.

"Welcome back," Mary said as he entered the building. "It's so good to see you Matthew. We heard from Ms Hamilton's office that there was some trouble on the trip."

"If you call what happened some trouble. Two very nice young people getting killed is more than, some trouble Mary."

"I'm so sorry. I understand that it is not right to say it that way, but I'm so glad you are okay. So tell me, besides that, how did the trip go, have you made a decision yet about going there?"

"Honestly Mary, I haven't talked with Julie yet, so until we have that discussion I'm not making any decisions about our future."

"Well Matthew, I've been making reservations for nearly half of the engineers and their wives to visit the Idaho Project. It would help if you could say something positive about Idaho as a place to live. I believe most of them are waiting for you to make a decision."

"Anyone that wants to talk to me may come see me in person anytime. Spread that word to them Mary. After all Mary, as you know, we are out of business so I'll have nothing much to do around here."

"I'll do that Matthew, by the way Matthew, how did Ms Hamilton handle the unpleasant situation?"

"Ms Hamilton is a professional all the way. She made all the necessary arrangements. Something I don't think I could have done, especially telling the parents of the two about the death of their boy and the teacher. Catherine Hamilton is a pro all the way."

"That's good to know Matthew." Mary said.

"I have made my decision and when this office closes, I'm old enough to take the retirement exit package and that's what I'm doing. My husband and I are going to visit places around

America that were never possible before. Frankly Matthew, I'm looking forward to ending my job at this place. It has been good place to work, but it is time to say goodbye and enjoy retirement."

"That's good Mary," Matthew said. "I'm happy for both of you.

"Incidentally Matthew," Mary continued, "TVA announced just after you left for Idaho that they are going to expand their nuclear power program. It seems they are going to build two more nuclear generation systems right here in the Tennessee Valley. Might be something you would want to explore. Several of our people are going try to get on with them."

"Like I said Mary, I have made no decision yet, but if some of them are doing that, I hope TVA is going to wait for the new Generation IV nuclear power units. Generation IV units are in the final testing stage as we speak."

The days went on; very quiet as expected. Answering the engineer's questions about the Idaho Project was the easy part, but he couldn't give them any idea about housing because his trip didn't get into such matters. He did tell them that it appeared they were going to at least explore the possibility of building the miniature nuclear power system and that any that decide to transfer to Idaho would be working on the new miniature nuclear power project if it is approved. That seemed of interest and excited many of them.

"If the government provides the funds for the project and that's a big if," Matthew explained, "it would take many years of research before it is decided, yes or no to continue. As is often said, this means built in job security for a long, long time for a whole bunch of people."

Discussions about the move with Julie were useless. She made it extremely clear to Matthew that she was not going to move. The considerable additional salary made no difference to Julie. Several times she said if he took a permanent job in

Idaho, he would be moving there alone. The reality of living as a happily married man with Julie for all of the past years began to sink into his thick brain. "I can't move way out there and live alone, I just can't."

This seemed like the right time for Matthew to mention some of his other choices. He told her about a job possibility with TVA in Chattanooga. Matthew tried to make that move seem like not much of a move, it being less than a hundred miles away. She nixed that idea also, it was very clear; Julie wasn't going to move, no matter what.

"Suppose I just retire," Matthew said. "I have enough federal government years to do that and the exit package for me is a healthy bunch of money. Julie, do you think you could live with an old retired husband being around the house all the time?"

"Certainly, why not, you could become a consultant for TVA or even for the new project in Idaho. That would keep your mind working and who knows, possibly keep you out of trouble and God knows you know how to get into trouble."

"Hmm," Matthew paused as he tried to ignore her comment, "I hadn't thought about consulting work. I guess I could do consulting right here in the house. Retirement and consulting, thanks Julie." Doing that would provide an exciting change and he could still have his hands in the Erickson Project. "I don't think I told you Julie, but they have decided to name the new project in remembrance of the Erickson boy that was killed."

"I'm glad the boy's name will be on the project for the boy's parent's sake, and I'm glad you have finally decided to stay right here in Knoxville with me. I love you so much for agreeing to stay here. After all, you are getting too old to make a move like you have been suggesting."

"Thanks very much Julie, but don't jump the gun just yet, we are just talking about a possibility. A lot of people in authority would have to agree to keep me on as a consultant and the money for a project like the Erickson has to first be formally approved by Washington. I'll talk to Jack Jackson at the Project site tomorrow and get his feel for an arrangement like that. Jack is in charge of the entire site and actually still believes I'm going there as the full time head of the Erickson project. The fact that I'm not coming to Idaho is going to make Jack an unhappy man."

"I'm sure if you asked Ms Hamilton to recommend you as a consultant, it would be done. I think she likes you a lot, right?"

"We get along Julie."

The next day at the office Matthew spent more time talking to several of the engineers about Idaho and the future possibility of relocating there. Their feelings were, why not move to Idaho and continue doing the same jobs they have been doing at Oak Valley for so many years. New challenges do excite engineers.

After lunch Matthew called Jack at the Project. It seemed Jack sensed that Matthew was not going to make the move. As Matthew said before, Jack seemed to always be one step ahead of whatever it is you are talking about. Jack was a true leader and certainly was the right person for the job he has. When Matthew told him why he wasn't coming, Jack seemed to understand. Jack said his wife wouldn't want him to transfer to a new location either. Having been honest with Jack by telling him the reason for not taking the job made Matthew feel a bit more relaxed, so he decided to bring up the consultant idea.

"Matthew," Jack said, "with today's new communication technology I don't know why that wouldn't work. We can keep you updated daily if necessary. If the boys here need help with development problems it would be good to have your expertise at their fingertips. With the scope of this project there will be some huge problems. I suppose you already know that you would make a lot more money as a consultant. Currently I am using several people as consultants for some of our current programs and boy does it cost big bucks."

"Run this by Washington and let me know the result Jack," Matthew said. "After this place closes in a few weeks I believe

Julie and I will take some much needed time off. There are some great fishing lakes in our area. Jack, you should come down when you get a break."

"Sounds like a good idea, but that is one sport that never appealed to me, but thanks for the invite anyhow."

Matthew was beginning to wonder how the government was going to close the doors at Oak Valley. In only days, Matthew received a surprise telephone call from a local business firm hired by Washington to inventory everything at the Oak Valley property. Matthew knew that everything was to be sold off at auction, but he had not expected the call so soon. Washington felt it would cost too much to transport the Oak Valley equipment to Idaho. Matthew agreed and furthermore most of his equipment in his old building was somewhat obsolete.

Several weeks after the call from the inventory people, Matthew received a conference call from Senator John Gandy and Catherine Hamilton. They congratulated him on being chosen as a consultant for the Erickson Project. Matthew had fully expected to hear that news from Jack himself. John and Catherine filled Matthew in on the details of the Erickson Nuclear Power System and they said the Erickson Project had been given the go ahead for a feasibility study. This is a long way from beginning to develop hardware for the project. They also told him, most of the finance people in Washington think this is a real stretch, but if it is possible, it could save this country and the world as well, trillions of dollars.

After John Gandy got off the telephone Catherine and Matthew talked for some time about the outcome of the funeral arrangements. She said that all went well except for Mark's mother. She had a mild heart attack during the funeral. She wanted to view her son's body, but the funeral director said no because the condition of the boy's body was not satisfactory for viewing. It was then she collapsed and was taken to the hospital. From what Catherine was told, the mother would recover after considerable time in rehabilitation and considerable therapy.

Of course, at the time, Matthew couldn't talk freely with Catherine. You never know who might be listening, but she did ask how he made out when he got home. Matthew assured her that nothing had been said about their time together in Idaho, at least not yet. Matthew decided not to say anything about the catty remarks Julie dropped recently. Nearing the end of the phone call, Catherine wondered if he would be coming to D.C. anytime soon.

"I would like to," Matthew said in a half hearted way, "but I know of no reason to come unless I have to come to explain some of our losses the inventory company might find during their inventory."

"Our government has put a lot of money into your place Matthew," Catherine said sternly. "Some of that equipment cost millions, so I might just have to insist you come here to explain if any of it is missing."

"Let's wait and see how the inventory company makes out."

He knew what Catherine wanted, but as good as they had it on their trips he hoped he could avoid being with her again. As it was, he was feeling extremely guilty.

After several days Matthew and Mary received an in-depth report about missing inventory. There were some missing items like chairs and desks and one microwave from the dining room, but nothing major. He was confident that the men and women working with him were, for the most part, very honest. On the other hand some of the tooling machines used here could have easily gone out the back door. They didn't, and that made Matthew and especially Mary, as office manager, feel like they were running a pretty tight ship. The things that were missing were not actually missing. They had been replaced years ago, but because of clerical errors had not been reported properly.

The weeks seemed to go by slowly as, one by one Matthew's crew of engineers began to leave. They had farewell parties for each, and tears were shed as they said their goodbyes. The goodbye that affected Matthew most was when Jim Adams and Marty Glessner left. They had been the successful core of the Oak Valley operation. The three reminisced about the long past years before Julie came into the picture. Jim was going to Idaho, but that didn't make his leaving any easier. He had dreams of the Erickson Project being the next big step in ending the fossil fuel crisis. Marty on the other hand had the same problem as Matthew had with Julie. His wife wouldn't move to Idaho, but she would go to Chattanooga; he took a job with TVA. He only had a few years before full retirement and he wanted to stay close to his grandchildren. You certainly couldn't condemn him for that.

Mary, being the faithful employee she had been forever, stayed with Matthew in their near empty office. She talked continuously about the travel plans she and her husband have made. Matthew was happy for her, but also very sad. She had saved his butt so many times. Mary had been a one of a kind office manager.

The last few days at Oak Valley finally came. It was nearly time to turn out the lights and bid the place an emotional fare-well. The relentless work of over two hundred dedicated, val-ued employees was over. Not a person left in the building except Mary and Matthew. The property auction was sched-uled, rain or shine, Friday and Saturday.

Friday's event was a surprise to Matthew. It never occurred to him so many people would show up to buy the old equip-ment left in the buildings. Friday, early a.m., the parking lot was jammed with prospective buyers from all over the country. Mary said a listing of equipment had been sent to the auction house who had advertised the sale nationally.

The auction went on all day long Friday and most of Saturday as well. It appeared people will buy anything, including the trash cans from the cafeteria. Some said that everything in the place represents a past piece of nuclear history and they defi-nitely wanted a piece of history. Matthew had to agree, the scav-engers just might be right. The only piece of history Matthew wanted was his name plate from his office door. Saturday night all the buildings were just empty shells. The tractor trailers and pickup trucks were all gone. It is now a ghost complex. It was time to lock the door.

In the parking lot by their cars, Mary and Matthew hugged as never before. Mary cried and so did he. This was a sad day for both of them. After all these years working together, this was how it ended, saying goodbye in a stupid parking lot, "it's just not right." Matthew said.

"Mary," Matthew asked as he wiped the tears from his eyes, "this isn't the way it should end, go home and get your husband. I'll call Julie to come meet us at Jimmie's Diner out on route 40. Please allow me to buy you and your husband a retirement dinner, that's the least I can do for you."

It was only a brief time until Mary's husband and Julie showed up. Although Jimmie's Diner is only a diner, it has the best steak dinners east of the Mississippi. They ate and talked and talked about the past years together. It was good, but how do you say goodbye. You don't, you just say so long. The four hugged as a group, shed more tears and they parted.

# CHAPTER 14
## STANDING IN A BOAT IS DANGEROUS

**M**atthew loved his job so much, thus it was rare he would take more than a few days off to go fishing. But now times had changed. Perhaps a week or two of vacation would be in order. The office had been closed for nearly a month. Where to go, that was the big question? His idea of a vacation is going to the big lake, in the hill country of Middle Tennessee. There were nice modern cabins, rental boats and lots of open water in which to fish.

Julie on the other hand preferred to visit her family that were scattered all over the place. "Men," she would say, "all they want to do is just sit around and fish and do nothing."

Matthew had to admit, she was right. He was happy to do nothing but fish. In his own words, "Fishing is a form of doing nothing, but very relaxing."

Julie's mother lived near Nashville. Her dad died several years ago so her mother now lived alone in Nashville. It was time for Matthew to try the old compromise trick so he said. "Julie, I'll take you to Nashville to see your mother. You stay there for a week while I fish. Then I will pick you up and we can come back and you can stay with me at the cabin by the lake for the second week, how does that sound?"

"I'll tell you what Matthew," Julie offered, "why don't you

spend two weeks at the lake alone and I'll not go anyplace. If we can't go some place together on vacation, I would rather stay here at home alone."

"Well, I don't want you to do that." Matthew said, defending his position. "After all that has gone on during the last month or so I just want to go where I can relax, and fishing relaxes me.

"Do what you must," she countered, "but I'm not going to the cabin and that's that."

About the only time we have heated discussions like this is when we talk about vacations, that's why we seldom take one together.

Monday morning Matthew had his car packed with enough food and fishing gear to get him through a week or so of relaxing by the lake. The weather was clear and slightly cool. The drive to the lake takes you across the Crab Orchard Mountain range for about fifty miles. Then you travel north on route 111 to Livingston, then a short drive north on route 52. Both roads are very curvy Tennessee mountain two lane roads. Unless you know where this place is on route 52, you could easily miss the turn off. The only indication of its location is a small, foot square sign, Sam's Fish Camp. Turn left and down a steep dirt road and there it is, a site to behold, a beautiful lake full of fish.

There are several cabins along the eastern shore of the lake. The place has a recreational boat dock and oddly enough only one person in charge, Sam, the owner. He rents the cabins and the boats and he also sells fish bait. The closest thing nearby is a tiny country store about five miles to the north of the dirt road turn off. This place is in the middle of nowhere. It has electric and Sam has a telephone for emergency use, but that is the extent of luxury. It is so far down in the valley that TV reception can't reach here. That's what Matthew likes about it, no communication with anyone.

After he settled up with Sam he unloaded his car and decided to make a little lunch before launching into the lake's fishing paradise. The thing he liked best about this place, except the fishing, is you don't have to be so fussy about anything. One cup, one dish, a knife, a fork and a spoon, that's it. The coat and tie are home in the closet and if he wanted, he could sit around in his shorts. As Matthew sees it, this is the only way to relax.

The sun was still high and warm so he decided to take his rental boat out and do a little fishing. The boat had a small gas trolling motor and a paddle that gets you around the lake slowly, but then who is in a hurry? The fishing spots he looked for are usually near the shore where there are shadows on the water from the overhanging trees. It's not a guarantee that fish are here, but generally he finds success, possibly at times even catching a fish or two. Today has turned out to be one of those days when he just fed the fish his bait.

Could it be his imagination or was he hearing someone calling for help. He looked around, but didn't see anyone. Again he imagined he heard a call for help. He quickly hauled in his fish line and began to go around the shoreline bend, traveling about two hundred feet to the west. There she was, a middle aged woman standing in her boat that appears stranded about fifty feet or more from shore.

"Thank goodness," she said as she saw him come around the bend, "my motor stopped and I can't get it going, could you help please?"

"Sit down, slowly sit down lady." Matthew called to her. "You could fall into the water. Just sit down very slowly and be calm. I'll pull beside you and get the tow rope and pull you to shore."

As she started to sit she shifted her weight to one side and into the water she went.

Matthew really had no desire to get in the water to pull her out, but she was going down, so he had no choice. Just as he was about to leap in she came splashing to the surface coughing and chocking from the water she had swallowed. At a time like this you don't think about how delicately you touch someone; you just grab any part and pull. Matthew pulled on the front and back of her dress and carefully slid her into the boat. It is not easy to drag a drowning person into your boat without upsetting *your* boat also. It can be done, and he did it.

Carefully he stretched her out as best he could on the boat floor, face down. She had taken on a considerable amount of water and it started to spurt out of her mouth as she coughed. What a relief, at least she appeared to just be wet and frightened, but she appeared to be okay.

"Just lay still, don't try to get up," Matthew said. "We're not far from shore so I'll get the rope to your boat and we'll go back to the dock." She was beginning to shiver uncontrollably. Julie used to tell Matthew that was a sure sign of shock. He would have to get her wrapped in something warm quickly.

As fast as the boat would go, which was slow and seemed to take forever, they went back to the boat dock. Sam was nowhere to be seen so Matthew realized he would have to take her to his cabin and get her into something dry and warm.

She was almost alert and partially able to walk, and so with some difficulty he managed to get her to his cabin. He was wishing Julie had come along, she would know how to handle a person that had almost drowned. But Julie wasn't here so it would be up to him to do the best he could.

Once inside the cabin he laid her out on the bed and put a blanket over her. She continued to shiver so the only thing he knew to do was lay beside her and hope the warmth of his body tight against hers would help her calm down and stop shivering.

"I have to get out of these wet clothes," she said, "I'm freezing, could you help me please?"

By now the sun has gone down and the room was getting a bit chilly. How could he refuse? "Sure," he said, "but before I do I'll light the heater, it's getting very chilly in here." Fortunately the big kerosene stove in the corner had fuel and it lit instantly with only one match.

It only took a few minutes for the room to warm. "Now," he said. "I'll take the wet blanket off you and get another dry one. You take the dry blanket and wrap yourself in it as I unzip the back of your dress and you can slide it down to the floor." Nervously Matthew fumbled with the wet zipper which ran all the way down her back. As the dress fell to the floor he quickly pulled the dry blanket around her back side. "Is that better?"

Still shaking uncontrollably she said. "Sure, but you look like you have never see a naked woman before? I just want to get out of these wet things."

Down on the floor went the rest of her clothes, the bra and panties. Apparently when he pulled her into the boat, grabbing the back of her dress, it tore the bra loose as well. As the bra fell to the floor she slid the wet panties down and completely off. *Control yourself*, he thought, *this is an emergency rescue and those nasty evil thoughts should vanish.* But he was a human and her standing before him in the buff left nothing to his imagination.

Again she lay down in his bed and he lay beside her. His arms were around her blanket covered, shaking body. Finally, after about an hour she stopped shivering.

"I think I'll be okay now." She said quietly. "If you don't mind I would like to go to the bathroom."

"Do you think you can manage alone?" he said. "Take the blanket with you; I don't want you to get chilled again."

The kerosene heater had now warmed the room to a cozy temperature. As she got out of the bed she stood before Matthew, totally naked until she managed to wrap the blanket around her young body. Being the man he is, he did notice the chill had made her firm little puppies point straight out.

She must be about thirty, possibility thirty five years old. Matthew guessed that using his rings on the neck theory. About five feet six tall with wet, but shoulder length brownish colored hair. It appeared she wasn't married. At least she had no ring on her finger. From the short glimpse he had of her, the skin on her entire body was very tan and smooth, making it appear she spent a lot of time naked in the sun. It's amazing what you notice with just a split second look. She had a kind, unmarred square shaped face complete with chilled, almost blue lips from the cold.

The pleasant warmth of the room was starting to have a good effect on her body. The color was beginning to come back in her youthful skin. Matthew was happy she was okay, now if he could just get her clothes dry and take her back to wherever she was staying.

As she walked back from the bathroom she began to talk. "I'm Susan; my cabin is next door to you I believe. I thought I saw you come in today about noon. I like to come to the lake every once in a while to take in the beauty of nature. Photography is what I do for a living. It doesn't pay much so sometimes I have to pick up odd jobs doing this and that. If you don't mind I would like to get in your bed at least until my clothes dry"

Wondering what she meant by picking up odd jobs doing this and that, and also waiting for her clothes to dry which could take all night, had the man thing in Matthew going again.

After a brief pause while he tried to regain his composure he said, "I'm Matthew. I recently retired from the Oak Valley Nuclear facility near Knoxville. A few times a year I come here to fish, but I must admit I have never caught a pretty lady like you before. I am certainly glad I was here today to help you. My wife hates anything about fishing so she never comes along."

"Matthew," she begged, "could you lie beside me again and hold your warm body close to me? I feel so comfortable with you near me, please hold me tight."

He wanted to ask if she was married, but he didn't know how. "Susan, I don't think I should do that. I'm married you know, and your husband; what if he found out?"

Reassuring me Susan said, "Oh I'm not married. I tried that a long time ago and found out it's not for me. Marriage tied me to one place much too long, I like adventure. Matthew, this is adventure for me and today has certainly turned out to be adventurous. Now lie down and hold me tight, I feel a chill coming on again."

A woman that takes charge, Matthew liked that. He couldn't

help think that this was a Catherine thing all over again. Julie will kill me if she finds out.

Being the obedient guy Matthew is he did lie down beside her. It wasn't long before she lifted the blanket and pulled him next to her naked body.

"You saved my life Matthew." she said. "Now I have to do something to thank you for that." As she said that she began to unbutton his shirt and pants. She was better at taking them off than he.

Pastor Bill would never understand why he wouldn't stop her from doing what Susan was doing. *Oh well*, Matthew thought, *he's not here, so have at it Susan*. And she did. Finally exhausted by the performance of this young lady he said, "Stop Susan I'm too old to completely satisfy a young lady like you."

"Nonsense," she said, "you're doing just fine. I have some experience with men like you so you do what I tell you and I guarantee you will satisfy both of us completely, now hush."

Afterwards, she began to cry and said, "If my husband had made love to me like you just did we would probably still be married."

"This old man thanks you for that," Matthew said still trembling, "but I believe we should find some other way to pass the time. Perhaps some food would be good for you and for me."

"That sounds good to me Matthew. Thank you again for saving my life."

He gave her one of his shirts and a pair of trousers to wear as they sat eating the only thing he had, a bowl of chili, a ham and cheese sandwich and some potato salad. Hot coffee seemed to hit the spot also. That's all she wanted. After a spill in the lake like she had you would think hunger would have set in big time, but it didn't.

They talked for hours about pretty much nothing. They exchanged work stories and home life stories. They talked about what she hoped to do now and in the future. She said she liked to jog and hike. Her tight and muscular body proved that she was telling the truth. So many times people tell you stuff like

I AM THAT I AM

that just to make them appear better than they really are. It was nice to have a pleasant conversation with Susan.

It seems that married people like Julie and Matthew don't talk much after all their years of marriage. It's not right, but that is the way it is with so many marriages today. How sad to have a dangerous situation like this remind you of the truth of your own marriage. Perhaps he would go home and take Julie out for a boat ride, shove her overboard, then rescue her. The excitement of it might put the spark back in their marriage. That's a stupid idea, so forgive me.

As Matthew said earlier Susan's clothing wouldn't be dry until morning and they weren't. She insisted that he sleep with her and he did, why, because it was the only bed in the small cabin so there was no choice.

Daylight came and with it she arose and put on her now dry dress minus the bra and headed out the door for her cabin. Before she left he offered to get her breakfast but she said, "No thank you, you have done more than enough."

He wondered, but never did ask why she wore a dress on an outing like this. One would think a woman would wear slacks. He never asked why and she never offered an explanation.

Apparently Susan decided she had enough excitement in the wilderness. She loaded her car and drove up the dusty drive to route 52 and was gone. So now it was just Matthew and the big lake full of fish. One simple problem, the fish wouldn't bite. For the rest of the week he tried to catch something, but without success. Totally frustrated he drove home without even one tiny little fish. Julie would never believe that he went fishing at all. He did wonder if he told Julie what really happened at the lake, if she would believe that...naaa... probably not.

His thought was that he had better stop and buy some fish, but there wasn't a fish store within miles of home. He had a better idea, drive into the city to the fish market place. If you have been fishing for days one must at least have a few fresh fish to show for it.

# CHAPTER 15
# WHERE TO DUMP WHAT?

Not much is happening these days where Julie and Matthew live. Big city life disappears when you turn off the main road that runs from Knoxville to Nashville. Every now and then in the distance you can hear the siren of a police car or an ambulance. Neither Matthew nor Julie has ever been drawn to find out where the action is.

Now that Matthew has lots of time on his hands, he tries to busy himself fixing things around the house. Julie pointed out a couple of times that there was a leaky faucet in her bathroom and her bathtub drips constantly as well. How to fix them has become Matthew's real problem? Perhaps, he thinks, he would go to the local home improvement center and have them show him how to fix the dumb things. Once inside the fixit center Matthew reasons with himself, in the past he never had to fix things around the house, so why start now. He decided to talk to the knowledgeable folks at the home improvement store and see if they have a fix-it person that would come to the house. After all, they have the stuff needed to fix the faucet and bathtub. If those folks mess up the fix-it job, they get the blame, not him. To Matthew that sounded like the right thing to do. Of course we all know all this would have to be done when Julie was at work.

Next day, after Julie went to work, a fellow from the plumbing department came and in a matter of a few hours repaired everything. Unlike some repair men, he was fast, good and really not that expensive. Matthew paid him cash so Julie would never see a bill. When Julie returned home that night she was surprised to see both projects completed and the bathroom cleaned up with not a sign of the repairs remaining.

"Amazing," Julie said. "I figured you might hire somebody to do the repairs, but you did this yourself, I'm proud of you Matthew. See what you can do if you put your mind to work"

"It was nothing," Matthew said. He didn't say he did it, she said that, he just didn't correct her.

When Matthew became totally bored with his new retired life of goofing around the house, he would walk the short distance to the neighbor's roadside vegetable stand. Most of the time he would spend time talking to Alf or Margaret about the price of vegetables or simply, engage in some small talk.

Matthew was aware his neighbor had a substantial garden behind and beside their large house where they grew vegetables they sold. Matthew, being an engineer, was fascinated by the fact that you could take a few tiny seeds, plant them in the spring and months later have actual vegetables to sell. Alf would say that doesn't happen without some difficulties.

Most of the talking was done by farmer Jones with his wife Margaret close by listening, but saying nothing. Patience, Alf Jones would say. His first name was Alfred, but Matthew called him Alf. At the time there was a hilarious comedy show on TV and the main character was Alf. Matthew liked Alf. Anyhow, Alf the farmer would say that's what it takes to have a business like this, patience. He said learning how to keep the bugs and birds from eating the harvest is the most difficult part and then he would tell Matthew just how you do that.

"Scarecrows keep the birds away most of the time and I use all kind of poison pesticides for the bugs." Alf hated the poison stuff. "But without pesticides the critters eat everything when it gets ripe." Extended conversations like that would pretty much take up most of Matthew's entire afternoon?

If you haven't picked up on what Matthew is trying to tell you, he was really bored with retired life. Why has Jack not called him about the Idaho project, he just wished Jack would call. Surely there must some type of problem that could use his expertise.

One day, after from his afternoon stroll, Matthew walked into the house and saw the telephone answering machine light was flashing. "Finally a message from someone, with a little luck, maybe it will be Jack." He listened to the call and sure enough, it was Jack. Jack wanted Matthew to call him about some problems the engineers were having involving The Erickson Project. Reborn life erupted within Matthew as he listened to the call. His spirits went from the cellar to the upstairs third floor. "Thank you, thank you, and thank you." He said aloud as he dialed Jack's telephone number.

"Jack," he said, "it is good to hear from you." They exchanged some small talk greetings and quickly Jack began the saga of a situation that had popped up. Jack explained there are some difficulties the boys, as he called them, are having concerning the Erickson Project. Using the design the engineering team came up with, they could not see how the steam and extremely hot water that is confined inside such a small cooling chamber would be cooled sufficiently. The engineers believed there must be a large cooling tower to perform the task and even then that would be questionable. The engineers feel the water temperature must be reduced to near cold before returning it to the nuclear reactor. To add a tower the size the engineering team suggests would make the system much too tall to use, as had been proposed.

"Send me the drawings overnight of where they are with the project Jack." Matthew concluded. "I'll take a look to see if there is a way around the problem. Give me a few days or maybe even a few weeks, but I will offer my opinion and hopefully a probable solution." Jack agreed and with that the telephone conversation was over.

A few days before the call from Jack, Matthew had the electrician man from the home improvement store come by the house to install a bright overhead light above his soon to be, new drafting table. Julie agreed to allow him to have space in the guest bedroom to do whatever consulting he planned to do. Matthew had asked the electrician to bring a large drafting table along from the store. After the electrician finished, Matthew was ready to do whatever business came his way. He now had a stay at home, work at home business, and was proud of it.

As Jack promised, the next day about noon, the overnight delivery truck arrived with several large rolls of the Erickson nuclear project drawings. Finally, Matthew now has days with a purpose.

Before taking on the consulting job Matthew talked to several local consultants about how to bill for the jobs. All agreed that even though one might see the solutions to the unresolved troubles immediately, you might want to drag the job out and pad the bills considerably. Otherwise the income might not be enough to support you. Matthew believed that was cheating, but as he quickly learned, especially with this job, that kind of mind set would be necessary.

The drawings indicated that Jack's boys were going to run the steam and water *down* from the top over the refrigerant cooling coils. Applying the scientific math he had learned in his many years of college would have the water running much too fast to sufficiently cool the water. Also they had not placed enough tubing inside the refrigeration unit. The water from the cooling coil outlet was at the bottom of the unit. Clearly, Matthew reasoned, the exit must be at the top and the water more slowly pushed *up* the miniature cooling tower and exit at the top. On the drawings he added about a hundred feet of tubing with hi temperature cooling fins on all the tubing inside the cooling chamber. He changed the water outlet from the bottom to the top of the refrigeration unit and changed the pumps to run the water at a much slower speed. According to Matthew's calculations the steam and hot water would be reduced to an acceptable temperature before it moved on to the large holding tank.

Over the next few days Matthew checked and double checked his calculations and determined that the changes would definitely get the water to a usable water temperature. He further suggested that the refrigeration tubing be extended all the way to the large final water holding tank. This modification should insure the water returning to the nuclear reactor be at tap water temperature.

During the next two weeks he studied the drawings over and over. He was curious to see how the uranium pellets would be changed without shutting the unit down which is the practice in the current large nuclear power plants. It is normal to shut down nuclear power plants to change the uranium rods. But because they were using pellets instead of rods in the new Generation IV plant, changing uranium is done by taking the spent fuel pellets from the bottom of the reactor and inserting fresh pellets at the top of the stack. Basically this miniature unit would be refueled the same way, according to the drawings. *Now if that will really work.* Matthew thought.

When he called Jack, Jack seemed impressed that the potential fix only took three weeks. To which Jack said. "Send me a bill and given the normal government payment cycle you should get paid sometime this year." Then they both laughed because he knew what Jack joked about was so true. Matthew returned the revised drawings and waited for the engineer's reactions.

During the next few weeks Matthew received several calls from Jack's engineers. The drastic changes he proposed were generally agreed upon by the boys back at the Project.

Several months passed and then one day he received a call from Christine Hamilton. She had received inquiries from several nuclear engineers of countries from around the world concerning the progress of the Erickson Project. They were wondering if the project was far enough along for them to take a look. Catherine told Matthew, "The interest is extremely high and several of the men want to go to Idaho and have a look-see at the progress."

"You do realize Catherine that a working model is several years away."

Catherine interrupted, "That doesn't seem to matter Matthew. These people simply want to see for themselves, the progress."

"Why are you asking me Catherine? Call Jack at the project. Jack knows the progress more than I. He is the one that would have to approve their visit."

Catherine did just that. Her next phone call was to Jack at the Project. "Sure, send them out Catherine. We have no secrets and perhaps the ideas those men have can help the project move along faster."

A month passed with no word from Catherine about the foreigner's visit to Idaho. A visit like that would not affect Matthew so he could care less what these men did. It wasn't long however before Matthew had to rethink his attitude about the foreign visitors. Another call from Catherine revealed to Matthew that scientists from ten International countries would be going to Idaho to examine the project. Catherine was excited because it demonstrated to the world; the United States is willing to be friendly regarding our nuclear power. Matthew, had for years, felt it was important to share the U.S. nuclear knowledge. The time to share had finally arrived.

It only took a few weeks for positive comments to come back from those that officially visited the project. Each comment included, "When will we see a working model?" Each of their comments ended with, "This surely is the future of electric generation and the spin off of hydrogen makes this project worth it all. The world wants the Erickson Project *now*."

Again, another call from Catherine, "Matthew, each country represented clearly indicated there is another unresolved dilemma we, in this country, and the rest of the world as well, must face." Catherine told Matthew the problem and Matthew had to agree with her. Matthew, you and I have talked about this in the past."

"I'm all ears Catherine." He said.

Catherine continued saying, "Their concern and mine, as well as NRC Chairman Johnson is, what to do with the nuclear waste our present reactors are creating? You and I know our storage waste facilities in Utah, Washington and Maryland are nearing full capacity. Yes, we could open more sites, but that's not a real solution. The very real problem Matthew is that water is seeping into our underground nuclear waste locations and minor amounts of radiation is beginning to leak into the underground water supply of those areas. Scientists from around the world are trying to deal with the same problem and are wondering if the U.S. has any promising solutions. I simply had to tell them that we are working on the problem. Of course that is a lie, you and I both know that Matthew."

"Are you asking me to come up with a solution Catherine?"

"You bet I am Matthew. Use your creative imagination Matthew. I have talked to our uranium waste storage site managers about this and collectively we have come up empty handed. They have engineers working on possible solutions, but I am asking you to help."

"Catherine, our largest waste site is in Utah. I'll talk to them about it and get back to you in a few days. I'm sure there is a solution, but whatever it is it is going to be expensive."

This presented a situation that had emerged several years ago. Oak Valley was not into the waste solution business so Matthew had cast it from his mind. It was his understanding engineers had solved the problem years ago. Apparently that had not happened. Besides, Matthew felt this was out of his field of expertise. Their job at Oak Valley was to help design the nuclear units, other engineers had to cope with the nuclear waste problems.

On the other hand, why would Matthew not agree to become involved in the problem? He was a nuclear consultant for the government and Matthew could foresee considerable financial gain if he agreed to look into the situation.

As agreed, Matthew had lengthy discussions with all three of the U.S. nuclear waste locations during the next few days. It had become extremely clear to Matthew that the United States had a big, a really big nuclear waste problem.

In a simplistic nut shell, this is what he was told. Each nuclear waste facility was built with what was supposed to be a permanent underground storage, leak proof protection plan. That protection is beginning to fail rapidly. Each facility is, as you would expect, buried deep into the side of mountains. The walls, the floors and the ceiling have a thick protective coating on them that is supposed to keep ground water from seeping into the underground caverns. But over the years that coating has begun to fail. Matthew knew much thought went into the design, but nevertheless, failure is happening.

Surface water leaking into the caverns would, by itself, not present such a huge problem would it not be for the nuclear storage containers themselves. Even though the containers are made of stainless steel that is supposed to last forever, fact is, they are beginning to disintegrate. Inside the containers is nuclear waste water with trace amounts of radiation that will last for thousands of years if not longer. NRC felt the waste water could be transferred into new containers. That idea was nixed because it was decided it would only delay the leakage problem for a few years.

A temporary solution, such as that, is not a viable option. Adding to the problem, the floor of the caverns is also beginning to leak. If only the groundwater leakage from above the caverns was the problem, water pumps could eliminate it, but that is not the case. The slightly tainted nuclear waste is mixing with the seepage nuclear water creating a near deadly mixture. That, of course, is not acceptable by any government standard. All of the facility operators agreed a solution must be found immediately, if not sooner.

Rarely was Matthew's mind so stymied. After days of de-

LEE A. DRAYER

liberation with himself, he had to admit there was no known
solution to such a monumental problem. For once his mind
was drawing only blanks. He called Catherine and asked her
to conference call with himself and several of the foreign scientists that visited the Idaho Project. To Matthew's surprise
the conference call revealed each of their countries represented
were having exactly the same problems. Why this subject has
never been mentioned before had Matthew scratching his head.
Several of the scientist said they were putting the stainless steel
containers, already located at their waste sites, in Casks. Casks
are huge concrete reinforced containers. As an engineering scientist Matthew knew the casks would eventually leak also.

In our country, Matthew told those on the conference call.
"We too are using the casks procedure at some of our nuclear
plant sites. We recognize the casks are only a temporary solution." Those listening concluded that there was apparently no
practical solution. "Don't give up," Matthew told those listening. "This is a problem we can and must conquer. Nuclear
power and hydrogen power must advance to the next level.
The world can not permit the waste disposal situation to deter
future nuclear power generation."

After several frustrating days Matthew called Catherine
and jokingly said the only way he knew to rid the planet of the
nuclear waste was to send it to some distant planet like Mars.
They both laughed about that for a bit as an absurd idea. "You
know Catherine; I wonder what NASA would have to say about
something as insane as that. Do you think we could set up a
meeting with some of their high ranking engineering folks?"

"You know Matthew, if I tell them something like that, they
are going to assume we are altogether crazy, but why not, this
could be the last straw for the U.S. and for the rest of world for
that matter. I'll let you know how I make out. If I can get an appointment with NASA and they agree to come to Washington,
you must come and stay with me in D.C."

Matthew was trying to ignore her comment about her place
so after a pause he countered with "Sure I could do that, but

why don't you suggest to them, we all meet in Florida or Houston. One place or the other might be the logical location. After all, that's where the NASA's power is and for questions like we have, it might be better if we are on their home turf."

"Okay, I'll speak to the folks at NASA and get back to you in a few days."

In the back of his mind Matthew still wondered if Julie had any inkling what he and Catherine had done in Idaho or Washington. Talking in his sleep had stopped; at least he wanted to believe it had. Matthew wondered if there was a pill that would discourage sleep talking. *I doubt it, probably not.* He thought.

Many times a person does things that they are ashamed of or at the very least, deeply regret. Matthew's romantic affair with Catherine, although extremely pleasant at the time, should never have happened. If Catherine was successful getting an appointment with NASA, Matthew was hopeful he could meet with them alone. He kept telling himself he must stop enjoying Catherine so much, but deep down he knew he wanted to be with her again.

You've heard the expression, "To be a fly on the wall." Those were Matthew's thoughts when Catherine talked to the folks at NASA, and explained why she wanted to meet with them. Catherine should be able to hear the gut shaking laughter coming from NASA all the way back in Washington after she hangs up from that telephone conversation. They would surely say that has to be the most insane idea ever, and to think, it comes from our own Secretary of Energy, Catherine Hamilton

Apparently that was not the case. Next day an excited and hurried call from Catherine advised Matthew they would meet the NASA people in Houston, not Washington, on the following Monday. She told him she would arrive in a private chartered jet at the Knoxville airport Monday morning about ten a.m. ... Hmm.

Matthew pondered the statement from Catherine. "I wonder how in the world she managed to get a private jet to take just the two of us to Houston?' This isn't what he wanted, but he would just have to wait to hear Catherine's explanation.

Later that day Matthew told Julie that he was going with Ms Hamilton to Houston to meet with NASA people for a day or so. Normally Julie's reaction was, "Call me and say you arrived safely." This time was different, not a word was said and her mood suddenly changed to being extremely cold. She turned blizzard cold when he told her that Ms Hamilton was picking him up in a private jet at the Knoxville airport. This is definitely not the response Matthew was expecting. "So, you are going off with your girlfriend again." Julie said. "It would be nice if you could keep her out of your bed this time."

The question of Matthew talking in his sleep had been answered, what could he say? There are times in a marriage relationship that a person doesn't try to come back with a quick answer to a comment like that. This seemed to be one of those times. He simply pretended that he had not heard her say anything. For Matthew the next two days, waiting for Monday, seemed like an eternity. Talking had all but stopped at the Wilson house.

Monday morning came and not soon enough for Matthew. Perhaps when he returned from Houston he would talk to Julie about Catherine, but definitely not now.

When he arrived at the airport Catherine was already waiting for him at the charter end of the departure building. She came up to him with her arms wide open like a long lost relative. "Good morning Matthew, I've missed you so very much." She said as she wrapped her arms around him and embraced him with a smooch on the lips. That sort of surprised him, but after the last two extremely frigid days with Julie it was a welcome touch. "Come along Matthew, there are a few people on board the airplane that are anxious to meet you. We have food and drinks on board."

As they walked to the tarmac he saw that this was not a little bird but rather a Comair commercial 707 jet. How did she manage to charter this overgrown bird? It didn't take long to find out. Once on board they immediately began to taxi to the departure runway. On board, in addition to Catherine and a stewardess, there were five foreigners. The engine noise required the introductions to the five men to wait until they were airborne.

Once airborne the stewardess announced that it was okay to move about the aircraft. Catherine began the introductions saying that these men were in Washington discussing with NRC Chairman Johnson and herself, their concerns about how the U.S. was dealing with the nuclear waste problem.

"Matthew, I told them you and I was going to the Johnson Space Center in Houston to investigate the possibility of blasting the waste, via some kind of rocket power, into outer space." Absurd as that sounded to you and I, they were willing to listen to any possible solution. Incredible, was their immediate response. They all became very excited and asked if they could come along.

Catherine went on to tell Matthew it would be good to have representatives from other countries along on the trip. It might help NASA realize, not just the U.S., but the entire world was serious about finding a solution to the problem. Catherine further explained what Matthew wanted to know. "They offered to charter this jet at their expense, if they could come along and join in the discussions."

"That sounds reasonable to me." Matthew said. So here he was with representatives from China, Russia, Canada, Japan and a man from Germany who was representing several European countries. Catherine said a gentleman from South America had hoped to come also, but was called home for an emergency. Catherine went on to say that man represented most of the countries in South America." *How odd*, Matthew thought, *our country can't have a decent conversation with Latin American countries, but here is a person representing most all of them.* That alone illustrates the seriousness of the problem.

As they all talked, Matthew realized that they had already been to Idaho and saw what we were planning for our nuclear power future. They realized that all nations must stop the use of fossil fuels, not just a few countries. Fossil fuel sources are being depleted all over the world which is one gigantic problem. Our atmosphere can no longer handle the smoke and smog problems created by our power generation plants. After talking with them it made Matthew feel that finally the rest of the world was also thinking nuclear power is the direction to go for all nations of the world. But before we can advance to the next generation of nuclear power, we must first solve the nuclear waste problems.

It seemed like such a short flight. When talking with experienced people about subjects that interested Matthew, time moved along very fast. The stewardess announced the all fasten seat belt warning. As the stewardess made the announcements she quickly collected the remaining refreshment items. Shortly afterwards they were on the ground in Houston. *If you have to fly*, Matthew thought, *this is the only way to go, by private jet.*

They taxied to a private charter area where a limousine awaited. Catherine had again pulled all the stops for this trip. At this point Matthew didn't know if this would be a hurried one day trip or if they would be staying overnight. He supposed he would just have to wait and see how the group was received by NASA. Matthew had packed an overnight case with an extra shirt and a change of underwear, just in case.

For Matthew it was confession time. His job at Oak Valley kept him close to his Tennessee home. Except for his short vacations to his fishing lake, Matthew seldom went beyond the Tennessee border. As you know he had been to Idaho and Washington D.C., but that is about it for visiting other states. Matthew had always thought of Houston as a fairly small city in Texas, but as they were landing Matthew could see the size of Houston was overwhelming.

Along the way from the airport to the hotel the limo driver gave them a brief tour of the city. He told them Houston was the fourth largest city in the U.S. Matthew had assumed the only big business in Houston was the NASA facility at the Johnson Space Center. The driver said the space center was about twenty five miles south of the city. But, he added they are not going there, instead he was instructed to take them to the Aldon Houston Hotel in downtown Houston. He explained that it was very nice and he hoped we would enjoy our stay. Boy was he ever right, the hotel turned out to be gorgeous.

When they entered the hotel Catherine and Matthew were surprised that the people from NASA were already at the hotel, awaiting their arrival. After a brief introduction the NASA folks explained there would be no need to go to the Space Center for this meeting.

After all, they said, "If you came all this way from Washington to discuss the possible use of a NASA vehicle, we should at least meet you all at a descent hotel." Included in the group from NASA were five men and a woman.

A gentleman from the hotel led our group to a small private conference room, totally isolated away from the public areas. It had become quite clear that this meeting had been classified as *top secret*. All present had to sign statements that any discussions during the meeting could not be discussed with anyone outside the room. For obvious reasons, if the U.S. population or the rest of the world for that matter, got wind of what they are about to propose, all hell would be raised, worldwide.

When Catherine set up the conference she disclosed vaguely what they had in mind. She gave the NASA folks enough information to whet their appetite, yet nothing that would cause them to shrug the two of them off as total loons, at least not to Catherine's face.

By now it is lunch time and the hotel staff requested permission to enter the room with a light lunch. Permission was granted allowing them to eat as they briefly discussed the mission. The NASA woman was curious about the foreign visitors. For security reasons she questioned them at length, but avoided asking directly what they hoped to gain from this visit. Matthew could see the NASA folks were anxious to delve deeply into our problem. After all, adding additional tasks on NASA could create additional space exploration and that meant more jobs for the private sector and the military as well, much more job security.

"Our reason for this visit," Matthew explained, "is the United States and the rest of the world foresees a huge problem approaching in the very near future. Our country is approaching near capacity for storage of its power plant nuclear waste material." The talk went on for considerable time about the increased direction nuclear power was going in the not so distant future. Matthew explained that power plant nuclear waste is going to increase dramatically in the near future.

"Presently our three nuclear waste containment facilities in the U.S. are beginning to fail. The stainless steel containers holding the nuclear waste water are beginning to leak into the caverns. The leakage contains small amounts of uranium which is already penetrating the underground aquifer of several cities. Most untrained people believe the reactor nuclear waste is simply spent dry fuel rods placed in small storage containers. That is not the case at all; those spent fuel rods are placed inside very large stainless steel containers that are, after the rod insertion, are completely full of radioactive water. The water keeps the small amount of nuclear fission left in the rods, inactive. As long as the rods are underwater, there is no nuclear fission."

The men from the represented foreign countries were quick to inform the NASA team they too were having the same problems as the U.S. That seemed to come as no surprise to any of the NASA representatives, but they said they had no idea how NASA could help.

At this time Catherine and Matthew began discussing the crazy sci-fi idea of using some type of NASA rocket to send the waste to some distant planet and dump it. "Would it be possible to do that?" Catherine said as though she was expecting an immediate answer.

The woman, who appeared to be the spokesperson for the six of them said. "As preposterous as that sounds, I believe we should take the suggested idea back to our base and discuss the possibilities with our knowledgeable engineering experts. After all, if we can build a space station and lug all of the necessary supplies and the parts into space, I for one can see no reason why we can't at least investigate the possibilities. The key word here is, investigate." As the lady spokesperson said that the other five NASA men nodded approval to at least have further discussions, but back at their home base.

Matthew was fully expecting to be laughed out of the meeting and sent home with a firm, "no way." But that didn't happen. They informed the group that it would take considerable time to figure a possible way to come up with the request.

"There are so many dangers involved with what you are suggesting," The spokeswoman said, "The current space shuttles could not be used for such dangerous missions. Placing cargo of that type in any manned rocket posed extreme safety concerns. Finding another planet to dump the waste would have all the peace loving people of the world up in arms, which is why this must be kept secret and never discussed beyond this room. Any telephone conversations concerning this discussion must be done over encrypted, direct secure phone lines to make sure this screwy idea *never goes public.*"

Matthew supplied the NASA group with the necessary information concerning the size and weight of the containers and the methods the U.S. uses to transport the waste to wherever it need be placed. The foreign guests supplied them with their container sizes as well and fortunately theirs were similar in size to that of the U.S. The guests said their countries were in need of immediate answers. They wanted action *now*, not years from now. It was explained to each of the visitors that a program of this magnitude, if it can be done at all, will take several years to be placed into operation. The visitors didn't like that answer, but understood.

They were again told that NASA would put their scientist and engineers to work on possible solutions immediately. That's all Matthew wanted to hear, some creative engineering solutions, not a political statement. The spokeswoman in charge, Ms Harrison said, "This will take some time to get even an intelligent opinion. I'll call Ms Hamilton when we come to some sort of yes or no decision."

That was it, the meeting was over. Having the foreign visitors present did provide the added weight to the meeting giving Ms Harrison and her fellow associates the picture of the situations seriousness. Furthermore it had given Matthew a day away from home at the government's expense.

Catherine had a discussion with the foreign guests concerning, whether they should return immediately to D.C. or wait until the a.m. of tomorrow. Seems they all wanted to leave in the morning because it would be the wee hours of the morning before they would be back in D.C. if they left immediately. She asked Matthew about it and he told her it didn't matter when they got back. Matthew's comeback, "Julie is already upset, so why hurry home."

Fortunately the hotel had rooms for the entire group. The group was escorted to their rooms and as Matthew suspected, Catherine's room was next to his, how convenient, oh well.

Later in the evening it was agreed that all would gather in the hotel lounge for dinner and drinks. The hotel lounge featured a small five piece band that played mostly old nostalgic music as opposed to an extremely loud band. The clientele the hotel catered to was an older generation. For Catherine and Matthew, quiet sounds of the past worked, however for those that prefers younger rock music, turns out there was another larger room that, as they say, really *rocks*.

All enjoyed a very pleasant and quiet relaxing dinner which incidentally was paid for by the gentleman from Germany.

Afterwards the foreign men excused themselves to find the room that rocks. The bellman had explained to the men that there are usually many ladies looking for action. That was all the guys needed to hear, they left Matthew and Catherine like a rocket for the place coincidentally named, the *Rocket Lounge.*

Catherine and Matthew stayed behind to enjoy the quiet music. It appeared that Catherine wanted to create her own action. She found a dimly lit table in the corner of the room. It became clear Catherine wanted to dance. She began dancing her fingers all over Matthew's body pleading with him to get up and dance. After a few drinks Catherine really got her motor running and the music demanded they respond by dancing. He was tapping his foot on the floor, but she wanted him on the dance floor. Finally she placed her arms around his neck and pretty much dragged him onto the dance floor.

It had been quite a while since Matthew had been dancing. Julie believed dancing was some kind of evil thing. "Christians," Julie would say, "should not be making obscene gestures in public like that." Matthew never understood that kind of rationale and this appeared to him, to be one of those times to forget Julie's teaching.

He had to admit it felt good to have a woman hold him close. As they danced, Catherine began to softly sing in his ear. Before long Matthew began to sing along with her. They danced and she drank. It didn't take long for him to realize that Catherine was getting drunk, oh so very drunk. At all costs he wanted to avoid a scene in the lounge. Many times, as a person gets drunk, they go over the top and start to get loud and then obnoxious. Matthew felt it time to take Catherine to her room. He could see, obnoxious for her was only about half a drink away. With a little persuasion he managed to get her to the elevator and to her room.

Somehow he managed to get her into her bed. The question in his mind was, "Should I or should I not get her out of her street clothes? What the heck I've seen her naked several times so why not remove her clothing. Besides sometime during the night she might get sick from all the booze. She has to wear these same clothes in the morning when we return to the airplane and I personally know how messy a person can get after all the drinking. And besides, she is too drunk to know how she got her night clothes on, assuming she brought some."

He looked and looked for her overnight case but didn't find it. Nothing left to do but slip her out of her clothes and pull the sheet over her. He was proud of himself for not even thinking of having sex with her although her body did look inviting. His thoughts went back to the time Julie found him passed out at the stadium in Knoxville. Putting that out of his mind, he left through the connecting door and went to his bed.

Matthew felt good to at last lie down; it had been a long day. Usually his mind didn't shut down quickly especially after such an unusual meeting like they had today with the NASA folks. Tonight was an exception however and after a few minutes he fell asleep.

Matthew stirred about four o'clock needing to go to the bathroom. As he started to roll toward the edge of the bed he realized he was not in bed alone. A warm pair of arms pulled him close to her soft body. "When did you come in?" he said.

Catherine said that she woke up in the bed about an hour ago and was hoping that he had been the one that put her in bed. He assured her he was the one and he wanted to be sure she got to her room okay. "You were having a few too many drinks and got to the point of needing someone to help you to your room. There were others in the lounge that would take advantage of your condition, but I didn't want that to happen. Incidentally I couldn't find your overnight case Catherine."

"It is under my bed." She said. "I didn't want to take my purse with me so I hid it in my overnight case under the bed. But removing my clothes was okay and I appreciate putting my clothing on a hanger in the closet. You really do care for me don't you Matthew?"

"Certainly I do Catherine." He was lying in bed with her, what else could he say? The fact was that he did care for her much more than he should. By this time he had forgotten why he was getting up.

Catherine was going to have her way with him. She rolled over and begged him to rub her back and shoulders like he had done before. As he began to ever so gently rub her shoulders she rolled on her back. To calm her, he softly kissed her below the breast. They lay there for a few minutes relishing the moment. Once again he began to gently caress her breast with his hands. How odd Matthew said, "Catherine, there is a lump here on the side of your breast."

"Oh that." She said as though it was nothing. "That has been there for years. It used to come and go when I would have my period, it's nothing."

Matthew had to admit that he didn't know much about a woman's body, but he did know that a lump on the breast was nothing that should be overlooked. "When you get back to Washington Catherine, promise me that you will go to a doctor and have them confirm that the lump is nothing."

"Sure," she said, fluffing his comment off. "Matthew, I promise I will see a doctor about it, but I know it is nothing to be concerned about."

By this time he really remembered why he was trying to get out of bed. Boy did he ever have to go. He reminded Catherine that they must be up by seven because their ride to the airport would leave promptly at seven thirty. After saying that, Catherine left and Matthew went back to sleep.

Matthew got up about six-thirty, took a quick shower, dressed and knocked on Catherine's door as he went by. There was no answer so he raced to the lobby area. Everyone was patiently waiting, including Catherine. After an intoxicating night like she had, Catherine had no appearance of a hang-over. Catherine Hamilton is an amazing woman.

The limo arrived on time and off they went. Their overseas guests were talking in some foreign language that only they understood. Apparently they talked about the fun time they had last evening. They spoke a bit, and then laughed a lot. A sure sign they were talking about their nightlife of fun in Houston.

The flight back to Knoxville was uneventful. Everyone enjoyed breakfast on the airplane, compliments of the charter airline. The flight time was the same as when they went to Houston, but the returning flight always seemed much longer. Along the way Matthew mouthed to Catherine to be sure she sees a doctor. She nodded that she would.

# CHAPTER 16
## NO WOMAN WANTS TO HEAR THIS

The weeks turned into months and Matthew had not heard any news from Idaho nor from Catherine or NASA. That bothered him a bunch. Surely she would call him if she had seen a doctor. He was also wondering if for some unknown reason, had he been cut out of the loop concerning the Erickson Project. At home in Knoxville, his life has been extremely quiet these days.

Julie had not mentioned the girl friend thing for which he was glad. They were getting along as well as old time married folks could. She would occasionally talk about current situations at the hospital, but they seldom talked to each other about anything. He supposed after you are married as long as they had been, this is normal.

For a week or so Matthew seriously thought about getting a small dog. At least he could talk to it while Julie was at work. He could tell a dog his most inner secrets and not have to worry about the talks coming back to haunt him later.

When Julie got home one night he mentioned it to her. "There is no way Matthew are we getting a dog, absolutely not." She said it in a way that definitively meant no. "Matthew, you wouldn't take care of it. They have to be trained to be house broken and they shed hair all over the place. Matthew, we are not getting a dog and that is that." Frankly Scarlet, Matthew recalled, he was beginning to get tired of her overuse of her expression, *and that is that.*

It would appear there would be no pitter patter of little doggie feet in this house. "Okay Julie, then why don't you retire from nursing and stay home with me. I just want someone to talk with during the long days while you are at work. After all you have enough years at the hospital and you are well past the age of retirement. Oops, that didn't come out the way I meant"

Julie seemed somewhat agitated by that last statement and returned with, "I have no intention of retiring. I will work until they make me quit. I enjoy nursing and *that is that*, the end of it Matthew."

Makes you wonder what makes nursing so enjoyable that you would work until you drop.

The tension was broken by the ringing telephone. Julie answered and said it is for Matthew. "It's some guy from Washington." Julie said.

When he answered a female voice said, "Hello Matthew, I had Charles my butler call you, I didn't want to cause you any more trouble with Julie. The reason I am calling is that William Johnson, you remember him; the Chairman of the NRC is hopping mad at both of us and demands that we meet him in his office in D.C. as soon as possible. It seems that he found out about the NASA request we proposed and left him out of the loop again.

Trying to be as respectful as possible Matthew said, "That's not true Catherine, Johnson knew exactly what we were doing. After all, he was in his office when you and the fellows from overseas discussed the problem. It doesn't surprise me though, he gets upset about everything."

"Well Matthew," Catherine coyly replied, "it's true, the foreign fellows and I were in his office discussing the Idaho Project, but after we left Johnson's office, it was then I told the visitors about going to Houston and our idea of using NASA, so Johnson didn't know anything about what we were up to."

"If you remember, Catherine, Johnson said he wanted every project proposal to go through him. Oh boy Catherine, I guess we are both in bad trouble. Catherine, if I must I'll catch the early morning flight and meet you at his office tomorrow afternoon and together we can see Johnson. What can he do to me, fire me!" They both had a good laugh over that statement.

Catherine advised that she would pick him up at Washington National. "Matthew, there is a direct flight to National that leaves Knoxville at eight-ten in the morning, okay." He agreed that he would be on the eight-ten and hung up the phone.

Now it is time for Julie to begin the questions as she said, "Sounds like you are going to D.C. again. You haven't been there for awhile. What is it about this time?"

He tried to explain to Julie that he is going to be chastised by the Chairman of the NRC for going ahead and becoming involved with the NASA nuclear waste thing. *Frankly*, I thought, *Johnson knew about my involvement*. But as it turns out he was not aware of what we were doing. The thing I don't understand is why I must go to Washington to hear what he has to say. We could have had that conversation over my secure, encrypted telephone."

Could it be this is Catherine's way of continuing the relationship? Of course he didn't say any of his thoughts to Julie, but he had the feeling she knew what is happening.

They say if one tells little white lies often enough, your mind begins to genuinely believe them to be true. Matthew believed by now he has reached that point. He still didn't like it, but it was better than trying to explain why Catherine would call him to Washington again. He really didn't like the confrontations with Julie, but she had a way of dutifully defining to him there is no such thing as a little white lie.

Julie would say, "A lie is a lie, the Bible teaches that Matthew." Unfortunately he knew she was right, but he still hated it when she brought it up.

"You must be in some real trouble this time Matthew." Julie said. "But at least you will have somebody to talk to for a few days while you are away."

"Julie, I have no idea how long this will take, I'll call you when I find out."

Next morning he was on the eight-ten flight to D.C. All along the way he couldn't help thinking about Catherine. Did she go to a doctor or had she neglected to do that as she had done for years. Many times he wanted to talk to Julie about the lump on Catherine's breast, but you know and he knew that would be insane because Julie would eventually want to know how he found that out. There are some matters no woman is going to talk about with a casual acquaintance. Until recently Julie believed his relationship with Catherine was just a friendship, acquaintance thing. Talking in his sleep had definitely changed her thoughts on that subject. Matthew figured it wouldn't be long until Julie found out the real reason for this visit to Washington.

Catherine was waiting to greet him with outstretched arms. A hug and a kiss and they were off to the parking lot to find her car. He had taken an over night case with him on the airplane so he didn't need to bother with the baggage waiting mess.

Along the way Catherine told him that their meeting with Johnson was in two days. Gosh, he wondered what they would do for two days. For starters they stopped at a small Italian restaurant on the way to her house in Georgetown. It was a quiet place that apparently Catherine frequented regularly. When you enter a restaurant, and everyone that works there calls you by your first name, it's clear you have been there many times before.

They talked a bit about how much trouble they might be in with Johnson and then Matthew had to ask. "Catherine, have you been to the doctor yet."

She tried to pretend she didn't know what he was talking

about, but he insisted that she answer him immediately. "Did you or did you not see a doctor about the lump?"

"Yes Matthew, I did. They did a biopsy and confirmed that it is a cancer tumor and it will have to be removed. The medical pictures show that it has possibly entered the lymph nodes which are not a good thing. They are talking about a radical removal of both breasts; do you know what that means Matthew?"

"Yes I do Catherine." he said. "But if that saves your life it will be worth it. Millions of women have that done and they are still alive, that is not the end of life. Besides, if they do the radical removal, the breasts can be replaced with implants."

"That is enough about that for now. Let's just enjoy the lunch, please Matthew, no more of that for now." She pleaded.

After their delicious Italian dinner they talked for an hour or so about the old days. We're talking the old, old days when they were both teens and then in their later college years.

She shared recollections of being a child growing up in the White House. For her, Catherine said, "You were always being watched by the Secret Service bodyguards. I always wanted to go out with my friends to the local shopping malls. It seemed that everyplace I went, George my personal bodyguard was with me always someplace lurking in the shadows watching. I just wanted to have the same kind of mischievous fun my girl friends were having. But I just couldn't get into trouble because George was always there."

Then she told Matthew about the one time she managed to slip away from George by going into a changing room in one of the department stores. George didn't know it, but there was another exit from the changing room. She said she and her two friends went to a movie with some boys they had met. In the movie house they sat in the very back row and made out big time.

"I have no idea what the movie was about." She said. "All I cared about was that the theatre remains dark." She went on to say it didn't take long for George and several other men with flashlights to go row by row looking for us. They found me and immediately took me back home. My father, President Hamilton, was furious.

"Incidentally, I don't think I ever mentioned that my dad was a single man." Matthew was learning something. Never new a divorced man could become President. That issue was never discussed in his childhood social studies class. Of course there must have been another divorced President, but Matthew was apparently asleep in class when it was discussed.

Then there was another time she almost slipped out during the night. She said she wanted to see her boyfriend and decided that if you tied a sheet to the bed post by the window, you could easily slide down the sheet to the ground. Catherine said what she didn't know was that there were very big, powerful guard dogs constantly roaming the White House grounds looking for intruders. The dogs create a lot of noise when they catch an intruder or as was my case, an escapee.

"That was the last time I tried sneaking out of my room at the White House." Catherine continued. "Once again, dad was really upset. After that he sent me off to a boarding school for girls. That wasn't much better. The old lady house parent in charge was worse than the Secret Service men at the White House."

They talked a bit about their college days. "Those were the really good old days." Catherine said. "Boys, boys well, they genuinely thought they were men, but they were actually still boys.

Catherine said her college years at Georgetown University were outstanding. The Secret Service man was only allowed to stay in the sorority lobby. The sorority house mom made sure the Secret Service man remained in his place.

The sorority mom watched every move that poor man made. "In our rooms we girls partied and partied until we fell asleep. "It amazed me that I was able to learn anything because most of us were hung over every morning as we stumbled to our classes."

By now she was over her boyfriend thing. Sneaking out was nearly impossible because all the windows in the sorority house had a silent alarm contraption on them. If you even opened a window, the sorority mom sent her assistant to check it out. Her only contact with men was during class. Life after class was nearly impossible.

Catherine finally realized that she must study and get through this hell-hole existence so she could at last be on her own. "Amazing how it has worked out. Here I am, in a government job that still has a bodyguard nearby watching."

"A bodyguard nearby," Matthew exclaimed. "Where, I don't see anyone?"

Catherine pointed out the window to the darkened street. "See that black car on the other side of the street. The man sitting in it is Cameron Markham. He's my grave yard shift watchdog. Actually he is a very nice fellow, but fairly new in the service and is low man on the totem pole thus he has the late night watch."

Matthew began telling Catherine that his days at Penn State were filled with wine, women and song also, but that was not the case. Even though he attended on a scholarship that paid the tuition, his mom paid for his study books. His mom worked so hard coming up with the money for his books he felt guilty, should he embarrass her by causing trouble. His academic studies were extremely difficult and his learning capabilities were being stretched to the limit in every class he attended. He needed to make his mom glad she struggled to help like she did.

Matthew said, "There were times I wanted to take a night off and go nuts with the rest of my classmates, but I couldn't. They would invite me to parties which, most of the time, I refused. It didn't take long for them to realize that I was not the social, partying person and therefore was no longer was invited to go with them anyplace."

"Catherine, on Friday nights before football games I would

drink, but usually alone. No one wanted to be associated with me. I shunned their parties because so many times the parties would get out of hand and the college security would raid the rooms. The cops would find drugs in their rooms and of course a bunch of underage drunks. I couldn't afford to get caught like that because a healthy number of the kids got expelled for using drugs, but not me, I was a good kid. I got drunk all by myself in my own room."

Catherine suggested they go to her house and get some sleep. "Tomorrow is going to be a rather trying day for both of us." It would be for sure, because Matthew honestly didn't know why Johnson had both of them come. Most matters of any significant importance were discussed over the telephone. The last time he came to Washington he became unemployed. Since then, he was only a consultant so why would Johnson be footing the bill for him to come to D.C.? Oh well it's his nickel, so Matthew felt he had better get a good night sleep and be well rested for whatever happens.

Remembering his last few encounters with Catherine, Matthew wondered if a good night's sleep would be possible. It didn't take long to find out that, he would in fact, sleep without interruption. He supposed Catherine didn't want him feeling her body looking for more lumps like he noticed the last time they were together. Surely that must be the reason he received no visitors during the night.

The next morning he was greeted by a very positive and happy Catherine. She explained that she had taken a couple of sleep aids and promptly went to sleep. His supposition was for naught, taking sleeping pills works for him and apparently works very well for her.

Washington is the pits, especially in heavy morning traffic, but Catherine took it in stride without even a cuss word when someone cut her off, which happens often. "Nothing surprises me here in D.C. traffic. You just get accustomed to it."

They arrived at Johnson's office almost on time. He was busy talking to another when they arrived. It was not the type of office Matthew expected. Johnson, being the principal man in the Nuclear Regulatory office, you would expect him to have a rather well appointed office. The last time Matthew met Johnson they met in a rather lavish conference room. Not so this time. Johnson's personal office was rather plain and nearly without furnishings. To be honest, a desk, several phones, a few chairs, a window and that's it. Oh, he also had a small closet where he could hang his coat. Of course he had an office assistant outside his office and tons of filing cabinets near her desk. It appeared that most of his business was done on the telephone and when he needs help with anything, the lady outside his door was quick to assist.

The two of them waited about ten minutes outside his office in the waiting area. Finally they were asked to step into his office.

As expected, the usual hellos and-so-forth took place and then Johnson suggested they get down to business.

"I suppose both of you are wondering why I asked you to come all this way. It has been brought to my attention Matthew, that you and Catherine sort of went over my head again with this project you call The Erickson Project."

Matthew's heart began to beat rather heavily. It would appear they are going to be chastised for not asking the committee's permission again. Had they done that, Catherine and Matthew both decided a long time ago, the project would be hung up in committee for months, if not for years and never given the possibility of a go ahead to at least explore the idea? Catherine and Matthew had discussed this in detail many months ago realizing there would be consequences for their forward actions.

Matthew and Catherine looked at each other with a confusing look. Neither said anything, but both thought he must be mistaken. Certainly he knew about the Erickson Project. He knew that Matthew was a consultant on it and Johnson had to give his approval for the project to begin in the first place. Both decided to say nothing and simply allow him to ramble on.

Johnson continued, "You both know that what you did is not how Washington works. But this is not a reprimand session, but instead in this case, I applaud your forwardness. Had you come to me with this idea I would have quickly told you our committee would have to discuss the idea, and that would have basically set us back years. Instead I am in constant conversations with our chief engineer at the Idaho Project. He tells me that it appears it will be possible to begin constructing a prototype miniature nuclear reactor within the year. What really interests me the most is the hydrogen benefit from this system? The President and I have been trying to find ways that we can have quick access to hydrogen fuel and we believe, along with the rest of my committee, the Erickson Project has the answer. Placing small nuke units in and around the electrical sub-stations in all cities and towns overcomes the transportation and storage problems that have hindered present hydrogen use.

Catherine, if I may call you Catherine, you and Matthew Wilson deserve national recognition for your efforts. That isn't going to happen however. The President definitely wants to announce a time line for converting all vehicular traffic in the U.S. to hydrogen powered vehicles. For your information, that time line will be twenty plus years from this date. It is going to be a hard push to make that happen. The President's announcement will be made even though we aren't even sure the prototype will work. With Jack Jackson at the helm of the project and you Matthew Wilson as a consultant, the Erickson Project will happen, I'm confident of that. I understand the Erickson kid and his teacher that came up with the creative idea will share the credit according to the President."

"That's as it should be." Matthew said and Catherine quickly agreed. "After all those two lost their lives perusing the dream and the world should know who they are."

Johnson was quick to respond. "Don't ever mention that they lost their lives again Matthew. The President doesn't want that fact brought to light. Now to the other reason I asked you two here."

"Some weeks ago I received a call from Nancy Harrison, the spokesperson with NASA in Houston. Can you imagine my reaction to the hair brained idea you two are suggesting? It seems that you feel the United States and in fact the world needs a way of eliminating the storage of the nuclear plant radioactive waste.

"That's correct." Matthew said. "I have done my own study of our nuclear plants here in the U.S. and after talking to several nuclear engineers from other parts of the world, we concur that this must be addressed now."

"Matthew," Johnson said. "Do you think I have no idea that this is a very real problem? Do you actually believe that I, Chairman of the Nuclear Regulatory Commission, sit here with my head in the sand? Absolutely not! We have been looking for new areas in this country to deposit the nuclear waste. The problem is that when the public gets wind of a new location all hell breaks loose. But suggesting what you two have, sending spent nuclear fuel into space is crazy. For starters, the costs of blasting it into space would be mind boggling. Another thing, even if the cost is not considered, sending a rocket into space could be extremely chancy. What if it didn't make it and had to be destroyed? The consequences of fallout would wipe out large sections of the country."

"Okay, so you know." Matthew said. If you talked to Harrison, does she have any suggestions on how to safely export the waste into space? You must have talked in detail about the progress NASA has made thus far."

"Yes I have Matthew." Johnson said. "The difficulty they are having is the weight. Do you have any idea what kind of weight you are trying to shoot into space?"

"Actually," Matthew said. "I know precisely what we will have to move. In the present containers you could not move them in any kind of rocket. I thought I had told Harrison and her committee about the size and the weight before."

Matthew continued, "As you know Mr. Johnson, we are currently storing spent nuclear fuel in temporary storage pools located next to most of our nuclear plants. Because they remove spent fuel rods every twelve to eighteen months from the nuclear plants, the on location, underwater water storage pools for the rods are rapidly running out of space. The spent fuel rods remain about a year in the temporary storage pools. After the nuclear fuel rods have begun to cool, they are being transferred to the stainless steel, water filled containers. Those containers are then placed inside the vertical and in some horizontal dry cask storage containers. The casks are fortified concrete vaults as you know."

"Mr. Johnson, these casks are the unresolved difficulty. As you know the trucks and trains that haul the casks to their permanent storage caverns are subject to accidents so the casks must be built to withstand extraordinary accident situations. If you eliminate the concrete and steel outer vault like casks, you have only the stainless steel cylinder containers that are welded and made leak tight thus eliminating radiation exposure to the handlers. To move the casks to a launch site is a must, but once at the site the stainless steel cylinders must be removed from the transport containment casks and loaded in some kind of space craft, but I have no idea what NASA is coming up with."

"I'm impressed, Wilson. Johnson said. "You have done your homework to some degree, but you are still talking about a lot of weight. I need to talk to my engineers in the field to see if it is possible to do what you propose. I have asked Nancy Harrison at NASA to keep you in the developmental discussion loop. It might not be a bad idea for you to contact her when you get home. Tell her of our talk and specifically give her the exact weights of the stainless steel containers again. She is going to need that critical information before they can come up with any possibilities. If we would be sending this stuff into space via our current space rocket systems I would have to say I don't think we could approve it. That would be far too dangerous."

"Well Mr. Johnson," Matthew said, "Ms Harrison already has the weight information, but I will call her as you suggest."

They both left Johnson's office completely surprised by the

discussions. They thought they would both be chastised for going over his head about the waste project. Apparently Johnson had been in discussions with others about how to solve the nuclear waste problem. It appeared, according to this brief meeting, the NRC actually was a thinking division of the government. It was nice to hear Johnson agree with us concerning the fact that something must be done now, not sometime in the distant future. It will be interesting to hear what Harrison has to say about NASA'S involvement and their progress.

The meeting was short and sweet. Matthew could tell that Catherine was not herself. Matthew was sure the thought of losing part of her body to surgery was constantly lurking in the back of her mind.

Before he left the house he had told Julie he would possibly be several days in Washington, so if he caught an earlier flight home she would be pleasantly surprised, he hoped. On the way to the airport he asked Catherine to call when she received word about a date for her surgery. Matthew needed to tell Julie about Catherine's surgery and this trip would provide him the right time to do just that. Catherine said that she would call, but wondered about the problems it might create with Julie. He assured her that he would tell Julie all he knew and that should clear up any possible problems.

# CHAPTER 17
## THE DOCTOR WILL SEE YOU NOW

It was a late flight so most of the passengers on Matthew's flight, once airborne, reclined their seats and were trying to get some sleep. Fortunately his seat companion was not the talker that you sometimes have sitting next to you.

He certainly didn't feel much like sleeping, but rather kept thinking about how he would tell Julie about Catherine's cancer. The last time Catherine came up in a conversation Julie became a bit hostile and mentioned that he was traveling to visit his girlfriend. Of course he wanted to deny that, but rather left it blow by as though he hadn't heard her remark.

As they got close to Knoxville the flight attendant announced the usual "Ladies and gentlemen we are beginning our descent into the Knoxville airport, please place your seats and trays in the upright position."

Not long ago Matthew recalled this same airline had a pilot that couldn't get the nose wheel to extend fully. He circled the field for an hour before landing with the wheel still stuck in the retracted position. How does a person deal with a situation like that? Pray, he supposed is about all one can do because one way or the other this aluminum tube they call an airplane is coming down. According to the newspaper reports of the episode there was a lot of praying and also a whole lot of screaming as the plane came to a sliding stop on the runway.

Fortunately for Matthew, this flight ended successfully. Not long ago he heard a pilot give the definition of a successful flight, "If you get the plane on the ground in one piece you have had a successful landing."

Julie was having a rough day at the hospital. Julie worked in the emergency room trauma center and today there seemed to be no letup in the number of messed up accident victims.

"Doctor Jordon," Julie said. "What in the world is going on today, I haven't had a minute's break from the time I got here this morning until now. Patients just keep coming, I'm sure glad my shift is nearly over."

Doctor Jordon, the kind caring ER doctor he is said, "Julie there is a full moon tonight and you know that the ER area is always busier when it is full moon. Why don't you sit here in my chair for a few minutes and I'll give you a good old, doctor approved, shoulder massage. I have ways to relieve all the tension from your body, top to bottom guaranteed."

"That sounds extremely good to me Doctor Jordon, my whole body and especially my back and neck is a total knot."

Julie moved to Doctor Jordan's chair in an empty ER room. As Doctor Jordon began to massage her shoulders and neck she began to ahh and oh my, as his expert hands did their magic. "Oh my goodness Doctor Jordon you are so good at this perhaps you should give up this ER doctoring and become a professional masseuse." In a half joking comment she continued. "You know Dr. Jordan; a girl would pay a man a bunch of money to do this, a massage I mean."

As Dr. Jordan continued to work on the neck and shoulders he began to move his hands up and down her spine. Julie began to call out muffled sounds of approval. She certainly didn't want any of the nurses outside the room to hear her sounds of extreme enjoyment. Julie knows doctors and nurses shouldn't do things like this together, especially in a private area like an empty ER room.

Julie thought for a few moments before saying. "You know Doctor Jordon, I'm sure it has been a long time since you have had a real home cooked meal. Why don't you follow me home after our shift is finished and I will fix you a good old fashioned home cooked meal? How does that sound to you?"

"Sounds great Julie," Doctor Frank Jordan said. "But I doubt your husband Matthew would approve."

"Oh, he's in Washington at some type of meeting," Julie said reassuring him it would be okay. "Matthew said he would call if he was coming home tonight, but so far he hasn't called so I expect he won't be home until tomorrow. My shift and yours ends at six, you can follow me home in your car."

It had been months since Dr. Jordan had a real home cooked dinner so, with some reservation, he responded with, "Nurse Julie, if you positively believe it will be okay, I will accept your very generous offer."

Doctor Jordon is a man about forty who obviously works out in the gym often. He appeared to have strong muscular arms and his stomach muscles were still tight and had not begun to sink as so many forty's men's have. Dr Jordan obviously took care of himself. In street clothes he dressed the part of a professional, always in a coat and tie. His six-three frame looked stunning to Julie, but she constantly had to remind herself that she was a happily married woman or at the very least, a married woman. His skin was lightly tanned and appeared to be so smooth, not a blemish on it anyplace. Julie was constantly saying to herself, "So what if he is a little older than me. He really looks, as the kids say, *hot*."

The temperature was in the comfortable seventies as they both walked to their cars in the hospital parking lot. As they walked, the sun was already beginning to slide behind the mountain to the west casting a beautiful golden glow over the city's landscape. For a moment Julie had an unusually warm feeling for the doctor as he walked her to her car. Julie immediately washed that thought from her mind. *After all*, she thought, *I'm only being hospitable to the kind doctor, nothing more.*

Before leaving the parking lot Julie told Dr Jordan, "I'll keep you in sight in my mirror, but if we get separated by some traffic, I will pull off onto the off ramp area and wait at the intersection for you to catch up. I certainly don't want you to miss your dinner tonight."

It is only about a half hour drive to Julie's house from the hospital if the traffic isn't heavy and this evening they both sailed out the four lane highway without a delay. Where she lived, near the foot of the mountain to the west, the evening sunset puts a shadow on their house early in the evening which makes it appear later in the day than it actually is. By the time they arrived at her house, the sun had gone completely behind the mountain revealing a lovely light blue-gray darkness on the small white cottage she called home.

At the house Julie parked in the garage and Dr. Jordan, just outside it in the driveway. As the doctor walked toward the porch he said, "This is so lovely Julie. It's so quiet here. Listen to the early evening birds. They're singing their goodnight songs."

"That's why I love this place so much Doctor Jordan, it is a peaceful, quiet place and the birds do provide beautiful music."

"You have such a quaint house, complete with porch, rocking chairs and a swing. I love it. It's the kind of place everyone dreams of having. Some day perhaps I'll have a place like this and a beautiful wife like you Julie."

Julie thanked him for the beautiful comment and invited him into the house and suggested that he take off his coat and tie and be seated on the sofa in the living room. "Relax while I fix us dinner, it should be only a short time until it is ready. I had the oven timer come on this afternoon so the roast beef, potatoes and vegetables should be almost ready now. I'll make a tomato, cucumber and lettuce salad and we will be ready to eat. Sound good to you Doctor Jordan?"

"Great Julie, that sounds really great, but please, Julie, my name is Frank, please call me Frank." As the doctor said that he closed his eyes and shortly, he was nearly asleep. The sofa was so comfortable. Julie had told him to relax so he removed his shoes and stretched his long legs on the sofa pillows. It had been a tiring day for the doctor also.

"Very well," Julie said. "Frank it will be."

Dinner was ready so Julie went into the living room and saw Frank asleep. *What a beautiful specimen of a man.* She knew she shouldn't think thoughts like that, but Julie is a woman, why not. This just proves she is a human being as well. Look, but don't touch her mom used to say. *Darn, darn, darn.*

The table was set complete with two dimly lit candles and soft music in the background. "What am I missing?" Julie said to herself. "Oh yes my guest, it's time to wake him."

He was sleeping so peacefully, but how to wake him. She could just call his name, but instead she went into the living room and placed her hand in his and said, "Frank, dinner is ready."

Surprised by her hand in his, he awoke pulling her into his lap. "Oh my goodness I'm so sorry Julie, you startled me, please forgive me."

"That's fine Frank," Julie said still in his lap. "You were sleeping so well and I didn't want to startle you, but obviously I did. I'm so sorry Frank, but I must admit I do feel so very comfortable sitting here, however we should eat before dinner gets cold."

Frank was impressed by the beautiful table setting. "The music calms the body and helps with digestion." Frank said. "Thank you Julie for going to so much trouble."

They ate and talked for what seemed like hours. Julie was enjoying the company of Frank ever so much. It had been years since Matthew and she had a quiet dinner like this. Matthew seemed to just gulp down whatever she made and then he would go to the living room to watch TV and fall asleep in his lounge chair. This, on the other hand is so romantic and she really didn't want it to end.

As always the worst part of cooking is cleaning up the dining room table and the kitchen mess. She quickly cleaned off the table and took everything to the kitchen and placed the dishes in the dishwasher. Frank helped clean off the table which she thought was a rather nice gesture, not many men do that these days. When they finished in the kitchen they went back to the living room. Frank on the sofa and she knew, she shouldn't sit down beside him, but she did.

Frank took her hand and once again thanked her for a most beautiful evening. Julie didn't want it to end just yet so she pulled up a foot stool and placed his feet on it. When she sat down again beside him, Julie took his hands and told him of her appreciation of having a quiet, beautiful evening with him.

They talked for a bit about their work. He apparently sensed the tension in her body building and pulled her head into his lap and began to allow those long muscular fingers to do the walking thing on her neck and spine. It felt so good. The reality was that as he rubbed her neck, spine and back Julie was aroused considerably. She tried not to let it be known, but he knew exactly what he was doing. If you haven't already guessed it, a light touch and a kiss on the back of her neck is one of those woman places that turns women on and Julie was no exception.

Boy was she turned on. As she rolled over on her back she looked into his beautiful brown eyes and said, "Frank excuse me for a minute, please don't go away. I will be back right back." She went to her bedroom and slipped off her work uniform dropping it to the floor and put on her finest silk rose colored robe.

"What am I thinking, I shouldn't do this but I am, please forgive me Lord." As she was saying that to herself she went back to Frank. He was still on the couch, but this time he beckoned her to come with his arms opened wide. And yes, Julie obliged him willingly as he placed his arms around her.

By now Frank appeared to be warming considerably so he loosened a few buttons on his shirt. "Would it bother you

Frank, as I lay on your lap, may I slip your shirt off?" She said rather nervously. "I just want to touch your soft tan skin and rub those large muscular arms. You are built like a rock." As she was saying that she finished opening the remaining buttons of his shirt. For a few minutes she stroked his chest and touched those beautiful big strong arms. "What a body!"

Frank came alive for sure. She could feel through his trousers his body had been alerted to Julie's hands. Suddenly he pulled her from his lap, lifted her to his face and kissed her like she had never been kissed before. His warm soft lips beckoned Julie to kiss and kiss. As they kissed her robe opened revealing her entire naked body.

"Oh Julie," Frank said, "you are so beautiful, your body so soft, but yet so firm."

Frank began caressing and kissing every inch of her body. She loved every moment of it. "I am alive for sure, oh God don't let these moments end." As he again lifted Julie's body ever so slowly by those big soft hands of his, they again were face to face kissing deep strong kisses. How much more can a woman take?

After a few minutes she regained her somewhat shaky composure and said, "Frank I need to take care of your needs also. You have given me feelings I have never ever realized a woman could have. Please, I must take care of you. If you would prefer we can go to the spare bedroom and I will do for you what you have done for me."

"Julie," Frank said, "what I need now is a cold shower or at the very least, to wash my face with ice cold water. I appreciate what you have done for me tonight, but I think its better we stop now. Feelings like this have a way of getting way out of control. I don't want anything to spoil our friendship. You already have a lover and have had one for many years. Let's not spoil the friendship we have, you are too kind and nice to end that. Frankly I could easily fall in love with you and certainly not because of the moments we have had here tonight, but because you are such a beautiful human being. Thank you for a most memorable dinner and especially for these moments. I must leave now before both you and I go totally crazy. I know I shouldn't say this, but I do love you Julie. I'll see you tomorrow at work. Good night."

Having said all those beautiful words Frank got up, put on his shirt, tie and coat and left, but not before going to the bathroom to refresh himself.

"Out of control, out of control, we went way past out of control." Julie said to herself. "How does a man satisfy a woman like that and then just get up and walk away? Surely it takes more than some cold water on the face to regain his composure after the episode we just had."

It was nearly eleven-thirty. Julie decided to sit up for awhile in her robe and try to settle her shaky nerves and as she added, *"to cool off."* There was a time when Julie used to say she perspired some, but not tonight, she was sweating profusely and in her own words Julie said, "My goodness, *It feels so good."*

Julie's sweaty body needed to cool off and sitting in the house was not working for her. The evening air outside seemed a better choice. Julie managed to lift her trembling body from the sofa and move to the front porch swing. As she sat for a few minutes on the squeaky swing, Julie looked toward the sky and saw an unusually bright star that appeared to be getting closer to earth.

As she stared at the star light she began talking to herself. "Oh God, I know what I just did was wrong, but it fulfilled a need that I desperately needed. Please don't judge me too harshly." That said, a chill entered her body causing goose bumps to appear on her arms and legs. Julie stood, rubbing her arms and pulled the robe tightly around her body and went back into the house.

Rather than go immediately to bed she decided to turn on the TV to watch the end of the Tonight Show. How to get over what had just happened is a question she would have in her mind for a long, long time? In a thousand years she thought she would never do something like this.

As she reached to turn the TV off, an announcement of *'Breaking News'* flashed on the TV screen. An excited TV newsman said, "A short time ago something, perhaps a meteor, has fallen in the mountain area West of the city. It is not know for sure what the object was. We will have a reporter investigate the situation and hope to have more details on the Early Morning Show. We are receiving hundreds of telephone calls, but for now, the Knox County Sheriff Office has nothing to say about the incident. Tune in at six a.m. tomorrow for further details."

She recalled a long time ago what Pastor Bill said to both Matthew and her during one of their many couple's retreats. "Always be aware that each of us can be seduced into doing something you could regret for the rest of your life. Being in the wrong place at the wrong time, each of us," and Pastor Bill included himself in this group, "can be tempted to misbehave. At all costs, fight off the urge."

# CHAPTER 18
## ALMOST GOT YA'LL

Exhausted, Matthew was finally home at last. It had been a long day in Washington. As Matthew pulled into his driveway at the house he noticed the lights in the house were still on. Julie was usually in bed by this time, he was hoping nothing is wrong. Julie usually went to bed about ten o'clock because as she says, she has to have her beauty sleep.

As he opened the door a startled Julie jumped up saying, "Matthew, I thought you were going to call me before you left Washington."

"I'm sorry Honey, but I barely had enough time to catch the last flight back and I guess I just forgot to call. I am a bit surprised you are still up, are you okay?"

Trying to act as normal as possible Julie said, "Well I went to bed, but I just couldn't sleep. We had such a nerve wracking day at the hospital and I just couldn't shut off my mind and go to sleep."

"I have days like that all the time Julie, the Tylenol sleeping pills I have do wonders for the mind, you should try them sometime." With that said, Julie went to the kitchen to get Matthew his usual evening treat, a dish of rocky fudge ice cream.

As Julie moved toward the kitchen her robe opened slightly. "I see you were apparently going to sleep in the nude tonight, your robe is showing nothing but beautiful naked skin. I like that."

Julie had to do some quick thinking about why she had nothing on. Matthew knew she always slept in her baggy, full length pajamas. "Actually Matthew, I was going to take a quick hot shower when I heard your car coming in the driveway."

"Really," Matthew said in a rather confused manner. "It looked to me like you were watching TV when I came in and startled you."

"I was." She replied, wanting to end the conversation quickly by handing him his nightly ice cream treat. "Here, enjoy your ice cream before it melts."

Julie quickly left the kitchen and went into the bathroom and took a hot shower using huge amounts of her own fragrant body wash. She certainly didn't want any of Frank's sweet smelling cologne to remain on her body. Immediately after the shower she donned her usual night clothes and climbed into bed.

Julie was feeling so relieved that Frank decided to forgo her beckon to come to bed. Another half-hour and Matthew would have found them both in bed. Matthew is a fairly liberal man, but even Julie didn't think he would be liberal enough to accept that kind of behavior. Especially since Matthew had met Frank and her in the restaurant in Knoxville some years back. Matthew really suspected something wasn't right, even back then.

It wasn't long before Matthew came to bed. They did the obligatory kiss good night and he went to sleep almost immediately. Julie on the other hand lay awake until at least three o'clock. She kept telling herself, "Go to sleep, go to sleep, I have to get up early in the morning so go to sleep," and finally she did.

Six o'clock the alarm went off waking Julie. Usually Julie woke without the alarm, but going to sleep around three a.m. had removed all of her enthusiasm for arising at all. Matthew on the other hand never moves when the alarm goes off. Like most men, it takes a bomb going off beside the bed to get him up. Sometimes, even that doesn't work. On this particular morning Julie was glad he didn't awaken. She just wanted to get out of the house before Matthew started asking more questions about last night.

Tip toeing around the house in the dark was not a good idea as Julie soon found out. As she made her way to the darkened kitchen her toe bumped the corner of a chair. She had left the chair out of its usual place in her haste getting to the bathroom for her quick shower last night. *"Ow! Ow! Ow! damn, Ow!"* She cried out loudly quickly slapping her hand to her mouth to muffle the cry of pain. Thank goodness there were no stirring sounds coming from the bedroom.

Usually Julie would have a light breakfast and coffee, but today she decided to forget breakfast. Instead she turned on the small light above the stove that provided enough light allowing her to get her travel mug. After placing a spoon of instant coffee and hot water in it from the kitchen sink spigot, she left the house and was on her way to the hospital.

Matthew used to tell her that you shouldn't drive and do anything that distracts you as you drive. Very carefully she sipped the coffee as she inched her way into Knoxville. "Where are all these people going at this ungodly time of the morning and why so slow?" She said to herself.

It suddenly became obvious why the traffic was inching along so slowly. A car had flipped over on the highway blocking one lane. As she was looking at the accident scene, the car in front of her stopped for no apparent reason causing Julie to slam on the brakes. The car slid to a stop, but not before spilling the coffee on the seat and nearly in her lap. Ouch, Julie's car barely touched the car in front of her that had been stopped.

The man that she rear ended quickly got out of his car and was running back to her screaming all kind of obscenities about her stupid driving. "A stupid woman driver, I should have known."

"Well sir you shouldn't have stopped; it's not my fault I hit you." Julie screamed back. Of course we all know that it was Julie's fault.

By now the cars behind them were honking their horns wanting them to move over and get out of the way. Both Julie and the screaming maniac she barely touched were out of their cars checking the damage. Fortunately there were none visible so they returned to their cars, but not before the man screamed more nasty comments about, stupid women drivers.

Once past the overturned automobile the traffic returned to the normal highway speed, very fast. Arriving at the hospital and still shaking from the slight accident, Julie went to the doctors and nurses lounge. She felt she needed a cup of real coffee to settle her nerves.

By this time several other nurses were in the lounge as Julie began telling her story of the accident. "Stupid men drivers," Julie said, just then the lounge door opened and there stood Frank or should I say Doctor Jordon. At the hospital a nurse never calls a doctor by his first name.

"Good morning ladies." Dr Jordon said. Then he walked toward Julie and stood by her side and said, "Good morning nurse Julie and how are you this bright sun shiny morning." Still steamed by the accident and her stubbed toe she wanted to grab him by his necktie, pull him down real close and tell him just how good her morning had been, but she didn't.

Rolling her sweet brown eyes at him and looking straight into his she said, "Good morning Doctor Jordon, why I'm just fine thank you." Of course the other nurses in the room picked up on that immediately, but said nothing. They thought plenty however.

All day long Matthew was pondering just how to tell Julie about Catherine's predicament. When Julie gets home from work tonight he decided he would just have to tell Julie about Catherine's need for breast surgery. He fully expected a lot of questions about why he was so cozy with Catherine and why she would reveal to him such personal information. "Let the chips fall where they must," he decided.

Julie arrived home at her usual time and went about making dinner. After they finished dinner Julie could sense that something was wrong. As they sat in the living room Matthew decided to tell her what was bothering him. "Julie, I went to Washington fully expecting a severe reprimand by Johnson and his committee for going over their head about the nuclear waste disposal project. That didn't happen, but that isn't really what is bothering me. What really is bothering me Julie is Catherine Hamilton told me that she must have radical breast surgery for cancer. I don't have to tell you the bad news about that, but they told her both breasts will have to be removed." Julie, being a nurse, knew what an ordeal radical breast surgery was. Matthew continued saying, "I suppose Catherine considers me a close friend and that is why she confided that to me." Matthew was hoping that simple explanation would satisfy her curiosity about why she took him into her confidence.

"I'm so sorry Matthew." Julie said. To his surprise Julie began telling him what to expect after Catherine's surgery and even suggested he go to visit her in Washington after the operation. Julie said that Catherine would need all the confidence from her friends that would assure her there is life after such surgery. He certainly didn't understand Julie's acceptance of the story. Why, all of the sudden would Julie seem so nice to him? Matthew certainly didn't understand Julie's lack of sarcasm, but he felt good there was none.

About a week passed when the phone rang Saturday afternoon. Julie answered saying, "I think it is Catherine, Matthew, do you want to take it in your office?"

"Yes, thank you Julie." He said.

Catherine and Matthew talked for some time about the Idaho Project and the nuclear waste thing. "I surely hope I'm around Matthew to see either one of them come to fruition." Catherine said, her voice trailing off. "But I have to be honest; the doctors are not giving me much hope. They tell me the cancer has moved way beyond the breast. They still want me to go through with the surgery however and they will try to get all of it by removing my lymph nodes. Not that it would be good, but according to the doctors, they are hoping that's as far as the cancer has gone. Time will tell Matthew, I'm scheduled for surgery at eight a.m. Monday next week." Julie had told Matthew if the cancer is in the lymph nodes there isn't much hope of recovery. Cancer in that region usually spreads to other parts of the body, but he said nothing to Catherine that would further alarm her.

"As your friend Catherine," Matthew said, "I'll be there. Julie and I have talked about your situation and I will be with you as long as you need me."

"That's so sweet of you Matthew." Catherine realized Matthew was far more than a casual friend and his words of comfort made her feel as though there might be hope of recovery. "Oh Matthew, thank Julie for me for allowing you to come." She continued, "Matthew do you remember my butler Charles? I will tell Charles to expect you and Julie. Please stay at my home in Georgetown for as long as you like. I look forward to seeing you Monday; thank you again for being my true friend. Till we meet again, I'll say good bye Matthew."

Julie overheard some of the conversation and expressed her sorrow about the prognosis. "Are you going?" Julie inquired. "Yes Julie and if you would like, why don't you come along? She has offered us her home in Georgetown."

That kind of surprised Julie but she said, "No Matthew, we are just too short handed at the hospital as usual. Besides, she will have plenty of nurses to take care of her. You do realize she will be in intensive care for several days and then they will eventually move her to a hospital room. I could never be off work that long. You go and give her the support she needs. After all, you are her friend; she will need friends like you to be with her for a long, long recovery time."

Julie suggested Matthew go to Washington Sunday because if

he went Monday morning, Julie explained, Catherine will have been prepped for surgery and already drugged to the point that she won't know anybody. That made sense to him so he did catch a flight to DC early Sunday afternoon.

When he arrived in Washington he rented a car and drove directly to the hospital. Catherine was in a room that was crammed full of flowers. Matthew shouldn't be surprised by all the flowers; after all, Catherine was a lady of national prominence. In addition to the flowers, there were reporters in the hallway and the waiting area from every part of the world. Apparently the world, not just the United States, is interested in the medical condition of The Secretary of Energy for the United States.

As Matthew approached her bed Catherine was alert and smiling. With open arms she welcomed him. As he hugged her tightly, their torrid personal past flashes quickly appeared in his mind. Happily the reporters were waiting in the waiting area which left them alone in her room. He was so glad because he wanted to kiss her so much. Not just a friendly kiss on the cheeks but on her lips. And they did, passionately many, many times. Her present situation had not cooled her desire to be loved and he had to admit he felt the same toward her. Catherine was so much more than a casual friend.

"You look great," he said. "I came alone because Julie felt that the hospital needed her. Her hospital is so understaffed."

"Good," Catherine said in a tone that sounded as though she was glad he came alone. "Now Matthew, if you will just get my clothes from the closet, we can leave this awful place."

As much as he wanted to do as she asked he, of course, had to say no. "Catherine it's time to take care of this thing. When you get better I will come and stay with you for a bit." I suppose everyone knows that surgery patients never want to go through with the surgery no matter what is to be done. "Catherine, we will have plenty of time to spend alone when you get out of the hospital. I'm just glad I am considered, one of your very best friends."

"You are a loving friend of mine Matthew." Catherine said in a warm loving voice. "I've been with many men throughout my years in Washington. I've told you that before, but none have had the lasting romantic effect on me like you Matthew. Please don't leave me, I'm so afraid."

"I'll be back here with you in the morning before you go to surgery," Matthew reassured her. "And I will be here when you come out of surgery. Incidentally, I'm sure that you know there are a lot of reporters from around the world awaiting the successful outcome of your surgery. The whole world is rooting for you"

"Oh, I know Matthew." She said. "Curiosity is what that is all about. Apparently it's a slow day in the world news departments."

"You know Matthew; I have had no close relatives any longer. You Matthew are the closest thing I have to a relative. But I surely am glad we aren't related because folks would think our closeness to be a bit creepy."

"Catherine," Matthew said. "I just heard them announce that visiting hours are over so I will have to leave, but I will be back early in the morning." They kissed a few more times and he left.

With the map the rental car company gave him he managed to find his way to Catherine's house in Georgetown. Upon arriving Charles told Matthew that he had taken the opportunity of fixing him a late evening snack. As he ate Matthew asked Charles to sit as he ate the late snack. Matthew wanted to talk about Charles employment years with Catherine. It seemed Charles needed comforting also. After all, Charles had been with her for the last ten years and was more like a relative than a butler.

Charles told Matthew how Catherine had rescued him from a rather run down section of Charleston, South Carolina. She had been vacationing in the area and had become lost while on a motorcar driving sight seeing trip of the area. Charles came to her rescue when the car she was driving had a flat tire. He appeared out of nowhere as an angel sent to change her flat tire. She offered to pay him for helping, but he declined.

Catherine begged of him and said, "Please sir, if you could just help me find my way back to the main highway, perhaps I could help you in some small way."

With that said, Charles pleaded with the stranded Catherine, "I don't want money lady, but there is something you could do for me, just put in a good word for me with someone so I could get out of this hell hole of a place. I guess she felt sorry for me and asked if I could work as a house man. That's a nice way of saying could I be her butler, and here I am. She paid my way to Washington and I owe Catherine Hamilton everything. Catherine has given me all that I have. She took me to the store and bought me nice clothes and taught me how to be proper when she has guests. Why she even bought me a car so I could do the grocery shopping for the house. I owe that lady every-thing; I surely do hope she is going to be ok."

"Catherine will be fine." Matthew said. "She will be in the hospital for a week or two Charles, but she will be fine. When she gets out of the hospital a nurse will come to the house to care for her."

"Mr. Wilson, before she went to the hospital she gave me an envelope and wanted me to give it to you. I have no idea what is in the envelope, but here." As he was saying that Charles handed Matthew the sealed envelope.

What could be in an envelope that is so important it couldn't wait until she came home? Matthew opened it and found a note and a check. The note explained that if she didn't make it back to her house, I was to give the check to Charles and thank him for his for the many years of faithful service. Of course Matthew didn't tell Charles what the note said nor did he mention the check for two hundred thousand dollars. Should Catherine die, the check would surely keep him for many years. What a gift, Catherine is a very generous woman.

The second piece of paper was an autopsy report about

Sheldon Blakely, the driver of the car killed in the Idaho accident along with Mark Erickson. Why in the world would Catherine want him to see that? An autopsy is performed any time there is a death related accident to see if drugs or alcohol could have been a contributing factor. As he read the report neither of those factors appeared to have any cause for the accident. The last paragraph did surprise Matthew however. It revealed that Sheldon was at least two months pregnant. Wow, he said to himself, Mark and she were way beyond the friendship thing, just as he had thought.

Catherine knew that also, but wanted Matthew to keep quiet about it. "I need to mind my own business." Catherine told Matthew. "Men are men and women are women. What they do is their business, leave them alone." He supposed Catherine just wanted him to know the whole story. That information would be a secret between the two of them forever. There was no need for either family to find out.

The envelope needed to be placed in a safe place, but where? For now he decided to keep it in his briefcase until he got back from the hospital tomorrow. Matthew was convinced everything would be fine and he would give the check back to Catherine when she got home. Having decided that, Matthew went to bed.

The next morning he arrived at the hospital early in hopes of seeing Catherine before she had been prepared for surgery. Unfortunately he was too late. Matthew was told she had been taken to the OR prep room earlier than expected. The surgeon had ordered the operating room an hour earlier due to the back up of patients waiting for surgery. Because Matthew was not a relative they would not allow him in to see her. The nurse in charge told him that it would be about a three or four hour surgery and asked him to wait with the media people in the waiting room.

# CHAPTER 19
## A FRIEND QUIETLY SLIPS AWAY

As Matthew walked past the family waiting area, which was on the way to the general public waiting area, he looked in to see if any of her non existent relatives were present. Catherine told him she had no immediate relatives however there was one person in the room, Charles, her butler. Clearly he was not a relative, but there he was. Being the curious person Matthew is, he entered the small relative waiting room to be with Charles.

The conversation with Charles picked up from the personal talk he and Charles had last evening. Charles told him that Catherine had been like a mother to him and he just wanted to be near in her time of need. As they waited for what seemed like hours, which it was, he described to Matthew what his life was like back in Charlestown.

Charles began to describe in gruesome detail, his life in Charleston. He began saying it felt like he was at the bottom of a slippery pit. Charles said the sides of the pit were so slippery that every time he tried to get out he would slowly fall back to the slimy bottom. Again and again he said he would climb up a few feet, always to fall back to the miserable slime filled bottom of the pit.

"At times," Charles said, "you just wanted to give up and end it all, but I knew God wouldn't approve of that. And then one day this princess, in the form of Catherine Hamilton, appeared and rescued me from the pits of hell. I owe Catherine Hamilton so much Matthew, she saved my life."

By now it was approaching fours of waiting. What could be taking so long? It would seem someone should come and explain the delay, but there was no word. Matthew decided to go to the nurse station and inquire. As he opened the door leading to the hallway, there appeared to be a lot of commotion in the general waiting area that held the media reporters at bay. Upon looking in that direction he could see a surgeon dressed in blue OR attire talking with the reporters. He went closer to listen. Matthew could not believe what he was hearing. Catherine had suddenly expired in the ICU recovery room.

After the reporters ran from the waiting room to file their news stories Matthew explained to the surgeon who he was and asked the surgeon to tell him what had happened.

"Catherine Hamilton," The surgeon said, "had a severe heart attack as we were moving her to ICU. We did every thing possible to revive her, but we were unsuccessful. The operation went off without a hitch however and we will therefore do an intense investigation to determine why a heart problem had not appeared before the surgery was scheduled. Had a heart problem appeared before surgery we would have certainly delayed her surgery. None of us on the surgery team saw any problem of this magnitude." Immediately, an extremely distraught Matthew returned to the small waiting room to see Charles.

Normally Matthew could handle difficult work related situations without even batting an eye, but telling Charles what just happened to his beloved princess savior, was out of his league. With no other way to say it however, Matthew decided to just tell it like it was, and he did.

"Charles," Matthew said fighting off tears, "Catherine passed away in the recovery room. The surgeon said her heart stopped suddenly and they were unable to revive her, I'm so sorry Charles."

Charles slowly stood up and as he did Matthew hugged

Charles tightly as though he was a close relative. Together they cried. They both lost a true friend.

After they regained their composure Charles asked, "Now what do I do?"

"You will be fine Charles." Matthew said with all the confidence he could muster. "Even with her passing, Catherine has taken care of you, so let's go back to the house and I will try to help you sort things out in every way possible. This is not the end Charles, this is only the beginning. I don't know why Charles, but I believe there is a future here for you and it will not be back in Charleston."

On the way back to Georgetown Matthew's mind went a million different directions. He knew the government would take care of the funeral for Catherine because she had been Secretary of Energy for quite a few years. She had been loved all over the world because of her devotion to her job. Matthew knew her burial would be done in first class style. There was nothing he could do at this point so he will simply step aside and fade from the picture.

His concern now was what to do about a butler that was suddenly without a home or a job. Yes, Matthew knew Charles has a sizable check waiting, but knowing so much more about the person he was now, Matthew felt as though he needed to help him move on to the next phase in his life.

As he pulled up in front of Catherine's Georgetown townhouse, Charles was already there. Of course he was, he knew all the shortcuts. Matthew on the other hand had to follow the directions given him by the car rental company. Good directions, but the long way. They didn't want him to get lost in Washington, which is easy to do.

Charles opened the front door and invited him in just as though nothing important had happened. He said he had quickly prepared a light lunch and had already placed it on the dining room table. "Catherine would have wanted me to feed you before you return to your home in Knoxville."

"Thank you Charles, but if I may, this is your house for now and I would like to stay here until after the funeral if that is okay. The funeral should be in just a few days."

"Stay as long as you like Mr. Matthew," Charles pleasantly offered. "The rent on the townhouse is paid for at least a month so we will both be able to stay that long."

"Charles, please join me at the table for lunch. There are a few things I want to discuss with you."

As they both ate they engaged in a discussion about his relationship with Catherine. Charles was curious how Catherine had become such good friends with Matthew. Matthew cleaned up his relationship as best he could. Frankly, it appeared that Charles could see through his explanation, but was kind and didn't show it. That showed Matthew that Charles was a very good diplomatic servant. Understanding the discretions, but keeping his opinions to himself.

They finished lunch and thus it became the time to reveal Charles' future wealth situation. "Charles, do you remember the envelope you gave when I arrived here yesterday?"

"Yes Mr. Matthew, I surely do."

"Well I have here in this envelope a portion of your future." Matthew said as he handed him the envelope with the check inside. He told him that Catherine wanted him to have something to tie him over until he could find work should something unexpected happen to her. His big black eyes welled with tears again as he looked at the check for two hundred thousand dollars. Charles rose to his feet as did Matthew and he began crying uncontrollably as they hugged. This time the hug was as though Matthew was a father looking out for his child.

He thanked Matthew over and over, but Matthew interrupted saying, "I didn't do this Charles, Catherine in her death wanted you to have a chance to continue on with your life."

That same afternoon, as Matthew sat in the living room flipping from channel to channel on the TV, something suddenly came into his mind.

"Charles," He said as though a light bulb had just exploded in his head, "would it be possible for me to look through some of Catherine's past telephone records? I want to see if I can find a phone number she used when we were in Idaho a month or so ago."

Matthew looked for hours and he began to feel as though Catherine had thrown away a very important phone number. "Surely the number has to be here someplace." Finally there it was, "Charles, would you mind if I use the phone. I need to call my wife in Tennessee and explain why I will be staying here for a few more days. Also, I want to call some people in Virginia that Catherine and I met some time ago."

Julie was as shocked as Matthew when he told her what happened to Catherine. "Stay as long as you need Matthew. I see things like that happening all the time at our hospital. People die for no apparent reason. The surgeons go to extreme lengths to be sure the patient is capable of withstanding surgery, but deaths do occur when least expected."

The second call was to the Erickson's residency near Reston Virginia when he and Catherine visited the Erickson's some time ago. At the time they appeared to be very well to do.

"Mr. Erickson," Matthew said when a man answered the telephone. "You might not remember me, my name is Matthew Wilson. If you recall, Catherine Hamilton and I visited you with your son."

Of course Mr. Erickson remembered them, how could he forget? He and his wife were still trying to get over the death of their son in the terrible auto accident. Matthew went on to explain that Catherine Hamilton has just passed away during surgery. Hearing the news, Mr. Erickson expressed his sorrow, but wondered what Matthew wanted.

Matthew paused, looking for words that would best describe the situation. "Mr. Erickson, there is a person that is no relation to Ms Hamilton, but has been a very close reliable butler friend to her for many years. The thought occurred to me that as busy as you folks appeared when we visited; your life could be far less stressful if you and your wife had someone you could trust to assist with your housekeeping."

As best he could, Matthew told Mr. Erickson about Charles. The conversation went on for awhile. As they talked Mr. Erickson asked if Mrs. Erickson could join them on the telephone. When she came on the phone Mr. Erickson explained to her what they had been talking about. "Absolutely delighted," Mrs. Erickson said. "I have been trying to get a helper in this house for months. I'll be home all day tomorrow. Would it be possible to bring Charles by tomorrow? We will both be here all day and would love to meet him." It was obvious that she wanted a house helper really badly because she thanked Matthew over and over.

Mr. Erickson gave Matthew very specific directions to their home which he needed and appreciated. Matthew was extremely excited about the up lifting conversation. Although it was not his business to interfere with Charles' future, for some reason he felt a responsibility to assist him.

Charles reaction was again deeply moving; clearly Charles had a tender heart and was capable of showing it. He felt extreme relief that anyone would go so far out of their way to help a total stranger. Until now Matthew was just an acquaintance, but now had become Charles friend, and that felt good to Matthew.

Next day Charles offered to drive and Matthew was glad because he had no idea where the Erickson' lived. Charles knew all the short cuts and had them arrive about ten a.m. The Erickson's appeared delighted and welcomed them with an extremely warm reception. Matthew was trying to recall the phone conversation from the day before. Had he mentioned in their telephone conversation that Charles was black, Matthew thought not. Judging by the reception, color didn't matter to either of them. Matthew was relieved to see their response.

Charles and Mrs. Erickson talked in depth about her idea of what he would do. The response from Charles was that he was very familiar with any and all parts of housekeeping including the meals. He described how he fed dignitaries at the Georgetown townhouse. That seemed to impress Mrs. Erickson. "Charles," Mrs. Erickson said, "When could you begin?"

Charles was not sure how to respond, so Matthew had to butt into the conversation and said, "Charles will need a few days to attend the funeral and then several weeks to close up Ms Hamilton's Georgetown house. I'm not sure what that will entail, but when that is all cleared up Charles will call you. I'm guessing at least three weeks."

It was set; Charles would have a new home. Mrs. Erickson showed Charles his quarters in the Erickson house. It was clear that all he need bring along was his charming self. His living area was to be a beautifully furnished living space with a sitting room, bedroom and private bath. All of it at the far end of the house with a private entrance. To say the least, his living quarters were very impressive.

Matthew was also impressed with the pay. Mrs. Erickson said that because there were two of them to look after, the amount of pay, as it turns out, would be considerably more than Charles was receiving from Catherine. The pay part wasn't mentioned until they were in the car on their way back to Georgetown.

The funeral for Catherine was, as funerals go, very impressive. It was certainly becoming for a government spokeswoman. People from all over the world attended. It was nice to see so many, even the Vice President took time out of his busy schedule to attend. It was clear that Catherine was a well liked government employee. All who spoke at the small chapel had nothing but glowing remembrances of their affiliations with her. And flowers, wow, the flower shops did an excellent job of supplying what appeared to be hundreds of arrangements.

Charles needed considerable help as he sorted through the reams of paperwork left behind by Catherine. Matthew tried to sort out the important papers and looked up the necessary parties to phone to determine what paperwork could be destroyed and what should be forwarded elsewhere.

As it turned out, all the furnishings in her home came along with the leased house. The lease for the house came completely furnished and even included the china and silver. Catherine was not a collector of anything and that was good. The lease company was notified and the important paperwork returned to its proper place which took only about a week. Charles was now free to call the Erickson's. Even Catherine's two automobiles were leased, that proved to be a blessing also.

When it was time for Charles to leave Matthew called the Erickson's for Charles and explained that he no longer had an automobile so they needed to come pick him up. After giving Mr. Erickson the address he said they would come early the next morning. Charles was extremely happy because his future employment had worked out so well.

Matthew had stayed almost two weeks longer than he had expected, but it was now time to go home. Before leaving for the airport in his rental car, both he and Charles stood in the driveway saying their good byes. They hugged knowing full well they probably would never see each again. As Matthew drove away from the townhouse he looked in the car mirror and saw a very appreciative man crying and waving good bye.

# CHAPTER 20
## NASA CREATES MAGIC

T he past several weeks in Washington has worn out Matthew. He was very happy he could do something for a person that was a stranger to him and now had turned out to be a person Matthew could call, a friend. Matthew had given Charles his home address and he promised to write after he got settled at the Erickson's.

A surprising new attitude had occurred magically, almost overnight with Julie. For example, Julie seemed genuinely happy to have him home again. It was good to have Julie talking a civil conversation for a change. Before Matthew's last trip to see Catherine, about the only talk that went on in the Wilson house were snips and snipes at each other. The discussions sounded more like a training exercise of a yipping, biting miniature dog that refused to listen.

Their recent talks were both sad and happy. Julie was especially glad Matthew took the time to help Charles, at what appeared another low in his life. Matthew explained to Julie that Charles would have been financially in good shape for a time, considering the large check Catherine left him. Both Matthew and Julie agreed nobody would ever know what kind of future Charles would have carved out for himself, having such a large sum of money given him. Charles would have never known about the Erickson's without the help of Matthew.

Julie, Matthew reminded himself, was a very caring person. After all she picked him up when he had hit bottom many years ago. He owed his life today to this kind lady, how many people would be as kind as she?

Their love life intensified now more than ever before. Perhaps it's because Matthew decided to use some of the techniques shown him by Susan. Remember Susan, she was the lady he rescued from the lake a long time ago. As Matthew had said before, married people tend to forget the tender moments that got them together in the first place and he was not just talking about sex. The last few days had been a refresher course that brought them both closer together than ever before.

Matthew was off on one of his morning walks to nowhere. Nearly everyday he enjoys his walk into the woods or going to the small stream located behind their house. He wished the stream was wider and deeper allowing fish to populate. He has tried fishing in it, but he says there are none.

Julie was enjoying her morning breakfast of a dish of cereal and coffee. She says, "I must have my coffee before going to the hospital." As she was doing the chore of washing the dish and coffee cup she thought she heard a knock at the door. She hesitated for a moment then realized it was a knock. Wondering who could be visiting them at this early morning hour, she opened it and saw her Pastor Bill and a very attractive young lady standing on the porch.

"Good morning," Pastor Bill said. "I have a huge favor to ask of you. May we come in?"

"Of course you may." Julie answered, holding the door open for both to enter.

Pastor introduced the lady, "This is Rachael. Rachael said she was lost in the mountains and luckily she found a hard road that led her to my church. I found her this morning on the front steps of the church crying. When I asked her what happened, all she could say is she was dropped off recently and was told to return to the same spot later for her ride back home. The problem is she can't find the spot where she was supposed to be picked up. She has looked for days and eventually ended on my church steps today."

"How awful," Julie said, "but how can I help?"

"Well, this is the hard part Julie. You are such a helping, kind person. Always doing what you can at the church for people less fortunate. You are the only one I feel I can trust to take care of her and supply her daily needs. That's what I am asking you Julie, to take her into your home until we can figure out where to take her."

"But I ..." Julie started to say more before being cutoff by Pastor Bill.

"Oh, thank you Julie ... God will reward you someday for this. He will, I know." And with that, Pastor Bill turned and walked out the door leaving Julie with her mouth hanging open, not knowing what to say.

Rachael, also not knowing how to react simply spoke using a very quiet voice, "Thank you so much Miss Julie. I can help you around the house. I'm very good at cleaning and I am a good cook also. I won't be any trouble to you, I promise."

Still not believing what just happened Julie said, "Rachael, I must leave now for work. I'd like to stay here with you, but I can't. In a short time my husband, Matthew will be back. He went for a walk and should be back soon. In the meantime, make yourself at home. There is food in the fridge and since you appear to be the same size as me, I have clothes in my bedroom closet. Feel free to use whatever you want. I'll be home tonight about six o'clock." That said, Julie went out the door and drove off to her job at the hospital.

Matthew was unaware of the situation in his house. After his daily walk he had decided he would go into Knoxville and check out the new fishing displays at his favorite fishing retail store, Mandy's Fish and Bait Center. Rather than enter the house after his walk, he immediately got into his car and drove to town.

As he began his hunt for a new reel for his fishing rod, his cell phone rang. It was Julie. "Matthew, have you been in the house yet?"

"No, not yet, I came back from my walk and decided to come to town. I'm in Mandy's store right now. Why do you ask?"

"Don't go home yet, I have a surprise for you. Meet me for lunch at that little Italian restaurant next to the hospital about noon."

"Sure Julie that would be a nice change from my usual sandwich I have at the house every day for lunch."

*What in the world could be the surprise,* Matthew thought as he closed up his cell phone. *Oh well, guess I'll just have to wait. I know it is not mine or her birthday. It's definitely not our anniversary. What in the world could it be*? Those thoughts ran through his mind as he continued checking out the fishing gear.

About ten o'clock Matthew was wondering what to do until time to meet Julie. Driving about town, he spotted a brand new Krispy Kreme store that had just opened. "Ah ha … that's how I can spend an hour or so. And he did, enjoying several donuts and their great coffee. Matthew feels they have the best coffee in Knoxville.

After drinking enough coffee to sink a battleship, he felt it was close enough to noon to head to the restaurant. Upon entering the restaurant he spotted an old friend he knew from years past. They chatted about much of nothing when Julie finally arrived. He bid his friend good-bye, excused himself and went to meet Julie at the front door..

"Well Julie, fancy meeting you here. Should we have a table back in the corner where it is quiet? I'm dying to hear the surprise."

"The back corner table is fine." Julie said as they walked to an area that had few customers.

The waiter came and they both ordered. With that out of the way Matthew said, "Now, what is the surprise?"

Julie hesitated for a time before saying, "Matthew, do you

remember a long time ago you asked me for something to help occupy your time." Julie decided to have a little fun about the surprise.

"Not really. Give me a hint." Matthew said scratching his head trying to remember anything, but he couldn't.

"You said you wanted something to occupy your time while I am at work."

"Oh no, what's broke now? Am I going to have to fix a broken water pipe or something like that when I get home?

"No, it's nothing like that Matthew. You don't remember asking me for something you can talk to while I work."

Excited, Matthew exclaimed, "You got me a little doggie. Oh, thank you, thank you Julie. I'll take good care of it, I promise. I'll have it housebroken in no time. I'll take it for long walks … I'll comb and brush its hair every day."

"Can you teach it to clean the house and cook and do the laundry?"

Those words had Matthew confused. "I don't think I can get it to do all that Julie. What breed of dog is it? I'll have to get a book about it to find out how to train it to do stuff."

One word is all Julie said, "Caucasian."

Apparently Matthew didn't catch what Julie just said. "I never heard of a Caucasian." Matthew paused before saying. "That's not a dog, that's a person."

"You are so right Matthew." Julie explained the little she knew about Rachael and how she arrived. Matthew understood why Julie had agreed to the temporary arrangement. After all, Julie had found him when he was at his all time low.

Julie suggested he not go home until they can both get home at the same time. Before leaving the restaurant they discussed giving Rachael the spare bedroom. Because Rachael brought nothing with her when she arrived at their house they agreed Julie would share her clothes. Matthew felt that was very kind of Julie to share her own personal belongings. Not many women would do that.

Matthew was anxious to meet Julie's new friend. Julie had asked him to not go home until after she got off work. To kill a few hours he decided to check out a fishing hole by the nearby Tennessee River. He had a fishing pole in his car and was anxious to see how his newly purchase reel would work. He wasn't too keen on fishing in the river but it would help him pass some time. The reel worked fine and he actually caught some fish, but he threw them back. "Not good eatin' kind of fish."

Darkness was fast approaching so he pulled in his fishing line, got in the car and headed home. As he pulled in the driveway he could see Julie and Rachael swinging on the front porch. Immediately Julie got and introduced Rachael.

"Good evening Mr. Wilson." Rachael said in a rather timid and extremely quiet voice. "I was just telling Ms Julie about my home far, far away from here."

"First of all Rachael, my name is Matthew." In a joking fashion Matthew said,

"Mr. Wilson was my father. ..." The response from Rachael was zero. It was as though she didn't know what Matthew was talking about.

Attempting to fill the void talk space Julie said, "Matthew, Rachael was telling me she is from a place called Seti. Have you ever heard of it? I surely haven't."

"No Julie, neither have I. ... I'm sure Rachael, in time we will find it on a map." After another brief pause Matthew said, "Rachael, we have never had anyone visiting with us for an extended time. Julie and I are honored to have you with us for whatever amount of time it takes to find your home land. Please, make yourself at home."

"Thank you Mr. Wilson. You and Ms Julie are so kind." A very polite Rachael said.

The three continued talking on the porch for a few more minutes when Rachael announced dinner is already on the table and getting cold. "Please, come inside and we will have a bite to eat."

Julie was very pleased with Rachael's work around the house. She was especially happy to have her as a cook. Julie said to Matthew, "I don't know how long Rachael will be here, but I must admit I love her help. As far as I'm concerned, she may stay here forever. And you should be happy also Matthew, you will have somebody to talk to when I'm at work."

"It will be interesting to see how this works out Julie. I only wanted a little doggie, not a maid," Matthew said.

It had been nearly six months since the meeting with Chairman Johnson in Washington. Matthew's special home telephone rang and to his surprise the voice on the other end was that of Nancy Harrison, the NASA spokeswoman from Houston.

"Mr. Wilson," she said. "I suppose you think we forgot about you and your insane idea, but I assure we haven't. I'm calling you to say we have been given the go ahead and the financing by the President and Congress to create a prototype vehicle capable of carrying the nuclear waste into space."

Ms Harrison talked for nearly an hour on the telephone about the plan and the vehicle proposal. She told Matthew it was not possible to use any type of present land propelled rocket vehicles. Instead, they were designing a new craft. The problem she said with current rockets is they could fail to reach orbit and have to be destroyed over land causing the nuclear waste load to come back to earth. This was nothing new to Matthew. Both he and Catherine had already ruled that type solution out. However, Matthew did not mention what he already knew. Instead he agreed with Harrison that an event like that happening would definitely be a catastrophe.

"So," he said, "how do you plan to avoid that?"

Harrison went in great detail about how the air force had a giant new aircraft capable of flying very near the edge of outer space. "The plan," Harrison explained, "is to attach a large, unmanned shuttle rocket loaded with at least two stainless steel cylinders placed inside the shuttle craft. When the aircraft carrying the rocket nears the upper edge of earth's atmosphere, the unmanned shuttle craft rocket ship would be released with enough fuel to get it into orbit speed sending it around earth and propelling it toward Mars."

Ms Harrison went on to say, we will use the same method to get it into the Mars orbit as we presently do with our Martian exploratory space crafts. "To lessen mishaps over land the shuttle craft would be released over the open waters of the Atlantic, the Pacific and possibly the Gulf of Mexico. Should an accident happen, the nuclear waste aboard would fall into water which would prevent further fission of the nuclear waste. That would not be a particularly good thing to happen, but it does lessen the possibility of any harm to humans."

"If foreign countries adopt this same plan, they too would launch their loaded shuttle crafts the same as the U.S., over open waters."

Harrison went on to explain that the shuttle craft would be built as an extremely stripped down version of the normal exploration shuttle. The shuttle would have aboard only the necessary guidance system and sufficient fuel allowing the use of a few necessary steering maneuvers, but that's about it. "This craft would definitely be a one way vehicle," she said.

They discussed costs and frequency of such a plan. Matthew told her in the U.S. there are twenty five reactors nationwide that are currently storing spent nuclear fuel in either reactor pools or storage casks. These facilities were running out of storage space within the next few years so it is urgent that this program be pushed ahead of any other space programs.

"It will take many daily flights and years to get the storage problems under control." Matthew said. "The casks will have to be shipped via truck and rail to the chosen rocket shuttle air bases. Then, just before being loaded into the shuttle crafts, the stainless steel cylinders inside the concrete casks must be removed from their holding casks. Ms Harrison, do you believe the air force is going to be able to handle the multiple daily flights necessary to accomplish the plan?"

"Matthew, the President and Congress are aware of the urgency and the cost." Using a very positive tone in her voice Ms

Harrison said. "We have recently had discussions with five air bases nationwide that are capable of performing this type of operation. First things first, we should have a prototype craft ready for test in about a year, but not more than two. A bid for the first has been awarded to two aircraft shuttle builders to begin design. These companies are presently working around the clock and in total secrecy to come up with the first test shuttle craft."

"You do realize Ms Harrison," Matthew said. "The world is looking to the United States for answers to this problem. If we are successful, our technology must be shared with any and all foreign countries, friend or foe."

"That too has been discussed in great detail." Harrison said. The President feels that this could help the U.S. regain the confidence our country has recently lost around the world, therefore we will share with whomever we must."

As a side comment Ms Harrison said, "I have heard that the U.S. is currently working on a practical solution to the fossil fuel energy shortage problems as well as the global warming issue being caused in part by the transportation industry. Rumor has it that you are involved in creating a miniature nuclear power plant that is capable of creating hydrogen, for use in autos, trucks and buses discharging no carbon emissions."

Harrison continued, "The President tells me that he is ready to announce to the people of this country that in twenty plus years all land transportation should be driving hydrogen vehicles. He is also going to tell the people that in the same time period the U.S. will be shutting down all coal, oil and gas fired electric power facilities. That is significant news and I wish you much success with your proposals."

"It is true Ms Harrison," Matthew said, "but I am just a very small piece of the pie that is developing that technology. The test research and development facility in Idaho is expecting to have a small nuclear electric power unit with hydrogen byproduct running in about five years."

"If this country can make that happen," Matthew said, "vehicle travel as we know it now will dramatically change. Most of us however are not going to like the cost. If you think gasoline is expensive now, wait until you fill up with hydrogen. Each of us will definitely need to rethink how we get around. Owning two cars, as most have now, will be history. Bicycling will again come into favor and bike paths along every road in America will become a must. Even lawn mowers and all other small gasoline engines will be affected. This will truly revolutionize our country and the rest of the world as well. The changes will be just as dramatic as when we went from the Stone Age into the Machine Age. I sincerely hope I'm around to see it."

"To say the least, that is exciting news Matthew. I have a feeling we will both be around to see the new age arrive."

It had been more than a year since Matthew has spoken to anyone about either of the two projects. Today he received a call from William Johnson of the NRC. He told Matthew, Nancy Harrison from NASA called him and said the Air Force has prepared one of their super sized jets to do a test flight. They have a prototype rocket shuttle craft attached beneath its massive body. The plan is to take the shuttle craft loaded with two dummy nuclear waste containers to the edge of space and release it. If all goes as planned, it should reach the back side of Mars in about seven months. The load would be dropped on Mars, then as designed the shuttle craft will self-destroy itself. After the nuclear waste cylinders are released from the shuttle, two huge parachutes attached to each cylinder will automatically deploy and gently lower the cylinders to the Mars surface.

Mr. Johnson, as a joke, told Matthew the destruction of the craft is done, "just in case there are any Martian people on the planet, as the comic books would have us believe. We certainly wouldn't want the Martians to be able to salvage any of our modern technology." The semantics of just how the flight engineers would make all this happen was way over Matthew's head. He simply accepts that they can make it happen.

Johnson went on to say. "Matthew, do you realize it will be

nearly seven months before we know of our success or failure. Johnson further explained the craft must have extensive communication equipment on board. Earth flight engineers must make several flight correction maneuvers to get it in the correct orbit of Mars and then maneuver it onto the back side of Mars where it will drop the load. The shuttle craft needs an onboard electric power unit to supply several sending and receiving radios. The onboard radio equipment will eventually tell us if the cylinders have had a successful soft landing and the craft has destroyed itself.

"I guess we will just have to wait and see what happens." Matthew said. "Thanks for the update."

"Matthew," Johnson said with a bit of excitement in his voice. "This is your brainstorm, why don't you go to the base at Panama City Florida and see the first test off for yourself?"

"Mr. Johnson, I can not see any reason to do that. After all, NASA knows what we genuinely expect to accomplish. My interest is in the finished results. If Ms Harrison told you it should work, that is good enough for me. If this works the U.S. and the world will have the beginning of a nuclear disposal system in place, incredibly expensive, but very necessary. I appreciate the thought however so please do keep me informed of the progress."

Matthew had said many times, time really flies when you have nothing to do. Sorry, just a bit of sarcasm here. Matthew had been wondering how Jack Jackson was making out with the Erickson Project in Idaho. Apparently it must be coming along quite well because he hadn't been asked for advice about any aspect of it for nearly a year.

While sitting on his front porch swing watching some squirrels dig holes to place some just found acorns away for winter, a car pulled into the driveway. Who could it be, no one called to say they were coming to visit and he didn't recognize the car. A tall slender man got out and as he came closer Matthew finally recognized him. Jim Adams, his former fellow engineer at the old Oak Valley Center. Jim had gone to Idaho to work on the Erickson Project after Oak Valley closed.

As he approached they hugged like the old friends they were and Matthew asked, "Jim you must be lost, what in the world are you doing in this part of the woods? I thought you were hard at work with Jackson in Idaho."

"It's true Matthew, we have been working hard," Jim said, "but from time to time they do give us vacation and I wanted to come back home to visit my folks. Thought I would come by and see how retirement is treating you"

They talked about the old times at Oak Valley. It was good to see Jim, he hadn't changed much. Got a little older and lost a lot more hair, but he was the same good ole boy he was when they worked together. They reminisced about their wild days in Knoxville. Jim said, "I sure am glad Julie found you when she did, things could have turned out really bad for you had she not rescued you."

"You got that right Jim," Matthew agreed, "So what news do you have about the Erickson Project, I haven't heard anything lately about the progress of the project?"

"I have to tell you Matthew," Jim exclaimed. "The reason I have been allowed time off is that the first test unit is now working flawlessly. We made some final adjustments to the unit last month and it is purring along perfectly. Actually Matthew, as we speak, Jackson is having a second unit built. This unit will be large enough to run several city blocks of mixed business and residential properties.

The first unit is currently running a village of about two hundred homes. It is really impressive to see it in action. The local electric company has been participating quietly and in secrecy, switching the power to nuclear without anyone being the wiser. The tests however will go on for another year or two.

They talked on porch for a long time about the apparent success of the project. Matthew asked him if the hydrogen byproduct of the system was working.

"Working," Jim's voice became excited as he spoke, "the

nearby electric and telephone companies as well as the college have been purchasing new, severely discounted hydrogen powered vehicles. These people have no idea where the hydrogen is coming from, but for now it is nearly free fuel. At this time these companies are only paying for hydrogen delivery transportation to their fueling locations. The Idaho Project public relations people have told them the government is working on a test project for now, but they are being assured the supply will continue indefinitely. By the way Matthew, the newest larger miniature unit will be placed near the college."

This was exciting news to Matthew, but he asked Jim why no one told him about the progress. He said Jackson didn't want to bother you with details until he was sure the unit was working properly. That made no sense to Matthew, but then a lot of things make no sense to him, after all, Matthew was no longer part of the Idaho operation.

He did ask Jim if anyone is in the nuclear science training program preparing for refueling the nuclear units. "Before the first unit was installed," Jim said. "Five men from the local power company were screened by security and placed in a secret project. They had no idea what they had volunteered to do; the only thing they knew was that the project, in which they were participating, was to be kept secret for the time being. They are now in the final aspect of reactor servicing and refuel training."

Jim and Matthew continued talking shop on the porch for hours and darkness was fast approaching when Julie came home from work. She was as surprised as Matthew had been when she saw Jim. "Rachael will have dinner ready shortly, please stay for dinner Jim." Julie said after giving Jim a warm hug greeting.

Jim, looking somewhat puzzled said. "Sure Julie, I can stay, but I didn't think you had any children."

Using a rather stern voice and glaring at Matthew. "We don't Jim. Don't tell me Matthew, you've been here on the porch all this time and never mentioned or introduced our house guest,

Rachael."

"Well I ..." Matthew began stammering as Rachael appeared at the door.

"Ms Julie," Rachael said. "Dinner is on the table, please come and bring your guest."

Jim stared for a moment, looking at Rachael admiring her extremely attractive body. For a moment Jim thought this lovely lady must surely be a sister of Julie, they look so much alike. "Julie, she looks and dresses just like you, she has to be related."

"No Jim, she is not related. As we eat I'll try to explain her situation." Julie casually mentioned as they took their seats at the dining room table.

After dinner Rachael served coffee in the living room. Rachael took a seat beside Jim on the love seat. Clearly, Jim was enjoying the closeness of Rachael being beside him. Jim's thoughts were, *Perhaps I have been much too hasty about wanting to remain single.*

Both Julie and Matthew assumed Jim would have been married by now, but earlier he said he was not. "My life," Jim said, "has been to enjoy life to the fullest and as a single man, I can do what I want and leave when I want without any nagging questions."

Boy, could Matthew ever relate to that. During their somewhat stirring conversation about the past, Julie blurted out that she was not *going* to retire but rather, *had* retired. Julie, *retire!* Matthew remembered hearing her say she was married to the hospital until death. "Julie," a stunned Matthew said, "that comes as a bit of a shock. What brought this on so suddenly?"

"Well Matthew," Julie said. "They announced today that the hospital has been sold and several people I work with have been given notice to leave and that includes several of our good doctors. The new owners believe they can operate, as they say, quite efficiently with less staff. We all know what they mean; the hospital can make more money by reducing the staff. In the ER where I am, we can barely keep up with the arrivals as it is. I am definitely not going to have emergency patients wait hours and hours for a doctor or an examining room. I have retirement money coming and I'm taking it now. I gave them two weeks notice today."

As the four of them sat in the living room discussing this very personal revelation Matthew said, "This has been an exciting day Julie. First, I heard nothing from anyone about either of the jobs I have been working on. Then I got a call from Johnson saying the test of the nuclear disposal test flight to Mars is about to happen. Then, while on the porch mulling that over in my mind, Jim arrives from out of nowhere telling me about the success of the Erickson Project. Now, you Julie, tell me you have retired. I honestly don't think I can take anymore good news today."

It had been two weeks since Julie gave her notice at the hospital. Today was her last day at the hospital, and so she invited Matthew to go along to the hospital. Julie told him several people she worked with were leaving today and apparently they wanted to have a going away party. Matthew opted not to go with her in the morning, but instead agreed to meet her in the afternoon. The only reason for agreeing to go was that Matthew hoped to see just how Knoxville Baptist Hospital would operate without their longtime dedicated employees.

It didn't take him long to realize what the new owners had done to fill the vacancies. The plan, as Matthew saw it, was to replace those leaving with new hires at much lower wages. Clearly they would have the bodies to fill the positions, but without the experience necessary to operate the place efficiently. This is the kind of strategy that industry, both large and small, has been doing for quite some time.

The party went on for an hour or so. During that time Matthew was introduced to those that Julie worked with in the emergency room. One that caught Matthew's attention was Dr. Jordon. He was the one Matthew saw with Julie a long time ago having dinner at a nearby restaurant. Nearing the end of the party he and Julie hugged for what seemed to be much longer than need be. Dr Jordon formally announced to all present that he was leaving to begin a new practice in Nashville. Julie seemed happy about that announcement. "Perhaps we can meet," Julie gleefully said, "when I visit my mother in Nashville."

To which Doctor Jordon responded. "That would be very nice Julie."

Several others went on to explain what they would be doing with their new found time off. Some said they were moving to other hospitals, others to private clinics and some had no plans at all. It appeared all of the ER personnel would be leaving. It soon became obvious to Matthew exactly how the hospital would continue operating. Just as the party was ending, the new shift of doctors and nurse replacements began arriving. Julie pointed out that all but two of the newly arriving doctors and nurses were brand new to the hospital. American businesses are sinking to new lows to keep their bottom lines profitable. That of course is only Matthew's view point and is not that of the hospital's new management team.

The next day was the first of Julie's forced retirement. What was Julie going to do with her new found time? She now had Rachael taking very good care of all the everyday household duties. How long would it take Julie to get sick of staying home? It didn't take long for Matthew to find out.

Early in the afternoon Julie announced that she was going to walk to the Jones place. They are the ones that have the nearby roadside vegetable stand. Alfred and Margaret Jones house and roadside stand is just around the corner from Matthew's house. Actually it is only about a five minute walk. Many times Julie would walk to their stand to buy fresh veggies. Julie especially enjoyed talking to Mrs. Jones. Every time Julie came back from the Jones' she would remark about how you rarely hear names of today's children like Alfred and Margaret, then Julie would add, "I guess those names are just too old fashioned for kids today. "Think about it Matthew, do you know any children named Margaret or Alfred today?"

Alf, as Matthew called Mr. Jones, was a large portly individual always dressed in bib overalls. It was Matthew's guess that in that kind of business; overalls were the dress code of the trade. As for Mrs. Jones, you would never see her without her bonnet that covered her entire head and it came complete with a large sun visor. In the farming business one needs to keep the skin covered as a protection from the sun. "Mr. Wilson," she would say, always calling Matthew, Mr., "you should wear a hat. The sun could cause skin cancer you know." What could he say, she was right, but Matthew couldn't stand a hat.

Today Julie returned from the Jones' house just grinning as though she had just won the lottery. "You know Matthew," she said. "I asked Margaret if they ever needed a break to get away from the business."

"Well," Margaret told Julie, "it surely would be nice, but we have to stay close so we can keep our eye on the vegetable stand."

"If you would allow me," Julie said asking Margaret, "I would be happy to help you. All you need do is provide me with a price list for the vegetables you sell. I could come over nearly every day if that would be okay with Alfred and you."

Julie told Matthew, Margaret gave her a big hug and as she did said, "You would do that for us? Bless you my child. Thank you so much."

And so began Julie's retirement job. It was a volunteer job that seemed to make her happy. Nearly every afternoon Julie would stroll to the Jones place complete with a book to read to pass the time. It was interesting to see Julie behind the stand wearing an old fashioned bonnet like Margaret's. Margaret insisted she wear one of hers. It was also good to see Julie come home with fresh vegetables. Alf insisted that Julie take whatever she wanted as a kind of pay, life is very good.

# CHAPTER 21
## MOM NEEDS MY HELP

The months passed without much happening. It would be good to hear from someone about how the Mars project was progressing, but Matthew heard nothing. Matthew noted that it was approaching the time for the test shuttle cargo ship rendezvous with Mars. NASA launched it just over seven months ago.

As Matthew sat back in his easy chair to watch the evening news his ears perked up as the TV network announcer was describing news that there had been an unmanned NASA successful soft landing on Mars. There was no mention as to the cargo carried; only that it had landed. The announcer said they would try to find out what is going on and would report on it later.

Matthew knew what was going on, the soft landing mentioned was the stainless steel cylinders being parachuted to the Mars surface. There was no announcement that the craft itself blew up as designed. Apparently the mission had been kept secret as planned. In this day of high tech news coverage it is rare when something of this magnitude gets past the media. In all honesty, when the world gets wind of the government's plans to ship the spent nuclear fuel to Mars, there will be demonstrations like never before. But this nation must do what it must.

As suspected however, it didn't take long for the country to learn the real reason for the project. Surprisingly there was little resistance to how America was ridding itself of the used nuclear fuel. The real problem was how to pay for the task. Media talk shows of all kind seemed to understand the painful developing problems as to why this was deemed necessary. The public's real concern is the cost. How will the bills get paid to accomplish the task?

Congress had to deal with that very dilemma and an upcoming battle would surely take place. Should the American people have to pay the billions and billions of dollars for the cost of the project? Of course, all America would have to pay, we are taxpayers and the taxpayers must pay every penny spent by our government and this is definitely a government project.

The radio talk show audiences expressed many opinions. The listeners would say the nuclear power companies are the reason for the problem in the first place and they should bear the largest portion of the expense. Why, because they are the ones that had not provided proper disposal techniques years and years ago.

Matthew had to confess his department at Oak Valley, right here in Tennessee was partially responsible for the current situation. Of course Matthew would never admit that, but it is true. Oak Valley should have been able to project future problems such as this and have made plans to handle the situation before it got out of control. Matthew recognized that the actual problem began long before he took the helm at Oak Valley.

A fierce battle raged for several months within Congress as they attempted to come up with a payment system for the nuclear waste project. In the end, the power companies decided a "disposal fee" of ten percent for each residential customer in the U.S. and a twenty five percent add-on fee for every commercial customer would be added to their monthly electric bills and it would begin immediately. That part of the program received the most flack. Congressmen began immediately receiving hate mail, even threats of death. These were comments a Congressman never wants to hear from his or her constituents. Those being never to vote for you again hate mail.

If you recall in the beginning, Matthew had said this would not be a cheap fix. As Matthew had said before, one way or the other, we the people will provide every penny of the expense.

Congress was dealing with an approximate dollar amount, but the final cost proposed, and it was a huge one, was hammered out after only a few months of deliberations.

NASA, in its present state, would take a hard hit. All fund appropriations for NASA would be re-directed to the nuclear waste program. Also the scheduled launch dates to send more investigative missions to Mars and beyond would be scrubbed for now and in the near future. After all why would we want to send anyone or anything to Mars if the world was going to use it as a radioactive dumping ground? The local concern around the country was that ending the Mars mission program would put so many people out of work. Congress explained those displaced individuals would be moved into the massive task of transporting the casks to various military locations around the country. The military bases would need hundreds, if not thousands of additional helpers to prepare for each daily launch.

Still short of money to finance the massive undertaking, Congress turned to other ways to get more money from the taxpayers? When government needs huge amounts of additional money who do they turn to, who else, the transportation industry? Diesel and gasoline users, and that includes air transportation systems, would be asked to provide an additional ten cents per gallon federal tax. It was explained that the tax would only remain in effect for about ten years. Somehow some genius in their ivory tower figured that would be the maximum time duration needed to bring the unpleasant situation under control.

In order to get some of the heat off congress the President asked William Johnson, head of the NRC, to announce via television, to all the people of this country that we have been testing for several years, a new electrical generation technology. Because of this, the massive nuclear waste problems would be a thing of the past. Actually, that was not an accurate statement as he would find out much later. Johnson was then told to describe in detail the miniature nuclear power plant and the benefits of localized power production. He also would explain that the miniature nuclear power plants would soon be ready to be placed in and around every town and city in the U.S. The message was to be strong, forceful and upbeat.

The President explained in no uncertain terms what he wanted Johnson to say when he addressed the people. Johnson was told to say; no longer will the United States be building huge nuclear power stations. No longer will the U.S. be held hostage by the oil producing nations of the world. The President went on to tell Johnson to tell the people our old nuclear power units are showing serious signs of old age and decay and must be dismantled in the very near future. The United States is prepared to do all it can to reduce our share of the global warming issue.

William Johnson did broadcast on a nationwide television message telling all that the President instructed him to say and more. While providing great detail, Johnson said testing had indicated the miniature nuclear units would be far more efficient and the additional good news was that each unit would be capable of producing hydrogen.

In his TV message, Johnson went on to explain how hydrogen powered transportation was the future, not just for the United States, but the entire world. "An infrastructure of hydrogen service stations will be in place within five to ten years to supply hydrogen to our newly developed hydrogen powered vehicles that are being developed and tested. Thus far, a nationwide infrastructure of hydrogen service stations has been the delay in implementing this type system. In the next fifteen to twenty years the United States will have eliminated the gasoline and diesel combustion engine."

Johnson, in his televised message continued saying, "During

the past few years the automotive industry has quietly been engineering and designing new hydrogen engines for the future. These new engines will be used not only in automobiles, but also placed in all new trucks and busses. The United States is sharing this technology with the world and in about twenty years the entire world should be running entirely on hydrogen powered vehicles. Our automotive engineers are now working on ways to retrofit today's existing vehicles to hydrogen power. It remains to be seen if that can be accomplished however. I would like to add that global warming as we know it today will be reduced to nearly nothing."

In spite of what Jim Adams told Matthew, the Erickson Project was still in early testing. The last time Matthew talked to Jack Jackson in Idaho, Jack indicated it would be about two years before the U.S. could be sure the test units were reliably working. Jack did tell Matthew that the test unit seemed to be doing a very safe job, "Time will tell." Jack said.

Political pressure was apparently mounting to make it appear as though the United States actually was ready to change our life as it applied to our nation's fossil fuel dependence. The President has pressured Johnson to take some of the heat off the President by announcing a start date of the Erickson program. Matthew hoped this didn't backfire and cause more problems than they already had concerning nuclear power. According to Johnson's television announcement, the country was moving ahead immediately.

Considering Matthew's involvement getting the two programs started, one would think his name would be mentioned along with that of Catherine Hamilton. Fortunately for Matthew, his name hadn't been mentioned during any of the news announcements, and for that he is a very happy man. Should something go wrong with either of the projects Matthew wanted to be far, far away from either of them?

Truth is, since the passing of Catherine Hamilton, the Secretary of Energy Czar, Matthew had been pretty much outside the new technology information loop.

Matthew and Julie, these days, were simply enjoying their senior retirement years and doing as little as possible. Most seniors, when they retire, have a desire to see the world or at least the back road areas of the United States. As you know, Matthew had expressed the idea that he might do a lot of local fishing. Several years ago a group of men insisted he go along on a deep sea fishing trip. Never again would he do that. For the entire eight hour fishing trip he hung his head overboard, feeding the fish some really awful stuff. He vowed to *never, never* do that again. Meanwhile Julie, on the other hand, continued her daily visit to the Jones' roadside stand which seemed to keep her content with retirement.

Matthew is becoming an expert at being his usual restless self. Trying to find something to do was becoming more painful every day.

He had asked Julie to go fishing with him a couple of times, but her usual answer was, no way. Today however, he again asked her to go fishing and there was a long pause before she answered. Matthew had the feeling she would say yes and go along. After the long pause Julie took a deep breath and did as she has done before suggesting, "Matthew, go look for fish alone." Julie has a way with words. She really didn't mean he should look for fish. What she meant was that most of the time he came back from fishing with none. Then she would say, "Matthew, you need to look harder, the fish are hiding from you. You should try the fish market in town. They seem to know where all kinds of fish are hiding." Matthew knew he should be offended by her catty remark, but he wasn't. After all, he had some very relaxing days doing nothing as he fished, or as Julie has said, "looking for fish." Matthew reminded himself of the time he caught the really big one, the lady that fell overboard. Now that was a big catch.

Springtime in Tennessee is an absolute delight. Julie, Matthew and Rachael sat in the living room late one March evening discussing the freshness of the newborn leaves on the trees and the smell of the spring flowers when suddenly Rachael exclaimed. "They're back, they have come for me. I must leave now. Thank you Julie and Matthew for all you have done for me all these years." That said, Rachael got up and ran to the door and went out, disappearing into the blackness of the night.

Shocked by the suddenness of Rachael's sudden departure, Julie and Matthew ran outside after her, but she was nowhere to be seen. "She seemed to know what she was doing. Apparently there is something about Rachael we will never know." Julie said.

Matthew and Julie had, years earlier, attempted to find out about her past and how she arrived in the Knoxville area. "Do you remember Julie, how Rachael explained she was dropped off on earth by a spaceship and all that crazy stuff about her life on planet Seti?" Matthew said with a kind of tongue in cheek tone in his voice. "Well, just maybe she was telling us the truth."

"Sure." Julie said, but not very convincing.

It had been a long time since Julie visited her elderly mother in Nashville. It didn't surprise Matthew to hear her say after coming home from a hard days work at the roadside stand, "By the way Matthew, I want to visit my mother in Nashville if that is okay with you. She is getting up in years and I would like to spend some quality time with her, maybe just a week or two"

What could he say, "Sure, go ahead. Take all the time you want, but call me from time to time with a progress report about how your mother is doing. You know, like kind of keep in touch with me."

The following Monday Julie left for Nashville. With her out of the house and Rachael gone, the house was really quiet. Matthew didn't know why that bothered him because Julie spent almost every day at the Jones vegetable stand. Matthew

I AM THAT I AM

was now faced with the task of the day, to go fishing or not go fishing. Funny, when you have all the time in the world on your hands, suddenly you don't feel like doing anything. Matthew had that kind of thought today and again he was faced with his reason for wanting Julie to go along fishing, it's really not fun fishing alone. Pulling that lady out of the water who had fallen out of her boat at the lake some time ago only happens once in a lifetime. It's not that you want somebody chatting all the time you are fishing, but it's just nice to have someone close, just in case you do want to talk. He sure did wish Julie would have allowed him to get a dog to talk to, but she didn't.

Matthew was talking aloud to himself again as he does so often, "Shoot, why not, why not go up to the lake and spend a few days fishing. He loaded the car with his fishing gear and some food provisions to eat while there and made the trip to the lake.

The lake looked beautiful as Matthew drove down the steep dirt road leading to the boat launch and cabins. He was looking for Sam, the owner at the bait shop. Instead there was a new man who introduced himself as Charles.

"What happened to Sam, did he retire?" Matthew said

Charles answered using a very noticeable somber Tennessee country drawl, "Nope, he didn't exactly retire. He was my brother and he died a few months ago. He had a heart attack. His wife didn't want to run the place so I bought it from her. I've been wondering if I might have made a big mistake. Business sure has been slow."

"I'm sorry to hear that about Sam, but don't worry Charles, business gets going really good in the summer. I come here a few times a year. Today I need a cabin for a few days and a boat for tomorrow."

"Got just what you need Mr. Got bait for ya to, if you need some."

"My name is Matthew, Matthew Wilson. For sure I'll need some bait Charlie. You can't catch the fish unless you have bait."

Matthew paid Charlie and unloaded his fishing gear and food placing it in his small, one room cabin. It was nearly dark and he walked outside to take in the fresh clean smell of the lake.

It was nice to sit on the cabin porch and listen to the sounds of the lake and the surrounding mountains. Darkness was fast approaching and the crickets and frogs were beginning there springtime music. *Life is good*, Matthew thought.

The sounds of the fish jumping in the lake were music to Matthew's ears. Matthew imagined he heard the sound of a small boat trolling motor getting close to the dock landing. In just a few minutes he saw the boat slowly pull into the boat slip. In it there was a lady and a child, Matthew guessed the boy to be about twelve or fifteen. Darkness had fallen over the lake making it difficult to distinguish if the lady was anyone he had seen before on any of his previous trips to the lake.

The lady and the boy walked by going in the direction of their cabin. As they walked past Matthew, the attractive lady, dressed in a long, brightly flower covered print dress made a grunting sound that could have been interrupted as, "hello." Returning the greeting, if that is what it was, Matthew said, "And hello to you too Maam. Sure is a fine evening for a boat stroll on the lake."

*That's odd*, Matthew thought to himself. *Neither of them has fishing gear. How do you fish without at least some kind of fishing pole?* Around the lady's neck and dangling by her side was a very expense camera. *Nah, it couldn't be, that was a long time ago and she wasn't married then and didn't want any kids.* By now it was completely dark and the two entered the cabin next door to Matthew's.

The night chill began to get to Matthew. He ever so slowly raised himself from the rickety old rocker, being careful to hold on to the arms of the chair as he lifted himself up. His thoughts were that he is getting much older now. These days he finds himself making slower moves, holding on to furniture and walls as he moves about. "Golly, I sure must be getting old. Oh well, happens to all of us." That said, Matthew opened the old squeaky screen door and went inside. The light switch to the room's single light bulb was on the wall, just inside the door. "It's much better with the light on. Now, if I can get the heater to work I'll have a warm room in just a few minutes. This place feels like a freezer." The small kerosene heater lit and quickly took the chill from the room.

Matthew imagined he heard a knock on his door. "Who in the world could be knocking on my door?" He carefully opened the door which revealed the lady that had just walked past him minutes ago.

Matthew soon found out the lady actually talks rather than just making grunting sounds as she did earlier. "I'm sorry to bother you sir, but I'm having a bit of trouble lighting my room heater."

Matthew felt he could show her how to light the heater in his cabin rather than go to her place. "Please Maam, come in and I will give you a lesson in, 101, lighting small cabin heaters."

As she stepped inside, the light lit a lady's figure that looked somewhat familiar. Both Matthew and the lady stared for a moment at each other before the lady said. "Remember me Matthew, you saved my life years ago in this very lake."

Just as quick to respond Matthew exclaimed, "Susan ... yes, I most certainly do remember. And in this very room we ..."

Susan cut him off as she said, "Yes Matthew, we did and in that very bed."

Immediately they both hugged and kissed friendly kisses on the cheek. Standing in his room was the very lady Matthew had, in fact, rescued after she had fallen overboard from her boat on the lake.

Matthew was dumbfounded by the happenstance of ever seeing Susan again. "Susan, it is so good to see you again. The boy Susan, you said you would never have children. Is the boy a relative of yours?"

"You could say that Matthew. He is my son, Matthew Franklin Marshall. Marshall is my last name Matthew."

The coincidence of the boy's name being similar to his own had Matthew wondering as he said, "Except for his last name, his name, Matthew Franklin, is like mine."

"That's the name I chose when I had the boy fourteen years ago. I wasn't married and the hospital required that a name had to be placed on the birth certificate so I chose yours, Matthew Franklin."

"I'm honored Susan."

"You should be Matthew. If you remember, we were both vulnerable the night we slept together. It was one of the most enjoyable and memorable nights of my life. If you recall, I had no sex protection and neither did you. The result Matthew … may I present, your son who is waiting for me next door."

Matthew, for once in his life was at a total loss for words. He slowly slid down onto the edge of the bed. "Susan, you never tried to contact me about the boy, why?"

"What was the point Matthew? I knew you were married and although it was a struggle for me for a time, my mother helped me during his early years. As it turns out, he is the joy of my life. I would have never known this kind of joyous life if it had not been for our happenstance meeting on that night over fourteen years ago. No Matthew, I thank you so much. I loved your name then and you gave me a life I would have never known."

The realization that Susan had come to his cabin requesting his help to light her room heater had dawned on both of them. Matthew said, "Susan, the boy is freezing in your cabin. Let's continue this discussion at your place."

They talked for several hours before Matthew went back to his own cabin. Matthew slept little that night. He was happy for her and sad for himself that he never had a boy to share his life experiences with. His thoughts were that the boy would have been even better than having a dog to talk to all these many years. From this night on and forever, this secret is one Matthew decided he would never share with Julie.

Matthew finally went to sleep early in the morning. When

he awoke late the next morning, he peered out his side window looking for Susan next door. She had driven off shortly after sunrise. That was the one and only time Matthew would see Susan or his son, Matthew.

Nashville is such a pretty place in the spring. The flowering dogwoods and the azaleas are all in full bloom. "I love this place," Julie said to herself as her car rambled up the lane leading to her mother's house. The old house appeared to be in need of some repairs and it definitely needed paint. Mom can't do stuff like that anymore and she no longer has her man around. It was about two years ago Julie's dad died, leaving her mom alone. That's why she tried to come to Nashville as often as she could. "If only Matthew would come along with me, he could do some of the necessary fix up projects. Well, maybe he couldn't do the fixing himself, but at least he knows where to get reliable help." Matthew proved that when he said he fixed the leaky faucet and tub in her bathroom. Julie never let on that she was on to his method of fixing things around the house. Julie knew he called the local fix-it center.

Mother as usual welcomed Julie with a big hug and a kiss. Mom was very loving in that way. The years she spent with her mother and dad were good times; they went places and always did things together. "Boy, I sure do miss those times."

They sat and discussed the immediate physical problems Mom was having. Mom wasn't one to complain, but this time she was having problems that needed attention that Julie couldn't handle. But where should she take her. Mom needed to see a doctor. "I wonder if Dr. Jordon could see you." Julie said to her mother. "He is one of the doctors that the hospital fired before I retired. I think I'll go through the phone book to see where he is and give him a call."

She knew her mother was feeling pretty bad when she agreed that Julie should call him. Mom's leg had swollen to nearly twice its normal size and she was complaining of pains in her chest. Mother was not one to complain about anything. Before

Dad passed away she used to complain to him. He would tell her that she was just imagining problems and to just tough it out. This time clearly wasn't the case. Mom really had problems that needed attention. What would Mom have done if she hadn't come today? Julie couldn't think about that, it would have been a medical disaster.

It was good to hear Frank on the telephone. No matter what calamity is going on around him he always had a certain calming demeanor in his voice that calmed a person. He had been that way forever and Julie thought that was why she always enjoyed talking to him in the past. Of course his looks didn't hurt either. They talked for a few minutes, getting reacquainted, and then Julie told him why she needed his help with her mother.

"Julie," Frank said, "my office hours are over in about an hour, why don't I come to the house to see your mother." *A house call, now that's what I call a doctor*, Julie thought.

In about an hour and a half there was a knock at the door. It was Dr. Frank Jordon looking just as she had remembered him. There he was, tall dark and handsome and dressed in his usual coat, shirt and tie and smelling extremely good. She wanted to kiss him for coming on such short notice, but she knew she couldn't do that, Mom was sitting close by. They did hug however, that seemed appropriate and Julie thanked him so much for coming to the house.

He examined Mom for a few minutes listening to her heart and taking her blood pressure several times. Finally he took Julie by the hand and led her to the hallway before saying, "Julie, your mother needs to be in a hospital now. I mean tonight, her blood pressure is extremely high and the blood circulation in her leg appears to be nearly completely blocked. Her heart is working overtime trying to get blood to the leg. It would appear to be clots that are causing the problem, but I can only be sure what is happening with additional testing at the hospital. Julie, it would be best if we transport her by ambulance, the leg needs to be kept elevated."

"Whatever you say is best Dr. Jordon." Julie said as they both went back into the living room. "Mom, Dr. Jordon wants you to go to the hospital tonight. Dr. Jordon is going to order an ambulance. The swollen leg has to be elevated and I can't do that if you travel in my car. I'll go with you and stay as long as the hospital allows tonight. You will be in good hands at the hospital, Dr. Jordan will see to that.

Frank called for a transport ambulance which arrived in just a few minutes. Julie rode along in the ambulance with her mother while Frank followed in his car. When they arrived at the hospital her mother was immediately placed in an ER examination room. This ER was unlike Julie's back at Baptist Hospital in Knoxville. Apparently the ER staff here had not been cut short as theirs had been. Frank had two nurses assisting him. Usually the on duty doctor comes in for patient problems like her mother's, but Frank asked if he could handle this patient. "Knock yourself out," the night ER duty doctor said.

It didn't take Frank long to come out and tell Julie that they had given mother a relaxing medication that would clearly put her to sleep. Dr Jordan had ordered a blood thinner that should begin working on the clot in her leg. Frank said she would be sleeping in a few minutes and suggested that they have some dinner while they wait. He assured Julie he would be nearby and the nurse would call him immediately if they needed his assistance. "The significant difficulty," Frank said, "would be if the clot begins to break up and move into the heart. I don't expect that to happen tonight, but if it does it could be fatal, but of course you already know that Julie." He didn't have to tell her that, she knew the danger, but the blood thinner had to be administrated to get circulation going in her leg.

Julie had not eaten all day, dinner sounded like a good idea although she was not sure she would be able to eat, considering Mom's serious medical condition.

Not far from the hospital Frank and Julie went to a very quaint small restaurant. It had a beautiful outside area for dining complete with a garden of freshly blooming flowers and vines that gave the area the fragrance of a perfect spring evening. How romantic this place would have been except for the seriousness of her mother's condition. To be here on the arm of such a good friend as Dr. Frank Jordon would have any normal woman swooning out of her mind.

Frank seated her at the table and he could see the worry on her face as he spoke in his most soft spoken doctor's bedside manner. "Julie, if there are any changes in your mother's condition the nurse will page me immediately. I don't foresee complications so please relax and enjoy the moment."

As they were finishing their meal, Frank's pager sounded. He immediately excused himself and went to a nearby telephone. In a few moments he returned saying, "The lead ER nurse just called to say they would keep your mother overnight in the ER and move her to a room early in the morning. The nurse said the pink color is ever so slowly returning to her leg and that's a good thing because it indicates that blood is beginning to circulate, to some degree, in her leg."

He reassured Julie that her mother's blood pressure was slowly returning to a near normal number, thus he suggested, "Julie I have a condo within walking distance of the hospital. You are more than welcome to stay there as long as your mother is in the hospital. But if you would rather, I will take you to her house, which would you rather do?"

"Frank," Julie said, "I would love to stay at your place, at least for tonight, but my overnight case is back at mother's house."

"Why don't I take you to your mother's house?" Frank offered. "On the way you can decide where you would prefer to stay."

This was a tough decision. Julie would really like to stay at Frank's condo, but she knew she shouldn't. Her inner conscience was getting to her because she knew almost certainly they would pick up where they left off when Frank came to her house in Knoxville. But what the heck, it would be so convenient so she said. "Sure, take me to Mom's place. When we get there I'll just be a minute while I go in the house and get my small overnight bag."

Arriving at Frank's condo Julie saw a well kept, very clean dust free place that reflected everything good about the doctor. Not what one would expect of a bachelor pad. Julie had to admit she was a little nervous about the sleeping arrangement. It didn't take long for Frank to pick up on her nervousness. Being the gentleman he was he suggested that she sleep in the bed and he would sleep on the pullout sofa in the living room. Julie thought, for a minute before she said, "Frank, we are adults, why would you sleep on the sofa? Please come to the bedroom with me. I could use the comfort of your arms holding me." After all, he had seen her totally naked before, so why not.

There they were in bed together, Julie in her nightgown and Frank in his pajamas. Yes, she knew that sounded like a night before Christmas thing, but it's not. For some reason she knew Frank would wear pajamas so why would that surprise her when she watched him modestly put them on?

It didn't take long for Julie to realize that Frank was not going to approach her so she had to make the first move. She reached over his tall outstretched body and took his arm and placed it over her shoulder as she said, "Frank please hold me tight." Without hesitation, he obliged her forwardness. It was so comforting to Julie.

"Julie," he said, "I can feel the tenseness all over your body. Roll over and I will give you my magic finger massage, you will never go to sleep in your present tense condition."

Relax her it did. His soft fingers went from her shoulders to her spine. What a masterful touch as her body melted as his ever so soft hands worked their magic. This could go on forever, but Julie must get some sleep. She felt her body temperature beginning to rise which she realized was not good thing to be turned on in such a sexual way tonight. Ending her feelings, she rolled over and gave him a thank you and a good night kiss. But his lips were so soft and when he returned the kiss his soft hands held her face for a moment as he gave Julie his final good night kiss. She could feel Frank was as turned on as she. However, Julie said what married women so often say to their husbands, "Not tonight dear, we both need our sleep."

Most doctors are extremely health conscience about what they eat. At least that is what Julie thought. So it came as a bit of surprise to her to wake up to the smell of frying bacon, eggs and grits cooking. "Good morning Miss. Sunshine." Frank said. "I usually have bacon, grits and eggs before I go to work; does that sound good to you? When we finish we can walk to the hospital together. I begin my rounds at the hospital about eight o'clock."

Of course it is okay with her, anything this doctor says is okay. He is the best medicine Julie could get at this most trying time in her life. Sure, she knew she was in the wrong place for a married woman, but she was just staying at Frank's place as a convenience to be near her mother. *Right!*

After breakfast the both left, walking hand in hand to the hospital. When they arrived at the hospital Frank immediately went into his doctor mode. First things first are the rounds of his patients. He told Julie he would be in her mother's room shortly, and she should go on without him.

Mother was having breakfast when Julie opened the door and saw her mom sitting up in bed, eating. Her leg was slightly elevated which revealed the swelling was beginning to go down. What an improvement a night in the hospital can do for the body. She said the leg pain was still there, but not nearly as bad. Of course Julie didn't tell her the pain medicine they had given her was still working in her system. Mom was a happy person again and as with all patients, she wanted to know if she could go home today. Julie advised her that Dr. Jordon would be in for a visit in a few minutes and he would make that decision.

It was only a few minutes before Dr. Jordon came to her mother's room. He examined her extensively. "Julie," he said, "your mother is responding nicely to the blood thinner medicine, but we will keep her for at least two more days. The clots are dissolving as I expected, but before I send her home I want to see the test results to confirm clear blood passage back to the heart. She still could have an unexpected clot release so we need to keep her here under observation."

Mom wasn't too thrilled to hear that she will have to remain in the hospital for two more days. Julie, on the other hand, in her selfish way, was happy to know she would be spending at least two more nights with Frank. Yes, she knew she was behaving badly, but she enjoyed Frank's company so much.

Julie remembered she had promised to call Matthew so she took a few minutes to place a call to him. To her surprise he answered the phone in what appeared to be a happy voice. He told Julie how he was helping the Jones' as Julie had before she left. It was especially nice to hear him say nice things about mother's condition. He wished his mother-in-law a speedy recovery and again told Julie to stay as long as needed. He ended the conversation with the "I love you and miss you Julie." That began to make her feel even guiltier, but only for a short time, after all, she knew about Matthew's affair with Catherine Hamilton. Matthew never knew she suspected anything, but if you remember, Matthew talks a lot in his sleep, enough said.

Frank and Julie did things in bed that she had never imagined. He was ever so gentle and yet so commanding. It was so good and as she says it, "I am so glad I am his bad girl." That's what he called her, his bad girl. To be manhandled like that should have hurt her, but it didn't and she felt good, oh so good.

Her two days staying with Frank went by so fast, but for mother in the hospital it seemed like an eternity. The time had come for mother to go home. Frank had given her the okay to leave. If you remember, Julie had left her car at her mother's house. Frank had taken time from his busy schedule to drive her back to mom's house to get her car.

As Julie pulled up to the front door of the hospital there was Mom in a wheelchair waiting with a nurse. Mother insisted she be allowed to walk, but all hospitals use wheelchairs when you are discharged so she had no choice in the matter. Usually you never see your physician at the time of being discharged, but Frank came out with her mother. After they got mother in the car and as Julie walked around the back of her car, Frank took her hand and pulled her close and gave Julie a farewell kiss. She didn't think mother saw that, at least she hoped she didn't.

Julie spent the next two weeks taking care of her mother the best she could. Her mother wanted to visit the grocery store and insisted on walking through the store. Julie had to use her best nursing skills to get her into one of those scooter cart things, allowing her to drive around the store. Then there were the household chores Mom felt she had to do. They really got into serious discussions about that. Trying to keep her down had turned out to be almost impossible. Finally Julie had to tell her that the problem with her heart and leg would come back if she didn't take life easy. "I won't be here," Julie said. "Mother I have to go home soon. What will you do if those problems return? What will you do?"

"Why I'll just call your Doctor friend," her mother said. "He seemed like such a nice person and I know he liked you. I could tell that by the way he kissed you after you put me in the car at the hospital. I'm not blind you know, by the way, did you stay at his house while I was in the hospital? I don't think you did because I saw your overnight bag in the back seat of the car when you picked me up."

What could Julie say, she caught her. The best thing she could say was, "Oh Mother, where do you think I stayed, with Dr. Jordon of course." Sometimes if you say the obvious, the one that is asking won't believe you.

"I suppose that was possible," Mother said, "he is single and rather good looking too. If I were younger I think I would have stayed with him rather than drive all the way home every day, but then that's just me."

"Now that is enough about that Mother." Julie did her best to change the subject. You wouldn't think older people would pick up on those kinds of things. Julie knew her Mom was old, but she's not blind and definitely not stupid.

Julie had been at her mother's house for over a month. She was doing so well and as long as she stayed on the blood thinner medicine she should not have more problems. But it is time for her to go home. If she stayed away any longer Matthew might find some young thing and leave her in the dust. It was hard to leave Mother at the house by herself, but she had to go. Julie had talked to a neighbor lady and asked her to look in on Mom from time to time, which relieved Julie somewhat.

As Julie rounded the bend in the road approaching their house there was her husband Matthew, behind the Jones vegetable stand wearing a long white apron. She pulled up to the stand, got out of the car and asked if he had some freshly pulled corn. Matthew stepped up and with a hardy laugh he said, "Lady, every vegetable you see here was taken right out of the vegetable patch this morning." Having said that Matthew came from behind the stand and hugged Julie as never before. That was nice.

They talked about her Mom for a bit and then Julie picked up some fresh corn to fix for tonight's dinner. As she got in the car Matthew said. "Julie I can't leave yet, I'm still on the clock, but I should be home about five o'clock. It's so good to have you back."

Matthew seemed like a changed person, he seemed to be a lot more relaxed. She couldn't put her finger on it, but she liked the change. Perhaps Matthew had finally dealt with the fact that he was retired. For some, retirement can be a death sentence. Matthew had always been in the mix of his former business. To leave his work had left him with a poor attitude toward life. People had stopped calling him about consulting work. Julie believed in time Matthew would tell her why the calls had stopped coming.

Julie was in the kitchen cooking when Matthew came home. He immediately hung his apron in the closet. Again they hugged and kissed as though she was his long lost possession. She said to him, "Dinner should be ready in just a few minutes."

As they ate, Matthew opened up a bit and began telling her the situation concerning the two projects with which he had been so involved. "Julie, this country, and the world for that matter, is shortly going into a new age. The changes that are about to happen in the electric industry are mind boggling. As we come to the end of our lives we will be driving very different automobiles. Our electric will come to us locally instead of from some far away power plant. Our local gas stations will no longer be selling gasoline. The service stations will fill our cars with hydrogen, not gasoline. It will take some years to get everyone converted, but it will happen by the time we reach our ninety's, in just a few short years from now."

Julie listened intently to what he was saying. Matthew seldom discussed any of the projects he had worked on, some were classified and she respected that. "Matthew," Julie asked, "that is a huge life changing event for us, but in view of the fact that we are running out of fossil fuel, this is good for all of us, right! According to what I read and see on TV the air we breathe is so polluted because of our love with the automobile. We hear so much about global warming, with these changes, air pollution should be nearly eliminated, if I understand what you are saying."

"That is so true Julie," Matthew said, "but it will take years for the world to see air pollution clear up. What really bothers me most is that we are sending our nuclear waste into space. I know I was part of the recommendation to do that, but I have had second thoughts about it. Sending the waste to Mars has already begun here in the U.S. and shortly the same program will begin in countries around the world. From what I understand, NASA is sharing the new technology with nations worldwide.

This is a world size problem and we have come up with a world solution, not just a United States solution. It's expensive and before long we will be feeling the financial effects big time. But I just can't help feeling the world is soon going to feel the effects of sending this stuff to Mars."

As the months went on it was interesting to see the infrastructure of the existing service stations as they began converting to providing hydrogen at the service station pumps. Matthew thought to himself. *If I were a bit younger I would invest heavily in the petroleum stock market. These people are going to make even more money than they ever have in the past. Of course we will be paying the price for their profits, but they will be huge nonetheless.* At his age though, investing in anything was useless. After all, with Julie's and his retirement money coming in each month, they get along just fine."

Nearly every country that had been generating nuclear power had started daily flight schedules sending their nuclear waste to Mars. There was not much discussion about it in the news. Matthew thought the media didn't think it was worth talking about. The feeling was that it is going to Mars, so why bother. About the only mention was the safety factor. What happens if the shuttle fails to reach orbit or falls back to land? The scenarios of that happening had been discussed in great detail. World governments had assured their people steps had been taken to control such an event. That seemed to satisfy most of the population's questions from around the world.

Nearly a year has gone by and the live loads of nuclear waste have begun their descent onto the planet Mars. So far so good, the experts have said. There have been no accidents. Some scientists have been concerned that during the long trip through space a shuttle could go off course, what then? Their answer was to simply let it go wherever. That of course, is no sensible answer, but that's the best official's can say. They say that if that happens we will deal with it at that time, end of the discussion.

# CHAPTER 22
## LIFE BEYOND EARTH

Have you ever wondered what is on the back side of Mars that is partially obscured from earth's eyes? Scientists tell us there is a cloud that appears to be miles thick that blocks even our most sophisticated satellites from seeing what is beneath it. The width and length of the cloud appears to be oval shaped and covers a space of several thousand miles. The scientists also say that nothing could live beneath such a thick cloud because sunlight could not penetrate the gaseous, vapor cloud. The land beneath the thick cloud would be in total darkness all the time. Well, the scientists are very wrong!

For thousands of years there has been a civilization of extremely intelligent beings that were created about the same time God created man on Earth. They were placed on a planet many light years away from Earth. Earths telescopes have just recently discovered it and have named this planet, Seti. Seti is about seven to eight times larger than Earth. The God that created people on this planet called them Setillians.

Setillians are different in many respects, but human nevertheless. The Setillians live and breathe an atmosphere very similar to Earth. They live and breathe much like earth humans with one or two significant differences. Setillians do age, but live for hundreds and hundreds of years.  Their life is extended much like earth human's lives were when first created by God because there is no disease on the Seti planet to shorten their lives.

After God created the heavens and earth, the seas and all the creatures, He created Adam and later, Eve.  Eve was created by removing a rib from Adam thus giving Adam a help mate.

Adam and Eve lived a good life in the Garden of Eden.  God said to the woman. "You may eat of every tree in the garden except one, *The Tree of Life*."

And the woman said to God, questioning Him, "We may eat the fruit of all the trees in the garden, but the fruit of The Tree of Life, we cannot eat of it, is that right."

God said, "You shall not eat of it, neither shall you touch it, lest you die."

But then a serpent appeared before Eve and was more cunning than any beast of the field which the Lord God had made.  And the *serpent* said to the woman, "You shall *not surely* die, for God knows that the day you eat thereof, your eyes shall be opened and you shall be as gods, surely knowing what is good from evil."

And when the woman saw that the tree was good for food, and that it was pleasant to the eyes, and the fruit of the tree to be desired to make one wise, as the serpent said, she took the fruit thereof, and she did eat it, and gave the fruit also to her husband Adam who was with her; and he also ate the forbidden fruit. But that was then that they messed up big time because he too also ate it.

Until that event occurred, both Adam an Eve were naked and had no need for clothing because neither knew they were naked.  God was providing all their needs.  However the moment they both ate the forbidden fruit, their eyes were opened and they knew that they were naked.  Now, realizing they were naked they sewed fig leaves together and made themselves apron like clothing.  From that time until now, life for man and woman on Earth was forever changed.  Man and woman now have free will to do with their lives whatever it takes to survive which means man and woman must work to survive from that day until now.

About the same time God created man and woman on Earth he also created a man and woman on Seti. On Seti, God's newly created man and woman were Aaron Grisemose and Esther Nacomi.

At the time, Seti was also a perfect planet, everything His newly created beings needed to exist was provided by God.

Like Adam and Eve who disobeyed God by partaking of the forbidden fruit, God's Setillian creations also disobeyed God and were tempted by Satan's promises. The result being the people of Seti live on a planet much like Earth that requires man and woman to live by the sweat of their brows. There is one huge difference from mankind on Earth however. Setillians learned by their mistakes quickly and chose to ask God through prayers for guidance to accomplish any problematical situations. That early knowledge has earned Setillians extreme advanced intelligence.

In the beginning, as on Earth, there were only the two beings, a man and a woman. Man on Seti, was shown the method by which he could impregnate the woman and immediately that knowledge had the Setillians beginning to multiply.

It soon became obvious to the Setillians, shelter from the hot sun would be necessary. Before the fall of man on Seti there were no clouds and no rain. As with earth's Garden of Eden, water came from below, up from the ground if you will. Because of Aaron Grisemose and Esther Nacomi's fall from grace, no longer would the Setillians be blessed with water from the ground, but instead would be subject to rain from the clouds above.

Many hundreds of years passed as the Setillian people struggled with the task of creating living areas for their families. For hundreds of years the people of Seti were living in caves located in the hills and mountains of their planet. Those chosen to create new methods of building shelter continued to only come up with nothing more than mixing the surface elements of the dirt and sand with water. The results being, a simple mix of mud baked by the sun that created a type of brick that would fall apart when the heavy rains came. And so, totally frustrated by failures, they moved back into their caves

Another notable difference from earth humans, they rarely spoke words aloud with each other. The Setillians needed only look at the person they were communicating with. No spoken words, rather, mind reading was the method of communication. As they spoke to one another using their special thought communication methods, they finally realized they needed help from their Creator, God. It was agreed by all that each individual would set aside a time for asking Him for help with their failed building methods. Each evening before the light began to fade; each person would take time out to pray, begging God for knowledge to help solve their construction dilemma. Years passed without even a hint of better ways to construct their shelters. Finally, after many years had passed, two men came forward and announced to those gathered, the solution that had been given them during their evening prayer session.

A gathering of the hundreds of Setillians listened intently as the two men spoke without words aloud of their findings. To the amazement of those gathered, the solution had always been present. The men said that inside the caves where they had been living were some very special elements. These elements, when heated enough would melt, allowing the molten material to be poured into molds that would be used to form walls and covers over the top of the walls. The men went on to say that the material, when poured very, very thin, could also be used in the open areas of the walls allowing light to come into the rooms and keep the wind and rains out. Earth humans would call this glass; the open areas would be called windows.

Those present were amazed at the revelation the two had explained, but wondered how they could make something hot enough to melt anything. "After all," they mentally questioned of the two men, "we can barely strike rocks together creating a fire capable of cooking our food."

Answering the question, the men explained that it had also been revealed how to create such heat. "There are several areas on our planet," they said, "that have a material, that when rubbed quickly with a rock, will burn with an intense heat capable of melting the new found building material." Setillians were now convinced their God would help the colony advance quickly, if only they asked.

The entire colony was now spending much of their time communicating with God. God responded to their prayers by providing extreme intelligence to a selected group of men who became the engineers and scientists for the colony. Thus the Setillians advanced rapidly. Very quickly the small villages became large towns and cities. After hundreds of years the knowledge to design and build protection from the sun blossomed.

God had also provided the seeds necessary to grow food. From the beginning of their time, as on Earth, animals existed which gave the Setillians meat for food. The selected group of men trained the other Setillians with the knowledge and skills necessary to build lighted domes over the fields of their fruits and vegetables, thus controlling the light and darkness which provided maximum food production. This came about, as the now very large colony, needed ways to provide maximum food production from the seed crops.

Although Setillians can talk aloud, it is rare that they do so. Some say that talking aloud is just wasted energy that could otherwise be used for doing something productive. Using their thought knowing sense processes usually eliminated discord, as Earthlings know it. Setillians do have mind discussions that at times become intense, but are almost always resolved quietly to the satisfaction of all.

After thousands of years the Setillians became curious about other planets within the universe. Using their extreme scientific knowledge given by Him, they discovered they had the ability, the tools and the materials to construct transportation that would allow them to travel the universe at light speeds. When the Setillians asked God's help in the design of these space crafts as they called them, they promised God that the crafts were never to be used as vehicles for destructive purposes. Thus God allowed the Setillians to explore the entire universe including Earth.

From time to time the Seti craft would venture into Earth's outer limits and simply observe from the vacuum of space. A few had been permitted to visit Earth for brief periods of time. Disguised as normal looking Earthlings, the knowledge they observed on earth made them realize just how good their civilization was on Seti. They saw with their own eyes the hurricanes and tornados, the floods, the pestilence and the work the Earthlings must do to just exist. They didn't understand all they were seeing, but they knew what they saw was not good. Each time they returned to Seti, after such observation trips, those that visited Earth would have mental discussions with their fellow Setillians wondering what the Earthlings did to deserve their kind of problems. "Yes," they would say mentally, "We have rain that supplies our water, but none of earth's other terrible miserys."

The Setillians do multiply as do humans, but with laws that prevent overcrowding, each man and woman is given the ability to have no more than three children. From the beginning of time the family surname of each man or woman continues on with each and every new child born. When a member of a particular lineage dies, the next born assumes the dead persons first name. As an example, the very first chief leader of the entire population of Seti was Aaron Grisemose. On the woman's side the very first woman was Esther Nacomi. Everyone on the planet of Seti is a direct descendant of Aaron Grisemose or Esther Nacomi.

To this day there is no pestilence and no disease on Seti. Because of this, Setillians live for nearly eight or nine hundred years. A few have lived over a thousand years. On Seti you are not considered old until at least six hundred years of age.

To maintain this system of assigning a first name to the next new born upon the death of someone, a very involved child naming method was developed. In the early years, a rider would travel by horseback to the King's palace and announce the birth of a child, a Grisemose boy or a Nacomian girl. Each new boy child's last name would be Grisemose. Likewise, each new girl's last name would be Nacomi. The King had a very large book containing the surname and the first name of every person, living or dead on the entire planet of Seti. At the King's palace, the person assigned the task of tracking the most recent death or birth would assign the new born a first name. The horse rider would then return to the newborn's parents and announce what the child's first name would be, a Grisemose boy or a Nacomi girl. The same would apply when someone died. The horse rider would ride to the Kings Palace and announce the death of a person thus making that first name available to the next born.

As the population grew it became apparent that a more modern tracking method of life and death had to be developed. That development was the beginning of what Earthlings now call, computers. Today a birthing and deceased information center is located in every large and small city and village. Each center has a computer-like device that tracks all new born children and all deaths. These devices are used to assign first names to the newborns. Yes, Seti has come a long, long way in the communication era.

By now you are probably wondering how the Setillians handle what Earthlings call, marriage. First and foremost as has been said before, the woman and the man keep their surname forever. During the wedding ceremony the man and woman exchange a unique gold necklace, one for the man and an identical one for the woman. These necklaces are created by the hands of the husband to be. That necklace is never to be removed from either the man or woman, even at the death of one or the other. Divorce, as Earthlings call it, does not exist on Seti. Should the necklace be removed for any reason by the married man or the woman, the partner may call for the execution of his or her partner, divorce is therefore, not a problem on Seti. Execution of a Setillian is performed by placing the guilty person in a prison cell alone with no food or water, eventually the person dies from starvation.

Age is critical when choosing a partner for marriage on Seti. When a male attains the age of one hundred or a woman reaches the age of one hundred fifty, the mate search may begin. The man must mate with a woman his own age plus fifty years. Setillians have found that women live longer than men. For example if a man, who is at least one hundred, decides to mate with a woman, she must be at least one hundred fifty. At times, this presents problems because the woman will say she is the proper age, but his extra sense ability knows she is lying. Lying on Seti has severe penalties also, including death.

A few years ago some of the Setillians migrated to Mars. To understand why that happened we should listen to Jacob Grisemose explain the situation.

Jacob Grisemose's immediate family obviously has been on Seti for thousands and thousands of years. On Seti his father, Joshus Grisemose, was the present King and died rather unexpectedly. According to custom, Jacob Grisemose, youngest son of Joshus Grisemose was next in line to become King of Seti. The King controls the entire *planet* of Seti, obviously a huge and very privileged position for him to assume.

As Jacob Grisemose tells the story, "At a very early age, less than one hundred, the age at which I would actually have taken over the Kingship of Seti, the courts decided to change the name regeneration system. The high courts ruled that on Seti each family would begin naming each new child born with a unique first name, chosen by the parents of the newborn child, the same as Earthlings do. This change, that even Jacob Grisemose still doesn't understand, made him ineligible to take over the Kingship of the Setillian Kingdom. The current ruler, or the high courts, in the event of the ruler's death, would choose whom they wanted to be the next King. Because the courts did not like the way my father, Joshus Grisemose had ruled Seti, it was decided I would not be appointed King. Instead the high courts appointed Samson Grisemose to be King. From that time forward he would be known on Seti as King Samson Grisemose, ruler of the entire Setillian Planet."

As time passed into years Jacob Grisemose's resentment grew to the point that he was asked to leave and find a new planet on which to settle. His choice was to find another planet to live on or be physically removed by execution. He chose to leave the colony of Seti, but where to go was the question.

By this time Jacob Grisemose's family had grown to be in the thousands. The news of his impending removal from Seti quickly spread through his family and his followers. His family had grown to nearly two hundred men and their wives. That sounds like a small group, but when you add brothers and sisters, their children, their children's children and so forth up the heritage line, it adds up to thousands and thousands of family members.

In many different areas of Seti, Jacob Grisemose's family members formed groups of vocal demonstrations. Vocal demonstrations were absolutely forbidden on Seti. It was felt mind to mind demonstrations were healthy, but never out loud demonstrations. For that reason King Samson Grisemose was forced to remove Jacob Grisemose and his family of dissenters to whatever land Jacob chose. In total there were about ninety thousand family members and followers needing a new home land.

Many years ago an exploratory mission from Seti had searched the universe looking for land on which Setillians could inhabit, should it ever become necessary. They had previously found Earth and mapped it extensively, but decided it was already overcrowded and not a fit place to live. They also discovered that Earth's atmosphere would be completely suitable for Setillians, much too dirty. They did however discover the back side of Mars to be a possibility. Why Mars you ask? They found the Martian land barren, but fertile and the atmosphere very similar to that of Seti.

A thick cloud covers nearly the entire back side of Mars. The early explorers found the cloud to be over two miles deep and thousands of miles long and wide. Needless to say this cloud cover provided no sunshine on the Martian surface. The lack of sunlight could pose a bit of a problem, but it was decided the obstacle could be overcome by using the Setillian advanced technology to create a dome over most of the land. It worked on Seti and certainly would work on the new found land of Mars. Overcoming the cloud problem would make Mars a safe habitat for the expelled Setillians.

Jacob Grisemose realized for the first time he was making decisions on his own and was not including God in any of his decisions, "Oh well, God gave me a brain, perhaps it is time I use it." He said those words under his breath, words Jacob Grisemose would regret later.

After considerable mind conferring with several chosen men of his family, a method for creating a dome over the large living area of Mars was determined to be possible. The dome would be supported by creating a synthetic air atmosphere beneath it. That air would support the dome and also provide the inhabitants an atmosphere much like that of Seti. The dome material to be used was similar to glass but not glass. If the heavy air inside the dome should become polluted, automatic vents would open in the dome and the dirty air would be released into the cloud dome above it. It would be very necessary however to keep the dome intact at all times. Failure to maintain a sealed dome could cause catastrophic problems.

The chemically light sensitive dome, when charged with a positive and negative electrical charge, would emit a brilliant light, simulating the sun. Using their past Seti knowledge, Jacob Grisemose knew they could control the duration of light thus having exact periods of night and daylight. It should be noted that the earlier exploration trips to the Martian surface discovered it had the necessary raw substances needed to create the dome material. When completed, the artificially lighted surface would supply plentiful amounts of fruits and vegetables and all the necessary products to support their new life on Mars.

They had discovered earlier, water on Mars comes up from the ground much as it did in the beginning on Seti. There appeared to be no weeds or unwanted plant life as they had found earlier during their close-up exploration of Earth. Jacob decided if he ever wanted to go to another planet, it would be to Mars. The backside of Mars is in a partially hidden part of the universe. God had created that area for beings such as Jacob Grisemose and his family knowing in advance he would someday need a new homeland.

The leaders of each family met with Jacob to discuss their willingness to move ahead with the departure plans from Seti. They were united about such a move and looked favorably to Jacob Grisemose for direction.

The question each asked, "How are we going to go about moving ninety thousand Setillians and everything it would take to start a new colony millions of miles away? In addition to moving our families we will need machinery to build the new colony."

Clearly it was up to Jacob to talk to King Samson about that very question. Much to Jacob's surprise, King Samson agreed to allow them the use of his Space Freighters for the task. He also agreed to the loan of his Mission Ships that could handle small numbers of his family.

Travel to far away places would seem nearly impossible except for the fact that Seti's newly created Space Freighters and Mission Ships travel at three to four times the speed of light. Space freighters and Mission Ships are Seti's newest transports replacing the aging, much slower space craft. Mission Ships can only accommodate about one hundred persons. Their primary purpose is for exploration. Space Freighters, on the other hand, are capable of moving tons of freight or thousands of people at a time.

Light travels at nearly three hundred million meters per second. At warp three, the Space Freighters and Mission Ships approach nearly a billion meters per second. To obtain light speeds the Space Freighters and Mission Ships are powered by an engine that is fueled by the inner most part of the atom. Earthlings are just now grappling with trying to understand fully, the Bosonic String Theory. Earthlings understand that inside an atom is a nucleus held together by what is called the Bosonic String Theory, but have no idea how to apply it. Through years of experimenting, Setillians discovered ways to create a Space Craft engine using this fuel theory that moves their space craft around the universe at warp speeds. As long as the crafts stay out of another planet's gravitational pull and remains in the vacuum of space, Setillian fliers can travel at up to a speed of warp three. At light speeds, if the craft gets too close to a another planet's gravitational pull, it would immediately burn and fall to that planet's surface.

During Seti's many trips of exploration, they have in fact been permitted to exit the vacuum of space and slow their Mission Ship speeds. Thus allowing the exploring parties to land and investigate distant planets close up, like Earth's surface and that of Mars.

Several space freighters loaded with machinery and several thousand men have been sent ahead to create a dome for light, and create a synthetic Setillian like atmosphere.

It is interesting to watch Jacob Grisemose's workers laboring without words being spoken. He had given a hundred men the decision making task of directing the entire construction of the dome. Telekinetic, or as you Earthlings would say, mindreading methods are working extremely well for the Setillians. As each worker finishes a task he simply looks in the direction of his supervisor for his next task and knows exactly what to do next. The result being, there are no mistakes and most important, no injuries.

The first stage of the dome had been given only one year to complete and Jacob Grisemose was happy to say the workers finished in record time. The first stage of the massive dome has been completed and tested. They now have artificial daylight and more important, an atmosphere similar to that of Seti and yes, similar to that of a cleaned up Earth's..

Before Jacob could bring the remaining Setillians he had to first import to Mars thousands of animals that would provide them with fresh meat for food. On Seti, the men tend the cattle and fish and also build the shelters. That process would be the same in their new Martian land.

You are probably wondering what the cattle would feed upon. As was said before, their new home on Mars had a special blessing from God; the water supply rose up from the ground below them. Using a much slower, older version mission shuttle, Jacob Grisemose explored the entire area beneath the cloud canopy. He was searching for large areas that could sustain animals of all kind and also for a body of water capable of harvesting fresh fish. Fish, they discovered on Seti, supplied a major nutrition supplement needed to give them the long healthy lives they enjoy. When they import the cattle from Seti, there would also be thousands upon thousands of male and female fresh water fish. The fish would reproduce quickly and give them the necessary food supplements their bodies needed.

One of Jacob Grisemose's chosen engineers recently approached him about a lack of light problem concerning the cattle and fish areas. It had not occurred to Jacob, the area over the grass lands and the ocean size fresh water areas would also need light to sustain proper creature and vegetation growth. The engineer correctly pointed out; the land is barren because there is no light. Our food cattle and other animals will need grass for food and without light, there will be none. The engineers also pointed out that the seas of water also needed light to provide plant life for the fish to survive. To think, Jacob was nearly ready to begin transporting the thousands of families left behind on Seti. Had Jacob Grisemose depended on God for Devine guidance, God would have shown him this very necessary, but skipped step. Clearly they must complete the lighted dome over the entire area beneath the cloud canopy.

It was time for Jacob Grisemose to face the music and call his engineers and scientists together for a thought discussion concerning the extended construction mission. Needless to say, there was much murmuring among the gathered men. It had been nearly a year without any of them seeing their wives and children. Clearly the men had no desire to delay the arrival of their wives and children caused by a mistake made by the almighty, Jacob Grisemose. The men felt the task of finishing the much needed lighted dome could wait. Many wanted to return to Seti without finishing the new lighted dome. That, of course, was not an option and Jacob Grisemose could not allow that to happen.

A solution was made by allowing the construction workers to begin immediately building temporary living areas for each of their wives and their children. The wives of the construction men could begin the huge task of sowing the grasses needed to provide food for the cattle when they arrived. While the wives were doing grass sowing, the men would continue the dome construction until it could be finished. The engineers projected it will be another two years or more to complete the entire dome.

Each week, the one and only mission ship Jacob Grisemose possessed, returned to Seti for the weekly supply of food rations. On the return trips, small groups of the workers families were brought back and reunited with their husband, construction men. The process of uniting all of the men with their wives was taking far too long. In a desperate attempt to hurry the process Jacob Grisemose decided to meet with Seti's, King Samson Grisemose. To Jacob Grisemose's surprise again the King allowed him an audience. As Jacob entered the Great

Room, King Samson had already read his thoughts. Without hesitation King Samson made arrangements for the entire remainder of the construction worker families to be transported on the King's new Space Freighter ships.

Jacob Grisemose thanked the King for his grand generosity to which King Samson looked at Jacob Grisemose, and with a gruff, very rare vocal voice said, "Go away please, and get your people off my Seti before I change my mind."

There was a jubilation celebration, the likes of which Jacob Grisemose had never seen. The negative attitude among the men workers had changed dramatically. The home site construction for the newly arrived families had begun at a pace never imagined possible. Only a few weeks after the wives arrived, their new temporary home sites were complete. The huge task of completing the lighted overhead dome has begun.

The women and children went about the task of seeding the fields as each new section of the dome lighting was completed. Amazingly the grasses were already showing significant life in only a few months of growth. The scientists had discovered a way to make the lighted dome over the water area have a very different color which gave the water a blue-green effect. All that viewed the vast body of water were quick to exclaim its beauty.

Food production had already begun because of the women's hard work of sowing the seeds to grow and harvest their own fruits and vegetables. The women tended the fields *and* did the household duties, as it was on Seti. The lighted dome over the vast harvest fields was providing an extended growing season. After the first initial food harvest, the scientists would adjust the lighted periods equally with light and darkness.

At last, Jacob Grisemose's fields had begun providing food supplies; the time of reckoning had arrived. His colony must, at last, be capable of completely sustaining itself. Until now, King Samson Grisemose has gladly provided all of the Seti family's needs concerning the initial construction and food supplies. The question in Jacob Grisemose mind was, will King Samson release the machinery necessary to build their permanent housing. More importantly, would he give Jacob Grisemose the thousands of breeder cattle and horses needed to sustain their new life on Mars? Jacob was thinking he had taxed King Samson's willingness to give to the maximum. There was only one way to find out, ask, and Jacob Grisemose did. To ask did however require another face to face meeting with King Samson. Jacob asked his Mission Craft flier to return him to Seti one more time.

King Samson was again expecting his Jacob's return. The King had anticipated Jacob's needs and when he asked for the additional machinery, cattle and fish, the King gladly approved.

His only question was, "When will you be taking the last of your dissenters?"

Jacob answered the King as best he could. "We will all leave your planet after we complete the cattle movement and fish movement." That appeared to delight the King Samson. King Samson Grisemose really wanted Jacob and his people off his Seti planet.

Using the huge Space Freighters, the transport of the cattle and fish occurred without incident. It did however require considerable cleaning of the Space Freighters afterwards. It is amazing how much fertilizer those animals leave behind. Speaking of that, Mars surface has very little material that can be used for, what you call fertilizer; therefore the animals would supplement an important useful element necessary to grow their fruits and vegetables. It was amazing the things you had to think about when you decide to begin a new life elsewhere on another planet. At times it made Jacob Grisemose wonder if he was capable of leading the thousands of his followers in their new land.

With the cattle mess finished, they began transporting the

remainder of the men, women and children to their new world. Each family was instructed to only bring along the necessary items to sustain themselves for a brief period of time. They were told that building permanent shelter would be their first task. It was explained that they had built the dome and created a Seti like atmosphere, but that was all. The exception was the temporary housing built for the families of the construction workers. Each new arrival man was instructed to bring along the building tools they used on Seti, nothing more. "For now," Jacob Grisemose said, "the new arrival housing will be temporary. Later we will improve our living areas."

When building the dome, they had to provide a safe entrance for the faster Mission Ships and the Space Freighters to come and leave. The crafts must land at very slow speeds, slowing from warp speed to less than two hundred nautical miles per hour. This became a tricky maneuver for the fliers. The entrance for the crafts had to be opened and closed as each space craft approached or left the dome.

Fortunately for Jacob, several men that were familiar with the Mission Ships and Space Freighter's communication systems on Seti had the foresight and the necessary knowledge to bring along communication computer equipment. Communicating with space vehicles as they come and go is extremely important. Jacob said he had not even thought about that little detail, communication equipment. This is just another piece of the puzzle that Jacob Grisemose forgot to ask for Devine help from God.

Bringing the thousands of people from Seti began and it took many, many trips to accomplish. It was interesting to see the faces of those arriving as they exited the Space Freighters. Disbelief best described the look as they saw, for the first time, the emptiness of it all. As Jacob looked at the faces of many of the arriving families, he could read their thoughts that they might have made a terrible mistake to ever leave the comfort of Seti. Life on Seti was good, not a worry ever, they took so much of life for granted on Seti.

Do you remember on Seti the Setillians depended on God's help in everything. God provided the knowledge to build and create all of their needs. On Mars however, God has been made number two, meaning every man, woman and child now had total *free will* to create their own destiny. Jacob Grisemose set the example for all to follow when he stopped conferring with God on all matters, especially the important matters. It didn't take long for all of his followers to realize that if their leader, Jacob Grisemose, could think without God's guidance; they should be permitted to do the same. The result being, God had, for now, abandoned the entire colony who must now work extremely hard to sustain their existence. Yes, they still had their mind thinking abilities to understand what others were saying, but that's about it. To exist on Mars was going to be very difficult for the new arrivals.

Before leaving Seti it had been decided that there would be one person to represent each one of the thousands of families. Jacob decided, not long after all the families had arrived, that he needed to discuss with the leaders, a new method of telling time.

"In our Mars settlement," Jacob explained to the gathered group of leaders, "we have to create our own system of measuring time. On Seti there was a day and night which was determined by daylight and darkness. On Mars, we will never see natural sunlight because we are on the dark side of the planet and beneath a thick cloud that blocks the sun from ever shining. Because of this, we are creating our own new calendar. One day will consist of one light and one dark period."

Jacob further explained, "For now, our dome will provide longer amounts of light than of dark. By doing this we will have the best food production season. Experience from our old planet taught us that some crops require more light than others. Depending on what crops have been planted we can program the most beneficial amount of light to shine over that particular crop area. The purpose on Seti was the same as ours, to control the growing seasons, however our dome also provides us with an artificial atmosphere similar to that of Seti. We will have workers on call day and night specially trained to repair damage to the dome immediately, should there be a penetration tear. Take this information back to your families and explain nothing has changed, daylight is day and darkness is night."

Their new city was beginning to take shape rapidly. Their building techniques were far more advanced than those they observed on Earth. A shelter on Earth took many months to complete. Here, they completed the same shelter in only days. Their construction methods of building are far too complex to explain. Each family helps the other until all shelters are finished.

The initial building structures had been completed in about thirty light and dark periods, or as Earthlings call it, thirty days. Discontent among the new settlers was beginning to fade, for that Jacob Grisemose was very happy. To himself he said, "I think I have made a wise decision by coming to Mars."

# CHAPTER 23
## AN INVASION APPEARS LIKELY

The leadership of the new colony on Mars had decided that Jacob Grisemose had earned the right to become the King of the Martian Colony. That right had been taken away from him and instead, Seti high courts appointed Samson Grisemose as King. Therefore, the leadership decided from this time forward, he would be known as King Jacob Grisemose.

Why had King Jacob Grisemose not married many years ago? He asked himself that question over and over. On Seti, many women had approached him, but when they realized his rebellious personality they chose not to pursue him as a mate for fear of retaliation by King Samson Grisemose. At age two hundred seventy, his desire for a woman companion grew stronger daily. After all, who would tend to his food needs and mend his clothing as he began to age. Now that he had been made King, he realized he must find a suitable woman companion to handle the daily task of running his new Kingdom Castle.

After the leadership of the colony named Jacob Grisemose, King, Nacomian women began to approach him constantly. He is a single man, why not? To become his wife would make them Queen Nacomi. She would live a life of luxury with him in his new home, his castle. The castle would be the most beautiful building in the new colony. When complete, there would be many rooms for those needing to stay for a time. For his wife and himself there would be a separate bedroom for each. For their prospective three children, should they decide to have children; a bedroom for each would be provided. Perhaps they would also have one large bedroom where he and his wife could discuss in detail their personal needs. Of course he would provide space for his many servants, one of the many bonuses of being King.

One day while riding his stallion observing the progress of the home shelters, he came upon a lady in distress. She had been riding and had fallen from her steed. As he approached her he could see she was crying as she lay on the ground.

"May I ask why you are crying?" King Jacob mentally asked.

Realizing it was the King, the young lady attempted to get up and bow before him, but she could not. "Oh King Jacob Grisemose sir, my horse stumbled and threw me on the ground and then my horse simply ran away. I think my ankle is sprained, but I will be fine.

"Nonsense," King Jacob said, "Please allow me to help you up on the back of my horse."

Having said that he dismounted and placed his long arms under the small body of the lady, and he picked her up. As he did, she placed her arms around his neck as he gently lifted her up and on the saddle of his horse. "I will take you to our medical shelter and get you fixed up good as new." It felt good to have the lady's arms around his neck; he could see and feel what he had missed so much by not allowing ladies to comfort him.

As they rode back to the medical shelter together she wrapped his arms around him. Her cloth wrapped body held on to him tightly. She was not looking at him so he could use his special senses to say thoughtfully, *You are much too young for me. Surely you must be only about seventy years old or perhaps even less, but she does feel good riding with me.*

Arriving at the medical center he lifted her from his horse and carried her to an examination table. As the examiner was working on the lady he felt it necessary to inquire as to her name.

"My name is Rachael Nacomi." She said.

"And, may I ask how old you are?" King Jacob inquired.

"In a few days I will be three hundred fifty." Rachael said as she looked directly into his inquiring eyes.

King Jacob was a bit surprised by her age and said, "I know many Nacomian women, but all are much older than you. I thought you must be a child of one of the older ladies in the colony."

To which Rachael Nacomi replied, "Well, that is right sir, but I told you the truth. I am nearly three hundred fifty years old." If you remember the people of Seti did not begin to show their true age until at least six hundred years. "I have always tried to keep my youthful appearance because sometime I hope to choose a mate that wants me for who I am, not just for what I look like. Most men don't want old looking, shriveled women. In time perhaps I will find a mate, but so far that has not happened. I suppose I am just too choosy."

The King hearing that she was nearly eighty years his senior made his heart beat faster. She looked straight into his eyes when she mentioned her age so he knew it was true. Could this be the one for him, she was youthful and spirited. He must explore this further. "If you would permit me Rachael Nacomi, I will return for you after you rest for a spell here in the medical center. It would be my privilege to feast with you tonight in my personal shelter. Would you like that?"

Somewhat stunned by the King's forwardness she said, "I would be honored King Jacob Grisemose."

To which the King replied, "Please Rachael Nacomi, you may call me by my first name, Jacob."

King Jacob could hardly contain himself as he rode about the colony examining the progress of the shelters. This lady had inadvertently entered his life and lifted his spirits to a new high.  The excitement of pulling this colony together had most certainly been uplifting but this; this had him jumping out of his skin with a renewed energy that had him smiling again.  He had almost forgotten what happiness was really all about.  Life, for King Jacob Grisemose, had taken on a whole new meaning.

As he was examining the last of the family shelters an alarm sounded indicating that the dome had been penetrated by falling objects from the cloud above it.  Immediately the security workers rushed to investigate.  As King of the new colony, the report immediately came back to him that several large objects had penetrated the dome on the Western edge of the city.  They had mysteriously floated to the ground surface.  The silver cylinder like objects had large cloth materials suspended above them as they floated down to the surface.  Security said that they had never seen anything like them on Seti and wanted King Jacob Grisemose to come quickly.  The report was that two such objects had entered their peaceful domain, piercing the canopy.

As the responsible person for the colony's safety, it was necessary for the King to visit the affected area immediately.  Nearing the area he could see the cylinders far in the distance, but a danger signal advised him there was a serious problem.  He stopped and read his dangemometer which indicated a foreign substance was leaking from the cylinders.  King Jacob summoned his Chief of Security, Ezra Grisemose.  Ezra Grisemose is an older security worker that had worked on Seti.  The King chose him to be his head of security because he trusted him and he had considerable knowledge, should there ever be a Terrestrial happening.  This appears to be such a happening.

People that were close to the King were addressed by their first name. "Ezra, "The King said. "My dangermometer is indicating we should not get any closer to these cylinders. Ezra, do you know what they are and from where they came?"

"King Jacob," Ezra said. "I have no idea from whence they came, but emitting from them is a liquid nuclear substance similar to what we use to refine and create our fuel for the Mission Ships and Space Freighters.

"Ezra," King Jacob said, "that would be the Micro Atom Neutron Liquid. A very dangerous liquid substance and will eventually destroy anyone that comes in contact with it."

Tell me Ezra, have any of our security people been closer than you and I?"

"Unfortunately two of our security members have." Ezra said. "Watching the cylinders fall to the ground, they were curious and wanted to see the cylinders up close."

King Jacob Grisemose was sorry to hear that because within only three to four lights they will begin to experience the effects of life failure. "We have not yet developed anti failure vaccines that could save their lives Ezra. Our rescue personal must quickly move the affected men to the medical healing shelter. Ezra, you must be sure the rescue people are properly clothed to protect them from the apparent radiation. After you rescue the affected men, we must move these cylinders to the exit bay. You must first wrap each one with a protective material before they are moved them from this area. That should stop the nuclear active solution from escaping. Later we will devise a way to dispose of the cylinders."

"King Jacob," Ezra said. "Could it be that King Samson Grisemose on Seti has betrayed us and sent these cylinders to destroy our colony?"

"I hope not," The King said, "but you and I will enter our new transporter capsule and visit Seti. King Samson is a hateful being, but I don't think he would go *this* far. After you supervise the movement of the cylinders we will visit King Samson Grisemose in person. Again I say, be sure to have the movement workers properly outfitted to protect them from the leaking nuclear liquid.

Just as they were leaving the area the alarm sounded again and the King and Ezra watched from afar as two more cylinders floated to the surface.

"Hurry Ezra, we must immediately visit Seti now. This invasion must be stopped. Make the announcement to all our families to remain calm and do not attempt to see the cylinders up close. They must stay at least a hundred kilometers away from them. Tell the container movement workers to begin their task now!"

Back at the operation central area, King Jacob and Ezra entered the transport capsule. The capsule was capable of moving only three to four people at a time. With the push of a button they were off and arrived in the receiving capsule at King Samson Grisemose headquarters.

"Well Jacob Grisemose or should I say King Jacob Grisemose," said King Samson using an arrogant vocal voice. I understand you finally received your all powerful Kingship, should I bow before your majesty? May I ask why you are back so soon? Are you coming to ask for assistance again? I have given you and your families all I can. I can give you nothing more, you must continue your lives on your own."

"King Samson Grisemose," King Jacob inquired, ignoring the King's nasty comment, "we have come to ask about the cylinders that are penetrating our canopy from the clouds above it. Have you sent them to destroy our city on Mars? Our dangemometer's are indicating the cylinders have a radioactive nuclear substance within them. Could it be that you have been kind to us and then turned against us?"

King Samson Grisemose denied he had any interest in destroying the new world settlers. "First of all, I have no idea what you are talking about. Besides, why would I do that now? I could have done that while you were here and saved me all the expense of moving your families." King Jacob could sense, using his inner sense abilities, that King Samson Grisemose was telling the truth. King Jacob felt relieved that his answer was honest. It is virtually impossible to tell a lie in the Seti society. "King Samson Grisemose," King Jacob said, "Allow me to apologize for even thinking you would do such an awful act, but once again I must ask your help. This is an extreme emergency and we will need many of your Mission Ships capable of transporting the cylinders off and away from our Martian settlement, would you help us please?"

It was good to hear the positive response as King Samson Grisemose said. "We have, but just a few Mission Ships. Yes King Jacob Grisemose, I will provide you with whatever we have during your emergency time of need." Having heard his positive response Ezra and King Jacob Grisemose concluded their visit to Seti and returned home.

Upon their return they found six more cylinders had fallen onto their pasture fields. It is imperative that they find the source of this invasion. The King asked for volunteer fliers to explore the solar system and locate the invaders. They now have only three Mission Ships at this time and thus only needed three trained fliers.

The volunteer fliers knew the assignment and were eager to begin. Any time the pilots can fly around the universe searching for anything is exciting. King Jacob always felt it was his duty to remind the fliers of the dangers when flying into the solar system. They must keep well within the vacuum of space as they near each planet. To get close to any planet's gravity system is instant death and the loss of a Mission Ship. Gravity at warp speed means instant loss of life.

"Report often as you travel." King Jacob said. "Remember you are only to find the location of the invaders. Do not attempt to destroy. We will take necessary actions later. Please, have a safe journey."

A few lights have passed. All of the reports have been negative as the fliers moved about within the Solar System. "Someone is invading us, but why?" King Jacob said to Ezra.

"Mission fliers," King Jacob called to the three from the Martian mission control center. "Has anyone been around Earth? I cannot imagine why Earthlings would want to destroy us because they do not even know that we exist. Just in case, at least one of you should circle Earth."

The response came from Ahab Grisemose. He was the youngest and perhaps the most alert of all the fliers. "Yes King Jacob Grisemose," Ahab Grisemose said. "I'm on my way to Earth now. I should be there in about one light."

One light had passed and as promised Ahab Grisemose called to report. He reported that from what he could see there were, what appeared to be, very large cylinder kind of aircraft dropping smaller space craft of some type, seemingly to propel them into space orbit. Ahab noted further that the earth space craft traveled at an extremely slow speed making it nearly impossible to follow it. This is the evidence that King Jacob Grisemose needed. It now confirmed that Earth was invading them, but why?

"All fliers return home." The King said. "As you approach our home Ahab, continue to orbit around us and look for any strange invading crafts as they approach Mars. I want to see for sure that they are the same type of craft you saw leaving Earth."

Ahab Grisemose did as requested and confirmed that they were in fact the same. "It is not the same one I saw leaving earth, but it is the same type." Ahab said. "As the ships carrying the cylinders near our area, they appear to open the doors of their craft and the cylinders are dropped into the cloud above us. The craft that dropped the cylinders then continue on for many miles and then suddenly disappear."

"You have done good Ahab, please return home." King Jacob said. The three fliers returned home without incident. The King greeted each and thanked them for a successful, informative mission.

King Jacob Grisemose received information from Ezra Grisemose that he was needed at the healing center. When the King entered the center he was greeted by the lady he had placed there to have her wounds attended to.

Again the beauty of Rachael Nacomi immediately received the attention of the King. "Rachael Nacomi," King Jacob asked.

"Are you the one requesting my presense? As you probably know I am very busy. How can I help you? Are they not attending to your wounds?"

"Yes, I am perfectly healed now, but if you want I can tell you why the cylinders you talk about are coming from Earth."

"You can tell me that. How could you possibly know the reason for such a terrible act? We haven't done anything to justify such an invasion."

As carefully as possible Rachael Nacomi looked directly into the eyes of the King and explained, "King Jacob Grisemose, do you remember many years ago on Seti a group of people were sent to Earth for a brief visit?"

"Yes, I do remember that eleven people went, visited and reported the awful conditions on Earth."

"That is true, but when they returned to Seti only ten returned. I was left behind on Earth because I was nowhere to be found when the group returned with the mission ship to pick me up. It was determined that another ship would return for me in a few years. That was to be my punishment for disobeying the commander of the mission ship. He had given us specific instruction as to when and where we were to meet the returning party."

King Jacob took her hand and spoke softly saying, "How awful of them to leave you in such a terrible place. I would have never have done that to such a beautiful lady as you."

"I doubt you would have, but it was really my own fault. The reason the search party couldn't find me was because I became lost in the mountain region and could not find the Mission Ship's return landing location. I wandered around the area for days before finally finding a nice man who took me to the home of an Earthling named Julie Wilson. I lived with Julie and her husband, Matthew for many years. For years I was with Julie and heard all the earthly problems her husband, Matthew was having."

Somewhat confused at this point, the King said, "I understand what you are saying, but how would you know anything about the cylinders."

Rachael Nacomi continued. "I will tell you King Jacob Grisemose, Earthlings believe they are the only humans in the entire universe. In fact, it is only in the last few years they have discovered the planet Seti. Julie's husband, Matthew and some other people came up with a way to move what they call, nuclear waste. It has something to do with generating electricity. That's the way they make Earth darkness look like day. Anyhow, the people decided that Mars had nobody living on it so they would ship the waste here. So King Jacob Grisemose, it is not an invasion, they just don't know about us."

"I thank you for that information Rachael Nacomi, but how did you get back here? Did Seti send a rescue ship to get you?"

"Several years ago Julie was beginning to get old. Did you know King Jacob Grisemose; Earth people start to get old and wrinkly at age sixty or seventy?"

"No." A dumbfounded King Jacob said.

"Anyhow Julie, Matthew and I were sitting in their house when I sensed a call from the mission ship. I received a message that a rescue ship was near Earth's surface. A mental call beckoned me to come immediately to the rescue ship. I went out on Julie's front porch and looked upward and saw the bright light of the ship's rescue beam. In just moments it landed near the stream of water behind their house and within seconds I was safely back in our ship and returned to Seti. I miss Julie, she was so nice."

"Did you know King Jacob, when Julie married Matthew her surname was changed to Matthew's?"

"Now that is interesting Rachael." King Jacob said.

"Yes, Julie's name became Julie Wilson. I like that and if I ever get married I would like to have my last name changed to my husbands. That sounds so romantic. Do you think you could make that happen?"

"Rachael Nacomi," the King said, "I will discuss that with you as a possibility later when I return. I will return for you

Rachael when we get this present situation under control. I have not forgotten our meeting to have dinner."

Meanwhile, The King had to resolve the problem at hand. King Jacob requested an immediate meeting with the family court of decision makers. "It is imperative that we return the cylinders that have now grown to thirty two, back to Earth." He said. "We have already lost two security workers and I will not allow any others to be harmed by the nuclear liquid that is within the cylinders. Our dome is being repaired as fast as the cylinders come crashing through. We cannot allow this to continue. I now know why Earth is doing this, but we will begin immediately to send the cylinders back to Earth. Our Mission Ship loading workers must be sure the cylinder's protective wrapping material is thoroughly sealed. A poor seal would subject our fliers to the nuclear radiation.

King Samson Grisemose has been kind enough to send us ten more new Mission Ships along with fliers to man them. Tomorrow at first light they will begin mission, 'Back to Earth.' May the God in Heaven have mercy on the Earthlings?"

# CHAPTER 24
## MYSTERY AT THE SPACE PLATFORM

As the workers began loading the cylinders into the mission ships the King held a mission briefing for the fliers. "Each of your mission ships have been programmed to fly a direct flight to the outer limits of Earth. As you approach the destination you will note that your craft will begin a very slight downward dive down toward earth. Do not be alarmed by this. The auto programming system will open the exit doors and release the cylinders automatically into the vacuum of space surrounding Earth. The slight dive will send the cylinders toward Earth's atmosphere at near warp speed. When the cylinders enter Earth's atmosphere they will begin to burn immediately and release whatever is inside. After that takes place, the automatic guidance system will redirect your ship back home and out of harms way. Are there any questions? If there are none, God's safety to each of you as you begin, 'Back to Earth' mission."

Never had there been an accident as the mission crafts moved about the universe. The craft programming had worked flawlessly. Ahab Grisemose was to be one of the fliers chosen for this mission. He was a bit anxious about the mission because he had never been on a mission to cause harm to another planet. "King Jacob Grisemose, has the Mission Craft been programmed to avoid the Earth's space platform?" Ahab Grisemose inquired.

Surprised that anyone would question the reliability of their superior advanced computer programming the King said sarcastically. "For your information Ahab, Earth's space platform is traveling very near the edge of Earth's gravity. Should you get that close to their platform and at your warp speed don't plan on coming back. Earth will suddenly have very tiny pieces of your Mission Ship raining down on them. Again I say to all of you, do not attempt to override the automatic craft controls. King Samson Grisemose has assured me that these new ships have never failed him and I don't expect them to fail us during this mission."

Even as the Mission Ships were being loaded for the first mission, the invasion of cylinders continued to fall on the small colony on Mars.

Over and over the Mission Ships left Mars with loads of cargo destined to Earth. The fliers were becoming tired of the boring trips with nothing to do but watch the planets whiz by as they traveled.

Back on his home territory of Mars, once again Ahab confronted King Jacob. "King Jacob Grisemose sir, I see no need for our fliers to make these trips. We have nothing to do, would you consider sending just one craft on a test mission without a flier on board? After all, the automatic guidance systems are working flawlessly taking us to the edge of Earth atmosphere and back,"

Again King Jacob is taken back by the boldness of Ahab Grisemose and said, "Ahab, the last twenty missions have been a test of the computer programming. I'm satisfied that the craft can in fact make trips without fliers. Beginning at tomorrow's light we will send all ten craft without fliers. I'm surprised you waited this long to ask that question. Thank you for being bold enough to even suggest it."

At next light the ten mission ships were loaded and sent on their way without incident. Back at the flight control center, The King entered the room to check the progress of the latest mission. He found the workers attempting to make contact with mission Craft Three. Over and over they were pushing buttons on their consoles. There was no sign of Craft Three, it had disappeared. Using their ability to tune to Earth's old fashioned radio communication, they turned some dials and heard Earthlings attempting to communicate with their space platform.

A very excited voice on the radio was calling over and over. "This is Houston can you hear me? This is Houston, can you hear me? This is Houston to the space station, can you hear me?" The voice then said that he was going to play back a recording of their last communication with the space platform.

The recording of the last communication between the space platform and Earth's Command Center began, "Commander, we are beginning to have radiation alarms going off all over the world as well as here in the U.S. Do you see anything unusual happening out there in space where you are?"

"Houston, this is Commander Billings on the space platform. Am I to understand that you have radiation alarms sounding all over the world? From our vantage point there is nothing unusual, but wait just a moment, something is coming at us fast, very...." Then complete silence. Earth tracking almost immediately systems began seeing large pieces of the space platforms fiery pieces streaking toward Earth.

King Jacob Grisemose sat down stunned. "I suppose we could tell Houston what happened, but we won't. We must find out what went wrong with the programming aboard our Craft Three. I am very glad we had no fliers on this mission. In spite of this setback we will continue with unmanned missions. If Earth continues sending the cylinders, we must send them back."

Many lights have passed as King Jacob Grisemose begins to recall his encounter with Rachael Nacomi. His past brief meeting with her was just now coming back to him as he realized that he never found out where this beautiful lady lived.

"When this is all over," The King said to himself, "I must find this lovely lady and take time to dine with her and discuss the name change situation she desires."

Back on Earth the TV news was reporting that the United States Space Platform has been hit by some object. It had been destroyed by something, but what destroyed it remained a mystery. Perhaps, the experts said, an asteroid hit it. NASA said that it couldn't be because they track every piece of space junk and asteroids as well. "Our tracking systems saw nothing even close to the space platform prior to the radio silence. Our tracking systems can see any object, even the tiniest speck moving at normal space speed. If whatever it was, was traveling at light speed, our tracking devices couldn't see it, but we all know we have nothing that can travel at that kind of speed."

Back on Earth it has been several years since Matthew had any communication with his friends in Idaho. The country had begun solving the fossil fuel problems by installing the Erickson Mini Nuclear Power Generation plants all over the world. The side benefit of that system has everyone driving hydrogen powered automobiles.

The experts said that global warming had begun to be reversed. Planet Earth was beginning to return to normal, the North and South Poles had stopped melting. Scientists had been worried that the oceans would eventually flood the earth. But now this, scientists from around the world were scratching their heads wondering what was happening.

Scientists with their telescopes had been scanning the skies, but could see nothing unusual. Occasionally one would say they saw tiny specks of light. Nothing, they would say that could be associated with nuclear radiation. "Nuclear radiation, you can't smell it and you can't taste it," the experts would say.

Julie and Matthew Wilson have now grown very old together. They had longed for the time they could just sit in their rocking chairs on the front porch and talk about the good old days. All of that good time was now beginning to fade. For months life had gone sour for everyone all over the world.

The actual problem began several months ago when, for some reason, the world began feeling the effects of nuclear poisoning. Geiger counters were showing alarming amounts of radiation. At first the scientific community thought there had been a melt-down of a nuclear reactor somewhere, but they had no idea where that could have happened. Then they said some foreign country, like the United States, must have set off a dirty nuclear bomb. That was not to be the case because reports of nuclear radiation were coming from countries around the globe. The United States was even accused of testing a nuclear war device in foreign waters. The U.S. government assured the world that was not the case because even the U.S. was feeling the same effects as their neighbors, Canada and Mexico. What was the origin of this disaster was the big question?

Julie and Matthew are in the safety of their home, yet their bodies are filled with open sores and so much pain. Julie had been a nurse years ago and through her hospital friends was able to get some pain medication. That is no longer available because the hospitals are quickly filling with extremely needy patients. The doctors and nurses are having the same problems as the rest of the population. Day by day people are dying by the hundreds, no not hundreds, but by the thousands. The world as they once knew it is beginning to shut down.

Television is showing horrible situations from around the world. There are no answers as to the source of the radiation. "Is it possible," the television reporters from around the world are saying, "that it could be we are being bombarded from outer space. Has the earth's protective shield from radiation disappeared?" There are no for sure answers concerning the source of the destruction.

The blood and yellow stuff is starting to ooze out of Matthew's and Julie's skin. Trying to stop it is useless. There is nothing they can do. Speaking as though in a quiet prayer

Matthew says, "Oh God, please take us home." At the top of his voice he finds himself screaming, "Take us, please take us now, we can't take this agony any longer."

Suddenly though, he looks around and realizes that Julie is gone. "Julie, where is Julie?" She had talked earlier of going out to look for some food and water. Matthew told her not to go because according to what is left of television news, most businesses have shut down. There are no deliveries to stores and no workers because nearly everyone is sick with whatever this is. "Where can she be?" he says. Matthew went to the front porch to see if her car was still there. "Her car is gone, now what?" Does he just wait for her to come back or does he get in his car and try to find her.

His car only has a little fuel and the hydrogen fueling stations have shut down so he is thinking he had better wait a while longer for her to return. He waits and waits, but no Julie.

Matthew cries out, "God, why are you keeping us alive?" His beautiful wife Julie had him believe there was a God that controls all things, but this; surely He wouldn't allow this to happen.

On the front porch he stands looking to the east. The sun is beginning to set behind him as it has done forever. The trees and the landscape are just as beautiful as ever, but nothing is moving. The children that usually play nearby in the fields are gone. The noisy teenagers that drive by with their loud booming radios have disappeared. They haven't driven by the house for weeks. He hasn't seen farmer Jones and his wife at the vegetable stand for over a week. The most noticeable missing thing is the birds fluttering and chirping in the trees. Silence, deathly silence! He would like to check on his neighbor farmer Jones, but he can barely move himself. Why is he wondering where they are, he can smell the answer. For days the disgusting odor of death has been in the air.

He places his head in his cupped hands and begins to cry hysterically. As he slowly pulls his hands away from his face it reveals that some skin from his forehead has come off in his hands. "Oh my god," He cries, "look at this, I'm coming apart piece by little piece." He shakes his hands trying to get the flesh to come off. He shutters as some of the skin falls to the floor.

His mind comes back to the reality of what he really wants: to find his Julie. He wonders if she has tried to call. He gave her a cell phone a year ago to use just in case she became stranded. But now he realizes she couldn't use it because the cell phone signals have been off for weeks. All he knows for sure is that she went looking for a store in hopes of finding some water and groceries. She actually thought there were a few people still in the stores, but she hasn't come back. Why she went, he doesn't know because she knew people were dying. There is no one left to talk to about helping him find her. Why would they help him anyhow, they have their own problems?

In a panic he says aloud, "I know what I'll do; I have a tiny bit of fuel left in the car. It's about enough to get me into town. If I don't make it, it doesn't matter. I might just as well die in the car as here in the house.

The sun is now low and he decides to wait no longer. He must leave now before it is completely dark. Slowly he backs out of his driveway and drives in the direction of town. He only travels around the corner from the house when suddenly he sees his neighbor, Alfred Jones and his wife Margaret. Alf must have given up and hanged himself on that that big oak tree right there in his front yard. "Oh my," he says. What an awful sight, Alf's wife sitting on the ground and leaning against the tree just under his dangling feet. She must have been trying to stop him from taking his life, but gave up. She sat down under the oak tree and died herself. Matthew thinks he should have taken his life also. If he had he wouldn't have all this pain and he would not be missing his Julie. Matthew knows he is going to die anyhow, why not take his life. But he keeps reminding himself of what Julie had told him over and over. God does everything in His own time. "Well God, it's time," He says out loud.

Matthew often wondered what would happen if the world

ran out of fuel, food and water. Now he knows, but then there is this unexplained awful thing that has been added into the equation. "It's the," he stops the sentence and stares across the road. "Oh no, my god no," he says, "That looks like Julie's car over there, and I think she's in it." His heart begins pounding really hard, he can't believe it that finally, he has found her. "Maybe she's still alive." He wanted to run to the car, but at his age and in his condition, he can hardly walk much less run. She must have run off the road, traveled up that little hill and overturned. "Oh God," he screams, "Help me get to her, I love her so much. I think I can make it, I have to make it to her car!"

After much effort he finally reaches the car. "Oh wow!" Talking to himself he says breathlessly, "Julie I'm at your car, but it's upside down, I know you are in there, but the door won't open. I'm trying to open the door Julie, but it won't open." He knows it's her, but he can't see clearly in the window. Again he pulls and pulls on the door handle, but it won't budge. "If I just had some tools with me, but I don't." Frustrated, Matthew says, "Maybe I can find a rock to break the window." He looks around and sees a big rock near the back of the car and picking it up he says, "Well, here goes nothing." With all the strength left in his body he slams the rock against the window, but it doesn't even crack. "I'll hit it one more time." Again, he slams the rock at the window. Glass flies everywhere revealing the lifeless body of Julie.

Sobbing he says, "Oh honey I'm so sorry." Clearly he can see she has been dead for just a short time. "Oh my honey I'm so sorry," sobbing out loud. "If you had just waited, I could have come with you. Why didn't you wait for me at the house?" His beautiful wife is gone just like all the rest of the people. Her beautiful face looks like she has been burned alive and her skin, that silky smooth skin is so shriveled, this is so awful. In total frustration he cries out and exclaims, "It's no use, I might as well go back to the house and die myself. I have found my Julie, but there is nothing left for me to do."

As he crawls back to the car, hand over hand and moving one knee forward then the other knee forward he is thinking, 'Why am I even trying to get to the my car. Why don't I just lay here on the road and die?' But he doesn't. Finally he makes it to his car, pulls himself into the seat and turns the key. It makes a few grunts as though trying to start, but it won't. "Ah damn, that must have been the last of the fuel. You stupid car start, come on, start!" Having screamed that he cries out, "Oh God, you took my Julie, please God, take me now!"

As he sits in his car staring into the wide open spacious sky he again cries, "Why God, why is this happening to the world?" As he gasps for what will be his last breath of air, the sky begins to get brighter and brighter. He holds his hand up to shade his eyes from the extremely white and brilliant bright light. As the sky gets even brighter suddenly he sees a vision. As the vision becomes more visible he hears a loud deep voice of God coming at him from all directions at the same time saying, because *I Am That I Am.*

As Matthew slowly slips into unconsciousness a hand is reaching out beckoning for him. "Come to me." The voice says. "Come, do not be afraid." Matthew extends his hands toward the brightly lit figure of a person. The hand of the figure takes Matthew's hand and they both begin walking toward the brightly lit pathway that appears to be going up into and beyond the clouds.

Matthew appears frightened as he questions, "Where are we going, and who are you?"

"The place will become apparent very soon. The second question you asked, I will tell you as we travel."

As they continued the walk upward she begins to explain. "I have been with you Matthew Franklin Wilson, ever since you became an adult. My name is Angelina, your appointed angel. You see Matthew; my job was to protect you and record every minute of your life up until the end. In fact Matthew, my task was to record your life story, which I have done by writing this book.  The purpose is to tell others of the many temptations of life an ordinary person faces during their lifetime.  It is important to your Maker to know how you reacted to the temptations.  He could be pleased or disappointed, in time you will find that out directly from Him.  In a sense, I was the second person ever present during your entire adult lifetime as your conscience and protector."

Pleading Matthew said, "I am so ashamed of the many times I behaved poorly, will God forgive me Angelina?"

Angelina tries to speak softly as she answers his question, *"You say you behaved, poorly!* Fortunately it is not up to me to judge you.  God is your judge."

"What upset *me* most was the way you and your people sent the nuclear waste to Mars.  That has caused the people living on Mars to retaliate by sending that awful material back to earth.  You could have found other ways to rid earth of it had you spent more time using your God given brain.  The mess you have created on Earth must be eliminated and God will do that in his own time.  God says the Earth will be turned inside out by earthquakes and volcanoes.  He has said there is no other way to cleanse it.  Once cleansed, He intends to place the people that are on Mars, back on Earth.  They will begin to re-populate the New Earth.  Those people have far more intelligence than you mere humans.  The world will, once again, be a pleasant place in which to live."

"Are you telling me there are other beings in the universe?" Matthew quizzed of Angelina.

"Yes Matthew, but we have now arrived at your temporary new home.  Look around, you should see people you recognize."

As Matthew looked at the masses of beings, complete now with their new perfect bodies, he spotted his mother, Thelma and his father, John.  The three gathered together for a loving welcome hug.  And behold, there she was, standing alone, his ever beautiful and loving wife, Julie.  Hugs and kisses abound in this, their new terrestrial life.  Matthew looked around and wondered where Catherine was, but he did not see her.

Hugging their loved ones was something that, unfortunately, rarely occurred back on their now forgotten place called Earth.

# ABOUT THE AUTHOR
## LEE A. DRAYER

I was born on October 4, 1934. Our house was located in a small Pennsylvania town, New Cumberland, located across the river from the capital city of Harrisburg.

I was born during the late depression years. Our family life was not fun, living in a house with no bathroom and no water, only electricity.

Day dreaming, now called ADS, was a serious problem for me. Lack of attention throughout grade school and high school presented a very real challenge for my school teachers.

At age eleven my mother died suddenly. My dad became a very frustrated parent as he attempted to deal with his unruly boy that I had become. The result, I was sent to an orphan school in Hershey. To some degree the school managed to change me into a better person.

It was there I met my first and last love. We spent almost fifty four years together before she died four years ago. Three great, and I might add very successful children later, here I am at age seventy four, still daydreaming, but using my extreme imagination to write books. At my age, you have to do something to occupy your time.